WE BRING YOU AN HOUR

OF DARKNESS

WE BRING YOU AN HOUR

OF DARKNESS

A NOVEL

By
Michael Bourne

DoppelHouse Press | Los Angeles

Publisher's Cataloging-in-Publication Data

Names: Bourne, Michael, 1965-, author.
Title: We bring you an hour of darkness / by Michael Bourne.
Description: Los Angeles, CA: DoppelHouse Press, 2025.
Identifiers: LCCN: 2025933249 | ISBN: 978-1-954600-26-3 (paperback) | 978-1-954600-32-4 (ebook) | 978-1-954600-33-1 (audio)
Subjects: LCSH Journalists--Fiction. | Ecoterrorism--Fiction. | Domestic terrorism--Fiction. | Colorado--Fiction. | Mystery fiction. | Thriller fiction. | Historical fiction. | BISAC FICTION / Mystery & Detective / Women Sleuths | FICTION / Small Town & Rural | FICTION / Thrillers / Suspense
Classification: LCC PS3602.O87 W42 2025 | DDC 813.6--dc23

DoppelHouse Press | Los Angeles

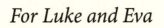

For Luke and Eva

Contents

Prologue

He stops only twice, *once to drink from a stream halfway up Elkhorn Ridge, and again a mile or two later for a handful of home-batch gorp; otherwise, for two long, sweaty hours he trudges up the switchback trail, taking care not to jostle the dangerous cargo in his pack. The ridgeline rises two thousand feet from the valley floor of the narrow box canyon formed by the West Fork of the Franklin River. To the east, past the canyon's mouth, he can just make out the northernmost tip of the county airfield and a short stretch of Highway 22 snaking through the Franklin Valley. Across the canyon lies the steep, forested hillside where the new ski resort is supposed to go in. If the Franklin Skiing Company gets its way, the entire south slope of Elkhorn Canyon, nearly twenty-five hundred acres of old-growth blue spruce and bristlecone pine will be clear-cut to make way for twenty-six freshly carved ski runs serviced by six high-speed lifts, transforming this pristine valley populated by elk and beaver and wildcats into a small, teeming American city of hotels and restaurants and parking lots.*

He set out hours ago, just a guy with a backpack and a rebuilt Schwinn Racer cruising the old railbed along the Franklin River. A couple miles out of town, he scaled a low wooden fence and followed a rarely used Forest Service road along the back side of Elkhorn Ridge. When the gravel gave way to dirt, he ditched his bike in a stand of chokecherry bushes and set off on the three-mile hike up the ridge. There are plenty of more direct routes to the West Fork Power Substation in the heart of Elkhorn Canyon, but at five o'clock on a

Sunday afternoon, those trails will be populated by tourists and locals out for a weekend hike, and he very much doesn't want to be seen. In any case, he's in no hurry. "The straightest line between two points is no fun," he says out loud, repeating Jack Frost's famous line from A Screwdriver in the Gears.

He has been hiking these remote woods for decades, first with his father hunting small game, and later with Bill Blanning, the man he has always considered his real father. It was Blanning who gave him the gift of patience, taught him to stand for hours at the edge of a meadow as the beavers built their dams and black bears foraged for roots and berries along the valley floor. Once, many years ago, they even spotted a lynx. This densely furred wildcat once ranged as far south as New Mexico, but it was nearly trapped out of existence below the Canadian border, and Elkhorn Canyon is one of its last remaining habitats in the United States. He's convinced that several breeding pairs are still out here. But if the three brothers who own the ski company get their way, the lynx will disappear from Elkhorn Canyon and quite possibly the entire country.

Dusk has fallen by the time he reaches the West Fork substation, but he hangs back in a patch of low-lying scrub oak, watching for any human presence and waiting. For weeks now, he and the other members of the Collective have been doing recon, taking up posts here or in a stand of willows along the creek using Zeiss binoculars. A few times, always on Wednesday and Friday mornings, trucks from the Mountain Power Company have pulled up at the service building and disgorged workers to recalibrate the sensors on the gauges and clear forest debris within a fifty-yard radius of the perimeter fence. These visits never last longer than a couple hours and the inspection crews are always gone by noon, usually much earlier.

Still, he waits for full dark before he snaps on a pair of surgical gloves, opens his pack, and begins assembling his materials. By the dim glow of his flashlight, he extracts the gauze-wrapped brick of industrial-grade TNT formed into a disk small enough to fit under a transformer box. The blasting cap, a thin rod of mercury fulminate, is rigged to a Seiko digital wristwatch bought two weeks ago at a Fred Meyer department store in Roseburg, Oregon. When it's fitted into the explosive, it will be set to detonate at five p.m. the next day, Monday, October 11, 1993.

When he finishes assembling the bomb, he repacks the remaining materials in his backpack, peels off his shoes and socks, and walks barefoot along a narrow deer path to the substation. The complex is ringed on four sides by a chain-link fence, but it's only eight feet high and unbarbed. He slides the bomb under the fence using a hole dug two days ago to look like the work of a ground squirrel, tosses his pack over the fence and begins climbing, his heavily calloused toes finding footholds in the diamonds of chain-linked metal.

Dropping down inside the complex, he makes his way to the central transformer housing, careful to tread only on grass or cement. With a screwdriver, he removes a metal panel protecting the transformers and slots the slim disk of explosive below a transformer box at the center of a long row of them. If his calculations are correct, the explosion will blow the transformer apart, sending a fireball thirty feet into the air and setting off the circuit breakers. Since this is only one of two substations serving the Franklin Valley, power company engineers will be able to quickly redirect the power supply. Power will be out in Franklin for at most an hour or two, possibly less if their sensors are better than he thinks they are. But it will go out.

He engages the timing device and reaches into his pack for one final item, a small plastic box containing five bright flakes of blasted aluminum harvested from a Seiko watch identical to the one used in the timing device. Using tweezers, he sets the glittering shards of metal, each coated with a nearly invisible dusting of explosive powder, in the grass and soil below the transformer housing in a broad blast pattern. The last, and largest, aluminum flake, containing a nearly complete serial number, he inserts into the dirt as if it had lodged that way after the blast.

He steps back to inspect his work, and when he's satisfied, he scans the site for any items – a glove, his sunglasses, a stray piece of clothing – that he might have dropped. Seeing none, he makes his way back to the fence line, once again careful to leave no footprints in the dirt, and draws a six-by-eight card from his pack. The hand-lettered note reads:

On behalf of the lynx, we bring you an hour of darkness. Next time we won't be so gentle.

     – The Jack Frost Collective.

He props the card against the base of the fence, well out of the blast radius. Then he tosses his pack back over the fence and clambers up and out of the substation compound. He has a long hike over the north rim of the canyon to the stand of chokecherry bushes where he ditched his bike, but at least now, at night, he can take main roads without being seen.

He turns back for a final look at the darkened substation, flicks on his flashlight, and sets off along the service road.

PART ONE

Fire on the Mountain

"You got a lot of balls, Jack, I'll give you that," Erskine said. "But you're crazy if you think an hour or two of darkness is gonna stop Boss Burroughs from cuttin' down all them trees."

"Then I guess we won't stop at an hour or two of darkness," Jack said coolly.

"You were raised up in this valley, just like me," said the old miner. "You know people here, they don't see things the way you do. Even if you're right."

"Don't you get it, Erskine?" Jack said. "That's the whole reason I'm doing this. I turned off their goddamn lights so they could see."

A Screwdriver in the Gears
Bill Blanning, 1971

Chapter One

When Tish Threadgill pokes her head into the newsroom a little before four that Monday, the reporters have pulled their chairs around Rod Arango's desk as he logs their story ideas on a whiteboard above a black-and-white TV silently playing CNN's coverage of the NAFTA hearings in Congress. In the Denver papers, NAFTA will run on page one, but here in Franklin, home to America's smallest newspaper war, local news is king, and going by the list on Rod's whiteboard, the staff of the *Daily Flyer* is crapping out. On the board, Tish sees nothing but process stories and a fluff piece about a pair of buskers who trained their dog to pick up dollar bills in her teeth. Moira Mangan, bless her black Irish heart, is on the phone from the courthouse where she's trying to rustle up news out of the day's court docket, while the new intern – Gina, maybe? Gigi? – sits in a corner chewing her hair and gazing at Hot Rod Arango as upon the face of God.

Tish would sooner eat glass than publish a newspaper this dull, but in the instant before they see her, she has to choke back an ugly impulse to cry. She hired everyone in this room. Some started out as interns. Others walked in off the street, their clip files consisting of a few exclamation-point-ridden editorials in their college newspapers. She trained them, mentored them, taught them how to write a lede and push back on a source. Her brother Doug, who founded the *Flyer* with her twelve years ago, is dead. Her mother died when Tish was in college, and don't even get her started on the subject of her father. She has no family to speak of anymore. This is her family, right here. And now, if today turns out the way she thinks it will, she'll have to come back in an hour and tell them they're all fired.

"Tish?"

Rod stands at the whiteboard, dry-erase pen in hand, watching her. The reporters all turn in unison, their faces craned upward like so many hungry baby birds.

"It's almost four," she tells him. "We should probably head out."

Silence. Some nods, a side eye or two. The newsroom knows something's up, but not what. The *Flyer* has been in crisis for months, and the reporters, being reporters, aren't idiots. And then there's the matter of what Tish is wearing. Most days Patricia Threadgill's clothing choices skew toward the preppily practical – Top-Siders and polos in summer, khakis and fleece pullovers in winter, Sorel boots and Columbia ski jackets when the snow flies. Clothes she doesn't have to think about, clothes so boring and predictable they serve as a cloak of invisibility. Tish is aware that the way she dresses and the fact that she hasn't shaved her legs regularly since the Reagan administration have led to whispers around town that she's a lesbian, but she doesn't care because a.) she isn't a lesbian; and b.) invisibility has always been her secret weapon. It's what makes her a great reporter and it's a big part of why she still owns a daily newspaper five years after her manic-depressive brother hung himself in a Denver hotel room, leaving the paper to her. Men still make most of the decisions, even here in tree-hugging, Anita Hill-believing Franklin, Colorado, and a woman that men don't see coming is a woman they underestimate every time.

Today, though, Tish has decided she needs to be seen. She may even have to do a little seducing, a gruesome prospect given that the seducee is Leo Mayer, publisher of the *Daily Bulletin*, her paper's competitor, and owner of a pair of wayward hands that unfailingly found their way to Tish's ass late at night in the layout room when she was fresh out of college and working for the *Bully*. Creep then, creep now, but Tish needs Leo thinking with his pencil today, so not only has she shaved her legs, but she's wearing a most un-Tish-like thigh-length sheath dress and pearl-gray Yves St. Laurent slingback heels that cost more than she spent on ink last year.

"Hubba hubba," Rod teases as he passes through the newsroom doorway.

"Bite me, Arango," she says.

In truth, Rod is looking pretty delectable himself in a pale blue button-down and khakis, his surfer-dude mane of jet black hair brushed girlishly out of his face. And here's another reason why Tish doesn't care what Franklin's overgrown ski bums think of her: She and Hot Rod used to be an item. Not for long, and technically her brother was the boss then, but still, Tish thinks as they stride through the *Flyer's* front office: Put *that* in your Coke can and drink it, Clarence Thomas.

"We've got to hit him hard on the layoffs," she says out on the sidewalk. "I'm not taking the deal if it means putting you guys out on the street."

"He's not going to take everybody," Rod says. "You know that. He can't."

"He's got to take the newsroom at least," she says. "And our ad reps are way better than his. Kendra is, anyway. Jason, too."

Rod nods, his finely sculpted face pensive in a manner that suggests he has thoughts he is wise enough to keep to himself. Which is cool, as far as Tish is concerned. Ad reps are ad reps. They'll find work at the Franklin Skiing Company and make more money doing it. But there are only two employers of newspaper reporters in the city of Franklin, and barring a last-minute miracle, in a matter of weeks there will only be one.

The *Daily Bulletin* is housed in an actual house, a two-story Victorian complete with gingerbread trim and an honest-to-God turret that dates back to Franklin's early days as silver-mining boom town. Tish worked here for two years in the seventies when the *Bully* was still a sleepy small-town weekly and she knows the way to Leo's office without having to ask for directions from the blonde Barbie doll Leo has installed at the front desk. Where Tish would like to go is into the *Bully* newsroom to get a peek at *their* afternoon news budget, or failing that, downstairs to the basement where Leo keeps his pride and joy, a single-tower Goss web-fed printing press with all the latest computerized bells and whistles. But Tish isn't here to fondle the Goss's parallel folders, gratifying as that might be, so she follows Front Desk Barbie up the carpeted stairs to Leo's office, located in what was once the home's master bedroom.

The last time Tish set foot in this room, twelve years ago, her brother was alive and Leo had called them in to tell them he was spiking a story Doug had reported that Hank Dunow, patriarch of the family that owned the Franklin Skiing Company, had fathered a child out of wedlock. Doug had spent months nailing down the story, which had circulated around town in one form or another for more than a decade, whispered in ski patrol shacks and late at night at the Lazy T Bar & Grill. When Doug called Dunow for comment, the old man threatened to pull the ski company's ads in the *Bulletin* if the story ran. When Leo agreed to kill it, Doug quit on the spot and wrote up the story that night. Then, with Tish's help, he distributed it the next morning to homes and businesses around town on a single double-sided sheet of paper under the banner, *The Franklin Flyer*.

Twelve years later, Leo presides over an ornate rosewood desk before a postcard-worthy view of Mount Boyd, grinning like the kid who ate all the gumballs. Because he has, in fact, eaten all the gumballs. The *Flyer*'s upstart success forced Leo to launch his own daily edition, which, over the last five years, has strangled the life out of Tish's business. Leo knows it, Tish knows it, and she senses that the price of avoiding economic ruin is going to be telling the handsy old prick what a genius he is for pulling it off.

Two tiny wooden chairs have been set out for Rod and Tish, as if they were misbehaving schoolchildren called to the principal's office, but this bothers Tish less than the presence of Kenny Carlisle at Leo's side. Carlisle is a nasty piece of work, round and balding, with an unwipeable smirk of Ivy League smugness on his lips, but more than anything he's expensive. Four hundred dollars an hour, last Tish checked. If Leo Mayer, that famous skinflint, has invited him here, it can only mean he thinks the meeting won't take long.

"So, Tish," Kenny says, once they've all settled into their seats. "Leo tells me you're finally coming to your senses on this."

"Well, I'm ready to talk about coming to my senses," she says. "I'm not sure I'm there yet."

"Of course," Kenny says. "But I think it's in everyone's interest to get this process moving. If I'm not mistaken, you missed payroll last month."

She shoots a glance at Rod, who eyes the floor, his long black hair a curtain over his eyes. This is *not* how she saw this meeting kicking off. She expected some flirting, some posturing, maybe even a few gauzy lies about the good old days. Not this, not so fast.

"It was just for a few days," she says. "Everybody's paid up now."

"It was almost two weeks," Kenny says. "And there's no guarantee you'll be able to make payroll next month. Leo can bail you out up to a point. He's prepared to cover your debts with your printer and pay your rent through to the end of the year, by which time hopefully you can get out of your lease. But let's not kid ourselves. He's doing you a favor here, not the other way around."

Still nothing from Rod, who only nods ruefully at this apparently self-evident truth. This meeting is less than two minutes old, but if screaming were an option, Tish would be screaming. Instead, she says: "I need to protect my people, Leo."

"I understand that," her old boss says. "And as I told you, we're happy to bring Rod on as a reporter here. I don't think there'll be any problem finding you a place as well."

"What about Moira Mangan?" Rod asks, piping up for the first time. "She's a hell of a reporter. She beats you guys on cops and courts practically every week."

"Maybe you can bring her on at the magazine," Leo suggests. "You'll need somebody to write the copy once it gets up and running."

Ah yes, the magazine. On the phone, and over lunch at the Hotel Franklin, Leo proposed launching a glossy lifestyle magazine, to be called simply *Franklin*, packed with four-color photo spreads of the valley's pricier real estate developments. As it happens, Tish ran the numbers for just such a magazine a few years ago and knows the math only works if the new resort is approved for Elkhorn Canyon. In other words, in exchange for closing her newspaper and laying off all but two of her employees, Leo will give her a job running a magazine that doesn't exist touting a proposed ski resort she's spent the past six years fighting to stop.

"I don't have to do this, you know," she says. "If I can hang on for another month or two, we're in ski season and ad revenue'll start picking up. We beat you on news most days, anyway. I can slim down, work with a skeleton crew until we get into the black. We did it before, we can do it again."

"You didn't owe the bank a hundred and fifty thousand dollars then," Kenny says, biting down hard on the word *dollars* as if the term might be unfamiliar to her.

Again, screaming feels like a viable option. The missed payroll is one thing, but how can Kenny Carlisle know the amount of her line of credit with the Franklin Savings Bank? She hasn't shown Leo her books. That was supposed to come later, after they'd finalized the outlines of the deal. Before she can work all this out, before in fact Kenny has finished counting her financial sins on his fat little fingers, Leo's eyes lock with Rod's. It's only a second, but Tish catches it out of the corner of her eye. And then Rod is talking.

"Mr. Carlisle's right," he says. "If you put this off, they'll just wait you out and you'll get nothing. You've got to think of yourself here. You could be wiped out by this."

A memory: It's five years ago, and Doug has just died, having hung himself from a light fixture at a Motel 6 on I-70. Tish is in Denver, gutted by grief, spending every waking hour talking to cops, talking to lawyers, and talking herself out of following her beloved older brother into the grave. For nearly a week, Rod stays in Franklin, covering multiple beats and taking business calls Tish isn't around to take. He isn't even the paper's editor yet. He's just a reporter, but thanks to their brief time as a couple, he and Tish share a shorthand, an honest way of speaking with each other, and she trusts him to do what she's in no condition to do herself.

"I think I need a word with my editor," she says.

"A word about *what*?" Kenny says.

But she's staring at Rod and in his eyes she can see he's trying to apologize. This had been their relationship, such as it was. Rod was beautiful and young, Tish was older and plain, and every few weeks she caught him with a different girl. He apologized every time, and every time he wore the same expression of stunned outrage, as if his transgression was something that had been done to him, not the other way around.

"You gave them my banking statements," she says.

"What? No way!" he sputters. "Tish, come on, I would never do that."

"Then you told them what was in them," she says. "That's how they know about the line of credit. That's how Leo knows how much I owe the printer and how far behind we are on the rent. You told them. You went behind my back and you told them."

"Now, now, let's dial back the accusations here," Kenny says.

He may in fact say quite a bit more, but Tish hears none of it. The seat of her too-small chair feels as if it's on fire; the very air around her boils. She is aware that this is only anger, and that she would be best advised to ignore it, that Rod is right that her only route to avoiding bankruptcy court is closing down the *Flyer* today. But none of that matters because before she knows it she's out of her chair screaming. The screams take the form of telling Kenny Carlisle he can go fuck himself and suggesting to Rod Arango that he can suck it, but the actual words are irrelevant. Her only real purpose is to throw up a wall of sound that will prevent the three men in the room from stopping her from leaving it.

She's out on Main Street, marching through the bright fall afternoon half a block from the *Bulletin's* offices when Rod catches up to her. He's out of breath, his runway-model cheekbones blazing with exertion.

"I didn't tell them anything," he pants. "They already knew. They already knew everything."

"How dare you," she shoots back.

"I'm telling you, Leo has some buddy at the bank," he says. "He's seen all the paperwork. He knew everything before he even called me."

"How dare you," she repeats. "When I met you, you were tuning skis, for God's sake. If it wasn't for me and Doug, you'd *still* be tuning skis."

"I'm married now," he says, as if this explains everything. "I've got a kid to support."

With that, she hauls off and slaps him. For weeks afterward, Tish will replay this moment, wondering what a therapist would say about a thirty-seven-year-old unmarried woman slapping a younger ex-lover when he dared bring up his responsibilities to his family. In the moment, however, it feels terrific. All around them on Main Street, people have stopped, riveted by the spectacle of the publisher of one of the city's two daily newspapers slapping her editor across the face. But she feels liberated. Vindicated. Rod Arango is a traitor. She loved him, first, very briefly, as a boyfriend, and then for six more years like a brother, but he never loved her back, not really, and now she's free of him.

The vibe in the *Flyer's* offices when she stomps through the door a few minutes later is off-puttingly normal. News of Tish's face-slapping incident on Main Street has not yet reached the office, and as far as everyone here is concerned it's just another drowsy off-season Monday afternoon. At the front desk, Jen, on the phone with an advertiser, hands Tish a thick stack of pink message slips, as Kendra darts in from Ad Rep Village to report that Marty's Liquor Mart is threatening to shrink its weekly ad buy, and Lydia calls from paste-up to say the waxing machine is low on wax again.

Tish ignores all this and heads for the newsroom, now a hive of pre-deadline activity. Moira is back from the courthouse and sits at her desk pounding out copy. Chuck Quigley, who covers county politics, is on the phone with someone from the sanitation department, and Perry Barlow, her dyslexic human-interest features guy, is pecking at the keys of his computer, stopping every few seconds to check a pocket spelling dictionary on his desk.

If the newsroom had a door she would slam it, but it doesn't so she claps her hands once, loudly, and announces: "Everyone, I'm going to need your attention."

Annnnd … nothing happens. Moira goes on banging out copy, Perry flips through his spelling dictionary, and Chuck chit-chats with his county staffer about Saturday trash deliveries.

"Chuck, put down the damn phone!" Tish snaps. "That goes for all of you. I need your attention right now."

"Sorry, sorry, gotta go," Chuck says, slamming the phone in its cradle. He's a long, skinny kid, all of twenty-three, with blocky glasses and a protruding brow. Half his body weight, Tish thinks, not for the first time, is forehead and Adam's apple.

"Thank you," she says, bringing it down a notch. "There's been a slight change of plans. It looks like I'll be editing the paper tonight."

Silence. Chuck looks at Moira, Perry looks at the intern Gina – or is it Gigi? – who stares back at him bewildered and chews her hair.

"What about Rod?" Moira asks.

"Rod Arango no longer works for this newspaper," Tish says.

"He quit?" says Perry in disbelief.

"No, he was fired," Tish says. "For cause. Obviously, we'll need to staff up to fill his place, but for now I'll be driving the bus, with Moira as my deputy. If I'm not in the room, Moira is the boss. Got it?"

"Wait, hold on," Moira says. "What the hell happened?"

"I fired his ass is what happened," Tish says. "He works for the *Bully* now." She turns to look at the whiteboard. "Chuck, how're you coming with that sanitation story?"

The young reporter's golf-ball-sized Adam's apple rises and falls, rises and falls, as he struggles to process the last minute of his life.

"Words, Chuck. I need words."

"Right, right, that was my last call just now," he says. "I've got it pretty well nailed down, I think. In response to citizen complaints, they're adding Saturday pickup in North Franklin and around the Airport Shopping Center."

"Okay. Boring, but okay," she says. "Give me ten inches. No, make it twelve and lead with the citizen complaints. Same with your schools piece, Perry. Short and smart, lots of quotes. But we need a front page, people. It's almost five and I'm not seeing a front page."

"You didn't take the buyout, did you?" Moira says.

Tish squares up, taking the punch. She's had her suspicions about Moira and Rod. Nothing definite, just noticing the nights Moira stayed late to help him write headlines, mornings they've come in to work together having "met" on the ski hill. Once or twice Tish has felt an urge to drop a dime to Rod's wife, Belinda, a Mount Boyd ski instructor, but never did. She's long past the day when Rod Arango's wandering eye is any business of hers.

"Could we maybe talk about this after we find a front page?" she says.

"No, we can't," Moira says. "I happen to like my job. If I'm not going to have it tomorrow, I think I have a right to know."

Lydia's hovering in the newsroom doorway now, Tish notices, having wandered in from paste-up. Come to think of it, the rest of the office is suspiciously quiet, too.

"Fine," she says. "For those of you who didn't know, there was an offer on the table for us to merge with the *Bulletin*, and long story short, I didn't take it. It would have meant firing all of you, and I couldn't be a party to that. But as financial decisions go, it wasn't a great one. We're low on cash and I doubt the bank will give us much more. If we can make it to ski season, ad revenue will pick up and we might be able to survive. But I can't promise that. I can't promise you anything. So if you have a line on a job somewhere else, or if you just don't want to live with the uncertainty, you should go right now. But if you stay, I will promise you this much: I will put my heart and soul into this newspaper every minute of every day until they evict me from this building."

The doorway is crowded now, nearly the entire office drawn by the sound of her voice. In their eyes Tish sees shock, but also long-held suspicions confirmed. For weeks, she realizes, just out of earshot, her employees have been arguing and speculating, laying side bets over beers at the Summit Tavern. Now the secret is officially out, and the next two days, maybe the next two hours, will decide if she can keep this leaky boat afloat until ski season or drown all by herself in twelve years of debt.

"Rod sold you out to Leo Mayer?" Chuck asks.

"No comment," Tish says.

"So, he did," Perry says. "Fucking Hot Rod sold you out."

"Look, I love you guys," Tish says. "I love this place. I love it like I love my lungs, like I love my arms and legs and my ten fingers. I'll do just about anything to keep this paper going. But I'm not going to lie: We're up against it. The only way we can survive is if we put out the best newspaper this town has ever seen, and the only way we can do that is if we look forward, not back. So Rod Arango works for the competition now. Forget him. Put him in the rear-view mirror and tell me what you've got that we can put in the paper tomorrow."

The silence is shorter this time, more galvanized, explosive.

"I've got that dog thing," Perry says.

"This is the dog that picks up dollar bills in its teeth?" she asks.

"It's pretty cute, honestly," he says. "The tourists eat it up. I took some decent photos."

"Great, that's our page-one bright," Tish says. "Give me fifteen inches, with art and lots of quotes. But we still need a lead. Moira, tell me you found me a lead story at the courthouse."

Moira has just opened her mouth to tell her boss that, no, she crapped out at the courthouse, too, when the lights flicker and come back up. From somewhere in the distance, so low she'll wonder later if she imagined it, Tish hears a muffled, snapping-tearing sound, like an errant crack of thunder bouncing around the glacier-formed bowl of the Franklin River Valley.

Then the lights go out for good.

Chapter Two

As she rounds the last curve in the dirt road that follows the meandering course of the West Fork of the Franklin River through Elkhorn Canyon, Moira Mangan sees two things that confirm she made the right call driving out here: 1.) there's no sign of reporters from the *Bulletin*; and 2.) the deputy at the scene is Ernie Ellis, the same slope-shouldered, weak-chinned horndog she's spotted at the Summit two out of the last three Friday nights she's pulled shifts there.

The lights were off for two hours the night before, and ever since, the word from Mountain Power has been *regrettable incident at the West Fork Power Substation, mumble, mumble, repair crews on site, mumble, mumble, we're looking into it,* but when Moira rolled into work this morning, she found a message from Sheriff Hayes' secretary saying there'd be a news briefing at noon. A news briefing about what no one would say, but you didn't have to be Bob Woodward to guess the sheriff had some new information on the mysterious outage at the power substation. With a couple hours to kill before the briefing, she'd hopped in her car, and now here she is.

She runs her hand through her hair, tousling it, and undoes the top button of her blouse. On second thought she makes it two buttons and climbs out of the driver's seat, all grins.

"Deputy Double-E!" she cries. "Missed you at the Summit last Friday."

Ernie Ellis looks over his shoulder, as if checking for hidden cameras that might be recording this exchange. "Had to pull a double," he says. "Derek was out sick."

Deputy Derek Hines, baby-faced, with hair the color of a five-alarm fire, sometimes rides wing on Ernie's Friday night pick-up missions. The kid is seriously cute, and Moira might well have jumped his bones already if he wasn't a cop. Ernie, whose idea of dressing to impress is putting on a fresh John Elway Broncos jersey, is another matter. Already, though, Moira can see past him to a length of twisted chain-link fencing and a wide blast ring of charred cement, so she cranks her smile up an extra fifty watts.

"Too bad," she says. "You know it's always way more fun when you're around."

Ernie laughs the sad laugh of a man who knows he's being played and wishes he wasn't.

"Sorry, Moira, but you'll have to get back in your car," he says. "This is a restricted area."

"Come on, I'm not going to touch anything."

"I mean it, you can't go back there. It's a crime scene. The FBI'll be here any minute."

He closes his eyes, embarrassed. He had one job, and only one job, and already he's blown it. Moira, for her part, sends up a silent prayer to Albertus Magnus, the patron saint of morons.

"FBI, huh?" she says. "They think it was some kind of sabotage?"

Ernie is quiet this time, knowing any answer gives her information she doesn't already have. But she's edged just far enough away from him to see past the red-brick service building to the fenced-in warren of high-voltage wires and transformers, which now looks like the filament to a blown light bulb expanded several hundred times.

"Oh, wow," she says. "They short-circuit the thing somehow?"

Ernie swallows slowly, as if physically forcing the answer back down his throat.

"Come on, the sheriff's going to say what happened at the briefing, anyway," she tries.

"Guess you'll just have to wait for the briefing, then."

He preens a little, proud of the snappy retort. He's showing off for her,

Moira realizes, that he can keep his mouth shut, do his job. It's not much, but she can work with it.

"If the FBI's coming, it's got to be some kind of explosion," she says. "Those guys aren't going to come all the way up here just because somebody crossed a couple wires."

"Not necessarily," says Ernie, the voice of experience. "They'd have to look into any kind of sabotage if it caused damage like this."

"So that's all it was, some crossed wires?"

She waits, watching the answer bubble up in him like fizz in a pop bottle. He wants to tell her. He *needs* to tell her. Anyway, she'll hear it all from the sheriff in a couple hours, right?

"Off the record?" he says. She nods, and he leans in, lowering his voice. "They found traces of TNT."

Like Moira, Ernie was raised on Saturday morning cartoons and together they picture Wile E. Coyote, singed as a struck match, stomping off to find the Roadrunner.

"They probably lifted it from a construction site," he says. "Had a timer and everything. I saw it myself."

From where she's standing Moira can see half a dozen Mountain Power employees fanned out across the meadow, bent over, eyes on the grass. Searching for metal fragments, she guesses. This is the front page of tomorrow's paper, definitely. She'll be able to sell the story to the Denver papers, too – maybe *USA Today*, if she's lucky. This is going to be a very long and lucrative day. The only thing that would make it more lucrative would be a nice, juicy photo of twisted metal and charred cement. She reaches for the camera on her arm.

"Uh-uh, no way," Ernie says, moving with alarming speed to block her view. "Absolutely no photos. I'm not bending the rules for you there."

"Hey, I'm a member of the press and this is public property."

"This is private property, owned by the power company. Give me that camera."

"I'm not giving you my friggin' camera, Ernie."

"You'll get it back," he says, taking it from her. "But the sheriff'd fry my ass if I let you take any pictures."

Moira hesitates, or rather she makes a show of hesitating. She has a plan now, a better one.

"Now that you have my camera, will you let me get a closer look?" she asks.

"Nothing doing. That's a crime scene. It's strictly off-limits to the public."

But she just starts walking toward the blast site, daring him to stop her. "I'm not the public," she says. "I'm press. And I'm not going to mess up your precious crime scene."

"Moira, I'm warning you. You need to stop right there."

She keeps right on walking. "Two minutes, that's all I'm asking. Two minutes and the beers are on me all night at the Summit this Friday."

He issues another ineffectual warning, but doesn't try to stop her or follow her. The second point is key. She worried he might follow after her like some hangdog rejected boyfriend, but he remains rooted to the spot waving her camera at her as if it were ransom for her safe and speedy return. So she moves quickly, making a show of inspecting the damaged transformers from all angles. Whoever did this, she decides, planned it carefully because while the metal of the transformers looks like so much blackened confetti, the wide meadow and the trees around it are untouched by flame. She can see no sign of the bomb itself, but little yellow evidence markers sit on the concrete pad of the complex pointing to what looks like a half-melted watch band.

She'd kill to have shots of these, but she has to keep moving around the complex until the brick service building stands between her and Ernie. The instant she's out of his line of sight, she reaches into her purse and pulls out her backup camera, a smaller, lighter Nikon EM she keeps in store for precisely for moments like these. It's a cheap little camera, not usually good enough for newspaper work, but now, aiming from the hip, she gets off five quick shots of the blown central transformer before she hears a voice behind her.

"Hey, you supposed to be taking pictures?"

She whirls around. It's one of the PowerCo guys, gray-haired and fiftyish with thick upper arms and a belly you could park a Chevy in. Tim, the tag on his shirt says.

"I'm with the *Flyer*," she says. "Deputy Ellis let me through."

"I thought they weren't letting people near this," Tim says, still suspicious.

"Different for press, I guess," she says, thinking – no, *knowing* – Deputy Double-E will never forgive her. "You were here last night after it blew?"

"Last night *and* this morning," he says. "I've been here sixteen hours straight. I'd give anything to get my hands on the guys who did this."

"It was some kind of bomb, as I understand it," she says.

"Environmentalists," he says, shaking his head. "They think they're so smart, so righteous. But it's just dumb luck they didn't send up the whole forest with this thing."

Moira reviews her mental tape recorder: Yes, she clearly identified herself to PowerCo Tim as a reporter with the *Flyer*. They're on the record here.

"How do you know it's an environmentalist?" she asks.

"I found the note myself," he says, indignant. "The Jack Frost Collective. Total crock, right?"

She can't help it. Her excitement gets the better of her. "There was a note and it was signed by something called the Jack Frost Collective?"

"Yeah. Like I said, I found the note. They didn't tell you that?"

"No they did – it's just, was there anything else in the note or did it just say 'The Jack Frost Collective'?"

He takes a half-step back, to get a better look at her. "You sure it's okay for you to be here?"

"It is, actually, yes, but" – she glances at her watch – "Ernie said two minutes and I think I'm overstaying my welcome. Nice talking to you, Tim. Hope you get some shut-eye."

The trick, she knows, is to walk fast without appearing to walk fast, so as not to set off alarm bells in the minds of either PowerCo Tim or Deputy Double-E, who has retreated to his patrol cruiser, where he stands brooding over Moira's camera.

"Ernie, thank you," she calls out, waving to him. "You're the best. Really."

"I shouldn't have let you do that," he says, sounding like a man who's just put down his dog.

She feels the weirdest urge to kiss him, not as a reportorial stratagem, but because in that moment she finds she genuinely loves the big, chinless goof. He will probably never speak to her again, but if he does, beers are on her until the end of time.

"Don't worry, you're good," she says. "Like you said, the sheriff is going to give us all the information at the presser today anyway."

"You won't say anything to Hayes, will you? About me letting you go look?"

"Are you kidding?" she says, starting for her own car. "I wouldn't do that to you, ever."

"Hey, don't you want your camera back?" he says, holding it up for her.

"Sorry, forgot," she says, dashing back to grab it. "I gotta fly. Can't miss that briefing."

She thanks him again from the door of her beater Honda and waves as she finishes her U-ey and pulls onto the service road, but as soon as she's out of sight her smile vanishes. She's dodged one bullet, but she needs to get the hell out of Elkhorn Canyon before PowerCo Tim and Deputy Double-E compare notes. She briefly considers stripping the film from the Nikon EM and stashing the cannister in her bra, but decides against it. Moira Mangan prides herself as having bigger *cojones* than any reporter, male or female, in the valley, but even she balks at the prospect of a roadside strip-search.

But no convoy of Elk County patrol cruisers swoops in to stop her when she reaches the mouth of the canyon and turns onto State Highway 22, heading toward the county airfield. It's quarter past eleven, leaving her just enough time to make it back to Franklin for the noon press briefing. Going by Double-E's squirreliness, she's guessing Sheriff Hayes plans to sit on the discovery of the note at least until the Feds get here, and if she asks about a group of eco-terrorists calling themselves the Jack Frost Collective, it will only tip off the *Bulletin* reporters and ruin her scoop. Then there's Bill Blanning, the crotchety old drunk who brought Jack Frost into the world. She'd like to get to him before the Feds do, too.

What the world needs, she thinks, is a little phone you can pull out of your pocket and call anyone whenever you feel like it. But the world doesn't always listen to the likes of Moira Mangan, so she pulls into the empty parking lot of the county airfield, which in the off-season boasts exactly one commercial flight in and out a day, and calls Tish from a pay phone outside the deserted car rental outlet.

"Can you pinch-hit for me on the Hayes presser today?" she asks her boss. "I think I'm onto something and I don't have time to come all the way back to town."

"Sure, but what do you have that's bigger than the sheriff's press conference?" Tish asks.

"Can it wait till I get back?" Moira says. "Let's just say, if I'm right, we'll be kicking the *Bully's* ass up and down the street for a week."

"I like the sound of that, but it's totally nuts here," Tish says. "Everybody's out following up on the blackout and I'm here all day trying to figure out how to make payroll."

"What about Gemma?"

"Who's Gemma?"

"The intern. Quiet, blonde, likes to chew her hair?"

"Her name's Gemma? How did I not know that?"

"I don't know, still waters run deep and all that. Look, I've been working with her and she's super green, but she's not stupid. And this is a Sheriff Hayes press briefing. He'll hand out the press release, give a couple quotes, and leave. A trained monkey could cover it."

"You sure you aren't just avoiding seeing Rod?" Tish asks.

Moira looks out at the parking lot, working through the many permutations of this question. Rod left her three messages last night, the first time to tell her he could still get her a job at the *Bulletin* and the last two times to ask why she hadn't returned his messages.

"He's covering cops and courts for them now?" she asks.

"That's what Chuck says," Tish answers. "He saw Rod poking around the cop shop this morning reading DUI reports. I thought you knew."

"Okay, actually, maybe that could work for us," Moira says. "Have Gemma tell Rod that's why I'm not there. I'm pissed and can't hack being in the same room with him, blah, blah blah. He's such an egomaniac he'll believe it and it'll throw him off the scent."

She hears her boss's giggle down the phone line, soft and girlish. A child's laugh. After a year and a half, Moira still can't get used to that laugh. Tish is such a bad-ass, taking on all these arrogant, preening men, and she laughs like a seven-year-old.

"All right, but bring this in as soon as you can," Tish says. "I'm going to need your help putting this paper to bed tonight."

Ten minutes later, as she pulls off Highway 22 at the sign for the Gilburne Saloon and starts up County Road 4 toward Bill Blanning's spread, Moira feels a familiar ache of homesickness flow into her like water into a sponge. She's only fifteen miles from downtown Franklin, but as soon as she leaves the freeway she's in country that looks and smells like the land around Corvallis, Montana, the flyspeck ranching town where she grew up. High in the upper folds of the canyon, she can see cows and their calves, red and black Simmentals mostly, along with a few hulking black Angus, heads down, feasting on the last of the tall summer grass. This is the other side of the Franklin River Valley, the working side. The un-silly side. The side that will be displaced if the new ski resort goes in. Strung out along the winding county road are a handful of mansions belonging to oilpatch millionaires and over-the-hill rock stars who couldn't castrate a calf if the directions were printed on the scrotum, but most of the families here inherited their small, whitewashed ranch homes from parents and grandparents who bought in after the silver bust at the end of the last century. If she had to, Moira could turn up at any corral in the valley, reach for a Newberry knife, and get right to work.

Moira Mangan, as she'll tell anyone who asks, is a ranch girl, born and bred. She could ride a horse before she started school, and almost from the day she could walk she was out tracking elk and deer in the Bitterroot Mountains with her father and brothers. In the winter of her senior year at Corvallis High, after spending eight hours tracking a gut-shot ten-point buck, she abruptly quit, disgusted by the waste and cruelty of the sport. Her father blamed *Blood Sport*, Bill Blanning's sulphurously funny account of his years as a professional hunting guide. Moira didn't need to read a book to feel nauseated at the sight of a pack of teenage boys in cammies chasing a wounded animal up a ravine in snowmobiles, but her father wasn't entirely wrong. Blanning was a hippie and a freak, but in his books he said everything she'd ever wanted to tell her father and her brothers – about the beauty of the land they'd inherited and all the stupid ways they were trashing it – but never had the courage to say out loud.

She was fourteen when she read Blanning's first book, *Mountain Man*, about the years he'd lived alone in a hunting cabin right here in Gilburne Canyon, and by the time she finished college she'd read it so many times she had to secure the binding with duct tape. But like everybody else, her favorite among his books is *A Screwdriver in the Gears*. Published in 1971, the novel follows a wise-ass hunting guide named Jack Frost and a band of disaffected hippies as they declare war on rapacious logging outfit in Southwestern Colorado, starting with a bomb that destroys a remote power station supplying a logging camp.

Blanning long ago traded the hunting cabin for a sprawling ranch house set back a quarter mile from the main road in a stand of cottonwood trees. The gated entrance is marked by two enormous signs reading "Private Property – Keep Out!" and "Warning: Vicious Dogs!" The gate isn't locked, however, and every few years, college kids from Boulder or Fort Collins, drunk, carrying out a fraternity dare, ignore the signs and get well and truly mauled by Blanning's Rottweilers. Moira, on the experience of two previous visits to Blanning's Gilburne Canyon lair, knows to stay in her car with the windows up as she cruises the long driveway from the county road. Fifty yards from the house, she sees them, four full-grown Rotts, a bitch and three of her pups, galloping toward her car, already at full bawl. She doesn't slow down or speed up, just keeps poking along the dirt driveway as the dogs lope alongside her tiny Honda Civic hurling their forepaws at the windows, barking and snapping and baring their teeth. She grew up around working dogs every bit as fierce as these, but still it's terrifying. Each of the dogs weighs a hundred pounds or more and looks fully capable of bashing its paws through her windows and devouring her whole. But she keeps driving until she reaches Blanning's yard where she waits, struggling to tune out the murderous racket outside her car windows, until the door swings open and Bill Blanning steps onto the porch.

It's noon, which means he probably just woke up, and he stands barefoot in a black-and-white checked bathrobe, a breached shotgun in one hand. Moira is surprised, as always, by how small Blanning is in person, five-seven, a hundred and fifty pounds soaking wet. His eyes are a grayblue smear and his long, silvering hair is wild as grass. The dogs continue flinging themselves at her windows, barking and snapping their teeth, their energy seemingly limitless until Blanning recognizes something about the young woman waving frantically to him from the front seat and inserts two fingers in his mouth, producing an ear-piercing wolf whistle.

"Brando, Jimmy Dean, get over here!" he shouts. "You too, Bardot! Knock it off!"

As if shot with tranquilizer darts, the dogs fall away from the windows of the Civic and retreat, whining plaintively, to the porch where they huddle in a protective clutch around Blanning's hairy legs. Moira counts a very slow five before cracking the driver's-side door and poking her head out, ready to dive back inside if the dogs stir. But they don't even growl, and Moira realizes her childhood literary hero is grinning at her, his pale belly peeking obscenely through his bathrobe.

"You're … uh …" he says, his voice husky from disuse.

"Moira Mangan," she says, "from the *Daily Flyer*."

He nods. "I figured one of you vultures'd be out here sooner or later."

"So then you've heard?"

"Sheriff called me himself this morning. Woke me out of a sound god-damn sleep to call me an eco-terrorist."

Inwardly, Moira smiles. This is her second confirmation. Her story is now officially gold.

"You have a few minutes?" she asks. "I'd like to talk to you about that."

Blanning's official position, repeated endlessly in magazine profiles and on talk-show couches, is that all reporters are vultures and parasites, but he's a lonely old man in love with the sound of his own voice. He's also a famous writer who hasn't published a book in twenty years. He can glare all he wants, but Moira knows he'll talk to anyone with a notepad.

"Aw, hell," he says. "Come on in. Give me a minute to make myself presentable."

This is Moira's third visit to the Blanning compound so she barely registers the fact that has appeared in every profile of Blanning published since the early sixties, that in this home of a lifelong hunter there isn't a single wildlife trophy: no antlers or elkhorns, no snarling wildcat or baying bear's head. What Moira notices instead, beyond the overpowering reek of wet dog, is how tidy the place is, all things considered. Blanning is a quart-a-day drunk who sleeps until noon and has been known to shoot out the lightbulbs in his own home, yet the scuffed pinewood floor is swept clean and every book on his floor-to-ceiling shelves sits neatly in its place. It must be true what she's heard that a steady stream of aco-lytes, mostly female, mostly from practical, ranching backgrounds like her own, pass through here, cleaning and dusting and laundering so the great man doesn't drown in a lake of his own filth.

When he comes out, he's wearing jeans ironed to a crease and a faded chambray shirt, his hair slicked back in an oily pompadour like a fifties lounge singer. Despite the decades of abuse he's heaped upon it, his face is still handsome: cleft chin, hawk-like nose, a narrowness around the eyes that gives him a perpetual squint. He limps, listing to his left like some broken-down rodeo cowboy, but there's a faint swagger in his step as he reaches for the bottle of Wild Turkey on the kitchen table and waves Moira toward the back porch, where the dogs rejoin them, the four exhausted Rottweilers draping themselves around his feet like hundred-pound lapdogs.

All this, Moira knows, is part of the standard Blanning treatment. From his back porch, the rude cabin he describes in *Mountain Man* is visible at the easternmost end of the canyon – or it would be if it weren't hidden under dense forest cover. Anyone even remotely acquainted with the Blanning legend knows the story, how he moved here in 1953, weeks after his discharge from the Marines, and built the cabin himself from reclaimed lumber on an abandoned mining claim local ranchers considered too marginal to be worth buying outright. Silver had crashed decades before and the ski resort was little more than a glint in Hank Dunow's eye, and the few people still living in the valley either ran cattle or sold supplies and drink to those who did. For two years, while his fellow Americans went to college on the GI Bill and raised their 2.3 children in suburban splendor, Blanning lived alone in Gilburne Canyon, growing his own food in summer and hunting and trapping what he needed in the winters. Since then, he's traveled the country working as a forest ranger, a guide for geology expeditions, and tracker and hunting guide, but like a salmon swimming hundreds of miles upstream past dams and waterfalls to spawn in the creek bed where it was born, he has always returned to this one unremarkable box canyon off the Franklin River, where he's lived and worked and drank for forty years.

"I didn't have anything to do with it, if that's what you're here to ask me," he says, pouring two generous fingers of Wild Turkey into a gummy-looking water glass. "If I did, I sure as hell wouldn't call it a collective."

"That's what they called themselves in the note, 'The Jack Frost Collective'?" Moira asks.

"According to Hayes, yeah." He makes quotation marks in the air. "'On behalf of the lynx, we bring you an hour of darkness. Next time we won't be so gentle,' signed The Jack Frost Collective."

Blanning sips his whiskey as Moira writes this down in her reporter's pad.

"You didn't have that, did you?" he says, with a chuckle. "Not till just now."

She ignores his question. "Did the note say anything else?"

"Are you quoting me?"

"On this, no. But I want to be sure I have the exact wording."

"Well, I didn't see it myself," he says. "But that's what Hayes told me: 'On behalf of the lynx, we bring you an hour of darkness. Next time we won't be so gentle,' and then this collective bullshit."

"Sounds like a threat," she says. "Like they're saying there's going to be a next time."

"Sure does."

"And they blew out a power station like Jack Frost does in *A Screwdriver in the Gears*."

"They sure did."

"So you can see why people could think you might be involved – not as an active participant, maybe, but behind the scenes."

His eyes have cleared by now, returning to their natural glittery blue, and when he fixes her with a stare Moira has an intimation, if only for an instant, of the charismatic holy fool who wrote three books that changed how Americans see the West.

"It's just a book, man," he says. "I didn't do any of those things I wrote about. I was making shit up, telling stories. Anyway, it was twenty years ago. I got paid to write another one just like it and I still haven't finished it. Probably never will."

This, too, is part of the legend of Bill Blanning, that after a run of three bestselling books, two nonfiction polemics and one antic novel, the muse abandoned him and he's published nothing since beyond an overpriced coffee-table book full of pictures he didn't take and a collection of early journal entries and magazine pieces cobbled together by his editors.

"Okay, here's my quote," he says. "You ready? I don't know who did this thing. Nobody approached me. Nobody asked my advice, and if they had I would've said, where were you twenty years ago when this might have done some good?"

"So you see this as a pointless act?"

"I applaud the effort," he says. "Somebody's gotta put a screwdriver in the gears every now and then. But is this going to save Elkhorn Canyon? Is this gonna save that poor cat up in those hills, hunting snowshoe hare? I'm not holding my breath. If you ask me, this is mostly about a few people trying to feel better about themselves and maybe get a little payback."

"Wow, you're really trying to piss everybody off this time."

He shrugs, granting her point, but his mind is already somewhere else. He drinks off the last of the Wild Turkey and gestures with his chin to the end of the box canyon, where his old cabin still rots deep in the spruce and pine.

"When I first came up here, it was just me and some traps and a rifle," he says. "I ate what I killed. How much damage could I do? Now, it's not just me. It's thousands of me. It's tens of thousands of me's filling up these valleys, and they're bringing their wives and kids and their big-ass cars. It's an infestation, man. We're like the leafy spurge. You ever see leafy spurge? Some people call it wolf's milk. Came over from Europe a hundred years ago, probably as an exotic in somebody's seed bag, and followed the wagons and railroads. And now it's everywhere, all over the West. You can't get rid of it. It invades a field of native grasses, sucks up all the water and nutrients, then poisons the ground under it so nothing else can grow. Sound familiar? That's us, Moira Mangan of the *Daily Flying Fuck*. We're walking, talking leafy spurge." He cuts a glance in her direction. "Sometimes, I swear, I think the most constructive thing a committed lover of the Earth can do is shoot himself. Quiet. Clean. A bullet to the temple. Boom, gone. One less weed in the garden, right?"

Moira finds she's closed her notebook. She's heard the riff about the leafy spurge before. He said more or less exactly the same thing, in more or less the same words, when he delivered a lecture at the University of Montana her senior year. But the last part is new. She's never heard Bill

29

Blanning say we should all do the world a favor and put a bullet in our brains.

Finally, though, the silence becomes unbearable and he laughs. "Of course, I'm not that evolved yet," he says, reaching for the whiskey bottle. "So for now, I just drink."

◆ ◆ ◆

It's nearly two by the time Moira gets back to the office, where Gemma is waiting with a copy of the press release Sheriff Hayes distributed at the briefing. As expected, the thing is a masterpiece of bureaucratic understatement. Citing vaguely defined "evidence of sabotage or tampering," Hayes says the "federal authorities" have been called in, but stops short of saying what caused the blast. Under questioning from Gemma and Rod Arango, the sheriff conceded that his "preliminary investigation suggested an explosive device may have been involved," but he insisted that tests were still underway, and that if it was indeed a bomb, it was too early to say what kind it was or who may have planted it.

An hour later, as Moira is batting out a draft of her piece, the phone on her desk beeps and Jen the receptionist comes on the line: "Moira, Sheriff Hayes for you. Line two."

"Mo's in trooouble!" Chuck and Perry sing out.

"You want me to take this?" Tish asks, ignoring them.

"It's cool, I got it," Moira says.

Still, she takes a moment, flipping to a fresh page in her notepad and squaring her shoulders for the shitstorm she knows is coming, before she hits the button for line two.

"Afternoon, Sheriff!" she chirps. "I was just about to – "

"What's all this I hear about you going down to talk with Bill Blanning?"

"Oh no, did Bill tattle on me?" she says brightly.

Nothing. Just dead air. Sheriff Lorne Hayes is a tall, erect man in his middle sixties with a former cattleman's native directness. He can't stand jokes, which is one reason why Moira can't resist making them.

"I'm sorry, Sheriff," she says. "I was just about to come down to talk to you about that."

"I'll save you the trip," he says. "You're not running any of that crap. I gave my statement this morning. The rest is embargoed."

"By 'the rest,' do you mean the note signed by the Jack Frost Collective?"

"I mean everything that wasn't in my statement," he snaps. "I don't know just what the hell went on at that crime scene today, but I'm trying to run a criminal investigation here. I've got the FBI breathing down my neck and I don't need some reporter putting out facts out of context."

"So, help me understand the context, Sheriff," she says.

Hayes was raised roping steers and castrating calves and keeps a Styrofoam cup on a corner of his desk where he discreetly spits tobacco juice while he works. Moira grew up surrounded by men like this. It's as easy for her to talk back to him as it would be to spit in her own father's face. But she has the contact sheet of the photos she took in Elkhorn Canyon on the desk in front of her. They're slightly out of focus, but you can make out the twisted metal and blackened cement.

"Sir, I mean no disrespect, but this story is running," she says. "We have photographs and multiple confirmations on the contents of the note."

"You have *photos*?" he roars. "Of what?"

Tish, crosses the room in two long-legged strides and puts the call on speaker.

"Sheriff, this is Tish Threadgill," she says. "My reporter had permission to be where she was standing when she took those photos."

"Well, she sure as shit didn't have my deputy's permission to take them," the sheriff fires back, so infuriated he's forgotten his usual rule about ladies and profanity.

"Sir, we would very much prefer to do this story with your cooperation and we definitely want to hear anything you have to say about what we're going to print," Tish says. "But the fact is a group calling itself the Jack Frost Collective blew up a power station, just like they do in Bill Blanning's book, and now it sounds like they're threatening to strike again."

"There is no goddamn collective," the sheriff says. "This is just some kids trying to scare the bejesus out of everybody and get their names in the papers. And you're helping them. You're giving them exactly what they want."

"We're reporting the news, Sheriff," Tish says.

"You're trying to save your little newspaper is what you're doing," he says. "And that's fine, but right now you're interfering in an active investigation. My deputy out at the crime site is a damn fool, but that girl had no business monkeying around back there. She knows it. You know it. If you print this, it could mushroom this thing all out of proportion. So I want you to think about what you're doing. I want you to think real hard."

Tish hits the key that mutes the phone and turns to Moira. "How solid are we on this?" she asks. "I need you to be honest with me. We don't have to do this now. We can run it tomorrow."

Moira has already walked her boss through the story twice, but now she does it again. The photos at the bomb site. The eyewitness report about the note from Tim at Mountain Power. He confirmed his full name, Tim Melton, and the wording of the note, though nothing else, in the thirty seconds she kept him on the phone before he hung up. Bill Blanning also confirmed the note, along with the language threatening more attacks.

But there's what it says in journalism textbooks, and then there's the real world, and in the real world, Franklin is a very, very small town. Moira can't imagine the pressure her boss is under, the landlords she's having to beg for extensions, the bankers she's having to beg for better terms, the employees coming to her talking about mortgages and small kids. If this all goes sideways, she has no safety net. And it won't just be her that gets hurt.

When Moira winds up her story, Tish nods, stares a moment at the bare wall, thinking, then presses the button for the speaker phone.

"We're running the story as is, Sheriff," she says. "If you have any comment you would like to make about the Jack Frost Collective or about the state of your investigation, we're all ears."

In the crackling silence, Moira could swear she can hear the steam whistling out Lorne Hayes' ears.

"You're going to regret this, Patricia," he says. "You and your half-assed little newspaper, you're going to regret this. Print *that*."

Tish nods to the notepad in Moira's hand and she writes down his words verbatim.

Moira's main story fills most of the front page under a massive double-decker head:

BOMBER'S NOTE REVEALED
Mystery 'Collective' Steals Page from Famed Novel

Inside, she has a longer piece recounting her interview with Bill Blanning and summarizing the relevant plot points of *A Screwdriver in the Gears*. Finally, at Tish's insistence, she put together a shorter sidebar offering a first-hand description of the bomb site and how she came to take the grainy photos appearing on the front page.

All told, it's more than a hundred inches of eleven-point Times New Roman, every word of it fact-checked and proofread by Tish four times before she lets Lydia run the text through the waxer and lay it out on her light boards. Only after Moira has turned in her final copy for the *Flyer* does Tish help her rework the text for the *Denver Post*, whose editors buy fifteen inches of her main story for page one and twenty inches of her Blanning interview to run inside. By midnight when she faxes a shorter version of her main story to *USA Today*, which will distribute it nationwide via the Gannett chain, Moira has made seven hundred dollars for one night's work.

When the edition finally closes, the rest of the newsroom hits the Summit for beers, but Moira decides to skip the revelries and walks home alone along Frederick Street, which follows the contours of north slope of Mount Boyd. Moira knows she should be nervous, knows it would be weird not to feel at least a little jittery after what she's just been through, but she knows what she heard and she trusts her instincts about the rest. Besides, what's the worst that could happen? If she gets something wrong and Tish fires her, she'll just take a few more shifts at the Summit until she finds a job at another paper, maybe in a ski town, maybe something bigger and better in a real city. Ever since Tish missed payroll in September, Moira has been sending out clip files and reading the want-ads in *Editor & Publisher*. Times are tough in the news business, but she's good at her job. Today is a case in point, but she doesn't need sixty-point wood and a byline in *USA Today* to know what she can do.

She's a ranch girl. She can take care of herself, always.

She's rounding the corner in front of her apartment building, rummaging in her purse for her keys, when she sees a man standing outside the main entrance, reading a battered copy of *Time* magazine by the light coming through the window. He's in his early thirties, tall and fit, with shoulder-length black hair and cheekbones to make a Kennedy weep.

"Jesus, Rod, you scared me," she says. "How long have you been out here?"

"Not long," he says, plainly lying. "You never returned my calls."

From the beginning Moira knew it was a mistake to sleep with Rod Arango, but for a long time it was a mistake she was happy to make. The man's freaking gorgeous, for one thing, and he's smarter and more sensitive than anyone that beautiful has any right to be. She feels guilty about his wife, but only so much. Belinda knew what she was getting into when she married him, or she ought to have, since she stole him from another woman herself. The fact is, Moira flat *likes* Rod. He bleeds newsprint black, and he's the kind of guy who would try to get his girlfriend, even his secret bit on the side, a job when it looks like her own might melt into the ether.

"I've been a little busy," she says. "Maybe you've heard, the whole valley's blowing up."

"It was weird you didn't come to the presser today," he says. "If that's really going to be a problem, I can switch to a different beat."

She laughs, shaking her head, trying to imagine being so madly in love with yourself that you'd believe everyone else is that madly in love with you, too.

"I had another story I was working on," she says, edging past him.

"Yeah?" A beat, then: "Wait, what story?"

"Don't worry about it. You'll see it tomorrow."

It's childish of her, she knows, but she can't resist twisting the knife. She and Rod will never break up in any official way, but when he sees the *Flyer's* front page tomorrow she wants him to understand she's done with him, once and for all.

"I'm serious about what I said on the phone," he says. "I can get you something at the *Bully* if you wanted. You'd probably have to start out in production or selling ads, but Leo knows what you can do. You'd be back in the newsroom in no time."

"Go home, Rod," she says, turning the key in the lock. "It's late. Go home to your wife and kid. We'll see enough of each other at the cop shop."

He's still standing outside the door looking like a kid lost in a grocery store when she peeks through the transom window on her way up to the second floor, but it's not until she's inside her apartment and sees the blinking answering machine telling her she has six new messages that she realizes what's been banging around at the back of her mind all day: She's staying put. She won't be moving to the *Bully* and she won't be taking another job outside Franklin. Tish Threadgill went to the mat for her today. Most editors would have caved. By all rights, Tish should have caved. But she didn't, and as long as Tish stays in that newsroom, with her *Preppy Handbook* clothes and her tween-girl giggle, Moira is going to stand with her.

Chapter Three

Tish has the press room print three thousand extra copies of the issue carrying Moira's big scoop, and by ten a.m. even those are gone, leaving the *Bulletin's* Jack Frost-free front page to languish unread in news boxes up and down the valley. At noon, when the story hits the AP wires, phone calls start pouring in from reporters and news directors around the country chasing a story with all the ingredients of a kick-ass bottom-of-the-newscast outro: a remote mountain town, charismatic wildlife, a flicker of violence, all of it liberally sprinkled with the serious topics of terrorism and the environment. Whenever possible, Tish has Jen direct the calls to the sheriff's office, but the lazier reporters insist on talking to Tish herself, hoping they can wrap up this strange-doings-in-snow-country piece in a single call. They want quotes, the weirder the better. Does one meet a lot of eco-terrorists in Franklin? This endangered wildcat everyone's trying to save – has anyone ever been eaten by it? Does anyone eat it? Is it true what they say that restaurants in ski towns place little shakers of cocaine on the tables beside the salt and pepper? Tish is coolly monosyllabic, knocking down the more outlandish rumors while avoiding saying anything quoteworthy except when talking up Moira's reporting and emphasizing, over and over, that the *Flyer* broke the story.

All day, between phone calls and meetings, she dips into her tattered UConn Bookstore copy of *A Screwdriver in the Gears*. She'd pulled it down from her bedroom shelves the night before, and already by noon she's halfway through the book, which is even better than she remembered, loose and funny, with a tough-minded pragmatism about the fragility of the Mountain West. Jack Frost, like his creator, is an ex-Marine turned hunting guide furious at the planned clearcutting of old-growth fir and lodgepole pine in a remote fifty-square-mile section of the lower Sawatch Range. But unlike his creator, who mostly drank and fornicated his way through the years the actual Sawatch Range was logged in the '50s and '60s, Jack Frost is a man of action. With his best friend, a Ute Indian hunting guide named Herbert Standing Bear, Frost recruits a dishonorably discharged Army munitions expert named Joey DiMaggio, the Yankee slugger's second cousin once removed, and together the threesome declares war on a local timber baron named Rupert Burroughs. The gang blows up the power station supplying electricity to Boss Burroughs's logging camp, spikes trees, pours sand into gas tanks, and, yes, sticks a humble screwdriver in the gears of a sawmill motor – all without injuring or killing a single living thing.

Tish is stuck in the office until midnight, laying out the last of Moira's follow-up stories to her own scoops, but she stays up another hour rereading her favorite scene in *Screwdriver*, when the Jack Frost gang sets fire to Boss Burroughs' hilltop mansion, after first clearing the house of every stick of furniture and every toy belonging to Burroughs' seven-year-old son and setting the furniture and toys in a forest clearing out of reach of the fire.

The next morning, on her walk to work, she sees the first TV news trucks setting up on Main Street across from the county courthouse. By noon, live trucks from all three Denver news stations are parked along Main Street, their radar dishes pointed skyward, awaiting a briefing from Sheriff Hayes and Elk County Commission President Cory Carr. This is Moira's story, but slammed as she is with the work of putting out a daily newspaper while simultaneously trying to save her business, Tish walks the three blocks to the courthouse to savor the spectacle of Lorne Hayes eating crow before a statewide television audience.

A few minutes before noon the TV lights flash on and teams of production assistants circulate through the crowd, asking people to shush. Who are these people? Tish wonders. Did they drive four hours from

Denver just to spend five minutes telling a crowd to be quiet? Is this, like, a paying gig? She's still turning that one over in her mind when the courthouse doors swing open and Hayes and Carr march together down the steps to the microphones, like some mortifying parody of a gay couple at a wedding. In his string tie and bone-white Stetson, Hayes looks like he just walked in off the set of a John Wayne movie while Carr looks like he's in a different movie altogether, maybe a different universe. A head shorter than Hayes, Carr is slim and gym-fit in a tailored gray suit set off by a full head of lustrous silver hair. His hair, though quite real, is like another immaculately tailored garment, wavy on top and swept back from his forehead, as if he were moving at great speed, perhaps behind the wheel of a fiery red Ferrari.

Hayes takes the podium first, and over the steady whir and pop of news cameras, recounts the basic facts of the bombing case, including the note claiming responsibility by the Jack Frost Collective and the uncanny parallels between the bombing of the West Fork Power Substation and an episode in a bestselling novel by local resident Bill Blanning. All of this is even more satisfying to watch than Tish expected. For two days, Hayes has stubbornly refused to comment on these two points, but now in a robotic monotone barely a notch up in enthusiasm from a hostage video he's reporting them to the world as established fact. Tish almost feels sorry for the man. Almost. Someone's out there, she reminds herself, with the skills to blow up a power station without setting fire to the pristine forest around it, and Hayes tried to sweep it under the rug. Well, Moira fixed his little red wagon, didn't she?

After Hayes answers a few questions in a low, aggrieved mumble, Cory Carr steps up to the podium and smiles, squinting in the bright noonday sun. *I have died*, this squinty smile says, *and landed in local-politician Heaven*. An old-school college lefty who spent a summer registering voters for the Mississippi Freedom Party in 1964 and who has spent the next thirty years working this fact into his every public utterance, Carr is a trial lawyer whose clientele ranges from drunk drivers to multinational mining conglomerates needing local counsel. He's in his late forties, old to be making a start in politics, but it's no secret that he has his eye on higher office, maybe a Congressional run, maybe even a shot at the U.S. Senate. And for a local pol seeking statewide office, there's just one route out of a backwater like Franklin, Colorado, and that is to get your face on every television screen in the Denver and Boulder media markets as often as possible.

"First, I want to thank Sheriff Hayes and his deputies for their unstinting efforts to bring to justice the person or persons responsible for this terrible crime," he begins, falling effortlessly into a minister's rolling cadence. "And make no mistake, we *will* bring whoever is involved in this so-called 'collective' to justice. Because we were attacked the other day. Yes, we were all attacked, even those among us – *especially* those among us – who have lawfully exercised their rights as residents of this community to oppose development in Elkhorn Canyon. Violence never solves anything. Destruction never solves anything. I learned this many years ago as a young man marching with Dr. King for rights and freedom. Violence only begets more violence. Destruction only begets more destruction. Now, we have a decision to make here in Franklin, a very important decision that will determine what our community will look like for generations to come. But we will not be cowed by threats of violence and destruction. We will not crouch in a corner waiting for these cynical nihilists to strike a second time."

Carr is still listing things the good people of Franklin will not do in the face of this threat when Tish feels a tap on her shoulder.

"Give me twenty million dollars and an airplane and I could run that hair for president."

It's Rod Arango, flashing the gap-toothed smile Tish woke up to all-too-few mornings over a three-month stretch six years ago.

"What are you doing here?" she asks, her voice perilously close to a screech.

"Same as you," he says. "Hearing what Brother Carr learned at the right hand of Dr. King."

"Fuck you, Rod," she says.

The childishness of her response, along with the sight of one of the twerpy TV network PAs elbowing through the crowd to shush them, sends a rush of warmth to her cheeks, and she turns on her heel, cutting through the crowd toward Main Street. Rod calls after her until he's silenced by one of the over-eager PAs, leaving Tish, still red-faced and angry, to walk the three blocks back to the *Flyer's* office alone.

All afternoon, as she pores over her budget spreadsheets, hunting for the three thousand dollars she needs to make payroll at the end of the month, the scene at the press conference plays before her eyes like outtakes from a low-grade horror movie. She can't believe Rod Arango still has the power to throw her so badly off her game. After all, Moira beat his ass this week in the most public way imaginable. She should be gloating, needling him for being too lazy to visit the bomb site the way Moira had, not lashing out at him like some jilted lover. It makes no sense because she hasn't been Rod's lover for a very long time and she doesn't feel jilted. Even at the time, it was a casual, open-ended thing, dependent as much how many beers they killed after deadline at the Summit as on any grand emotional or pheromonal convergence. But she keeps replaying their shouting match on Main Street after she walked out of the meeting with Leo Mayer, the one that ended with him reminding her that he had a wife and child to think about. That's the nub of it, right there. Not because she wishes she could be in Belinda's place, but because Rod *has* a Belinda. He has a kid he has to put first. At age thirty-seven, Tish has attended more than a dozen weddings and been a bridesmaid in half of them. She's watched countless reporters and ad reps and paste-up queens cycle through the *Flyer* offices for a year or two and move on to real jobs in the real world, with spouses and children and mortgages. And she's still here, still single, still living in the same one-bedroom apartment she moved into after Doug died, still struggling to make her ragtag local newspaper turn a profit.

Not for the first time this week she considers throwing in the towel. Leo Mayer will never again offer her a cushy job running a non-existent lifestyle magazine, but even after her scene the other day in his office, it's probably worth fifty or sixty grand to him to put the *Franklin Daily Flyer* out of its misery. Tish would be paying down the debt till the ice caps melt, but she would be free. She could move somewhere else and start a new paper. Or she could shake the trees in Denver or Dallas, see if she can find work at one of the bigger papers there. Or she could get out of the business altogether, go back to school, become a lawyer or an accountant, anything but a newspaper editor.

"You wanted to see me?"

Gemma the intern, Tish realizes, is standing in her office doorway, looking like a frowsy blonde mouse poised to scurry from sight if a cat should appear.

"Yes, yes, come in," Tish says, waving her in. "Thanks for stopping by."

Tish cannot for the life of her figure out Gemma the intern. Her last name is Seagraves, and according to Moira, she's distantly related to the Roosevelts – Teddy or FDR or maybe both. Her father is the CEO of an agricultural supply conglomerate in Chicago, and she actually lived in Franklin as a kid for a few years before she shipped out to prep school, but for now she's living in a spare bedroom at one of her family's many homes on Rodeo Road east of town. In the normal course of events, all this would make Gemma Seagraves loud, careless, and stupid. But the young woman – okay, girl, really – standing in the doorway to Tish's office in jeans and hemp-cloth loafers is just the opposite: soft-spoken, thoughtful, and so far at least a halfway decent reporter.

"I wanted to let you know how much I appreciated the way you handled the sheriff's press briefing the other day," Tish says, gesturing for Gemma to take a seat. "It was all very last-minute and you knocked it out of the park."

"Thanks, ma'am," Gemma says. "That means a lot coming from you."

The "ma'am" sits weirdly. Tish knows the girl is just trying to be polite, but it makes her feel old and dowdy, like her own grandmother with her tennis bracelet and her Pimm's Cup at the New Canaan Country Club.

"You've probably noticed we're a bit shorthanded these days," she says. "So, if you're up for it, we'd like to see you step in and do a little more reporting."

Gemma's round, freckled face brightens. "I'd love that. I'd *totally* love that."

Tish nods, but she can't help it: the "totally" grates. If there's a newspaper in Heaven, it will dock its reporters a day's pay every time they use "totally" as an adverbial intensifier. And if, God forbid, they ever use "literally" to mean "figuratively," they will be shot on sight.

"Okay, but you need to understand, I'm strapped here," she says. "I've spent the last two days going over the books and I can't free up the cash for another full-time reporter."

"That's fine, I don't care about the money," Gemma says. "I just want the experience."

"Well, I can't just not pay you. We have laws against that in this country."

"So go on paying me the freelancer's rate – two bucks an inch or whatever it is."

The *Flyer's* freelancer's rate is in fact three dollars per column inch of published copy. The rate Gemma is quoting is one Tish dreamed up a few winters back to scare off the loud, careless, and stupid rich kids who persist in turning up at the *Flyer's* offices hoping to give their parents an excuse to keep paying their allowances while they ski their butts off on Mount Boyd. It's criminal to pay this rate to an actual reporter, but Tish needs another body in the newsroom, now, and Gemma Seagraves clearly doesn't need the money.

They talk for a few minutes about the City Council meetings Gemma will need to cover and how she can always ask for help from the other reporters, but as Tish is escorting her out, the younger woman stops to admire a framed single sheet of paper on the wall next to the door.

"This is the first edition, right?" she asks.

"Yep, Issue No. 1," Tish says. "In twenty years I'll get a good price for it on the collectors' market, along with Doug's old Spider-Man comics."

This is Tish's go-to line whenever anyone takes an interest in the framed sheet of paper, one of a thousand she and Doug ran through a Xerox machine at Lawton's Drugs on the night of September 17, 1981. Usually, people chuckle and move on, but Gemma takes a step closer, as if she plans to actually read Doug's lead story about Hank Dunow's secret love child.

"That was a totally amazing scoop," she says. "He got fired for reporting it, didn't he?"

"He did, yeah," Tish says, discreetly checking her watch.

"Wow, you even ran a picture of the woman and her kid," Gemma says, pointing to it.

Tish smiles, in spite of herself. This was the one thing she and Doug had argued about that night. Doug had insisted no one would believe the story unless they saw a photo of the spurned mistress and her son, and of course he was right. In the cheaply photocopied broadside, you can barely tell the figures in the picture are human, much less what their faces look like, but it was all anyone remembered: There's a picture.

"Listen, let me introduce you around at City Hall," Tish says, finally. "It's a small office. You can meet them all in an afternoon."

This seems to pierce Gemma's fascination with the *Flyer*'s inaugural issue.

"Oh no, you don't have to do that," she says. "I covered a few stories over there before."

Before Rod Arango got his traitorous ass fired, seems to be the unstated dependent clause of that sentence. Which surprises Tish. Did Gemma Seagraves write a bunch of cityside stories without her noticing? Or did Rod send the intern out to do his reporting and then publish what she came back with under his own byline? It bothers her that she suspects it was the latter, but her budgeting spreadsheets beckon so she's relieved when Gemma thanks her one last time and heads back to the newsroom.

The Lazy T Bar & Grill is packed on Friday morning when Tish arrives at nine for her breakfast with Scott Sage, who manages her credit accounts at Franklin Savings. The Lazy T, located at the edge of town a block from the wide bend in the Franklin River that marks the city's southern boundary, is an old roadhouse with plank floors and rows of dusty rodeo trophies behind the bar. This is where old Franklin, the parts of town that have as little to do with the resort as possible, does its drinking and fighting. At night, ranch hands from across Elk County roll in to drink Pabst Blue Ribbon and hit on whatever dark-eyed ski bunny the Lazy T's owner Patti Murray has hired to tend bar for the season. In the mornings it's quieter, the kind of place where contractors gather to plan out their workdays and a person can order two eggs with meat, hashbrowns, and coffee, and settle up for less than three bucks, including tip.

Two years ago, when Scott Sage pitched the corporate line of credit as a solution to Tish's cash-flow problems, he'd taken her for a martini-soaked lunch at the Alpine Grill in the Hotel Franklin. Now, it's three-dollar eggs at the Lazy T, but as he banters with Patti, who chips in to wait tables in the mornings, it dawns on Tish that he's invited her here because he relishes, as she does, the Lazy T's raffish roadhouse charm. She's always had the sense that Scott is a little sweet on her. Nothing gross or harass-y, just occasional lingering glances, laughing at her jokes even when they aren't funny. She's never reciprocated. Scott is plenty good-looking if you go in for square-jawed Americana, and he's from her corner of Connecticut, the tonier zip codes along the Metro North corridor where people know what you mean when you say someone went to Rosemary Hall before it got Choated. And maybe that's the problem. Tish escaped the Connecticut suburbs for many reasons, but one of them was so that she'd never have to settle for a square-jawed guy who manages corporate credit accounts at a bank. Then there's the fact that he's managing her corporate credit account, which, given the state of her finances, is a bit like a cokehead dating her dealer.

She's come bearing circulation audits and revenue spreadsheets, and after some preliminary chit-chat about his daughter, who lives with her mother in Fort Collins, Tish lays out her case, which is that even six years into a bruising newspaper war, the *Flyer*'s daily readership is still only a thousand lower than the *Bulletin*'s.

"If I can just get back on my feet financially," she tells him, "hire a few new people, bring back a few of the ad contracts I lost after last ski season, we could get back to parity with the *Bulletin*. Then in a year or two, we could be beating them again."

"Tish, look, I like your paper," Scott says. "It's scrappy and smart and I like your politics. But your own numbers show that ad revenue dropped twenty percent last year."

"But we're a better newspaper. I mean, look at this week."

"Yeah, that was something," he admits. "You guys put Franklin on the nightly news. But it's only one day. Look at today's paper. They've got the same front page you do."

He reaches for the morning papers and holds them up side by side. Both the *Bulletin* and the *Flyer* play the Jack Frost story top of the fold, with nearly identical screaming headlines.

"Imagine you're a real-estate agent trying to sell second homes to corporate honchos from Chicago and Dallas," he says. "These guys, they're only here a few weeks a year. They couldn't find Elkhorn Canyon with a compass and a map. If you were trying to sell to them, which one of these newspapers would you put your ad dollars in?"

In spite of herself, Tish forces herself to look at the two papers. The *Bulletin*, thanks to Leo's spanking new Goss web-fed press, is bright and crisp, with photos that pop and headlines you can read even through the scratched plastic of a sidewalk news box. The *Flyer*, on the other hand, is ragged and smudged, with muddy photos and a glaring typo in the lede of Perry's Man in the Street piece about the Elkhorn Canyon bombings.

"A little birdie tells me Leo might have had some inside information on my finances ahead of our meeting this week," she says, to change the subject.

"I wouldn't know anything about that," Scott says.

He fiddles with his fork, his square, handsome face twisted in embarrassment. He isn't the one who leaked the numbers, Tish decides. But someone did. His expression confirms that much.

"So I should probably be looking for a new bank about now," she says.

"It wouldn't be the worst move you could make," he says, carefully. "But no bank is going to take this off our hands right now. And no one, truly no one, is going to extend you more credit than you've already got."

"So what can I do?"

"Start making money," he says. "I'm on your side, okay? I'd give anything to see you pull this off, but I can't extend your line of credit, and – you know Stan Bucholtz, right?"

"Sure, he's your boss. I go back a long ways with Stan."

Tish's relationship to Bucholtz, never chummy, permanently soured when the *Flyer* ran a story identifying him as the leader of a pro-development group that included the *Bulletin's* Leo Mayer and half a dozen other local businesspeople who had quietly financed the campaigns of Elkhorn Canyon-friendly County Commissioners, including Cory Carr. If she had to list five people who might have leaked her banking info, six of them would be named Bucholtz.

"Well, I'm here to warn you that if you don't start paying it down by the new year," Scott says, "Bucholtz is going to call in your loans, everything you've got."

"New Year's? It's October now."

"You need to start making money, Tish," he says. "Like, yesterday. If it was up to Bucholtz, you'd already be out of business. If you can prove him wrong, I'll go to bat for you. But if it's still like this in January – I'm sorry, my hands are tied."

After breakfast, Tish decides to walk to her office, both because it's shaping up to be a another gorgeous fall day and because after what Scott told her she's not so sure she should get behind the wheel of a car. Tish was raised by a mentally unbalanced single mother, whom her father had briefly and unhappily married before returning to his older, wealthier, and saner first wife. Among other things, this meant that, as a girl, Tish belonged to the New Caanan Country Club and went to prep school, but everything else about her daily existence was hand to mouth. One winter, when her mother took to her bed for weeks after a failed suicide attempt, she and Doug showered at the club for a month and charged their meals to their grandmother's account. Crazy as they were, Doug and her mother were wildly creative when it came to hustling cash, and thanks to them, Tish had never truly run out of it. Now, both are gone – her mother from an overdose of barbiturates, her brother with his own belt in a Denver motel room – and Tish is on her own. Everything she told her staff after she rejected Leo's buyout offer is true. She loves the *Flyer* like she loves her lungs and her fingertips. But what if none of that matters? What if they keep breaking story after story and she still goes broke?

She's turning onto Mountain Avenue when she spots a tousle-haired kid in jeans and a hoodie tacking a flyer to a telephone pole with a stapler gun. A small crowd has gathered around him, and when Tish sees the words on the flyer, she understands why.

"I turned off their goddamn lights so they could see." – Jack Frost

Keep the canyon wild.
Keep Franklin weird.
Support the Jack Frost Collective!

"Excuse me," Tish asks the kid with the stapler gun. "Did you make these?"

"Yeah," he says. "Not just me, though. A bunch of us made them."

Lanky and tanned, his eyes shielded by mirrored Vuarnets, the kid with the stapler is a male of the species *skibumus Coloradii*. Without asking, Tish knows he's living four to a room in a repurposed miner's cottage in East Franklin and subsisting largely on ramen and granola.

"Aren't you worried the cops are going to come after you?" she asks.

"For what?" says Vuarnet Boy. "I had nothing to do with that bombing and I don't know who did. I just think they have a point."

"They could've set the whole canyon on fire with that thing," Tish says.

"But they didn't, did they?" he says. "I've been coming here all my life. A lot of us have. This is our home. Our *real* home. And the Dunows, they want to ruin this place. They want to turn it into freaking Aspen. I'm glad somebody stood up. It's about time."

Tish is carrying neither a notepad or camera, so she has Vuarnet Boy write his name and phone number on one of his flyers and asks him to wait until she can get a reporter out to talk to him. But when she makes it back to the newsroom, the reporters are huddled around Rod's old desk staring at a copy of the same flyer Tish has in her hand.

"They're going up all over town," Moira tells her. "They're talking about holding a rally at the base of Mount Boyd."

"A rally at the ski hill?"

"I just got back from there," Perry says. "A dozen or so people are already setting up."

Tish sends Moira to the courthouse to get a read on how Sheriff Hayes plans to handle any potential civil disobedience and Perry back out the ski hill to get a read on the crowd. Gemma and Chuck she keeps in the office covering their usual beats in case the whole thing fizzles out, which, with the likes of Vuarnet Boy in charge, is the most likely scenario. Tish, meanwhile, holes up in her office to work her sources at the Franklin Skiing Company.

It takes her fifteen minutes of dialing through her Rolodex before she gets a call back from Sheldon Dunow, the founder's youngest son and FrankCo's director of operations, who, as he gently reminds Tish at the top of the call, prefers not to speak for attribution.

"What're we going to *do*?" he says, answering her first question. "We're going to sit here like good corporate villains and wait until all the little eco-terrorists get bored and go home."

Tish laughs in spite of herself. This is Sheldon Dunow's gift. An Oz-like figure, pudgy and cherubic, his large head shaved clean as a newborn's, Dunow rarely goes on TV or allows himself to be quoted, but he manages the ski company's reputation as a snow-country Death Star by playfully leaning into it, making the joke before you can.

"How many of them are there up there, anyway?" she asks.

He pauses to look out his office window. "I don't know, twenty, twenty-five."

"An hour ago, it was just a dozen."

"Have you seen these people, Tish?" he asks. "They're kids. They're up here playing hacky sack and throwing frisbees around. Trust me, they'll be gone by lunchtime."

But Sheldon Dunow is wrong. The crowd is still there when Perry reports back from the ski hill at one, and a few hours later, when Tish can tear herself away from her budget spreadsheets long enough to look for herself, more than a hundred people have gathered on the grassy lap of Mount Boyd, where during ski season skiers step into their skis before joining the lift line. A local pick-up band is playing earnest U2 and R.E.M. covers when Tish arrives, but their cheap nightclub amps are no match for the miserable acoustics of a grassy meadow in the open air and after a few songs they give up. But they don't leave. Nobody leaves. The crowd keeps growing, spilling out onto Mountain Avenue like some sprawling, impromptu block party. One section of grass is roped off for a game of ultimate frisbee, complete with regulation end zones. Elsewhere, the buskers with the dog who picks up dollar bills have set up shop at a disused fire ring, cracking jokes and performing magic tricks. A few yards away, an off-duty forest ranger has set up a makeshift chalkboard on an easel and delivers a campfire-style lecture on the ever-shrinking habitat of the lynx.

As she wanders the meadow, asking questions, taking down names and quotes, Tish feels as though she's seeing her own town through a fun-house mirror. Ever since Hank Dunow died and left the company to his three sons, Franklin has been at war with itself. A Texas oilman, the elder Dunow had poured millions of dollars into Franklin's makeover from dying mining town to elite ski destination, but by the eighties the company he'd built, outmoded by corporate-funded behemoths like Aspen and Vail, was going bankrupt. Dunow had been dead less than six months when his sons laid off twenty percent of FrankCo's employees and announced plans to expand into Elkhorn Canyon, which their father had steadfastly refused to do. The town has never really forgiven Dunow's sons – the Three Amigos, locals call them – for this breach of their father's legacy, but even ardent opponents like Tish, who has been editorializing against Elkhorn Canyon for the better part of a decade, have always assumed the new resort will be built. The money's just too good, and the opposition is too fragmented and flaky.

But tonight, to her surprise, the Jack Frost attack appears to have brought them all together, and as the sun dips behind Mount Boyd organizers pass around small candles and the crowd begins to sing. Along the perimeter of the brickwork plaza TV reporters shrug on blazers and start doing live standups before a backdrop of four hundred wholesome young Americans holding candles and singing "This Little Light of Mine" at the foot of a mountain. It's great TV, but also faintly ridiculous. The crowd is lily white, the over-educated sons and daughters of bankers and corporate middle managers fighting to keep a wealthy tourist town high in the Rockies from becoming a filthy rich tourist town high in the Rockies. Earnest as they are, serious as they may be about stopping development in Elkhorn Canyon and saving the endangered lynx, these kids can smell the irony, can sense how it's all going to look refracted through the lens of the nightly news back home in Brentwood, California, and Rye, New York. After a few half-hearted rounds of "We Shall Overcome," no one seems to know what to sing next and one by one the candles flicker out.

Standing at the edge of the meadow taking notes, Tish feels the energy flow out of the gathering like air from a punctured tire. Along the lip of the grass, cameramen are packing up, and there's a palpable sense, unstated but real, that they've blown it. They had their chance, they had the eyes of the world on them, and when it mattered most they had nothing to say.

"Where do you think you're going?" a voice rings out over the meadow. "We aren't done here. We haven't even gotten started."

Half a dozen flashlights home in on an older woman near the back of the crowd holding one of the pick-up band's stage microphones. It's Patti Murray from the Lazy T, Tish realizes, still in her pale blue waitress uniform, her steel-gray hair piled up on her head in a tight bun.

"Look here, I know you kids," she says. "You come to my front door every season looking for waitressing gigs, and when the money runs out, some of you come to my back door hungry, looking for table scraps. You could go anywhere – Aspen, Vail, Steamboat Springs – but you keep coming here because Franklin isn't just a resort. It's a town. It's a real place full of families and schoolteachers and cops and folks like me who run small businesses. It's been that way since I was a little girl growing up in a miner's shack across the river in East Franklin. It's why we're all here, and right now it's as endangered as that poor wildcat out there in the woods."

Green lights blink on again above the TV cameras, and Tish scribbles even faster, racing to capture Patti's words. This, she sees now, is the real news event, the moment when old Franklin joins forces with new Franklin against the Dunow brothers and their millions.

"I have a hard time taking sides with anybody who'll blow things up to make a point," Patti is saying. "It's not my way. I believe in laws, in the democratic process. But I don't know how else to get people's attention. My granddad came to Franklin in 1884 on the back of a mule and my people have been here ever since, mining and farming and running restaurants. But if this new resort goes through, I'll be gone in five years. And it won't just be me. I saw Rudy Lawton here a little while ago. His drugstore'll be gone, too. And Vern Browder at Franklin Hardware. And Sally Ambrose at Sally's Notions. I could name a hundred more. They'll all be gone. There'll be nothing left here but art galleries and jewelry stores and rich people in fur coats trying to remember the name of the town they're in."

As the crowd lifts its voice in a collective *Noooooo!* Tish spots Lorne Hayes, his bone-white Stetson cruising shark-like through the mass of bodies toward Patti Murray, trailed by two uniformed deputies.

"What I'm trying to say is you're not alone," she says. "It might seem like it, but you aren't. We're with you. We won't be blowing up any power stations, I can promise you that, but we're with you every step of the way. Because we're fighting for our lives. We're fighting for our homes, our very livelihoods."

A scuffle breaks out not far from where she's standing: shouting, shoving, bodies tumbling to the ground, followed by still more shouting.

"Just wait one minute," Patti shouts. "Get your goddamn hands off me, Lorne."

But the tall figure in the Stetson hat wrests the microphone away from her and steps into the blinding glare of flashlights, drawing a lusty round of boos and catcalls.

"This is Sheriff Hayes," he calmly intones. "You are on private property and you will have to disperse. You have five minutes to collect your belongings and leave. After that, you will be ticketed and fined. Those who resist will be arrested and jailed."

"Let her speak! Let her speak!" the crowd chants, drowning out his words.

Fearing an all-out riot, Tish pushes through the jostling crowd to the rows of TV cameras. It's only there, in the relative safety of the press area, that she hears the first distant, thudding explosions. *Pop! Pop! Pop-pop! Pop!* She's scanning the dark mountain, trying to fix a position on the sound, when a flash of bright orange and yellow lights up the night sky. There's another flash, this one bigger and brighter, followed by the air-sucking *whoomp* of a roof being blown off a building.

As if some unseen hand has pressed the mute button on the world, the crowd hushes and four hundred pairs of eyes gaze up at the fiery orange glow emanating from the ridge at the top of Mount Boyd's main ski run.

"It's the Highline Chalet!" someone shouts.

And so it is. The Highline, an upscale beer garden a hundred yards from the gondola shed, is the oldest of the ski company's three on-mountain restaurants. Celebrity couples hold weddings there. At least once a week during high season somebody proposes marriage on the back deck. And now, Tish realizes, it's very publicly on fire.

"Holy shit!" someone else shouts. "It's Boss Burroughs' house!"

Like that, Tish is transported back to the scene from *A Screwdriver in the Gears* she'd reread earlier that week in which the Frost gang painstakingly removes every piece of furniture and every toy belonging to Boss Burroughs' son before setting fire to the greedy timber merchant's mountain-top home.

As the flames climb ever higher into the night sky and the soft tinkle of shattering glass rolls down the mountainside, Tish shakes her head, knowing that every table and chair in the Highline's dining room, every dish and plate in its kitchen, has been carefully set on the ground outside the restaurant where it will remain untouched by the flames.

He's in the crowd, *too, standing twenty feet from Tish in mud-splattered racing shorts and a backwards Ski Franklin! ballcap. He hasn't been there long, having arrived just in time to see Patti Murray grab the megaphone. The Lazy T has never been his scene - too much chambray and tooled leather for his taste - but his mother waited tables there for a season when she first came to town and always told the story of how Patti advanced her a week's pay when she fell behind on her rent. Tonight, he was so caught up in Patti's speech that he was as shocked as everyone else when the first burst of yellow flame rose from the crest of Mount Boyd. He wanted to shout,* No, wait, not yet! She's got people listening down here!

Now, though, standing in the crowded meadow, four hundred people pointing up at the burning mountain chalet like it's a Fourth of July fireworks show, he has to fight to keep the grin off his face. First the power station and now this, all of it like clockwork, just like they drew it up on the dirt floor of an abandoned hunting cabin on the back side of Mount Boyd. That morning, he and the other members of the collective had taken the Motherlode gondola up the mountain with their bicycles. There are no cameras in either gondola tower, nor in the cars themselves, and they didn't have to show ID to buy a ticket. Each of the saboteurs simply boarded the gondola a few minutes apart, blending in with the other mountain bikers in their padded shorts and decal-covered helmets enjoying one of the last days FrankCo allows bikes on Mount Boyd. Already, in mid-October, there's snow at the higher elevations, but they all spent the day happily cruising the mountain's muddy back bowls and taking afternoon siestas in secluded sage thickets alongside the trails.

At 5:35 p.m., when the last gondola of the day disappeared over Highline Ridge, taking all remaining FrankCo workers with it, he'd biked down from his hiding place and snipped the wires that linked the alarm system at the Highline Chalet to the ski company's main office at the base of the mountain. A minute later, he snipped the wires connecting two surveillance cameras mounted on trees outside the chalet to a VHS player in the restaurant's basement. That was it for on-mountain security. The system was designed to stop foraging bears and drunk teenagers, not four activists determined to burn the place to the ground. So, snip, snip, snip went his wire cutters, and five minutes later, right on schedule, three other members of the collective swooped in from the hills above the chalet.

A rock through the de-alarmed window, half a minute fiddling with knobs and deadlocks, and they were in. The work of hauling out tables and chairs, plus any kitchen equipment on wheels, took even less time than they'd planned. Twenty minutes, tops. When they were done, they filled four five-gallon water bags with gasoline siphoned from the ski company's own on-mountain pumps and doused the floor and walls of the now-empty building with accelerant. They placed igniters rigged to simple kitchen timers, each bought at a different Fred Meyer department store in Central Oregon, in the four corners of the building. At a signal, they set the timers for one hour and hopped back on their bikes for the long ride back down the mountain, each Collectivist taking a separate path home.

His route had been the most direct, skirting Mount Boyd's South Peak bowls and ending at a quiet stretch of Highway 22 a few minutes south of town. So it was that he'd pulled into downtown Franklin fifteen minutes before sundown, locked his bike at the bike corral on Mountain Avenue and sauntered up the stairs to the base of the ski hill just as the TV lights were blinking to life to film Patti Murray comparing old-time residents of Franklin to the endangered lynx.

Now, as the Highline Chalet burns at the top of the mountain like a Roman candle, a new song starts up in the meadow:

Nana-na-na, nana-na-nah, hey, hey, goodbye!

At first it's just a few rowdy ski bums at the edge of the crowd, but before long others pick up the tune, locking arms and swaying to the rhythm of their own mocking harmony. The cruelty of it shocks even him. The fire will cost the Dunows a million dollars or more and put Franklin on the front page of the nation's newspapers again. But that was the whole point, wasn't it? To get out the word. To put the world on notice. He locks arms with strangers on either side of him, a bearded guy in his twenties and a skeletal brunette who looks even younger, throws his head back, and belts out the song:

Nana-na-na, nana-na-nah, hey, hey, goodbye!

Nana-na-na, nana-na-nah, hey, hey, goodbye!

PART TWO

A Missing Cat

To one side of the boss's home, now reduced to blackened sticks and rubble, stood the Burroughs' family furniture set out on the lawn in clusters as if it were still indoors: the living room settees and rugs gathered around the Zenith television set, the beds neatly made, water glasses and unread books resting on the night tables. The most curious sight of all was the boy's bedroom, a riot of clothes and comic books and erector sets laid out across the grass just as they had on the floor of the boy's room.

When he reached the kitchen furniture, Sheriff Fontine stopped. On the table, stabbed through with a footlong silver carving knife, lay a note written in Jack Frost's unmistakable schoolboy scrawl:

HOWDY, GREEDHEADS! ARE WE HAVING FUN YET?

A Screwdriver in the Gears
Bill Blanning, 1971

Chapter Four

A little before noon on Monday, three days after the fire, Tish and Moira climb into a six-seater forestry jeep for the ride to the top of Mount Boyd, and a minute later, Rod Arango and Andy Minturn, editor of the *Daily Bulletin*, settle into the seats in front of them. There's a round of awkward hellos and some embarrassed chuckles at the seating arrangements, and then for the twenty long minutes it takes to drive up to the site of the fire no one says a word.

It has been a very strange weekend. The Highline Chalet fire, and the crowd that sang as it burst into flames on live TV, have captured the nation's imagination, and the satellite news trucks that had lumbered into town after the power station bombing are joined by half a dozen more, lining both sides of Main Street, their radar dishes and spiky antennas broadcasting a steady diet of reporting on the mysterious Jack Frost Collective. Franklin made the front pages of the *New York Times* and the *Washington Post* (lower right-hand corner, but still). *Saturday Night Live* worked the fire into a sketch, and President Clinton, angling for another Sister Souljah moment, railed in a speech against "environmental extremists who in their zeal to save the planet risk undermining the very political system that could help them reach their goals."

Like everyone else, Tish spent the weekend watching the aerial footage on CNN, but this does nothing to ease the shock of her first sight of the hundred-seat Highline Chalet reduced to a handful of charred two-by-fours. On the patio, she can see, like the setting for some mad tea party, the restaurant's chairs and tables arrayed on the grass, each with its own yellow evidence marker. A few men in government-blue windbreakers mill around the crime site, taking measurements and collecting samples, but they're outnumbered by the small army of reporters and camera techs corralled into a press pen thirty yards from the ruined building, facing a podium bristling with microphones.

Not long after Tish and Moira take their places in the press pen, a dozen middle-aged cops file onto the makeshift stage, led by FBI Special Agent Art Monkiewicz, head of the task force investigating the Highline fire. Monkiewicz is here, as even the most casual follower of the Jack Frost story knows, because of his success against a loose network of environmental activists who call themselves Mother Earth's Avengers, but when he steps up to the podium, he nimbly sidesteps any mention of the Avengers or eco-terrorism more generally. Yes, he tells the cameras, this investigation is a top priority for all jurisdictions involved. No, as yet there have been no credible claims of responsibility. Yes, investigators are aware of the writer Bill Blanning's work and its seeming implications for this incident, but at this early stage they are ruling nothing in and ruling nothing out.

This, Tish realizes, is less a press conference than a photo-op, a chance for the nation's TV crews to shoot enough B-roll footage of the crime site that they'll quit sending news helicopters up the mountain every fifteen minutes. She nudges Moira's arm and hisses, "Back in a sec."

Before Moira can even look up from her notepad, Tish is halfway to a stand of bristlecone pine near the shuttered gondola terminus where she's spotted a familiar-looking shaggy head of silvering blonde hair belonging to Jimmy Lachlan, director of Mount Boyd's ski patrol.

Tish knows Lachlan, a sinewy, perma-tanned Aussie, from her pre-*Flyer* days when he used to lead her and Doug on illicit early-morning powder runs on Mount Boyd's out-of-bounds South Peak bowls. Back then, he was a ski bum's ski bum, skiing a hundred and fifty days in Colorado before jetting off to New Zealand's Craigieburn Valley or Argentina's Las Leñas for the Southern hemisphere's winter. A spinal injury that would have landed a lesser man in a wheelchair put a stop to his wanderings, and now as ski patrol chief, it's his job to keep people out of the very avalanche-prone South Peak bowls he used to shred.

"Shouldn't you be down there?" he asks, gesturing to the scrum with his stubbled chin.

Tish shrugs. "Whole lot of talking, not much being said."

"Beats listening to that FBI bloke when he *is* saying something, trust me."

This stops her. She'd come up here to ask Jimmy about rumors that the arsonists siphoned the gas for the fires from the ski company's own fuel tanks, but this could be even better.

"Why, what's he been saying?" she asks.

But Jimmy just laughs. "You know I can't be talking to you."

"That's good because you aren't talking to me." She shows him her hands, visibly empty of notepads or recording devices. "This conversation never happened."

He gazes off at the assembled press corps for such a long time that she starts to wonder if he really has decided not to talk with her.

"Put it this way," he says, finally. "If all you've got is a hammer, everything starts looking like a nail."

She looks at Lachlan, then at the long line of windbreaker-clad cops on the podium. "You're saying Monkiewicz's got the Mother Earth's Avengers on the brain?"

"I'm not saying anything, am I?"

"Okay, but they've got more than a dozen agents on this. And this Monkiewicz guy's supposed to be Eliot Ness and J. Edgar Hoover all rolled into one."

"He's Barney-fecking-Fife, is what he is. They hit the ski patrol hut, Patricia."

This much Tish already knows: In addition to the Highline, the fire destroyed a ski patrol warming hut located in the restaurant's basement. So far, though, in two days of wall-to-wall coverage she's heard no one attach any special significance to this fact.

"We have three restaurants up here and the other two are bigger and more visible from town," Jimmy says, as if explaining the point to a toddler. "But the arsonists chose to hit the Highline, which is attached to the ski patrol hut. Which most people don't even know is there."

"And now your guys will have to find a new place to keep warm," Tish says, lost.

"It's more than a warming hut," he says. "It's the communications hub for the whole top side of the mountain. That's why you couldn't ride the gondola up here today. If something went wrong, we'd have no way of coordinating a rescue with our people down in Franklin."

For Tish, the most interesting thing about what he just said is that she hasn't heard it before.

"So the mountain's effectively shut down," she says.

"For the moment," he says. "And it'll cost a hundred grand to get it back up and running – double that, probably, to get it all done before we open next month."

"I don't get it. Why hasn't any of this been reported?"

"Not much to get," he says. "Corporate's in no hurry to tell the world we can't run our lifts a month before ski season, and so far, apparently, none of you lot has asked."

"Okay, well, I'm asking."

"Not a chance. This conversation never happened, remember?"

"Come on, you can't give me a story like this and then tell me I can't report it."

"I most certainly can. I've spoken about this internally and the Amigos are panicking about early-season bookings. If you report this, it'll come right back and bite me on the arse."

Tish feels an unseemly urge to grab the shaggy-haired ski patrol director and toss his blokey arse over the side of mountain.

"When you get back to town, you can ask the PR folks when the gondola will open again," he says. "They'll give you the usual song and dance, but if you push, sooner or later they'll have to admit they don't have a date for reopening. Then all you have to do is ask why."

Tish can only smile. Jimmy Lachlan, media guru. Not only has he figured out how to leak a story he wants on the record, but he's found a way to keep his name out of it.

"Thank you, Jimmy," she says.

"For what?" he says. "I've no idea what you're talking about."

Across the narrow grassy swale the press conference is breaking up, the TV crews begging Monkiewicz, again, for a guided tour of the burnt-out building with their cameras. That's never going to happen, as they all know, and already sheriff's deputies have begun gently herding the reporters toward a line of waiting jeeps.

"I don't like this, Patricia," Jimmy says. "It's like these guys are taunting us. Like they're saying, 'We know how this mountain works and we can shut you down any time we like.'"

Tish's story – "Ruined Radio Gear Forces 'Indefinite' Mt. Closure" – runs across the top of page one of Tuesday's paper, though to honor her agreement with Jimmy Lachlan, she has to write around the question of whether the communications gear was the arsonists' real target. Still, it's a solid scoop, one she knows will generate waves of follow-up stories about what it means for local businesses if Mount Boyd can't open in November as planned.

At noon she's at her desk eating a Yoplait cup and reading the fine print of her office lease when Jen shouts from the front desk: "Tish, you need to come out here!"

"In a minute!" Tish calls back through a mouthful of blueberry yogurt.

"No, right now," Jen cries. "You need to see this."

When Tish pokes her head out of her office, her receptionist is standing a few feet from her desk, on top of which is a tall pile of mail she's been opening.

"This just came in," Jen says, pointing like a character in a horror movie to a folded sheet of paper next to a torn envelope and a plastic letter opener. "Go ahead, read it."

Jen's panicked cries are attracting a crowd so Tish takes Jen's seat at the desk and reads the printed message:

"HOWDY, GREEDHEADS! ARE WE HAVING FUN YET?"

The Dunow brothers and their loyal henchmen at the U.$. Forest Service plan to clear-cut 2,000 acres of pristine forest, one of the last known habitats of the lynx south of the Canadian border, to create a winter playland for millionaires. We refuse to stand by and let this happen. Until the Franklin Skiing Company abandons its plans to develop Elkhorn Canyon, we will continue to disrupt winter activities in the Franklin Valley. It really is that simple. Drop Elkhorn Canyon or you can kiss your ski season goodbye.

— The Jack Frost Collective

P.S. Check the gas levels at Pump #1 on Mount Boyd. You may find a few gallons are missing. Sorry to pump without paying. We'll catch you next time.

Tish checks the torn envelope for a return address. There is none, of course, just the *Flyer's* business address, rendered in the same computer-generated typeface, and a postmark showing that the letter was mailed on Saturday in Twin Falls, Idaho.

"Has anyone else touched this?" she asks.

"No, just me," Jen says. "I was going through the morning mail."

"No one else, you're sure? Not even the outer envelope?"

There's a thoughtful silence as, one by one, her staffers shake their heads.

"Okay, I'm going to call the FBI," Tish says. "Nobody touches this until they get here. No one even gets close to it, understood?"

In her office, she dials the task force hotline and spends an exasperating minute being passed around between secretaries and public information flacks before she blurts out the magic words: "We got a letter from the Jack Frost Collective." In ten seconds flat, Art Monkiewicz himself is on the line.

"You've had a communication from the arsonists?" he asks.

"It just came in," Tish says. "My receptionist opened it thinking it was a letter to the editor."

"Does anyone else know about this?"

"Outside of my office? No, not yet."

"Good. I'm going to have to ask you to keep it that way. These direct communications, they're some of the best investigative tools we have."

"Sir, with all due respect, we're a newspaper," Tish says. "I'll give you the letter itself, but this is news. We're going to print what it says."

"I understand, Ms. Threadgill, but in the interests of justice, I'm asking you to hold off for a few days. As I say, these are powerful investigative tools."

Tish can hear her brother in her ear reminding her the letter came to the newspaper, not the police, and that as a legal matter, she isn't even obligated to tell the Feds she'd received it. Doug was a born muckraker who got off on telling people in power to fold it five ways and shove it where the sun don't shine. But Tish isn't her brother. She stood up to Sheriff Hayes when he wanted her to suppress the first note, but this is different. This is the FBI.

"You wanted an interview, right?" Monkiewicz says, filling the growing silence.

Like every other journalist within a fifty-mile radius, Tish has submitted a formal request for an interview with Agent Monkiewicz, but she never expected to actually get an interview.

"Work with us and I'll make that happen," he says. "I'll still have to be circumspect, but I'll be as honest as I can about the state of the investigation."

This is better than she expected, better in fact than she has any right to expect.

"Today?" she asks.

He chuckles. "Let me deal with this note first. How about tomorrow? Around eleven?"

First thing the next morning, Tish visits the periodicals room of the Elk County Public Library to read up on Art Monkiewicz and the Mother Earth's Avengers. In a perfect world, the one Clinton's wonkish vice president keeps promising is right around the corner, she could type "Art Monkiewicz" and "Mother Earth's Avengers" into a computer and call up every article ever written about them. But for now that world exists only inside Al Gore's head, so she searches the only way she knows how, flipping through old issues of *Time* and *Newsweek* until she finds a story about Monkiewicz or the Avengers, then switching to the Denver papers, looking for more in-depth versions of the same stories pulled from the news wires.

It takes all morning, but she learns that Monkiewicz is a former beat cop from Washington DC who put himself through law school before joining the FBI in the early eighties. A year ago, he set up a task force in Oregon near the state's public university, where several of the core members of the Mother Earth's Avengers reputedly met as students. Since then, his agents have stopped a husband and wife team transporting ten kilos of high explosive they intended to use to blow out a logging bridge. More recently, in Eastern Washington state, his task force arrested four activists responsible for disabling turbines at the Rock Island Dam on the Columbia River. And now he's in Franklin, along with a dozen agents from the FBI and ATF in a warren of windowless offices in the basement of the county courthouse, sifting through leads and canvassing whole neighborhoods, looking for anyone who might have seen something in the hours before the fire at the Highline Chalet.

When Tish and Moira arrive outside Monkiewicz's office a few minutes before eleven, they find Rod Arango and Andy Minturn loitering in the hall, looking, if anything, even more non-plussed to see Tish and Moira than Tish and Moira are to see them.

"You guys got a letter, too, huh?" Minturn asks.

"In the interests of justice, I'm afraid I can't answer that question," Tish replies.

Polite laughter. But at least now Tish understands why the FBI agent was so quick to offer her an interview. He had two newspapers to silence, not just one.

Sure enough, when they're ushered into his office, Monkiewicz leaps up from behind his desk like he's greeting old buddies from Quantico, shaking hands all around and butchering their names in his gruff, street-cop way. "Call me Monk," he says to each of them, as if they would fucking dare. On TV, Monkiewicz is a news director's wet dream of a gumshoe cop, short and bald and thick, a walking side of beef in a too-tight gray suit. But here, away from the cameras, Tish can see how exhausted he is, his suit badly rumpled, the pouches under his eyes turning a sickly yellow. If Monday's press conference is any guide, Monkiewicz is no closer to making an arrest now than he was when he landed in Franklin five days ago. He probably hasn't slept more than an hour or two since then, either.

He glowers at them from behind his desk, a crooked smile pasted on his face, as a young Public Information flack walks them through the ground rules: In exchange for their fifteen minutes with Special Agent Monkiewicz, they agree to embargo the contents of the Jack Frost letters and this interview until Friday. In the meantime, Monkiewicz will give no other interviews and no other news outlets will be told about the letters. After Friday, they can write whatever they want about the letters, but the interview will remain on deep background – no names, no direct quotes, all information attributed to "sources in federal law enforcement."

"Are we good?" Monkiewicz looks around at the four slightly cowed local reporters squeezed into folding metal chairs. "Okay, then. Fire away."

"Can you give us an update on the status of the FBI's forensic investigation into the letter we received yesterday?" Rod asks.

"We know they were mailed from Twin Falls, Idaho," Monkiewicz says. "Beyond that, no comment."

"I meant, did your agents find any fingerprints or identify any distinguishing features of the language used in the letters?" Rod asks.

"I know what you meant," Monkiewicz says. "Still no comment."

"How about the reference to the missing gas in Pump #1?" Moira asks.

"Is that real? Did they siphon gas from the on-mountain pumps to set the fire at the Highline Chalet?"

He purses his lips, considering her question. Then he nods. "It would appear so, yes."

"So then, the letters are legit," Moira says. "That fact hasn't been reported, so only the actual perpetrators could have written that note."

"That's our working supposition at this point."

"Twin Falls, Idaho, is almost precisely midway between here and Eugene, Oregon," Andy Minturn says. "So is it your working supposition that the arsonists dropped off these letters on their way back to Oregon?"

"No comment."

"Are you saying that because you don't know or because you do know and don't want to put it on the record?" Andy asks.

"I'm saying I have no comment."

Tish chuckles to herself. She's starting to like this squat little FBI agent. He's bought himself three days to investigate the letters and in return all he'll say is that they're probably real.

"I've been reading up on the eco-terrorist cases you've investigated," she says. "I've noticed that the Mother Earth's Avengers often claim responsibility for their actions under different names. For instance, the activists you arrested this summer in Washington State claim to belong to something called the Earth Action Coalition, but you've linked them to the Avengers."

Monkiewicz waits, impassive, neither agreeing nor disagreeing.

"So my question is: Are you investigating the possibility that the Jack Frost Collective is just another name for the Mother's Earth's Avengers?"

"We're investigating a wide variety of possibilities," he answers.

"One of them being that the Earth's Avenger's are now calling themselves the Jack Frost Collective?"

He shrugs. "We know the core membership of the Earth's Avengers have long admired the work of Mr. Blanning. We also know this was a fairly sophisticated operation. It's certainly an avenue that bears investigation."

Moira and Tish exchange a look. Finally, some actual news. Monkiewicz has been asked this question a dozen times, in a dozen different ways, and he's never given more than a terse no comment. Now, for the first time, they can report what everyone from Ted Koppel to the drunks at the Summit Tavern have been saying, that Monkiewicz is here because the Feds suspect the Jack Frost attacks are the work of the Mother Earth's Avengers.

"But this did seem like a pretty targeted attack," Moira says. "I mean, whoever did it knew enough to take out all that communications equipment."

"You're assuming they knew it was there," Monkiewicz says.

"But it *was* there, and only a local would know that," Moira says.

"Not necessarily," Monkiewicz says. "As I say, this is a complex investigation, and I would submit that you don't have all the evidence."

He's tossing them a bone, and all four reporters jump on it. Tish gets there first.

"What other evidence is there that we don't have?" she asks.

A tight cop smile. "No comment."

For the next few minutes the reporters pepper him with questions. Is he suggesting the FBI has a witness that can put one of the known Avengers in Franklin? Are there more letters they haven't heard about. A government informant? Some other forensic evidence he hasn't mentioned? Through it all, Monkiewicz is calm and polite and gives them exactly nothing.

"But, just to be clear," Tish says, finally, "you're saying you have evidence that makes you confident this was an Earth's Avengers operation, not just some locals making trouble?"

"As a matter of fact, I don't recall saying that," he says.

"Well, no, not in so many words – "

"Not in *any* words that I can recollect," he says. "And I will ask that the stories you write accurately reflect what I said and did not say."

In the stony silence that follows he turns to the young Public Information flack.

"How're we doing on time, Daniel?"

A large clock hangs on the wall above Monkiewicz's desk, but Daniel is no fool and knows a cue when he hears one.

"Ladies and gentlemen, it's eleven-fifteen," he says. "I'm afraid we're going to have to wrap this up."

"But we started a few minutes after eleven," Moira protests.

"Be that as it may, Special Agent Monkiewicz is on an extremely tight schedule and we're going to have to wrap up," Daniel says, standing. "I'll see you out."

"Just a couple more questions," Rod tries.

"I wish I could," Monkiewicz says, shaking his hand, "but like Daniel here says, I'm already late for my next appointment."

Once again, he shakes hands all round, thanking each of them for their time, and then there's nothing to do but follow officious Daniel out of Monkiewicz's office and up to the main floor of the courthouse. Outside, TV crews are setting up on the sidewalk for their midday news hits, and for a minute the four of them watch Kelly Cherry, an anorectic blonde from Denver's Channel 4 News, run through her standup, her camera tech feeding her questions the anchors will ask. There's a job for you, Tish thinks. You wake up in the morning and read the local papers and then a couple times a day you put on a foam-padded blazer and tell the world what you've read.

"What was that all about?" Andy says, waving toward the courthouse basement.

"I don't know," Rod says, "but I say twenty bucks goes to whoever figures out what his other evidence is."

"Make it fifty," Moira says.

"You're on," Rod says, shaking on it.

He turns to Tish to shake her hand, too, and to her own surprise, she lets him. She'll never forgive Rod for giving aid and comfort to her enemy at her hour of greatest need, but her anger, so raw at first, is already beginning to fade. As deep in debt as she is, she has Rod to thank for keeping her from selling out to Leo Mayer. If he hadn't betrayed her, she might be sitting in the *Bulletin's* offices mocking up a lifestyle magazine that would never publish a single issue, and the battle that has given her life meaning since her brother died would have been lost.

A minute later, crossing Main Street, Tish and Moira spot Chuck Quigley coming the other way, head down, lost in thought.

"Chuckles!" Moira calls to him.

He looks up and his elongated face, brooding in repose, breaks into a lopsided grin. Tish hangs back while Moira fills him in on their interview with Monkiewicz. She can't help worrying about Chuck. Every day the kid looks a little more pale and underfed, as if the high mountain air is depleting him of some life-sustaining fluid. His is a classic ski-town tale. When she hired him, he had just flunked out of law school and was crashing on a college buddy's floor in East Franklin, and for the first few months he'd been too ashamed to even tell his parents where he was. They found him eventually when a family friend saw Chuck's byline on a story he sold to the *Denver Post*, but he's still rooming with that same college buddy and every day Tish expects him to tell her that, upon reflection, he's decided to go back to his real life.

"Where are you headed now?" she asks him when Moira finishes her story.

"Commissioners' meeting," he says. "Russell Canavan called this morning. The Wildlands Coalition is going to stage a protest."

"Has anybody checked out this Canavan guy to see if he's connected to Jack Frost?" Moira asks.

"Have you met Russ Canavan?" Chuck asks.

Clearly, Moira hasn't. Canavan, the owner of a local wellness retreat, the Flying Y Ranch, is a gangling New York transplant with a spray of silvering hair and a habit of rubbing his hands together like a nervous grasshopper. His group, the Mountain Wildlands Coalition, has long opposed the Elkhorn Canyon project, but to imagine Canavan firebombing a building is to imagine Jiminy Cricket as an eco-terrorist mastermind.

"Didn't they protest at the last meeting?" Tish asks.

"And at the one before that," Chuck says. "But the TV cameras weren't here then."

The three of them turn to the courthouse lawn where Kelly Cherry is applying lipstick in a side mirror of the Channel 4 news truck. Up and down Main Street, producers and camera techs are sunning themselves in beach chairs while the on-air talent, all of them young and blonde and some variety of drop-dead gorgeous, check their makeup or walk in circles running their lines.

"You bring a camera?" Tish asks.

Chuck reaches into his backpack for one of the loaner Pentax LXs the *Flyer* reporters use.

"Shoot the TV cameras this time," Tish says. "They're the story now."

"Aye-aye, Boss," he says, snapping off a quick salute as he sets off across the street.

Chuck's meeting doesn't start for another hour, which is fine because it gives him time to make the rounds, checking in with his courthouse sources. His excuse, today and always, is that he's gathering items for his "Valley News" column, which catches locals up on a week's worth of marriages, births, deaths, and notable real estate transactions. In each office, when Chuck pokes his head in the door, secretaries throw open the books for him, eager to point him toward the latest juicy bit of local news. But that's just the start, because as Tish explained when he took the job, secretaries know *everything*. When a concerned citizen calls in to report that the county clerk's breath smelled of gin at noon on a Tuesday, a secretary puts through the call. When the health inspector finds rodent droppings in the walk-in refrigerator of an overpriced local restaurant, another secretary types up the report and files it.

So, in each office, as he takes down the names and birth weights of each newborn child, he chats up whoever's behind the counter, asking after their kids and bantering about John Elway's passing efficiency rating. Today, though, Chuck is preoccupied by a letter he received from his mother telling him that his grandfather, a senior judge on the Missouri Court of Appeals, has put in a word for him with the dean of the University of Missouri Law School. He'd have to retake the LSAT and give a full accounting of his decision to drop out, but if they like his answers, his mother had cheerily informed him, he "could be back at Mizzou next fall!"

Unremarked upon in the letter is the galling irony that his parents never wanted Chuck to go to Mizzou Law in the first place. His father wanted him to apply to his alma mater, Yale Law, and his mother wanted him to follow in *her* father's footsteps and become a doctor. Neither of these was a realistic possibility for Chuck given his grades and interests, but now, thanks to his spectacular flameout at Mizzou, his beloved, beetle-browed Grandpa Charley is sucking up to the law school dean to get Chuck reinstated at a school his family thinks is beneath him. All morning he's been mentally composing the letter to his mother telling her and his grandfather to kindly quit meddling in his life. But he knows what she'll say in return. It's what he'd say to himself if he were in her position: *Do you really see yourself spending the rest of your life chatting up secretaries at the Elk County Courthouse?*

"You grew up in Franklin, right?" Chuck asks Troy Martin in the county assessor's office.

Troy works for his mother, Clarice, Elk County's elected county assessor. *Friend* may not be the right word for a guy who you pump for information several times a week, but Troy is the only person in the courthouse Chuck would talk to if he wasn't getting paid to do it.

"That's right," Troy says. "My parents grew up here, too. And their parents before that."

Chuck nods, recalling Troy telling him once that his great-grandparents had come to the valley in search of cheap land not long after the turn of the century. Maybe that's what Chuck likes about him. Troy seems settled, rooted in place in a way no one else Chuck knows seems to be.

"You ever think about moving someplace else?" he asks. "Doing something else?"

"I did, man," Troy says. "I spent three years being all I could be for Uncle Sam. Got as far Okinawa. That's pretty damn far."

"And you didn't mind coming back?"

"To come work for my mom?" Troy holds up a hand to stop Chuck before he has a chance to pretend that wasn't what he meant. "It's funny,

Mom says the same thing. Get out, see the world. The Dunows are gonna turn this place into downtown Disneyland, so go to college, move to Denver, move to Dallas. But I don't want to live in Dallas, man. I like it here. This is home."

The bell over the door to the clerk's office jingles and a young woman pokes her head in the door, looking lost. She's pretty, in her early twenties, long-boned and slender in ratty jeans and a sloppy sweater. She is wearing glasses even thicker than the ones Chuck wears, and chunky in a way he finds it hard to believe a girl like her would choose.

"Can I help you?" Troy says, responding to the same single-guy Bat-Signal that has made Chuck forget all about Mizzou Law and the letter from his mother.

"I hope so," she says. "Is this where you keep property records?"

"Some of them, yes," Troy says. "But if you're looking something up, I'll need the parcel number. You can get that from – "

"Oh, I have that right here."

She hands him a folded sheet of paper on which she has written a long string of letters and figures. Troy glances at the paper and cocks his head, giving her a slow once-over.

"This is way out in the boondocks," he says. "You know that, right?"

"Yes, my family owns it," she says. "Or they did, anyway. My great-grandfather mined the land out there."

"He patented the claim?"

"I guess," she says. "I don't really understand all of it. I just know he walked away from the land and it was supposed to go to the county, but it never did. We still own it. That's what my aunt says, anyway. It's out where they're building this new ski resort so it's got to be worth something, right?"

The two men's eyes graze one another's long enough to read the thought bubble forming above the other's head: *Did she just say her family owns land in Elkhorn Canyon?* Then, nodding, Troy turns toward the back room where the property records are kept, leaving Chuck alone with her. He busies himself pretending to take down real estate transactions for his column while he checks her out. She's about his age, he decides, unusually long in the face, with full red lips and pert button nose, but he can't kick the nagging sense that something's slightly off about her. It's not just the glasses. She's dressed like she threw on whatever she found on the bedroom floor, her white-blonde hair tied off in a messy ponytail, but she strikes him as several ticks too refined, too poised for that. But hey, who says pretty girls can't dress like slobs? And this one, he reminds himself, is related to someone who owned land in Elkhorn Canyon.

"Here you go," Troy says, emerging from the back room with a thin manila folder. "If you like, I can set you up at one of our reading tables."

"You don't have it on computer?"

"Afraid not, ma'am. We're just now starting to digitize our holdings," he says. "This old stuff, it's all still on paper, and I'm going to have to ask you to be careful with it. The older documents are in plastic sleeves, but they're super fragile. Some of these deeds, nobody's really looked at them since the 1890s."

She opens the folder on the counter and begins flipping through its contents. She only makes it a few pages in before she looks up, panic flaring in her eyes.

"God, I have no idea what I'm even looking at," she says.

"You can have a lawyer look it over if you want," Troy says. "In general, though, the most recent documents are going to be at the front. That's who owns the property now. Then you can work backward to see the history of land transfers, going back to the original claim."

"What's this, then?" she asks, holding up the top sheet of paper. "FEC Corp – do you know what that is?"

"They're the current owner?" Troy asks.

"I don't know. It's the first thing in here. But how can they be the owner? *We* own it."

"Ma'am, would you mind if I had a look at that?" Chuck asks, stepping forward.

He keeps his voice light, casual, just a fellow citizen here to lend a hand, but she turns on him, her eyes narrowed behind the big glasses, unnerved.

"Do you work here, too?" she asks.

"I – no, I don't." He looks over at Troy, now openly smirking at his stuttering. "My name is Chuck Quigley. I'm a reporter with one of the local papers here, the *Franklin Flyer*."

"A reporter?"

"Yes, and I couldn't help overhearing what you were saying about this property your family owns. It's in Elkhorn Canyon?"

Now it's her turn to look at Troy, who, damn him, still hasn't wiped that smirk off his face.

"I don't mean to be rude, but this is kind of a private family thing," she says.

"No, sure, I totally get that."

"I'd appreciate it if you didn't put this in your newspaper," she says. "At least not until I've had a chance to talk this over with a lawyer."

"Sure, sure, of course," he says, digging in his pocket for his wallet. "I respect your privacy, totally. Here's my card. Give me a call once you talk with a lawyer, Ms. – ?

"Thanks, I will," she says and smiles, dismissing him. But now that he's close up he finally understands what's been bothering him about her. Chuck has worn prescription glasses as long as he can remember, and for as long as he can remember, he's stared into the mirror and despaired at how the lenses distort his features. With lenses that thick, this girl's brown eyes should be twice their normal size, but they're not. The glasses aren't real.

"Right, sorry," he says. "I should head out. The commissioners' meeting's about to start."

He means to loiter in the hall and catch the brown-eyed girl on her way out, to see if he can at least get a name out of her, but as soon as he steps through the door he hears a low-level drone of voices coming from the street.

"What do we want?" one voice shouts.

"No development!" a dozen more answer.

"When do we want it?" the first voice calls.

"Never, ever!" the others respond.

"Shit," Chuck swears under his breath, racing for the courthouse doors. But before he gets there, they swing open and Russell Canavan bursts in, waving for the crowd to follow. "C'mon, everyone!" he cries. "The commissioners' room is this way!"

He marches off down the corridor, his long arms flapping, leading a dozen or so protesters holding signs and shouting slogans, followed by an even larger crowd of reporters and camera techs carrying forty-pound video cameras. At the rear of the throng Chuck spots his competition, Dana Teig of the *Daily Bulletin*, scribbling in her notebook.

For a split-second Chuck considers bailing, just marching out to the nearest pay phone to call his mother and tell her he's coming home. But he doesn't do that. Instead, he joins the media scrum, trying to peek at Dana Teig's notes, until they've all poured themselves into the commissioners' meeting room, where the five county commissioners are taking their seats behind a crescent-shaped table, Cory Carr at the center.

Chuck reaches for the Pentax, and remembering Tish's directive, snaps half a roll of the TV cameras filming Canavan and his Wildlands crew as they run through two more rounds of their "What do we want?" chant before Carr pounds his gavel for quiet.

"Before you call this meeting to order, Mr. Commission President," Canavan declares, "the members of the Mountain Wildlands Coalition demand an opportunity to address the most important issue facing this county, the development of Elkhorn Canyon for skiing."

"So I see," Carr says. "And you brought a few friends of yours from the media to watch you make this demand?"

Laughter skitters through the crowd. Even Chuck laughs, not because the joke is funny, but because Carr seems so in control, so unruffled by the sight of camera crews turning his meeting room into a makeshift TV studio.

"They're here to hear the truth, Mr. Commission President!" Canavan proclaims, rubbing his hands together. "The citizens of this county aren't the only ones concerned about the wholesale destruction of our wild-lands. The entire nation is concerned. They're sick and tired of the dou-ble-talk and obstruction on this issue from their elected officials."

"Well, this is just a working session of the commission," Carr says. "We're here today to see to the routine business of the county. As I explained to you at our meeting last month, we won't be taking up the issue of Elkhorn Canyon until the Colorado Department of Conservation issues its report on the status of the lynx."

"The people of this county are plainly divided on this issue, Mr. Commission President," Canavan says. "We came today to demand that you delay any consideration of the proposal until the entire community has had a chance to educate itself on all the issues."

"But we *are* delaying – until the state issues its wildlife report," Carr says.

Canavan's hands are moving faster now, palm against palm, in frantic little circles. Any faster, Chuck thinks, and his hands might spontane-ously combust.

"We understand that," he says. "But in light of recent events, we believe a more sweeping moratorium on the proposal is called for."

"Which events are you referring to, exactly, Russ?" Carr asks. "Do you mean the arson fire at the Highline Chalet? Or the bomb that nearly set an entire forest on fire?"

"You know perfectly well we abhor violence in any form," Canavan says, indignant. "We were among the very first groups to condemn the firebombing of the Highline Chalet last week."

"And yet here you are using that very same act of violence to further your cause," Carr says. "You know, thirty years ago reactionaries with a very different political agenda attempted to use violence to thwart progress, and liberals like yourselves – good, well-meaning, reform-minded folks – pointed to that violence when they begged Dr. King to wait. They told him that his efforts to nonviolently protest segregation in Birmingham, Alabama, were 'unwise and untimely.' And maybe from their perspective they were. But in his justly famous 'Letter from a

Birmingham Jail,' Dr. King wrote, 'This "Wait" has almost always meant Never.' Isn't that what you really mean? Never? Isn't that what you and your friends were chanting just now? Not *delay* taking a vote, but *never* take a vote, ever – isn't that what you really came here to ask us to do?"

"We are *not* a bunch of Southern bigots," Canavan says. "We're environmentalists. We're trying to save a pristine forest from predatory development."

"Oh, I believe you're sincere in your intentions," Carr says, playing to the cameras now. "But the fact remains that you're trying to leverage violence, or at least the threat of violence, to thwart the democratic process. And I cannot allow that. Now, you and your friends are more than welcome to stay as long as you like. This meeting is open to the public. But we are going to follow our published agenda and the first item on that agenda is consideration of a new stoplight at the Valley View Shopping Center."

A dozen camera techs, knowing their business, have trained their cameras on Russ Canavan, whose hands have ceased their mad stridulation and hang uselessly at his sides, beaten. Carr's comparison of environmentalists to Southern racists is outrageous even for him, but in the chopped up soundbite that will run on the six o'clock news, viewers will hear "Martin Luther King" and "threats of violence" and when the camera cuts away to file footage of the crowd singing while the Highline Chalet burns, the mental circuit will be complete.

Canavan takes another run at Carr, demanding a place on the agenda for his protest, but the camera crews are already packing up, the hot lights blinking out one by one as techs fold up tripods and stuff cameras into padded cases. In ten minutes, they're all gone, leaving Canavan and his Mountain Wildlands Coalition to sit forlornly in the back row under their posters and banners while county engineers drone on about the need for a stoplight outside the Valley View mini-mall. Half an hour later, when the stoplight discussion gives way to a report on persistent sewage backups at a mobile home park along Highway 22, first one or two, then whole clusters of Canavan's troops fold up their banners and head out, until Canavan himself is alone. When, some time after that, the subject switches to leaf abatement in a culvert next to the county library, even Canavan grabs his poster and his manila folder of talking points and treads solemnly toward the hallway, leaving the commission, county staff, and two local beat reporters to ponder an eight-page memo on failed efforts to clear leaves from the library culvert.

Ten minutes into the discussion of the culvert memo, Chuck leans over to Dana Teig, the only other reporter in the room, and whispers, "Notebooks down, Teig. I gotta pee."

Dana, every bit as bored as Chuck, laughs and makes a show of setting her notepad in her lap. This is a joke, but also not. Once, a couple months after he started at the *Flyer*, when he missed an hour of a commissioner's meeting due to a persistent case of the runs, Dana surprised him by letting him copy her notes. Then again, with a story like wet leaves clogging a culvert, who would even notice if it wasn't in the paper?

As soon as he's out of the commissioners' meeting room, Chuck strides across the tiled lobby to the assessor's office.

"Figured you'd be back," Troy says, reaching for a folder below the counter.

"That girl who was in here looking at this – did she give her name?" he asks.

"I wish she had, man," he says. "Hella cute, right?"

"Hella," Chuck agrees. "You see her glasses, though?"

Troy eyes him, confused. "What about them?"

"Nothing," Chuck says, waving it away. "Could I have a copy of everything in that file, please? Put it on the *Flyer's* tab."

Chapter Five

Late on Friday afternoon, Tish makes the rounds of the office handing out paychecks to each of her seventeen employees. Normally, she stuffs the checks into envelopes and leaves them in each employee's mail slot, but getting payroll out, on time and in full, merits its own small victory lap. To make the numbers work, she had to stiff several of her vendors and cash out some of the last mutual funds in her own dwindling portfolio, but her single biggest savings came from swapping her most expensive employee, Rod Arango, for her cheapest, Gemma Seagraves. Now, two weeks after she fired him, Gemma is covering Rod's beat almost as well as he did and Tish has survived a whole pay cycle without firing anyone else.

That night, after she hands off the paper to Lydia in paste-up, Tish takes the ad reps out for beers at the Summit Tavern and stays much later than she planned chatting with Moira at the bar, where she's pulling her regular Friday night shift. That morning, less than an hour after the Jack Frost letter ran in the paper, the news hit the AP wires, and every news crew that had left town rolled right back in again and Tish spent half the day on the phone with reporters and sitting for interviews. Channel 4 in Denver has been teasing the story all night, and when the local news comes on at eleven, the bar breaks into a raucous cheer at the sight of Tish's face on the screen.

"I'd say we've got a pretty neat real-life mystery on our hands here," she hears herself say. "We know someone is going to extreme lengths to come to the defense of the lynx, but we don't know who that someone is and we don't know when they'll stop."

The camera cuts to week-old B-roll of the gutted Highline Chalet as Kelly Cherry reads from the Jack Frost letter the *Flyer* and the *Bully* ran on their front pages that morning. Tish keeps waiting for the story to cut back to her and the rest of her interview, but instead they run footage of Monkiewicz at his Monday press conference and interviews with locals talking about the arson and the Elkhorn Canyon resort. After a couple minutes, Cherry signs off and the anchorwoman pivots to a report on a fresh round of construction delays at the Denver airport.

In the bar, another big cheer goes up, and for the next hour, drunken ski instructors and construction workers buttonhole Tish to offer their own alcohol-infused takes on the Jack Frost story. Each time one of them leaves, she tells herself to call it a night, but when the next one arrives, she's still sitting at the same barstool, watching the same endless news loop on TV. The *Flyer* doesn't publish on Sundays, which makes Saturday the one day of the week she can sleep in, and she doesn't want to go home. Home is a carton of faux French yogurt and bags of wilted carrots and celery in the fridge. Home is turning on CNN to have some conversation in the apartment. Home is where she sleeps, and she's not ready to sleep just yet.

But when Moira clocks out at midnight, Tish finally settles up and sets off for home. It's a cool, clear fall night, a sprinkling of early-season snow dusting the tops of the trees, but she sees none of it, her appearance on Channel 4 News still cycling in her brain. Did she actually say "pretty neat" on statewide TV? And would it have killed her to put on a little makeup? Or wear something other than a pink and green Polo with the collar turned up? But what rankles most is what a local rube the piece made her out to be. She'd sat under the hot TV lights for half an hour telling Kelly Cherry everything her viewers needed to know about the lynx and the Elkhorn Canyon debate, and in the end she used the only two sentences Tish had uttered that had no actual news content.

At home, she considers breaking out the Stoli bottle she keeps in the freezer to finish the job she started at the Summit, but instead she downs a tall glass of ice water, fills a bag with a week's worth of dirty clothes, and hauls it down two flights of stairs to the laundry room. Some people have time and money for therapy. Tish has laundry. Laundry, as she'll tell anyone who will listen, is nothing like real life. Life is one long series of compromises and muddled choices. With laundry, you throw your dirty, foul-smelling clothes into a machine, put in a few quarters, and a couple hours later they come out clean and smelling faintly of flowers. Every time.

In the cave-like quiet of the laundry room, Tish lights her third cigarette of the night, a habit she only indulges when she's been drinking, and lets her mind wander over her hectic week until it alights, as she halfway knew it would, on a picture of Scott Sage sitting across from her at the Lazy T. Even a few weeks ago she would have thought Scott Sage beneath her. More accurately, a few weeks ago she wouldn't have given Scott Sage much thought at all. The guy's pleasant enough, and one of a vanishingly small number of age-appropriate single men in Franklin whose employment doesn't involve ski wax or a nametag. But how else to say it? He reeks of suburban niceness, of 401k plans and Volvo station wagons. She's never seen him on a bike, but she'd bet her next month's payroll that he wears one of those dental-mirror-looking things affixed to his helmet so he can see the traffic behind him. He is, in short, the kind of man her Pimms Cup-tippling grandmother was forever telling her she should marry, which makes him the kind of man Tish would never marry in a million years.

Yet for a week now she's been replaying the moment during their breakfast, just before she broke out her spreadsheets, when Scott showed her a wallet photo of his eight-year-old daughter. At the time, the gesture struck Tish as odd. If he really is sweet on her, and he is, why show off the last remaining entanglement of his messy first marriage? Isn't that like hanging a great, honking "Please don't date me" sign on your forehead? But here, in the dank privacy of her laundry room, Tish decides the moment had very little to do with her. His daughter, he'd explained, had spent the summer with him in Franklin but is now back in Fort Collins with his ex and he won't see her again until Christmas. So, no, he hadn't been trying to scare Tish off. He wasn't hitting on her, either. He was simply trying to communicate to another human being how much the prospect of a long, daughterless autumn was killing him.

Glancing at the curling ash of her cigarette, Tish discovers, to her abject mortification, that this thought has made her wet. Only a little, but still. Here she is a grown woman sneaking a smoke while doing laundry on a Friday night and she's getting a lady boner because a man she barely knows displayed outward signs of being a loving dad.

Stubbing out her cigarette, she marches back upstairs where, on second thought, she decides she *will* have that shot of vodka from the fridge. She's furious with herself. She can't be mooning around after a guy like some horny teenager. She has a business to run, and a once-in-a-lifetime story to cover. She might sound like Daisy Dipstick on the eleven o'clock news, but she's the only reporter in town with the contacts and skills to chase down the evidence Monkiewicz hinted at in their interview.

She changes into a nightgown and brushes her teeth, planning to catch a few hours' sleep before heading into the office, but despite all she's had to drink, or maybe because of it, her brain won't power down. All week she and Moira have been working their sources at FrankCo and law enforcement, sniffing around for evidence of outside involvement in the Jack Frost attacks. But maybe, she thinks now, they've been coming at this the wrong way. They've been hoping someone in the know might slip up and tell them something they shouldn't. What they haven't done is ask themselves why *Monkiewicz* slipped up and told them something he shouldn't have. He had seemed so in control, guiding Tish and the other reporters to the facts he was prepared to release, and shutting them down whenever they steered toward a line of questioning he didn't like. A guy that smart, that wise to the ways of the media, doesn't tell a bunch of reporters they don't have all the facts unless he wants them to go lamming out after them.

So, why?

Tish stares at the bathroom mirror, trying to see the Jack Frost case from Monkiewicz's point of view. She assumes he hasn't solved the crime yet. She assumes, too, that if he doesn't solve it soon, the Kelly Cherrys of the world will drive their satellite trucks back to Denver and New York for good and the FBI brass will rotate his investigators onto other, more urgent cases. So, what does a man in his position need? Well, obviously, bad guys in handcuffs wouldn't hurt. Failing that, he needs manpower and time, which means he needs the national media to keep beaming live shots from the lawn of the Elk County Courthouse. And one very good way to do that is to quietly leak evidence that a notorious national eco-terror group is behind the attacks. Of course, the FBI's special agent in charge can't do the leaking himself. But if someone else leaks it *for* him – that could work.

But who might that someone be? It won't be anyone at FrankCo, because they're too scared of Monkiewicz, and it won't be a cop because they hate the media on principle. No, it would have to be someone outside the direct chain of command but who's close enough to the investigation to know the facts and politically astute enough to know why Monkiewicz might want to get them out.

She sets down her toothbrush and laughs. She knows just the man she needs.

Dry-mouthed and queasy, dressed in baggy sweats and a rumpled Ski Franklin! sweatshirt, Tish cautiously approaches the leg-stretching bar at the first station of the Franklin River parcourse. She ran this mile-long parcourse for a story on the day it opened, but that was at midday in full summer. Now it's eight in the morning in late October and the steel bars of the fitness station are like icicles in her hands. If she had known it would be this cold, she would have brought gloves, but then, if she'd known it would be this cold, she would still be in bed, sleeping off her hangover. But she's here now, decked out in this fantastically ugly jogging outfit, so she steps up to the bar and stretches her calf muscles, first her left, then her right. A hundred yards down the trail, she comes to a second parcourse station where she dutifully executes ten sit-ups on the angled bench, chasing away all thoughts of her warm bed and the sour taste of bile rising from her stomach.

Half an hour later, she's two stations from the end of the parcourse, afraid she's missed her quarry, when she spots a man with a halo of silver hair chugging up the path behind her, his head bobbing to the Motown tune pulsing through his Walkman earphones. Tish executes one last pull-up and drops to the ground mere feet from County Commission President Cory Carr out for his regular Saturday morning run along the Franklin River trail.

"Well, well, if it isn't our very own Katharine Graham running the fitness parcourse," he says, tugging his earphones down around his neck. "Don't remember seeing you down here before."

"Just getting in shape for ski season," she says brightly. "I gotta tell you, this parcourse is kicking my ass."

Carr offers a pitying nod of his regal head. First thing in the morning, slathered in sweat, he still looks like a cross between the Marlboro Man and the crown prince of a European city-state. Here, she thinks, is the man Robert Redford has been playing in the movies all these years.

"Which way you headed?" he asks.

"Same as you, I think. But you don't want to run with me. I'll just slow you down."

"I'm due for a break, anyway. Come on, you can set the pace."

She shrugs and they set off together at a companionable trot. Freed from the tyranny of the exercise stations, Tish can finally take in the beauty of the trail, which follows the winding path of the Franklin River through the east side of town. Here, Franklin's few remaining teachers and cops and postal workers own tidy wood-frame Victorian homes with steeply sloped roofs and small, gated front porches. This is the red-hot center of the opposition to Elkhorn Canyon, and jogging past it isn't hard to see why. It's a slice of high-country Americana, middle-aged guys reading the morning papers on the porch, surrounded by Halloween pumpkins and kids building tiny snowmen in the fast-melting snow. In ten years, if the Dunow Brothers get their way on the new resort, all this will be gone, replaced by luxury hotels and gated condo villages.

"Nice job on Russ Canavan," Tish says, breaking the silence. "I'm guessing that's the first time he's been compared to a drooling Southern bigot on national TV."

The commissioner shrugs, the faux-modest tilt of his head saying, *We should all be so lucky in our enemies*. "And I appreciate you guys waiting to release that letter," he says. "I told Monkiewicz how lucky he is your brother isn't still around."

She laughs, only half-feigning her surprise. She knows Carr is in the inner circle on the arson investigation – it's why she's here, freezing her ass off – but she's startled that he's the one to bring it up.

"They're going to catch these guys, Tish," he says. "Give them a week, maybe two, tops. Then I'll make sure you guys are first in line for the full story."

"'These guys' being the Mother Earth's Avengers?"

"We aren't on the record here, right?"

Always this question. Tish can't ask a politician to pass the salt without him wondering if it's going to end up in the newspaper. When they both know that, of course, it's going to end up in the paper. If he didn't want it there, he wouldn't have brought it up.

"Nope. Just two locals shooting the shit."

"Then, yeah, the Avengers. Elkhorn Canyon's a walking billboard for their cause."

"You don't think the arson attack wasn't a little targeted?"

Carr side-eyes her again. "Someone's been talking to Jimmy Lachlan."

"Who, the ski patrol guy?"

"Save it, Tish. You're hardly the only one Jimmy's been whispering to."

"Okay, but you have to admit, hitting that communications gear was pretty darn lucky," she says. "They had three restaurants to choose from and they picked the only one that can shut down the mountain."

"Maybe they recruited some locals to do recon, but this was a national operation," he says. "It's too sophisticated, too well-planned to be a bunch of kids pissed off at the ski company."

"Someone's been talking to Special Agent Monkiewicz," Tish says.

He doesn't respond, just chuckles. How much easier her life would be, Tish thinks, if she could just sit in on their meetings, instead of sneaking around ambushing politicians on their morning runs. But politicians have their jobs and she has hers. Luckily, she's good at hers.

"Monkiewicz has been dropping hints about evidence of this being an outside job," she tries.

"Yeah well, I can't help you there."

"He wants it out, Cory. He wouldn't have mentioned it if he didn't."

"You think he's trying to plump his budget?"

"I think he's trying to catch some bad guys and he's worried CNN's going to get bored," she says. "And CNN *is* going to get bored if they think this is just some local kids."

They run a little ways in silence, Carr staring stonily ahead. Tish waits, watching this cagey politician scope out the angles, weighing what's best for him and his constituents. At last, he slows to a stop and waits for her to circle around to face him.

"They traced the explosive to a quarry in Oregon," he says flatly.

"Which explosive?" Tish asks, struggling to catch her breath.

"From the first bombing, at the power station," he says. "The FBI traced the residue to a batch of industrial TNT stolen from a quarry outside Roseburg, Oregon. Which, as it happens, is about an hour's drive from the state university in Eugene."

"Okay, but anyone could have bought that explosive and brought it here."

"It was taken a week before the bombing. That's not a lot of time to organize a theft and a sale. And that's not the only thing they found. They recovered a partial serial number from the watch the bombers used in the bomb."

"It survived the explosion?"

"Most of it didn't, but a few fragments got lodged under a girder near the blown transformer. It's only a partial number so they can't trace the exact point of sale, but they know it's part of a lot sold in Fred Meyer stores in central Oregon."

Tish wishes suddenly that she had a pen and notepad. Her fingers are actually twitching, as if they're already typing out the story on an invisible keyboard.

"A knowledgeable source in county government," she says.

He laughs. "And here I thought we were just two locals shooting the shit."

She ignores this. "No quotes, no names, just a source in county government."

"Keep the county out of it," he says. "And you're going to have to go light on the details. You're probably right about Monkiewicz shopping this around, but he's keeping a close hold on that serial number. Even some of the local cops haven't been read in on that."

"All right, how about: The FBI has traced parts of the bomb used to blow up the West Fork Power Substation to Roseburg, Oregon, according to a source close to the investigation."

"Go with 'Central Oregon.' They don't know where the watch came from, exactly."

Tish repeats her lede for him, substituting "Central Oregon" for "Roseburg, Oregon." Carr cocks his head, listening, calculating not just the odds of the story being traced back to him, but whether he wants the story out there in the first place. No cop, federal or local, would leak this information because it could impede the investigation, but Carr isn't concerned about the integrity of the investigation, which, despite his brave talk, could drag on for months. He wants everyone to know, now, that this is the work of outside agitators and he wants to send the bombers a message that it's too hot for them to come back to Franklin.

"One last thing," he says. "Give the byline to Moira Mangan."

"Moira?" she protests. "She's sound asleep in bed right now."

Carr shrugs, unmoved. After all she's gone through to get this story, it galls Tish to think of giving it to another reporter, but she can't fault his logic: If the news appears under Moira's byline everyone will assume it came from law enforcement, not a local politician.

"Okay, fine. Done."

They stare at each other, each smirking at their knowledge of the other's ulterior motives.

"You crack me up, Threadgill," he says. "You didn't have to come all the way down here. You could've just called me."

"Would you have given me this if I'd called you?"

He gives this a moment's thought, then laughs. "Probably not, no."

Their business done, they part ways, Carr to continue his morning run, Tish heading back to the empty *Flyer* newsroom to type up her notes. She hates when editors speak of news stories as "packages," as if they were little Christmas presents to be set out under the tree each night, but if ever a story called for a package this is it. She doubts she'll find anyone to corroborate Carr's information, and the FBI flacks will issue their standard "no comment," but maybe she can find an expert to talk to her about tracing explosives. It would be great, too, if someone – Gemma, maybe – wrote up a sidebar laying out the history of the Mother Earth's Avengers. And Tish herself will have to write a thumb sucker piece looking at what the arrival of a national eco-terrorist group means for Franklin and for the future of the Elkhorn Canyon project.

Passing the courthouse, she sees the local CNN correspondent – a young kid, Anderson somebody-or-other – doing a standup on the courthouse lawn. Over the past two weeks, watching TV news correspondents deliver live reports outside the courthouse has become a local sport, and Tish barely breaks stride until she remembers that it's nine o'clock on a Saturday morning. Across the TV dial, kids are watching Rocky and Bullwinkle, so what is little Anderson what's-his-name doing reporting live from Franklin, Colorado?

Out of the corner of her eye, Tish spots Kelly Cherry sharing a smoke with her producer in the open doorway of the Channel 4 News truck. Marching over to where they're standing, she asks, "Kelly, what gives?"

She hands Tish a fax copy of an inside page of the *New York Times*. A hundred copies of the *Times* are flown in daily on the afternoon United Express flight out of Denver and circulate a day late at the Hotel Franklin and the front counter of Lawton's Drugs. Tish reads it every morning because even a day late it's still the best newspaper in the world. But this isn't Friday's *Times*. This is the Saturday morning paper, and she can see the headline splashed across the page:

National Activist Group Tied To Attacks at Colo. Ski Area

"I don't believe it," Tish says, tossing the page to the ground. "That asshole gave my story away."

Kelly Cherry's finely featured face twists in confusion. "Wait. Which asshole?"

But Tish is already gone, headed for home and her warm bed.

◆ ◆ ◆

"What you got there?" Gemma asks.

Chuck looks up from the papers on his desk, startled. It's Monday morning around ten, more or less the crack of dawn in newsroom-time, and he'd thought he was alone.

"Honestly?" he says. "I'm not sure. You know much about property law?"

"Aren't you the guy who went to law school?"

"No, I'm the guy who flunked out of law school. I've been staring at this stupid thing for a week now, and I'm still not sure what it means. Or really, if it means anything."

But he has her attention, so he tells her the story, how he'd been making his regular rounds at the courthouse when a young woman wearing a pair of non-prescription prescription glasses showed up at the clerk's office asking for the file on a property deep in Elkhorn Canyon.

"Her glasses were fake?" Gemma asks.

"I don't know, maybe I made that part up," he says. "The point is, her great-granddad mined the land out there but now this other company owns it, FEC Corp. And if it's where I think it is, it's close to where they're talking about building this new ski hill."

"FEC Corp?"

"Yeah, I asked around. Nobody's ever heard of it. All I have is an address in Denver, which, when I looked it up, turns out to be a big law firm."

"What'd they say when you called them?"

"Well, nothing yet. I wanted to do some more legwork before I burned that bridge, you know?"

Gemma waits, expecting to hear about all this legwork he's been doing, but the fact is for the past week, every minute he hasn't spent writing stories for the next day's paper, Chuck has been on the phone with his mother and writing the letter to the dean of Mizzou Law explaining why he wants to reapply next year. He's written three drafts, retyped it onto thirty-two-pound-bond paper, and folded it into an envelope. But he hasn't sent it. He told his mother he'd sent it Saturday morning, and he spent all weekend planning to send it, but here it is Monday morning and it's still sitting on top of the TV in his bedroom, unsent.

"I better get going on this," he says, holding up the property file.

"Want a hand?" she asks.

These are, bar none, the three kindest words Chuck has heard in months – years, possibly.

"You sure?" he asks. "What about your own stuff?"

"I have Planning & Zoning at noon, but I'm good till then. What's the first thing you need to do?"

The first thing he needs to do is look at the county maps in the assessor's office to figure out where the FEC Corp property, known officially as Elk County Parcel 135-65-A25-R, is located. On the walk to the courthouse, Chuck fills her in on what he's learned about Parcel 135-65-A25-R so far, which isn't much. The original deed, dated October 12, 1886, lists the owner as Byram Milton, who had patented a mining claim to ten acres of federal land. Three years later, Milton added an adjoining fifteen-acre parcel, bringing the total to twenty-five acres. He paid his taxes, in full and on time, each year until 1894, at which point he mysteriously stopped. For the next decade, notes in the file show tax liens in gradually escalating amounts until even those stop, and the file has no new entries until 1946, when someone, presumably an employee at the assessor's office, scratched out a note indicating the tax arrears and the clouded title to the land. For the next forty-two years, the property sat unoccupied, its taxes unpaid, its title unchanged, until July 16, 1988, when FEC Corp bought the land from the Milton Family Trust for $50,000, plus $34,795 in back taxes.

"Fifty grand?" Gemma asks.

"Not a bad price, really, for twenty-five acres in the middle of nowhere without even a road leading to it."

"Or the steal of the century if it happens to be right next to a brand-new ski resort."

At the assessor's office, Troy Martin is hunched over his desk behind the counter typing in data from handwritten property forms onto a spanking new Dell computer.

"I'm here about the parcel that girl asked for last week," Chuck tells him. "I'd like to check out the plat maps, see where it's located."

"No problem." Troy shoots a glance at Gemma, then turns back to him, eyebrows raised.

"Right, sorry, this is Gemma Seagraves," Chuck says. "She's a new reporter at the *Flyer*. She's kind of helping me on this."

"Nice to meet you, Gemma," Troy says, holding her hand a tick longer than is strictly necessary. "You didn't happen to grow up here, did you?"

She laughs, high and startled. "I did, actually. Well, I moved away for high school. Did – you're from here, too?"

"Born and raised," he says. "I was a couple years ahead of you at Franklin Elementary, I think. Your name rings a bell, though. Your mom, she was, uh…"

"A teensy bit wild?" Gemma says. "That's my mom. The talk of the town, in every town she's in."

"Yeah, doesn't take much to get us Frankbillies talking." He looks over at Chuck. "Sorry. You guys are looking for some old plat maps?"

Troy leads them to the records room where he and Gemma trade tales of teachers they remember from Franklin Elementary School. But after ten minutes of flipping through the county's official maps, they still haven't found Parcel 135-65-A25-R.

"I don't get it," Gemma says. "How can it be in your files, but not on these maps?"

"You say this guy Milton vacated the land and quit paying taxes on it, right?" Troy says.

"Yeah. So?"

"So, after silver gave out here in the 1890s, thousands of miners walked away from their claims, just like this guy did," Troy says. "Abandoned properties are supposed to be auctioned off on the courthouse steps to pay the back taxes, but pretty much the whole valley had emptied out. Stuff slipped through the cracks – for decades. When Mom took over the assessor's office, she tried to clean up the files, but, well, it's a big county and this is a tiny office." He looks up, realizing what he's said. "You're not going to quote me on that, are you?"

"No, you're good," Chuck says. "Does the county still have any of the original maps from the 1890s?"

Troy's eyes light up. "You ever been in the courthouse vault?"

The courthouse vault is the size of a small bedroom, complete with a steel-reinforced door and boat-wheel combination lock, built for a time when miners paid their taxes in silver ingots. A hundred years later, it's mostly used to store old documents, including hand-drawn plat maps from the county's earliest days. From a drawer high on the vault's rear wall, Troy pulls down an ancient leather-bound case labeled "Elk County Plats #135-40, 1891," on which, after several minutes of searching, they find a faint, kite-shaped island of private property in a sea of federal land on the south slope of Elkhorn Canyon: Parcel 135-65-A25-R.

"Is there any way of saying how close it would be to the new resort?" Chuck asks.

Troy leans over the map, studying it from several different angles. "Okay, see this creek?" he says, pointing to a dotted line winding across the center of the map. "That's the West Fork of the Franklin. And this little bend here, I'm pretty sure that's the base of the new ski hill."

Using his index finger, Chuck traces a line from the bend in the river to Parcel 135-65-A25-R. If he's reading the scale correctly, Byram Milton's old mining claim, which hasn't appeared on any official map in nearly a century, is less than a mile due west of the proposed Elkhorn Canyon ski resort.

Walking out of the courthouse, Chuck tries not to feel spooked by his visit to the assessor's office. He knows he should tell Tish what he's seen. Now. Do not pass Go, do not collect $200. But he also knows that if he does that before he has all the facts, Tish will hand the story off to Moira, or more likely just take it for herself. Which, honestly, is what *should* happen. He's no investigative reporter. He has no idea how to uncover the identity of a mysterious corporation buying up land next to a proposed ski area. A year ago, he was flunking out of law school. Next year, if he sends that letter to the dean, he'll be back in law school, flunking out all over again. The smart thing, the obvious thing, is to give Tish the story and walk away, go back to his birth announcements and clogged culverts. But if he does that, he might as well mail the letter to the dean and be done with it.

"Are you going to try to get this in the paper today?" Gemma asks as they turn onto Main Street.

"Not yet, no," he says. "I think I need to do some more … "

He almost says *more legwork*, but stops himself. He looks over at Gemma, this slip of a girl in an oversized parka and jeans. She's just a kid, he realizes, every bit as young and clueless as he is, but he watched her with Troy. She isn't pushy like Moira, but whenever they got off-track, whenever it felt like they were hitting a dead end, she gently steered them back on course.

And, maybe more to the point, she's too green to steal the story from him.

"Could you – would you like to work with me on this?" he asks.

"Like, divide the work?"

"Right. I mean, it'd still be my story, but you'd get credit for additional reporting."

"Oh, I don't care about all that." She smiles, beaming. "Thank you. I'd love to."

"You would?" Chuck catches himself before he does something dumb, like hug her. "Okay, look, we've both got meetings now, but let's get started first thing tomorrow, see if we can't figure out who's behind this FEC Corp thing."

The next morning, early, they meet in the reference section of the county library to bone up on federal mining law and its complex inter-actions with Colorado property law. The day after that they spend hours scouring business listings across the state for the FEC Corp and the Milton Family Trust. When that goes nowhere, they divide up all the Miltons in the phone books for every town in the western half of the state and call every one, hoping to find someone with a great-grandfather named Byram.

It's a big fat waste of time, all of it, but when they're not paging through dusty law books and dialing their way through thin rural phone books, they talk. Gemma was born in Chicago and went to prep school and col-lege back East, but she spent much of her early life here in Franklin, where her mother landed after the divorce. Her mother's present whereabouts are sketchy – last Gemma heard, she was living on a private island off the Caribbean nation of Curaçao – and for now Gemma is living alone in a six-bedroom fieldstone castle on Rodeo Road, high above East Franklin. She has other habits that read to Chuck as rich-kid affectations. She's often late and can't understand why this bothers him. She never carries money and lets Chuck pay for everything. Then there's what she won't eat. She isn't merely vegetarian, which at least Chuck can understand; she won't eat or wear *any* animal products. So, milk and butter are out, obviously, but so is mayonnaise, which contains egg yolks, and honey, which is made by bees.

"*Bees?*" Chuck says, incredulous. "You're fighting for the rights of insects?"

They're in the reference section of the library, law books spread out on the table in front of them, and Chuck's outburst causes several patrons to glance up from their magazines.

"I'm not fighting for or against anything," she says, dropping her voice just above a whisper. "I'm not saying *you* can't eat honey. I just won't eat it myself."

In that same calm, placating voice, she ticks off her other restrictions. No shellfish. No animal oils, even as additives. No wearing leather, silk, fur, wool, or down.

"Around here, wool and down are the tough ones because I also try to avoid synthetics," she says. "Polyester's just another word for plastic, which is just another word for oil. Try putting a match to your parka there. It won't burn. It'll sort of smolder and then melt."

"What's your jacket made of, then?" Chuck asks.

"This here?" she says, fingering it. "The outer shell is hemp-oil cloth and the lining is a faux down made from a blend of cotton and dried wildflowers."

"Does it keep you warm?"

"What do you think? I'm wearing freaking ganja oil and flowers." She laughs, a soft, pretty trill. "Lucky for me, my moral superiority keeps me nice and toasty."

This, for Chuck's money, is her saving grace: Gemma is a kind of rich he can't really wrap his mind around, but she never brags or talks about money, and she can laugh at herself. Maybe for that reason, or maybe it's just that he's found someone to talk to who isn't answering phones at the county courthouse, over the course of the week a funny thing happens: he quits worrying about Mizzou Law. He still takes his mother's calls because he's never known how to say no to the human freight train that is Marilyn Quigley, but his letter to the dean stays where he left it on top of the TV, unsent.

"Hey, hey, look what I found," Gemma says.

It's a Monday morning again, a week after their trip to the assessor's office, and Gemma is at her desk holding a ring of papers from the *Flyer*'s morgue. At a big-city daily, the morgue is a climate-controlled library staffed by professional librarians who cross-reference each archived article in dozens of different ways. At the *Flyer*, the morgue is a supply closet in the corner of the newsroom containing a few hundred smudged copies of the paper hanging from binder rings.

"What am I looking at?" Chuck asks.

"These are legal notices for July 18, 1988," she says, pointing to two columns of 5.5-point agate type in the paper's classified section. "Now look at the last item in the second column."

ELK COUNTY PARCEL 135-65-A25-R
Sold July 16, 1988. By Milton Family
Trust, Inc., c/o Catherine Milton Boggs,
Lakeland, Fla. to FEC Corp, c/o Brandt,
Lewis & Thurgood, LLC, Denver, Colo. in
consideration of $50,000.

In a matter of minutes, he's gotten the home number for Catherine M. Boggs from an operator in Lakeland, Florida, and is dialing through, with Gemma listening in from the extension at her desk. When Mrs. Boggs picks up, Chuck has to identify himself three times, raising his voice to explain that he's a reporter working *for* a newspaper, not a telemarketer selling subscriptions to one. When he manages to jog her memory by mentioning Elkhorn Canyon, she turns indignant, asking why he's bothering her when she doesn't even own the land anymore.

"Ma'am, that property is near a proposed ski resort," he explains. "It's coming up for a vote early next year. The land your family owned, it's less than a mile from the bottom of the ski hill. Somebody could build condos or a hotel there."

"Well, that's never going to happen," she tells him. "The folks who bought the land, they're environmentalists. They're trying to stop people building things there."

"FEC Corp is an environmental group?" he asks.

"Uh-huh, the Friends of Elkhorn Canyon," Mrs. Boggs says. "You can call them yourself if you want. Ask for Anna Pitlor. She'll talk to you, I know she will. That girl's dedicated her whole life to saving that poor wildcat you have up there."

"The Canada lynx?"

"The Canada what?"

"Lynx," Chuck says. "It's an endangered species of mountain wildcat."

"Okay," she says. "All's I know is they're trying to save it. They're going to preserve that land forever, so nobody can ever build on it."

"This organization, do you know how I could contact them?"

"Anna, you mean?"

"I guess, yeah. Do you know how to reach her?"

"I'm sure I have her number around here someplace," Mrs. Boggs says, "but you can look her up. Anna Pitlor. P-I-T-L-O-R. You'll like her. I've never been one to warm up to strangers, but she's just good people. You can tell right off. Do you have kids – Chip, is it?"

"It's Chuck. And, no, actually, I don't."

"Well, I do. Two girls, Ginny and Jo. You know what an aesthetician is?"

"I'm sorry?"

"Aesthetician. Do you know what that is?"

Catching Gemma's eye across the room, Chuck mimes banging the phone receiver against the wall.

"Chip, you still there?" Mrs. Boggs says.

"We're here, Mrs. Boggs," Gemma says. "Chuck doesn't know what an aesthetician is, but I do. It's someone who does facials and styles your hair."

"Who's this?" Mrs. Boggs asks.

"Gemma Seagraves, ma'am," she says. "I work with Chuck at the *Flyer*. And my cousin's an aesthetician. She does my hair every time I see her."

Gemma Seagraves, daughter of an agribusiness CEO and descendant of presidents, no more has an aesthetician for a cousin than she has anyone "do" her hair, but Mrs. Boggs sends up a high, cackling laugh.

"See now, Chip, you need to listen to your friend there," she says. "I didn't know what it was myself until Ginny said she wanted to be one. But, Anna, she knew all about it. Gave Ginny some of the best advice of her life. She was still in school then, trying to make up her mind did she want to be a dental technician or an aesthetician. When Anna heard that, she got right on the phone and they talked for hours, just the two of them. You wouldn't think a woman like that's got time talk with a school girl about her future, but Anna, see, she – "

"Mrs. Boggs," Chuck cuts in. "Ma'am, do you have any of the paperwork they sent you? Contracts, deeds, anything like that."

She stops, thrown. "You're just all business, aren't you?"

"I'm sorry. It's just, we're kind of on a deadline. We have a paper to get out."

"Oh sure, I understand," she says. "I'm plenty busy myself. It's not like we sit around all day down here watching "Days of Our Lives." You hang on a minute and I'll go get that file."

Chuck stares at his cluttered desk, avoiding Gemma's gaze, painfully aware of two things: 1.) Catherine M. Boggs will never, ever tell anyone that he is "good people," and 2.) three weeks into her newspaper career, Gemma Seagraves is already a better reporter than he will ever be.

"Here it is," Mrs. Boggs says, coming back on. "Not much to it, to be honest with you. There's a copy of the deed, with my granddaddy's name on it, and a bunch of legal stuff saying I'm really his relation and I have permission from the rest of the family to sell the property. That was the real job, rounding up everybody. Lucky for us, we pretty much all of us live here in Lakeland, but poor Anna, she must've made fifty phone calls to get everybody on board."

"And you're sure you got everyone?" Chuck asks.

"What's that, Chip?"

"I met a woman here the other day who was looking up the property records," he says. "She said her family had a claim to the property, but she'd never heard of FEC Corp."

"You get this girl's name?"

"I asked, but she wouldn't give it. She said the claim belonged to her great-grandfather."

"Then I'd say someone's pulling your leg there," she says. "Anna did a right thorough search, and she got everybody. Even the ones who didn't want to sign at first, they signed up. Fifty thousand dollars is a pile of money, even split between all us Miltons down here."

"The contract you signed, does it mention conservation easements?" Gemma asks.

"Conservation easels?"

"Easements," Gemma says. "When environmental groups want to protect land from development sometimes they'll put special language in the contract stating it can never be built on."

"Well, I don't know about that," Mrs. Boggs says. "But Anna and the people she works for, they're environmentalists themselves. They're not going to build anything there, and I don't know who would. It's way out in the woods, isn't it? How would you even get to it?"

Chuck closes his eyes, wanting to tell Catherine Boggs she's signed a contract giving the FEC Corp the right to do anything it wants with her grandfather's property. But what good would that do? So he takes down the Denver address listed for FEC Corp on the sales contract, which he already has, and asks Mrs. Boggs to fax him a copy of the contract, which he is certain she'll never do. Then, after another five minutes of listening to how Ginny Boggs's career as an aesthetician is working out, he and Gemma say goodbye and hang up.

"That law firm on the contract," Gemma says, "it's the same one you found in the county assessor's file, right?"

He nods. "Yeah, it is."

"So, are you ready to burn that bridge?" Gemma asks.

He is. Chuck calls the number for Brandt, Lewis & Thurgood, LLC, the law firm listed in the legal notice, and asks to speak with Anna Pitlor.

For half a minute he and Gemma sit listening to hold music before a breathy receptionist comes back on the line to say, "I'm sorry, but no one by that name is employed by this firm."

"Then can you put me through to whoever handles the account for the FEC Corp?" he says.

More hold music, more breathily conveyed corporate puzzlement before at last they're put through to a "communications specialist" named Jake Orlan who asks, in coolly reassuring tones, how they came to believe that Brandt, Lewis & Thurgood represents the FEC Corp.

"FEC Corp is named as the buyer in the sale of a property located near a proposed new ski resort here and they listed your office as their representative," Chuck says.

"I see," Orlan says. "Well, I'm sorry to say, as a matter of policy, we don't comment to the press on legal matters."

"Can you at least confirm that your firm represents FEC Corp.?"

"No, as a matter of policy, I'm afraid I can't confirm or deny that."

"Why would they list your name on their sales documents if you're not their lawyer?"

"I wouldn't want to speculate," Orlan says. "I'm sure you're very busy, Mr. Quigley, and have better things to do than listen to me profess my ignorance on these matters."

"Jake, this is Gemma Seagraves, Chuck's colleague at the *Flyer*," Gemma says, jumping in. "We're writing a story about an organization called the Friends of Elkhorn Canyon. They claim to be an environmental group working to save a portion of a national forest from development. We have a source who tells us that the Friends of Elkhorn Canyon and FEC Corp, which put your firm's name on its sales contracts, are one and the same."

"I'd really like to help you, Ms. Seagraves."

"But you're not actually going to," she says.

"I'm afraid I'm not, no."

"You realize we can just call Denver and get its incorporation statements," Chuck says.

"You could, yes, assuming it still exists."

Chuck and Gemma look at each other. This is a turn of events they hadn't anticipated: FEC Corp could have dissolved itself and reincorporated under a different name.

"Thank you, Jake," he says. "I appreciate your time."

"Not a problem, Mr. Quigley," Orlan says brightly. "Always happy to speak with members of the press."

Chuck sits a minute looking over his notes of his non-interview interview with Jake Orlan, then opens a fresh file on his computer and starts typing. It's time to take the story to Tish and he wants to have something for her to read – not a finished piece, exactly, just a simple account of his reporting of the story, starting with his visit to the assessor's office. When Gemma sees what he's doing, she logs onto her computer and starts doing the same. Moira and Perry arrive for work, drink their morning coffee and read their copies of the *Denver Post* and the *Rocky Mountain News*, and leave again, heading out to report the day's news. Through it all, Chuck and Gemma type, laying out the known facts about Byram Milton and Parcel 135-65-A25-R and emptying their notebooks of quotes from Catherine Milton Boggs and Jake Orlan.

It's almost noon when they type up the last of their notes and print out their files. Quickly, they read each other's accounts, making handwritten notes in the margins, before sweeping it all into the manila folder containing the assessor's office file for Parcel 135-65-A25-R and setting off together to find Tish. Any thought Chuck had of hogging the byline for himself is gone. This is *their* story now.

But when they reach her cramped business office, the door is shut.

"Sorry, she's gone for lunch," Jen tells them.

"Lunch?" Chuck asks. As long as he's worked at the *Flyer*, lunch for Tish Threadgill has been a blueberry Yoplait cup and an oatmeal raisin cookie at her desk.

"Yes, with Sheldon Dunow at FrankCo," Jen says. "Word is they're talking about bumping up their ad buy for the season."

"FrankCo?" Gemma says. "I thought they hated us."

This, as it happens, is precisely what Tish is thinking as she walks the three short blocks up Mountain Avenue to meet Sheldon Dunow. As long as Sheldon's father was alive, FrankCo rarely advertised in the *Flyer*, the old man wielding his considerable clout to starve the upstart newspaper born out of a scandal involving his illegitimate love child. Even after he died, the ski company's ad team favored the *Bulletin*'s superior production values and wider readership among second homeowners. Then there's the politics. Ever since the Three Amigos proposed opening Elkhorn Canyon to skiing, Kendra Graves, the *Flyer's* ad manager, has begged Tish to tone down her opposition to the project during the fall shoulder season when the ski company formulates its winter advertising strategy. And every fall, including this one, Tish has run editorial after scathing editorial railing against the new ski area.

So why now? Why, just weeks before Mount Boyd opens for the winter, is the Third Amigo inviting her to lunch at the Tenth Mountain, the chicest of FrankCo's chic *après-ski* restaurants, and dangling the possibility of tripling his company's winter ad buy? But then this is one gift horse Tish is not inclined to look too closely in the mouth. She made payroll for October, but as she's all too aware, the paper is still running at a loss, and it won't be long before has no more stocks to sell or vendors to stiff. So, today she has once again wriggled into a tight skirt and strapped on her trusty Yves St. Laurent heels to meet Sheldon Dunow.

The Tenth Mountain, named for the U.S. Army's legendary Tenth Mountain Division, which fought on skis high in the Italian Alps during World War II, is built to look like a military mess hall, with rows of long pinewood tables and a cast-iron pot-bellied stove. This fools no one. The restaurant is a two-minute walk from the Motherlode gondola, and in high season a lowly cheeseburger, the cheapest item on the menu, will set you back twenty bucks. When Tish arrives, Dunow, a short, round, perfectly hairless man in a black Bernini tracksuit, is seated near the back, looking like a Bond villain just returned from a jog around the parcourse. One table over, completing the portrait, sit two enormous neckless men in ill-fitting dark suits eyeing Tish over untouched club sodas. She nods, flashing the pair a friendly salute.

"I see we've stepped up our personal security," she says, taking a seat.

Dunow's eyes slide, half-disgusted, in the direction of the two hulking ex-cops at the next table. "Orders from Dallas," he says. "They go wherever I go these days."

"Afraid you'll catch a bucket of blood?"

He smiles mirthlessly. Early in *A Screwdriver in the Gears*, the Frost gang dumps a bucket of fresh elk's blood over the head of Boss Burroughs' second-in-command, Tad Snively, at his daughter's sixteenth birthday party. For weeks, in warring letters to the editor, readers of the *Flyer* and *Bulletin* have been speculating about which local luminary would receive a dunking.

"I keep telling them we're wasting our money," he says. "Nobody's coming after me. I'm brother number three, a mere cog in the corporate wheel."

Tish isn't so sure. Dunow is good at keeping his name out of the press, but for locals he's still the face of the ski company. If Tish was an eco-terrorist bent on dousing someone in town with a bucket of blood, Sheldon Dunow would be at the top of her list.

"So then, where do you think they're going to strike next?" she asks.

"You want to know what I really think? I think we've seen the last of these guys."

"Well, that makes one of you."

"I'm serious," he says. "The Mother Earth's Avengers couldn't give a rat's ass about Elkhorn Canyon. They're trying to make a broader political point and they've made it. Why would they hang around here waiting for the FBI to lock them up? No, the ones who worry me are the locals, all those fine citizens who sang while the Highline Chalet burned. They scare me."

"There's still a lot of anger left over from the layoffs," Tish says, treading carefully.

"All due respect, Tish, I don't need you to tell me people here are pissed off. I've worked every job on that ski hill. I've run lifts. I've worked ski patrol. I spent an entire winter driving a snowcat. But what do they think, if we don't do Elkhorn Canyon, it's going to turn back the clock to 1975?"

"A lot of people are just afraid they'll get run out of town by this new resort."

"My dad was a genius, he really was," he says. "Everything you see here, he built it brick by brick. But that was thirty years ago. Half the people coming to a ski resort these days don't put on a pair of skis. They come for the shopping and the nightlife and maybe a chance to watch Mick and Keith party with a bunch of starlets. Aspen has that. Vail has that. We don't. And you've seen our numbers. You know the hole we're in."

Tish has seen FrankCo's skier numbers and they are indeed dismal. In 1977, at the zenith of the Hank Dunow era, for every skier who traveled to Aspen or Vail, two skied Franklin. Now those numbers are reversed, even though a day pass for Mount Boyd is five bucks cheaper than either Aspen or Vail.

"And don't kid yourself, this makes us a buyout target," Dunow is saying. "The money guys in New York, they look at us and they see an undercapitalized family business with plenty of cash flow and two thousand acres worth of room for expansion."

"These New York money guys," Tish asks, unable to resist, "have they approached you and your brothers about a buyout."

"You know I'm not going to answer that. But I promise you if we can't get that new ski hill built, they will approach us and it's going to be very hard for us to say no. And then *they'll* build Elkhorn Canyon, except it'll be twice as big with half the character." He smiles. "Ah, look. Lunch." He bows to a silver-haired Japanese man approaching their table carrying a polished wooden block bearing a dozen dark red slices of uncooked fish. "*Domo arigato, itamae-san.*"

"*Ie-ie, Sheldon-san,*" the Japanese man replies, bowing deeply.

The two men converse briefly in rapid Japanese before the elderly chef bows again, first to Tish and then to Dunow, and withdraws.

"Is that what I think it is?" Tish asks, eyeing the dismembered fish.

Dunow laughs. "Come on, you're not telling me you've never had sashimi."

To Tish food is fuel, nothing more. She has eaten the same meal for lunch for five years because it means one less decision in a day packed full of them. But she has one ironclad rule: If it once had eyes, it should be cooked before you eat it.

"Last I checked, tuna is a saltwater fish," she says, "and last I checked, we were more than a thousand miles from salt water."

"That's the insane part," Dunow says, unsheathing a pair of gleaming black chopsticks. "This time yesterday this tuna was alive and swimming. They catch them off Catalina Island one day, pack 'em in ice, and fly them here overnight."

"*Fly* them here?"

"Three times a week in high season. In the off-season, *Itamae* Akira puts in an order once a week, as a favor to me. This is *otoro*. It's found only in the belly of a mature bluefin tuna. Put one of these little honeys in your mouth and it melts like butter. Go on, try it. You'll love it."

So much for Sheldon Dunow, man of the people, worker of every job on Mount Boyd, Tish thinks as she spears a sashimi slice, struggling to grasp it with her slick wooden chopsticks.

"Is this why you invited me here today?" she asks, setting the fish on her plate, uneaten. "So you can give me the company line on why you need Elkhorn Canyon approved?"

"Of course not. You asked me a question and I answered it."

"So then, why am I here?"

"I told you, we'd like to triple our ad buy at the Flyer," he says, popping a slice of fish in his mouth and pausing to savor it. "Every year about this time we have to play advertising roulette, and this year we've decided to put our money on Tish Threadgill. You've done a terrific job with that paper, considering."

Considering the regrettable handicap of your gender appears to be where he's going with this. Tish has known Sheldon Dunow long enough to know that this is his idea of a compliment, and she's been a woman running a marginal small business long enough to know she'd be crazy to point out to him how insulting this is.

"You do know the demographics, right?" she says instead. "The *Bully's* reach among second-home buyers has always been better than ours."

He cocks his head, eyeing her. "Are you trying to talk me out of my ad strategy?"

"No, just trying to understand it. We've been a thorn in your side for a decade now."

"Believe me, we're well aware of your editorial position," he says. "And it should go without saying that we have no intention of asking you to soften or shift your position on our behalf."

"But at some point you might have to reconsider your advertising strategy."

"It's always possible that we might have to redirect ad dollars. If circumstances merit." He pops another sashimi slice in his mouth and chews slowly, emitting a low, faintly sexual groan. "Take the money, Tish," he says. "This town is better served with two healthy newspapers."

"Oh, I'm going to take the money," she says. "I just don't want you to think you're buying anything other than ad space in the best newspaper in town."

"Then I won't." He leans in across the table, looking more Bond villain-ish than ever. "I've never kidded myself, Tish. If my last name wasn't Dunow, I'd be stuck in an office somewhere with three kids and a house in the Dallas suburbs, eating tuna salad instead of tuna sashimi. But here I am, and here you are. And it's not so bad, is it? Lunch is on me today, so let's enjoy it. If otoro isn't your cup of tea, Chef Morrison does a delicious brook trout."

"This brook trout, is it cooked?" Tish asks.

"Pan-fried," he says. "Let's order you a pan-fried brook trout and we'll get a little day-drunk on extra-dry martinis. And the rest of it will just work itself out, eh?"

♦ ♦ ♦

The brook trout *is* delicious, all the more so when washed down with two very strong martinis, which is two more martinis than Tish is in the habit of drinking in the middle of the day. As a result, she's feeling no pain when she rolls into the *Flyer's* office a little after two to find a note from Chuck saying he and Gemma wants to talk to her about a story. By then, however, they're both out working their beats and the rest of the day is a mad sprint to put out a daily newspaper with four reporters and an editor who is also the paper's publisher and business manager.

So it isn't until the next day that Chuck and Gemma corner her in the newsroom to pitch the FEC Corp story. After handing her their typed notes from the day before, the two reporters walk her through it step by step: the bespectacled blonde at the assessor's office, the search for Parcel 135-65-A25-R on county plat maps, their interviews with the chatterbox Catherine Boggs and close-mouthed Jake Orlan. Midway through their account of the phone call with Mrs. Boggs, Moira turns down the volume on her police scanner and wanders over, drawn in by their story.

It's a hell of a story, Tish thinks. Some loose ends, yes, but still a killer piece of investigative reporting from two very young, very green report-ers, one of whom was an unpaid intern a month ago. But the whole time they're talking, Tish keeps seeing Sheldon Dunow in his glossy Italian tracksuit tongue-fucking a slice of tuna sashimi. She hates herself for seeing it, but that doesn't stop her from doing it.

"Give me your lede," she says.

Chuck looks at Gemma, then lets his eyes roam over his notes. "Okay, how about this: A shadowy organization calling itself an environmental group has – "

"Define 'shadowy,'" Tish says.

"Fair enough," he says, and starts over: "An organization calling itself an environmental group has bought a remote parcel of land in Elkhorn Canyon near the site of the proposed new ski area, the *Flyer* has learned, but the group is not registered as an environmental group and its purchase contract makes no provisions for preserving the land for conservation."

"What does that mean, not registered as an environmental group?" Tish asks. "Is there some official registry of environmental groups I'm not aware of?"

"You're right, you're right, I can take that out," Chuck says. "It's not crucial to the story."

"It's a problem, though," she says. "For all we know, they could be legit. They could be buying up the land to stop it from being developed."

"So, if they're the good guys, the story will flush them out," Gemma says. "They can come out and take their bows."

"What if they don't want to take a bow?" Tish asks. "What if their whole strategy depends on flying below radar?"

"Since when do we care what their strategy is?" Moira says. "Tish, you've been saying for years the hotel at the base of the ski hill was a Trojan horse for what FrankCo really plans to build. Well, maybe we just figured out where they're hiding all the soldiers."

This, of course, was Tish's first thought when she heard Chuck's pitch. Six weeks ago, even six hours ago, she would've cleared the decks to get this in tomorrow's paper. But once again she sees Sheldon Dunow's post-coital grin as he pops a gleaming slice of sashimi in his mouth. The first FrankCo ads are due to run this weekend and already she can feel the injection of cash flowing through her system like a hit of pharmaceutical-grade cocaine.

"Okay, but that's a pretty big claim," she says. "Do we have any actual evidence of a link between FrankCo and this FEC Corp?"

"They probably *aren't* connected now," Moira says. "Not on paper, anyway. But in a few years FrankCo can just buy them out."

"Are you guys hearing yourselves?" Tish says. "We're implying deep levels of corporate corruption with zero evidence to back it up."

She is, she realizes too late, shouting, and for a brief, awkward moment all eyes hit the floor.

"Look, we'll run the story eventually," she says, recovering. "We have to. But we need to bulletproof it first. Chuck, Gemma, see if you can't track down this Anna Pitlor. The Friends of Elkhorn Canyon, too. Somebody's got to have heard of this thing."

"Okay, we can do that," Chuck says.

"Aye-aye, boss," Gemma says.

"Really good work, though," Tish says. "I mean it. Both of you, this is first-class reporting."

But they're already walking off, Gemma back to her computer, Chuck to the piles of notes and photocopies on his desk. Moira, too, has retreated to her desk, too disgusted, apparently, to look her in the eye. Tish wants to make another speech, call in the whole staff and tell them they'll make payroll this month and that there's a fighting chance they'll make it to the new year and beyond. Instead, she reaches for the coffee she was drinking before Chuck and Gemma called her over and heads back to her office and her budget spreadsheets.

Chapter Six

The following Monday, a little after eight in the morning, Perry Barlow emerges from the bedroom of his snug North Franklin apartment, sleepily hitching his bathrobe. His wife Sarah is already at the kitchen table, a mug of Darjeeling tea in front of her, scratching out a poem in her notebook. She's been there since six, and she'll be there for another hour while he showers and silently eats his breakfast, until it's time for them to leave for work – Perry at the *Flyer*, Sarah at Eagle's Nest Books.

When they met six years ago, in a creative writing class at Colorado State, Perry was the writer and Sarah was the girl two seats over who kept telling him he really ought to consider publishing his stories. He listened to her, and with Sarah acting as his editor and agent, he published a handful of gently satirical stories in campus literary magazines. The magazines paid in contributor copies, but the publications encouraged him to start a novel, and Sarah's enthusiasm for its early pages encouraged them to dream of moving to New York City where she could take a job as a secretary to pay the rent while he finished the novel they were both certain would make him famous. Their college loans put the kibosh on that plan, and Perry started working as a reporter at a neighborhood weekly in his hometown, and then a year later, at a slightly larger paper in the Denver suburbs. It was Sarah who'd urged him to apply for the job at the *Flyer*. Bill Blanning, one of Perry's literary heroes, lived in Franklin and she thought the town's natural beauty and lively arts scene might push him to finally finish the novel he started in college.

He still owns the second-hand Compaq computer he typed the first hundred pages of that novel on, but Sarah uses it more than he does now. She writes poetry mostly, but lately she's been writing essays, too, about her strict Mormon family back in Loveland, about Colorado history, about hikes they've taken in Elkhorn Canyon and along the Continental Divide – about anything, really. Once a month, like paying the bills, she sends off a sheaf of poems and essays, and increasingly now they come back with acceptance letters. They pay, too. Not much. Ten dollars for a poem here, twenty-five for an essay there, but it adds up, and now there's talk of a small press bringing out a collection of her poems. Perry knows he should feel jealous, and he does a little, but mostly what he feels is proud. Sarah is heavy-set and pale, five-foot-nothing with freckles and a frizz of pumpkin-orange hair, the sort of woman the world looks through rather than at. It doesn't help that she's so shy around strangers that they had to move her from the front counter of the bookstore to the office because a simple request for a book recommendation can leave her tongue-tied and humiliated. But somehow, at six in the morning with a pen in her hand, she's found a way to make the world see her.

At ten after nine, Perry whisks away her cooling cup of tea, their agreed-upon signal that it's time to put away the notebooks and get dressed for work. They hardly talk on their walk into town, Sarah lost in the poem she's writing, Perry thinking about a school board meeting he's supposed to cover that night and what he can do to get out of going. But just before they reach Founders Park, where they will part for the day, Sarah asks, with soft insistence: "Are you going to talk to Tish today?"

"She's pretty busy, Sare," he says. "She's trying to keep the paper from going under."

"Which is why you should talk to her," she says. "You have more experience than anyone at that paper. Even Moira, she was tending bar a year and a half ago."

Perry just nods, refusing to be goaded by the mention of Moira Mangan, and they walk in silence through the snow-covered park. He and Sarah have been having a version of this argument ever since Tish fired Rod Arango and hired Gemma Seagraves to take over his beat. This incensed Sarah, who thinks it's absurd for his boss to hand a plum assignment like the city beat to a twenty-two-year-old blonde trust-funder who literally walked in off the street while Perry is stuck writing fluff pieces about dogs who pick up dollar bills with their teeth.

"In case you hadn't noticed, this town is in the middle of a national news story," Sarah says, finally. "I mean, look at Moira. Her articles are in *USA Today*."

"Well, I'm not Moira Mangan," he says, for possibly the five-hundredth time.

"You could be. She's just persistent, that's all. She sees what she wants and she goes for it."

Perry could point out the obvious, which is that Sarah loathes Moira, and that the few times they've met Sarah fled the room like a field mouse from a hawk's shadow. Instead, he says: "I like writing those features. I'm good at it. It's really the only thing I am good at."

She turns on him then, her stocky frame nearly vibrating with outrage. "You have got to stop saying that," she snaps. "I read that newspaper every day. You're a good reporter and you're a *great* writer."

"Come on, Sare, I can barely even spell."

She turns away, furious. He'd like to believe it's just because he shouted at her, but he knows better. He knows he disappoints her. No one, not his teachers, not his parents, not the editors who published his stories, not even himself, has ever believed in him the way Sarah did. The way she still does, despite an unwritten novel's worth of evidence to the contrary. He loves this about her, with the same force of desperation that he wishes she would stop.

They're approaching the corner of Park and Union where both papers have news boxes, and he rushes ahead for a copy of the *Flyer*, which carries his story about two brothers, ages six and eight, who showed up at the *Flyer* office late the day before to report the results of their rock-skipping contest on the Franklin River. This is precisely the kind of story Sarah sees as beneath his talents, but Perry can't help it: He's proud of it. He captured something, he thinks, in his description of the boys' solemn faces as they presented him with the tally sheet of their contest as if they were handing over the last extant copy of the scorecard of the 1919 World Series. If he has a talent, it's this: Making a story funny by treating it with dead seriousness. That, and being friendly. People underestimate the power of a friendly guy who asks a lot of questions.

"Oh, wow," Sarah says, reaching for the *Bulletin* news box. "They're saying there's no lynx in Elkhorn Canyon."

"What?" he says, snatching the newspaper from her hand. "Let me see that."

No Lynx in Canyon, State Report Finds

By Rod Arango, Bulletin Staff Reporter

A Colorado Department of Conservation study due for release later this week finds that the endangered Canada lynx has "in all likelihood not been resident in Elkhorn Canyon for some time," undermining a key argument in the long-running battle against a massive new ski resort in the area, the *Bulletin* has learned.

According to the state study, portions of which have been shared exclusively with the *Bulletin*, the few traces of wildcats found in the canyon likely belong not to the lynx, but to bobcats, a far more common near-cousin to the lynx which is believed to pass through the region during the warmer months.

A small but viable population of lynx are believed to have settled in the Laramie Mountains near the Colorado/Wyoming border, wildlife specialists say.

The lynx' retreat from the canyon may be due to a natural drop in the population of snowshoe hare, which provides the bulk of the wildcat's diet, according to the report.

"We're seeing a steep decline in the numbers of snowshoe hare in the canyon, and it looks like the lynx may have gotten the message and moved north," said one high-ranking state conservation official, who requested anonymity to discuss the report prior to its official release. "This may just be a case of nature taking its course."

◆ ◆ ◆

"This is a big deal, isn't it?" Sarah says, watching him.

"Huge," he says, rereading the *Bulletin*'s headline. "If there's no lynx, the whole environmental case against the new ski area falls apart."

"You better get into the office," she says.

"This isn't my story, Sare."

"So, make it your story. You know that guy, right? Paula's husband, the biologist."

He stares at her, lost, half his brain imagining the state of abject panic in the *Flyer* newsroom, the other half struggling to form a picture of a woman named Paula who has a husband.

"Paula from poetry group," Sarah says. "We went to their house last summer, remember?"

"You mean Rick Sheffield?"

But of course she means Rick Sheffield. Perry remembers him now, a wiry little guy with a scraggly beard and rimless glasses. His wife had invited Sarah and Perry to their house last summer for a backyard barbeque. Over the grill, the two men chatted about telemark skiing and the new baseball team in Denver – anything to avoid tripping over the fact that Perry was a local reporter and Rick was the wilderness biologist in charge of documenting the Canada lynx in Elkhorn Canyon.

"Why would he talk to me?" Perry says. "I met him once at a party."

"Fine," Sarah says. "Why don't you go and write another story about kids skipping rocks?"

"Don't be like that," he says. "It's not my beat. I've never covered Elkhorn Canyon."

His wife makes a low snort of disgust and marches off down Lupine Avenue, waving one hand in the air, dismissing him. He considers chasing after her, but doesn't, knowing it will only cause a scene, the two of them shouting at each other in the street. He wishes he didn't love her, this orange-haired madwoman pumping her legs down the sidewalk, but he does. What's more, he knows she loves him, despite the many ways he disappoints her. So instead of doing what he'd like to do, which is crawl back into bed and stay there for a week, he folds the morning's newspapers under his arm and sets off for the *Flyer* office.

It is an inviolable rule of small-town journalism that nothing news-worthy happens before noon, and on most days the *Flyer* newsroom is empty at nine-thirty. This morning, Perry is the last to arrive, the other reporters having already passed through the first three stages of grief – denial, anger, bargaining – and settled into wall-gazing depression. First Tish pulls her punches on the FEC Corp piece, and now this: They get beaten, badly, on one of the biggest stories of the year by none other than Rod Arango, the man who had been their boss until Tish fired him.

"Rod, that self-important prick," Moira says, breaking the silence. "Did you notice how many times he used the word 'exclusively'?"

"Eight times," Chuck says. "The story's barely a thousand words and he says it eight times."

"Well, he did get an exclusive, right?" Gemma says.

The other reporters glare at her, and it doesn't take a degree in psychology figure out why: *She's* what they've got instead of their old editor, Hot Rod Arango.

Tish chooses this moment to sweep into the room, notepad in hand.

"I just got off the phone with the Department of Conservation," she says. "It's fifteen versions of the same thing: They'll have a statement when the full study is released Wednesday. It's incredible. They won't even confirm what's in the *Bully*."

The mood in the room, already black, grows still blacker. If Rod is this far ahead of them on the story, he could very well have another bombshell waiting to explode tomorrow, too.

"The whole town's talking about it," Moira says. "We have to cover it. This is the biggest story since the Highline fire."

"Cover it how?" Tish asks. "We don't have a story. All we can do is rewrite what Rod says in the *Bully*."

"What about Rick Sheffield?" Perry asks. "Didn't he do most of the field work on this?"

"I've been calling him all morning, too," Tish says. "Home, office, everywhere. He's not picking up and I don't blame him. The word for months has been that he thinks the lynx is still out there, and now they're saying he's wrong."

"I know Rick a little," Perry says.

Tish turns, one eyebrow cocked. All the reporters turn to look at him, even Gemma.

"Sarah's in a poetry group with his wife," he says. "They've had us over once or twice."

No one has a response to this. They've all tried, at one point or another, to make friends with Perry's shy, intense wife with the cloud of orange hair, but it's like talking to a tree stump – a very judgmental tree stump. It's hard to imagine her having a friend who would invite her over for anything.

"You think he'll talk to you?" Tish asks.

"It's worth a try, right?" he says. "He's a decent guy and this has got to be eating him up. I'm thinking I could go visit him tonight, after he finishes work."

"Maybe one of us can come with you," Moira offers.

Perry wants to hate her for the insinuation that Perry Barlow, king of the cutesy-pie human-interest feature, needs adult supervision on a real news story, but the truth is he'd have suggested it himself if he didn't know Sarah would kill him.

"I appreciate the offer, but I think I better take this one myself," he says.

That evening around five, just as Perry is heading out for the drive to the town of Humble, where Rick Sheffield lives, Tish shows him the hole on the front page she's holding for him. If he can get Sheffield to talk, he has the whole top half of page one to himself. If he can't, they'll lead with her own lynx follow story, despite the fact that it says nothing more than what everyone's already read in yesterday's *Bulletin*.

"No pressure, though, right?" Tish says brightly.

The town of Humble, twenty-three miles from Franklin, is named for the Humble #1 mine, which for six years, from 1887 until the collapse of the domestic silver market in 1893, was the most productive silver mine in the continental United States. A hundred years later, the mine shaft is stoppered with cement, and the word "town" is probably too grand for the three short, haphazardly paved streets of modest clapboard homes half a mile from Highway 22. Humble has no post office and the nearest grocery store is a dozen miles away in Gibson. There is a school, Humble Elementary, a grim, single-story excretion of cinderblock and steel at the end of the last block of houses, looking out over miles of open ranchland.

This is where Perry parks his off-white VW Bug before walking the two blocks to Rick Sheffield's cozy vinyl-sided rancher. The lights are on inside and kids' bikes lay abandoned on the lawn, a boy's dark green Schwinn and a girl's powder-pink Strawberry Shortcake with Malibu handlebars. It's the dinner hour, Perry realizes. Maybe he should take a walk, come back in an hour when Sheffield might have more time to talk. Then he recalls Sarah at Founders Park that morning, her round Mormon face aflame with impatience, and he thinks: Would Moira Mangan come back in an hour? No, she would not. She would knock on the damn door and demand to speak to Rick Sheffield.

He does knock on the door, but the demand dies in his throat when Paula Sheffield answers, squinting at him in the fading twilight. She looks disheveled, her hair in a frowse, half moons of exhaustion gouged into the skin under her eyes.

"Hi, Paula," he says. "My name's Perry. I think you know my wife, Sarah. From your poetry group. You had us over for a barbeque this summer."

"Sarah from poetry group?" she says, as if he's speaking Serbo-Croatian.

"Right. I work for the *Flyer* up in Franklin and I was hoping I – "

"He's a reporter," a man shouts behind her. "He's here about that wild-life report."

"Rick, honey," she says, shushing him, but he's already at the door, having elbowed his wife aside. A slight, bearded man in jeans and a red-checked flannel shirt, Rick Sheffield looks like a college-poor grad student, not a government employee with two kids and a mortgage. At the moment, though, he's wild with fury, his astigmatic eyes popping out behind his rimless glasses.

"How dare you?" he shouts. "How dare you come to my house when I'm having dinner with my kids."

"Look, I know – " Perry tries.

"No, you don't know," he fires back. "You people have been hassling me all day and I've had it. Get out of here, man. I mean it, get off my goddamn property – now."

"I didn't … I'm really sorry for – " Perry stammers, backpedaling.

"Stop talking and leave," Rick says. "Tell your boss I refused to speak with you. Not no comment. Say I refused to speak with you. Print *that* in your fucking newspaper."

Any thought of channeling his inner Moira Mangan has vanished, wafted away like smoke, as Perry marches back to his car, red-faced and sweating. Ditto the news hole at the top of page one. All he cares about is finding the nearest pay phone so he can call Tish to tell her he struck out. After that, he can drive home and tell Sarah he's done with the newspaper business. He'll find a job at an ad agency, or maybe in public relations, something that pays enough that Sarah can stay home and write the books that will make her famous.

Even once he reaches his car, his humiliation is still so raw that he has turned the key in the ignition and is throwing the car into gear before he notices the tow-headed kid riding toward him on a dark green Schwinn, leaning hard into the pedals. Christ, Perry thinks, the guy's sending his kid out after me, too? But when the boy swerves his bike alongside the VW and motions for Perry to roll down his window, he does so.

"My dad says you should wait for him," he says. "Out behind the school."

The boy is a smaller version of his father, slight-built and intense, a nine-year-old grad student minus the beard and the shouting. He even wears the same cheap rimless specs, oval with silver arms.

"He wants me to wait for him here at the school?" Perry asks.

"Yeah," the boy says. "He'll be here as soon as we finish dinner."

With that, he leans into the pedal and rides off without so much as a backward glance. Perry sits in the idling VW, watching the boy's receding silhouette, stunned. He has no idea what just happened, but whatever it was, it means he'll be getting his interview. Dyslexic, let-me-get-that-page-one-bright-for-you Perry Barlow scored an interview with the wildlife biologist who's been ducking Tish Threadgill's calls all day, and if his luck holds, he'll bring home the story that will blow a hole in Hot Rod Arango's big scoop. And all he did was knock on a man's door and ask him to talk. Maybe that's Moira Mangan's secret, too. Not the J-school degree. Not the free-floating badassery she so loves to flaunt. She just knocks on a lot of doors.

Fearing being seen and scaring Sheffield off again, Perry drives the VW Bug two hundred yards up a dirt road its creaky German suspension isn't really built to withstand and parks behind a grove of willow trees. By the time he makes it back to the school it's dark and a chill has set in. He takes a seat on the bleachers behind the softball backstop, freezing in jeans and a light parka. Once, an elderly woman in sweats passes by with her dog and waves, thinking she must know him. Otherwise, Perry is left alone with his thoughts, which, to his dismay, focus not on the questions he'll ask or the story he'll write, but on all the things he'd rather be doing than freezing his butt off at an elementary school softball field in Humble, Colorado. Having dinner with Sarah, for one. Reading a book. Watching Monday Night Football. Even sitting in a school board meeting is starting to look pretty good.

When Rick Sheffield at last appears at the far side of the ballfield, tossing an iridescent green tennis ball for a knee-high Jack Russell terrier, it's almost eight o'clock. They take their sweet time coming across the grass, Rick tossing the ball far out into the outfield, the dog racing after it, leaping high off the ground to snatch it out of the air. Finally, cold and sick of waiting, Perry stands and marches out to meet him near second base.

"Thanks for coming out to meet me," he says.

"No problem, man," Rick says, with a shrug. "I take the dog out here most nights, so nobody'll think twice."

Perry knows he should say something, but he's new to this kind of reporting and he doesn't know how it's supposed to go. More than anything, he would like to suggest they walk to his car where at least they could have a little heat. Instead, he digs his notepad out of his back pocket and says, "Sorry about hassling you at your house."

Again, that non-committal shrug. "You're just doing your job. I get it. I just can't be seen talking to you."

It's eerie: All the anger, all the testosterone and finger pointing, is gone. This is the guy Perry chatted with over sizzling burgers and brats at the barbeque this summer, the hippieish perpetual grad student who skis telemark and calls everybody "man."

"Okay, so what happened with your conclusion on the lynx?" Perry asks. "Everybody was expecting you to say it's up there, but now the report comes out and you're saying it's gone."

"Yeah, I can't talk about that," Rick says.

"You can't talk about it – like, not at all?"

"Not if you're going to put it in the paper," Rick says.

"How about if I don't use your name? Say it's an anonymous source or whatever."

"Sources. With an 's.' If it's just one, they'll know it's me."

"Okay, I can do that."

Actually, Perry isn't sure he can do that. Can he pretend he's talked to more sources than he really has? Is that legit? He would kill to have taken just one actual journalism class in college. Surely, they went over all this.

"Then yeah, completely anonymously, that story in the paper today is true," Rick says. "They leaked it to the *Bulletin* over the weekend."

"Who did?"

"I don't know, man. My boss, I guess. Deborah Benton, the district chief. But I can't tell you for sure because I wasn't consulted. I wasn't consulted on any of this."

"So then it's true? They reversed their finding at the last minute?"

Rick has been tossing the ball for the dog, tossing and picking up, tossing and picking up, but now he lets the ball sit at his feet untouched.

"You gotta understand, I'm the field-science guy," he says. "I go out and collect evidence and write it up. I don't write the final report. That's way above my pay grade."

"But the evidence you collected, did it show the lynx was living there?"

"I'm not going to answer that."

"Come on, Rick. You have to see how this looks. It looks like they're cooking the results. It looks like they're cooking *your* results."

Rick picks up the tennis ball from the ground and turns it over in his hand, examining it like the footprints of the Canada lynx might be imprinted on its side. The dog is going nuts, jumping in the air and snapping at the ball, but Rick ignores her, thinking.

"I've got a wife and kids, man," he says, finally. "Trust me, there aren't a whole lot of jobs for field biologists who have gotten themselves fired from the Colorado Department of Conservation."

"Okay, but you came out here," Perry says. "You could have let me drive away, but you sent your son out to tell me to wait. You didn't do that because you feel good about what happened."

Rick rears back and hurls the ball high over the outfield and the dog fires off after it like she was shot from a cannon.

"It's Barry, right?" he says.

"Perry. Perry Barlow."

"Okay, Perry, a lot of what I found, especially at the lower elevations, it did come from bobcats. They got that part right. And bobcats and lynx, they're not that far apart taxonomically. Same genus, different species. But bobcats aren't built for deep snow. They have shorter fur and smaller paws. And I found footprints in the snow high up on the ridgelines that, in my opinion, could only have come from a lynx. It wasn't much, honestly. In two years, I only found the one set of tracks. But I found other evidence up there, too – fur and scat, that kind of thing."

"Didn't you keep any of that stuff?"

"Of course I kept it. I took pictures, too, but they're not in the report. I went looking for the negatives today, and I couldn't find them. Same with all the other stuff I collected. All that's left is the evidence that points to the bobcat or is inconclusive."

"You're saying they destroyed scientific evidence?"

"I don't know, man," he says. "When I mentioned it to Benton and her people, they looked at me like I was out of my mind. All day I've been wondering, Did I just make this up?"

"Wow," Perry says.

"Exactly. I know what I saw, but I don't have any evidence. And without evidence, how am I going to go up against the chief of the Franklin River District of the Colorado Department of Conservation? I mean, even if I wanted to, what would I say? Who'd believe me?"

The two men stand staring at the panting dog, patiently waiting for its master to toss the iridescent tennis ball.

"What about the other part," Perry asks, "that the lynx has moved north to the Laramie Mountains?"

"I mean, it's possible," Rick says. "I know those mountains, and the terrain doesn't seem right – not enough snow in the winter, the wrong kinds of prey animals. But is it possible? Sure. It would be great if it was true."

"And there's other places, right? Further up the spine of the Rockies?"

"Oh sure, we believe there's still a few cats north of here near the Canadian border, but they're struggling up there, too. Same deal: too many people, not enough snow."

"So it's possible they'd die out even if Elkhorn Canyon never gets developed."

"Anything's possible, man, but that canyon's been prime winter range for those cats for thousands of years. Probably would be for thousands more if we leave them the hell alone."

In the distance, a child's voice calls: "Hey, Dad!"

Rick's son has ridden his bike to the edge of the field and is walking it across the grass toward where they're standing. Rick calls the boy's name – "Kevin!" – and waves him over.

"I can't publish any of this, can I?" Perry says.

"Look, I came out here tonight because I needed to tell somebody," Rick says. "I've spent all day sitting in my office wanting to puke. I mean, if I'm right and those cats are out there, we signed their death warrant today. We might as well have taken a rifle into the woods and shot them ourselves. And it's not just the lynx. That's a fully intact alpine ecosystem up there. Or it was. We used to have dozens of canyons like that all up and down the Rockies and we're knocking them out, one by one. This was one of the last ones left anywhere in America."

"That's why we need to get this into the paper," Perry says.

"Well, that's not going to happen, not under my name. If you print any of this, I'll call Rod Arango at the *Bulletin* and tell him I never talked to you. I'll say I told you to get the hell off my property and you just made up the rest. Okay? Are we clear?"

"I'm sure my boss can find a way to – "

"No, you can't tell her, either. You *especially* can't tell her. That woman's relentless – she'll get me fired for sure."

"Dad, Mom says you have to come in now," Kevin says.

"Okay, Kev, I'm coming," Rick says. "Could you take Connie back for me?" The boy picks up the ball from the turf and tosses it for the dog, who sprints off after it. When the boy follows him, Rick turns back to Perry. "So now you know. I hope like hell you find some other way to get the word out. File a lawsuit. File an Open Records Act request, whatever. But if you report this conversation, I swear to God, I'll make sure *you* get fired."

"C'mon, Dad," Kevin calls across the field. "Monday Night Football's on!"

"Coming!" Rick calls after him. "See you, man," he says to Perry. "Good luck. I hope you find some way to get that story out."

Perry watches Rick trudge across the field to where his son is waiting, then turn toward home, the dog at his heel. Perry looks at the notepad in his hand. He's written Sheffield's name and nothing after that. He remembers it all and if he sat down on the softball bleachers he could write down every word, and then tomorrow he could start working methodically to prove what Sheffield said. It would be a hell of a story if he could get it. If Sheffield is telling the truth, high ranking officials at the state's Department of Conservation destroyed evidence, apparently to help grease the wheels for a major development. Reporters win prizes for stories like that. But where would he even start? What evidence there is is missing and only person who could attest to its existence can claim, quite credibly, that Perry never spoke to him.

The pay phone is out of order at the first gas station he stops at so he has to drive another five miles upvalley before he sees a QuikMart with a phone out front.

"Did you get him to talk to you?" Tish asks when she comes on the line.

"I tried," he says. "The guy wouldn't even let me on his property."

In the silence, he imagines he can see his boss' long, angular face in the smoked glass of the phone booth, her mouth a taut line of dismay.

"Nothing, huh?" she says. "No comment all the way?"

"He wouldn't even give me that. He told me to say that I refused to speak to him. He said it really loud, too, so all his neighbors would hear."

She sighs. "Well, we tried, right? I'll run the follow piece without anything from Sheffield. No point in getting the guy fired for refusing to speak to us."

After he hangs up, Perry stands a minute in the parking lot, watching the traffic sail past on Highway 22. He'll get that Open Records Act request going later in the week, but he knows enough about government records requests to know they can take years, longer if the officials in charge drag their feet. He'll be long gone from the *Flyer* before those records come back, and when they do, they won't contain anything like a smoking gun. These people are professionals. They know how to cover their asses. But he'll file the request and hope that whoever's covering Elkhorn Canyon two or three years from now can nail Deborah Benton's ass to the wall.

In the meantime, he has Sarah to face. Most nights she'd be in bed by now, but he told her he was driving to Humble tonight to see Rick

Sheffield. She'll be waiting up for him and she won't be as easy to lie to as Tish was. She knows him too well. The hardest part will be the look of disappointment in her eyes. He can see it already, a little light in her pale blue eyes going steadily dimmer. How long before it goes out completely? Can he find something that he's good at that she respects before it does?

Chapter Seven

All week Rod Arango is a day ahead of them on the lynx story, and then, on Wednesday, hoping to track down the ever elusive FEC Corp, Chuck skips a County Commission meeting and gets scooped the next day on the news that the commission will open hearings on the Elkhorn Canyon proposal in January, months ahead of schedule.

For Tish, all this is doubly grim. She hates being scooped, but she hates even more knowing she has no one to blame but herself. She's never had the money to pay her people what they're worth. True, it's a ski town, which is a built-in job perk most employers can only dream of. It's also true that she works harder than anyone at the *Flyer* and has been a mentor to everyone from the greenest interns to her head pressman. But that's not why she's still in business, not really. The *Flyer* is still alive because the people who work for her like her and trust her to make the right decisions, from little stuff like which photo to use on page one, to big things like when to run stories and when to hold off. This is an asset that appears nowhere on her budget spreadsheets, but she's convinced it's the only thing keeping the lights on. Which is why, first thing Thursday morning, while the rest of Franklin is reading Dana Tieg's front-page scoop on the upcoming Elkhorn Canyon hearings, she calls Gemma and Chuck into her office.

Chuck is, of course, mortified that the one time all year he missed a commissioners' meeting he got beat on a lead story, but Tish waves it off.

"When you get scooped on the state wildlife report we've been waiting two years to get, we can talk," she tells him. "In the meantime, tell me, where are we with the FEC Corp story?"

The two reporters look away, their floorward glances saying: *Basically, nowhere.*

"I was afraid of that," Tish says. "Look, I know I've been a little gun-shy on this. That's on me. But I'd like to get something in the paper before the county starts its Elkhorn Canyon hearings. Ideally, I'd like to have a story ready to go by the start of ski season."

"That's in two weeks," Gemma says.

"More like ten days, but I think we can do it," Tish says. "We're going to report this by process of elimination. We'll look everywhere we can think of, and if we don't find anything, that becomes the story. So, Gemma, you keep looking for Anna Pitlor. And, Chuck, have you talked to Russ Canavan to see if he's ever heard of the Friends of Elkhorn Canyon?"

The phone on Tish's desk beeps. "Scott Sage, Franklin Savings, line two," Jen says.

Scott's name in her receptionist's mouth brings up an image of Tish, drunk, in her building's laundry room at one in the morning going moist in the box because he showed her a snapshot of his daughter – not an image she relishes contemplating in front of her staff.

"I'm in a meeting," she says, hitting the talk button. "Can you tell him I'll call him back?"

"That's what you said last week," Jen says.

"He called last week?"

"Yeah, and you never called him back."

Even after Jen signs off, Tish remains suspended in that moment of arousal in the laundry room. She had been drunk then, but she isn't now, and still she feels it: a deep, low flame in her middle. Tish dated plenty in her twenties, and briefly lived with two extravagantly inappropriate men, one a Swiss-born former slalom champion, the other a Harley-riding weed dealer, but in the years since Doug died, men have come to feel like a chore, yet another set of needy employees to be managed. Still, she can't deny it, this stray flicker of midday horniness feels awfully good.

Gemma and Chuck, she realizes, are watching her, their expressions studiously neutral.

"Sorry, where were we?" she says.

"Russ Canavan," Chuck says. "I haven't talked to him, but it's a good idea."

"Good," Tish says. "Talk to him and some of the other enviros in town. In the meantime, I want you to start drafting a story. You can build on the notes you already have, but I want to get a sense of where we are. We'll meet on Monday to look at your first draft. Okay?"

◆ ◆ ◆

Friday night, after the paper goes to bed, Tish takes everyone out for drinks at the Summit Tavern, putting the first two rounds on her maxed-out company AmEx. A little before midnight, taking a break from the foosball table where the newsroom is in the process of thrashing the ad reps, Tish spots Scott Sage alone at the end of the bar nursing a beer.

"I think I owe you a phone call," she says, taking a seat beside him.

"You do," he says. "Two, in fact, as I recall."

"How about I buy you a beer, to make it up to you," she says. "That is, if it's kosher for a client to buy her banker a beer on a Friday night."

"Actually, that's one of the reasons I called. I'm not going to be your banker much longer. I gave my notice Monday. As soon as I get my year-end bonus, I'm out of there."

She fixes him with a look. "Seriously? You quit your job?"

"Well, more like changed jobs. I start at Mountain Equity in January. That place was getting me down. I didn't like how they treated you. I didn't like how they treated a lot of people."

"And so now you're here celebrating your escape."

"No, I'm here because I know this is where you go."

Their eyes meet and there it is again, that low-burning flame. Time was, not so long ago, sexual attraction felt to Tish like someone had taken a blow torch to her insides. Now, the fire burns lower and slower, but it still produces a marvelous glow.

"I'm afraid I'm the captain of this ship," she says, tipping her head in the direction of the foosball table where Gemma and Chuck are finishing off two hapless ad reps.

"And those are your sailors?" Scott says.

She nods. "It's a very, very gossipy ship."

A roar goes up around the foosball table as Chuck slams home the winning goal. In a minute, Tish knows, they'll all come tumbling back to the bar, shouting for Jello shots.

"Okay, here's what we're going to do," he says. "I'll finish what I'm having and take off. You wait twenty minutes and tell them you're going home. Then we'll meet at the bar of the Franklin Hotel."

Tish likes this idea, very much, but it will never work. She's the editor of the local newspaper. If she shows up at the Franklin Hotel bar on a Friday night with the banker who handles her credit accounts, everybody in town will know it by nine o'clock Saturday morning.

"I have a better idea," she says, reaching into her purse for one of her business cards and a pen. "Give me half an hour and meet me at this address."

She hands Scott the card with her home address written on the back and it's worth the whole night to see his eyes pop wide in surprise. But after a beat, he stuffs the card in his shirt pocket.

"See you in half an hour," he says, draining the last of his beer.

On the walk to her apartment, fifteen minutes later, Tish flirts with the idea of meeting him at the door wearing nothing but her YSL heels and a smile. Back when she was twenty-two and lithe enough to keep up with a Swiss slalom racer, she could pull off a move like that. Now, she settles for bare feet and a floor-length silk kimono, midnight blue with a yellow dragon spewing fire up the back. If she'd given herself a little more time, she could have put on some makeup and done something more with her hair than simply free it from the ponytail she's been wearing all day. But when she answers the door and sees Scott's eyes go wide again, taking her in, she realizes it would have been a waste of time.

He's brought a chilled bottle of Veuve Cliquot and two glasses, but by the time they get around to drinking it it's lukewarm and they're in bed pouring out their life stories like a pair of post-coital undergraduates.

Tish wakes up sometime after noon the next day to the smell of coffee and fresh-baked muffins. Scott has been up since nine, and unsure what to do with himself, he drove into town to pick up ingredients for blueberry muffins and omelets.

The whole presentation – the dusting of flour on Scott's shirtfront, the tawny brown muffins nestled in a bowl at the center of the table, the expert way he whisks and fluffs the eggs – is so powerfully erotic Tish can barely keep her kimono on long enough to eat her Denver omelet. But she's glad she did. Scott put himself through college working as a sous chef, and everything he sets before her is hearty and delicious. But it's not just the food. It's the process of eating it, setting two places at her white-topped kitchen table, pouring fresh cups of coffee, taking her time over her omelet and home fries, savoring every bite. When was the last time she ate a meal in her own kitchen with another person? Two years? Three? She misses it, not just the tastes and smells and the incidental chatter, but the indolence of it, its wondrous purposelessness. Normally at this hour on a Saturday she would be in the office going over her budget spreadsheets or getting a start on Monday's paper. That's where she should be right now. Instead she's here in her brightly lit kitchen, stuffed full of eggs and blueberry muffins, while outside the windows the season's first decent snowstorm covers the world in white.

They spend the day in bed, talking and talking, about anything and everything but their jobs. As the afternoon progresses, Tish comes to see Scott's square-jawed suburban blandness for what it is: an elaborate cover for a childhood that was, if anything, even more Dickensian than her own. He grew up in a cramped coachman's cottage on an estate in Greenwich, three towns over from New Canaan, where his father was the groundkeeper and his mother cooked and cleaned. His mother still lives there, except that now she's divorced from his father and lives in the main house with her widowered former employer.

"Whoa," Tish says. "I'm guessing going home must be pretty weird for you these days."

"It is," he admits. "But honestly, it's less of a shock than you'd think. Even when I was a kid, the gossip was that Mom took the job so she could be near Mr. Tattinger."

"So, did she?"

"Oh yeah," he says. "My sister looks just like him."

At first, Tish is more circumspect about her family, prettying up her mother's descents into mental illness and saying as little about her father as possible, but Scott already knows about Doug, which makes it easier to talk about him. Tish spent the last decade of her brother's life covering for him, running the paper during his depressive episodes and cleaning up after his first, amateurish attempts at suicide. Now, telling the story to Scott, she finds it hard to believe how normal all this seemed to her. When she was eight, her mother tried to kill herself with Seconal and three years later she tried again with a razor. Both times Doug cleaned her up and kept her out of the hospital. The lesson Tish took from this wasn't that mental illness kills, but that her job was to make sure the doctors didn't find out because doctors meant hospitals and hospitals meant drugs and expense and public shame.

"Jesus, listen to me," she says, eyeing him across the pillow. "Usually I wait until at least the third date before I let it drop that crazy runs through my family like the mighty Mississippi."

"Hey, my mom moved us into a cottage at the edge of an estate so she could be close to the man who owned it, and we all pretended we didn't know – even my dad," he says. "So, you don't have the corner on crazy here. Not even close."

At nightfall, as the snowstorm begins to let up, they shower together and make themselves a meal from their breakfast leftovers. It's almost seven on Saturday night, a fact that astonishes them both. Tish has blown off an entire day of work. Scott has missed his weekly phone call with his daughter in Colorado Springs. They're at her front door, fumbling through their goodbyes, when he takes a step back to look at her.

"Is this going to be okay?" he asks.

"Is what going to be okay?"

"I don't know – this, us, here."

"Well, you aren't my banker anymore, right?" she says. "I mean, isn't that why you came to the Summit last night, because you're quitting your job?"

"Yeah, but I wasn't expecting *this*. And I am still your banker until the end of the year."

She watches him, aware that for the first time all day he won't meet her gaze.

"What is it, Scott?" she asks.

"What do you mean? I just wanted to check in, make sure we're good."

She shuts the front door. "We're good. Now, tell me, what is it that's bothering you?"

He's quiet a moment, eyeing the closed door. "Okay, it's probably nothing, but last week Bucholtz asked for your credit file. Then a couple days later he called me into his office and started asking all these questions. Why are you so far behind on your payments, why I aren't doing more to make you pay up, on and on like that."

"You think he's planning to close out my line of credit? You said I had until January."

"That's what I thought, too. And, look, it's not like he had me draw up any papers. But it was weird. I just had the sense you'd done something to piss off the wrong person, somehow."

"Pissed off who?"

"I have no idea. I shouldn't be talking to you about any of this, anyway. I'm breaching twenty different fiduciary rules divulging internal bank processes to a client whose bed I was in an hour ago."

He says more, making more excuses for why he didn't mention it earlier, but she ignores him, panic bubbling up in her chest, mentally flipping through two weeks of *Flyer* front pages, trying to think who she could have pissed off. She pissed off her own staff, royally, by spiking the FEC Corp piece and firing the man who beat them on the lynx study. It's true, of course, that Chuck and Gemma never really stopped asking questions about the FEC Corp. But that's crazy. How could that have gotten back to

Stan Bucholtz, and why would he care if it did?

"I don't care that you didn't tell me before," she says. "I just want to know what I can do about it."

"Same thing I told you last month – you need to start making money," he says. "That way he's got no leverage over you."

"I could probably scrape together fifteen or twenty grand. Is that enough, do you think?"

"It's a start, but I think you need to figure out what this is really about. Because maybe I'm crazy, but I get the sense the money is just a means to an end for him."

"Which is what, exactly?"

"I wish I knew," he says. "All I know is Bucholtz and his buddies run this town, way more than Cory Carr and the County Commission do. If you've done something to tick them off, they're not going to get off your back until you stop."

For a long time after Scott leaves, Tish paces her small living room in her kimono, thinking about her least favorite subject: money. She had been hoping to hold off on any payments on the credit line until January, but if it gets Bucholtz off her back, it's worth it. But what if Scott is right and it isn't really about the money? She keeps coming back to the FEC Corp and the mysterious Parcel 135-65-A25-R. Clearly, she's going to have to back off on that again, at least until she's on firmer financial ground. If Sheldon Dunow pulled all his FrankCo ads, she'd still have a month or two before the *Flyer* truly hit the wall. If Bucholtz slaps a lien on her assets, her other creditors would panic and she'd be out of business in a week.

But even as she works all this through, her internal news detector is pinging, telling her that her reporters' conspiracy theories about the FEC Corp might not be so conspiratorial after all.

Ever since Doug's suicide, Tish has edited the Monday paper, working from noon till nearly midnight on Sundays, alongside whichever reporter has the least seniority and is therefore least likely to complain about having to work on a weekend. For the past six weeks that reporter has been Gemma Seagraves, who took over from a supremely grateful Chuck Quigley when she was elevated from intern to staff writer.

But this Sunday when Tish rolls into the office with a thermos of milky coffee and two of Scott's fist-sized blueberry muffins, both Gemma and Chuck are at their desks in the newsroom pounding out copy. Tish knows what they're working on without looking at their screens, but she bustles around the newsroom, doling out chunks of blueberry muffin and issuing orders: Gemma needs to start sorting the letters to the editor, and Chuck, if he's up for it, could maybe knock out ten inches on the effect the weekend's snowfall will have on ski conditions on Mount Boyd.

"You mind if I finish up this draft of the FEC Corp piece first?" Chuck says.

"Okay, but I'm not sure you need to be in such a hurry," Tish says.

Chuck turns to face her, his Adam's apple bobbing, up and down, up and down. "I thought you wanted to get this in the paper before the season opens," he says. "That's this week."

"I know, I've been thinking about that," Tish says. "There's a reasonable chance the Jack Frost gang will strike again this week, and even if they don't, it's all anybody's going to be talking about. We'd be throwing away a terrific piece of reporting."

Chuck cuts a glance at Gemma, the frustration in his eyes hard to miss.

"What if we get scooped?" Gemma asks.

"Have you heard anything that tells you the *Bully's* on this story?" Tish asks.

Their silence gives their answer: No, they haven't. The longer this goes on, the more Tish is convinced that even if the *Bulletin's* reporters did pick up rumors about the FEC Corp property, Leo Mayer wouldn't let them run a story.

"Don't worry, we'll run the piece," Tish says. "We just need to pick our moment. In the meantime, you can take another week or two to beef up your reporting."

"A week or two?" Gemma says.

"Or less. Or more," Tish says. "We'll know better after this week. In the meantime, how are we doing for letters to the editor? Monday's paper is looking a little light, so the more letters you can find, the better."

With that, she takes her coffee and what's left of the blueberry muffins to her office, where she spends the afternoon avoiding Gemma and Chuck and taking calls from news directors in Denver and Chicago wanting to know if the Jack Frost Collective will strike again on the opening weekend of ski season. The PR flacks at FrankCo must be getting the same calls because a little after four the ski company faxes out an upbeat news release talking up its heightened security measures, which instantly becomes the day's lead story. By then, Chuck has filed his snowfall piece and gone home, leaving Tish alone with Gemma, whose sullen silence forms a third, glowering presence in the newsroom.

By the next day, her disappointment has spread to the rest of the staff. No one mentions the FEC Corp story or directly questions Tish's authority, but when she enters a room, conversations trail off, all eyes dropping a few strategic inches, and pick up again, louder than before, after she leaves. Tish tries to ignore it, consoling herself with mildly smutty memories of her sex-soaked weekend with Scott Sage. But it hurts. Of course it hurts. In her five years as the editor of a struggling small-town newspaper, Tish has allowed herself few vanities, but one of them is that she has earned her employees' respect. Their love, even. If she loses that, she's just another thirty-something single lady who stuck around a ski town too long.

So, naturally, she's overjoyed when Gemma pokes her head in her office doorway, smiling, her eyes meeting Tish's straight on. They chat about the spell of mild weather that has already melted away much of the weekend's snowfall, but Gemma is plainly working up to something, and finally it comes out: "I hear FrankCo's holding a press conference on the mountain tonight."

"Oh, that," Tish says. "It's a glorified photo op. They want to get TV cameras up there to show all the skiers coming in this weekend they have nothing to fear."

"So, who were you thinking of sending?"

"I was going to go with Moira," she says. "Why, are you saying you'd like to go?"

"I've got some time on my hands now, right?"

Tish leans back in her chair, trying to remember the last time she caught Gemma chewing her hair. It's been weeks, maybe more. She's dressing better, too, less like a teenager throwing on whatever happens to be clean and more like a grown-up with a job: skirts and low heels on warmer days, stone-washed jeans and hemp-cloth sweaters when the mercury drops. And now this, throwing Tish's loss of nerve back in her face to ace another reporter out of a byline.

"Let me talk to Moira," she says. "It might be good to keep her in the office tonight to drive the paper."

"It's cool, I can tell her," Gemma says. "What time does the presser start?"

Tish laughs, thinking: *Watch your back, Mangan. Somebody's gunning for your job.*

"Four o'clock, at the base of the ski hill," she says. "Bring cold-weather gear and a camera."

At ten past four, a crowd of reporters and producers files onto the gondola for the ride up to the site of the Highline Chalet, where TV crews have spent the afternoon setting up generators and radar dishes for a live shot timed for the start of the five o'clock news. Two weeks ago the ski company released preliminary drawings for a new, expanded Highline Chalet on a craggy outcropping further up the mountain. For now, the site is mostly empty, the rubble of the torched restaurant cleared away and replaced with a squat temporary ski patrol hut set up on a hillock of heavily trodden snow behind the podium bristling with network-branding microphones.

At the stroke of five, the TV lights blink on, blanketing the clearing in blinding white light, and Sheriff Hayes steps to the microphones flanked by Cory Carr and Jimmy Lachlan, making his first public appearance in his new role as FrankCo's director of mountain security. Behind them stand a dozen security guards in sky-blue FrankCo ski parkas and snowpants along with an equal number of local deputies and officers from the Colorado State Patrol. Hayes, in a dark suit and his trademark white Stetson, takes the lead, announcing a tripling of security staffing levels, along with twenty new ski patrollers, extra video cameras outside all on-mountain buildings, and an unspecified number of movement sensors along the ski area's boundaries.

These are canned remarks – Tish has the script he's reading from in her hands – so she lets Gemma take photos while she surveys the edges of the crowd, where the TV cameras don't reach. Monkiewicz is rumored to be back in town for the start of ski season, but if he's here, she doesn't see him. Ditto the State Patrol brass. A few local deputies stand in disorganized clumps, ready to corral the media scrum once the presser ends, but that's it. Her gaze pans back to the stage where Cory Carr is now speaking. Inside the camera frame, the police presence is overwhelming. Off-camera, nothing.

As soon as Carr finishes his own canned remarks, the TV lights go dark and a row of snowcats parked beside the gondola terminal roar to life. Led by the deputies and a platoon of blue-parka'd FrankCo security goons, the reporters pile into seats jerry-rigged onto the snowcat's cargo bays to start the mountain tour. By now, the sun has dipped behind the rocky peak of Mount Boyd, casting the slopes in a cold, blue-gray light. Down below, three days of warm weather have caused unsightly brown spots to bloom across the lower slopes, defeating the efforts of hundreds of droning snow-making machines, but above the Highline, on Mount Boyd's North Peak, the powder is several feet deep and nearly trackless, glittering under the snowcat's high beams like drifts of pure, granulated sugar.

As they tour the North Peak, Tish keeps a running tally of FrankCo's security measures, silently costing it out in her head. Six cameras at

Lucy's Grotto. Three security guards outside the new ski patrol hut. Four more at the snowmobile pen. A dozen more driving snowcats or zipping around in snowmobiles. And that's just what she can see from the back of her snowcat. Combine that with the sheriff's deputies and State Patrol officers back at the Highline site, and there's at least thirty overnight security guards, to say nothing of the cameras and movement sensors.

At their last stop, outside Herbie's Hideaway, the largest of the company's three mountain restaurants, Tish shadows Jimmy Lachlan, slipping into the spot next to his on the snowcat.

"Jesus!" he says. "You again."

"I missed you," she tells him. "Mr. Director of Resort Security."

"No thanks to you, I might add."

She laughs, but when he says nothing more she waits until the snowcat's engine rumbles to a start before she leans over again.

"I talked to your boss a couple weeks ago," she says. "He thinks the Avengers already got what they came for and won't be coming back."

Jimmy just stares forward, stone-faced, and together they gaze out at the town of Franklin lit up below like a train set village, and beyond that, at the distant headlights on Highway 22 strung out across the valley floor. Tish wishes, just for a moment, that she wasn't working and Scott was here. That morning they'd talked just long enough to agree they'd meet on the mountain for a ski date on Saturday. All day she's been replaying snippets of their conversation, giggling in the middle of the four o'clock news budget meeting at a joke he'd made about the wilted vegetables in her fridge. She hates how this makes her look, how girly she's become all of a sudden, but she'd trade a month of front page scoops to be alone with him right now, holding hands and sharing this heart-stopping view.

"What's your point?" Jimmy says finally, snapping her back.

"My point is I've been counting," she says. "Twenty cameras. At least thirty security guys. Twenty extra ski patrol. God knows how many more guys monitoring all those cameras and sensors. And the snow is lousy and Jack Frost has been national news for six weeks. I'm betting your bookings are down forty, fifty percent."

Jimmy says nothing, but his tight smile tells her that her numbers aren't far off.

"You know what I think?" she says. "I think this is all one big Potemkin Village."

"I don't even know what that means."

"It means I think you're putting on a show for the cameras. As soon as they leave, you'll wait a week or two and then you'll scale back your security."

"The cameras and the sensors, they stay no matter what we do."

Tish nods, making a mental note. This is, in its way, a backdoor confirmation of her point.

"I know you, Jimmy," she says. "I know you fought for every bit of police protection you could get. If I'm right, I know this has got to be chewing you up."

He turns away again, ignoring her. In the distance, across an expanse of glittering powder, she can see the lights of the gondola terminal, the last glass-walled car waiting on the platform. In two minutes, less than that, she'll be on their way back down the mountain.

"I didn't burn you last time, did I?" she says. "They *promoted* you, you big lunk."

She laughs, and then he does. It is funny. Jimmy Lachlan, the Aussie ski rat twice banned from the mountain for racing avalanches in Mount Boyd's South Peak bowls, is now the director of resort security. It's like hiring John Gotti to break up the New York mob.

His voice drops to a whisper. "Between you and me?"

"Of course," she says, wondering why anyone would ever believe a reporter who says this.

"Count the lights."

"The what?"

"The lights," he says. "All the security personnel, all the snowmobiles, they can't work without lights."

It takes a second, but then she gets it. After dark, each light is a person

– on a snowmobile, at a guard post, walking a fence line. Ipso facto, the more lights, the more people on the ski hill.

"There's plenty now," he says. "There'll be less later, unless I start winning more battles."

"Thank you, Jimmy," she says.

He waves this off. "Just don't screw me on this, Threadgill. I'm trying to stop some bad guys here."

Later that night, after she hands the paper off to Lydia, Tish climbs up onto the roof of her building, scaling a flimsy exterior ladder technicians use to reach the satellite dish that connects the *Flyer* to the AP wire. Over the next ten minutes, she counts twenty lights on the mountain. By itself, this number doesn't mean much. She can't know how many lights are hidden from view behind trees or inside buildings, just as she has no idea how many she's double-counting because they're on the move. She also doesn't know how many are blue-jacketed FrankCo security staff and how many work for the county or the state.

But she has some baseline numbers: twenty lights equals thirty security guards.

The next night, Thursday, the count is even higher, twenty-two, which by her crude system means there are thirty-three security guards on the mountain. That's twice her payroll at the *Flyer*, all working overnight, ten or twelve hours a night, seven days a week. If even half of them work for FrankCo and they average fifteen dollars an hour, that's close to twenty grand a week in extra security costs. And that doesn't count the hundreds of thousands of dollars it cost to replace the firebombed ski patrol shack and wire up the mountain with cameras and electronic trip wires.

Bottom line, Tish thinks as she climbs down the cold metal ladder from the roof, the ski company is spending hundreds of thousands of dollars, quite possibly millions, to protect Mount Boyd from a threat Sheldon Dunow doesn't believe exists.

Chapter Eight

In 1960, when Tish was four years old, her family drove out from Connecticut and spent two weeks in Colorado, first in Aspen and then in Franklin, where Hank Dunow had just the year before opened five short ski runs serviced by a single two-seater chairlift. Tish can see that lift now, or rather the upgraded version of it built in the 1980s, through the rear window of a Motherlode gondola car, where she stands with five other skiers heading up the mountain for her first run of the season. The original lift carried skiers less than a thousand vertical feet from the valley floor, at which point skiers wanting to take on the mountain's more demanding upper slopes had to put skins on their skis. Every time she rides the gondola, Tish pictures her mother on the snow below, the twenty-five-year-old former ski instructor marching through the trees on wooden skis as her much older husband struggles to keep up. She'd had her first psychotic break a year before, leaving Doug and Tish watching *The Mickey Mouse Club* while she drove the family station wagon to the Bridgeport ferry, where she was prevented from leaping into the Long Island Sound by an alert ferryman. Now, though, climbing Mount Boyd, her lungs filled with sweet-tasting mountain air, the suffocating atmosphere of the New Canaan Country Club behind her at last, she was alive, free, fully herself.

This is the picture Tish carries in her mind as she steps off the gondola and into her freshly tuned Salomon 4S boards a few yards from where the Highline Chalet once stood. In the years after her father went back to his first wife, a department-store heiress he's still married to today, her mother took them to local ski hills because it was all she could afford, and most of the time she couldn't even afford that. But it was never good enough. It was never Mount Boyd, where, in her mother's telling, the slopes were never crowded and the powder was like sailing across a fat, fluffy cloud. Tish was in college when her mother ingested the fistful of barbiturates that killed her, so she never got to ski Mount Boyd with her, but she feels her mother's spirit with her now as she leans into the first turn, then powers out of it, cutting across the Highline Bench toward Gravy Train, a steep, twisty run cut through the heavily forested south flank of Mount Boyd past the entrance to the South Peak bowls, blocked off with a bright yellow warning barrier.

It's a popular run, famed for its tight corners and gut-tightening drops, but today Tish has it almost to herself. The mountain had opened the day before without incident, but the lousy early season snow and the steady drumbeat of Jack Frost stories has taken its toll. The day is cloudless and bright, perfect bluebird conditions, but there's no line for the lift at the bottom of Gravy Train, and the powder, though still mushy from the mild weather, is nearly virgin from top to bottom. Coming off the lift after her second Gravy Train run, Tish makes a mental note to check with her sources at the ski company for skier counts. But she quickly shelves that thought, along with any lingering memories of her late mother, when she sees Scott Sage stepping into his skis twenty yards from the lift.

Their story, if anyone asks, is that this is a work meeting, but she's hoping no one will ask, which is why, after a few words of greeting, she starts back down the hill, taking the Highline Highway this time, a gentle intermediate run. Scott's turns are a little stiff and he's tentative on the steeper drops, but he's nothing like the suburban-soft newbie she'd feared he might be. Halfway down the run, they skid to a stop and neck like teenagers, their cheeks raw with cold, their goggles and gloves scattered in the snow around them. Twenty minutes later, on a run called Gravity's Rainbow, they topple over and flop around in the foot-deep powder at the edge of the trail, giggling at the spectacle they're providing for passing skiers.

"Get a room!" one shouts as he flies by.

"Know where we can find one?" Tish calls back.

Then they're up again, shaking the snow out of their hair and from under their parkas before hopping back on their skis and racing down the mountain side by side.

At four, they part ways with a handshake at the bottom of the hill, only to reconvene five hours later at Scott's sparsely furnished condo overlooking the river on Franklin's North End. They're up until two drinking red wine and when Tish wakes up the next morning she's still half drunk. For a few queasy minutes, she fights off a headache and watches Scott snore softly on the pillow next to hers. He's pushing forty, with faint crow's feet at the corners of his eyes and a sprinkling of gray at the temples, but she can see the boy in him, the pudgy kid picked in the middle of the pack for kickball, the somewhat over-earnest teenager he'd been in high school. Would she have been attracted to him then? Probably not. At Choate, Tish went for the bad boys, pot-smoking, class-cutting teenage versions of her own bad-boy father, a Korean War fighter jock who raced imported Ducati motorcycles and ran off with his ski instructor.

So the tenderness she feels for this man beside her surprises her. He's a serious foodie who reads old cookbooks for fun and has a seemingly bottomless repertoire of food-related knock-knock jokes. But he's a good guy, gentle and kind, a listener. For a few hours, cuddling on the couch watching Bergman and Bogie in *Casablanca*, Tish had felt there was no place else on earth she'd rather be. But now at nine a.m. on Sunday, her mouth tasting like a small mammal has crawled up in it and died, she wonders just what she's doing here. Her business is hemorrhaging money. Her staff is still furious at her. She has no idea how she'll get a paper out tomorrow, much less how to keep it from going under. And her solution to all these problems is to spend her Saturday afternoon necking on the ski hill with her nerdy credit manager?

Steeling herself for the wash of nausea she knows is coming, she rolls over and sets her bare feet on the floor. Then: one, two, three, and she's up, searching for her clothes.

"You're leaving?" Scott mumbles from the bed.

She turns around, realizing, too late, that she's naked. Her instinct is to cover up, but he's smiling, taking her in, and she decides, just this once, to let him.

"It's Sunday," she says. "I've got a newspaper to put out."

"Right. Of course." He closes his eyes, working his jaw over the same desiccating mammal that filled her mouth earlier. "What time do you have to be in?"

Not until noon is the honest answer, but she fears that if she doesn't get out of this man's apartment in the next ten minutes, she might not ever leave.

"About an hour," she says.

"That's still enough time to make you breakfast. I've got everything all set up."

She starts to argue, but the tender feelings flow back into her. *He's got everything all set up.* The whole night had been like that. He'd cooked dinner, bought the wine, rented *Casablanca*, along with two other movies in case Bogart wasn't her mojo. Tish had planned ahead, too, packing fresh underwear and a clean shirt, along with a small toiletries bag, so she takes a leisurely shower and sits down at his kitchen counter for coffee and home-baked blueberry muffins. But by the time her omelet is ready she's doing math problems in her head, calculating how long she can hold the FEC Corp story before somebody at the *Bully* finally picks it up, and whether she'll have enough cash coming in to save her when she does pull the trigger.

"Everything okay?" he asks, eyeing her untouched plate.

"Yeah, all good," she say, forking in a bite of omelet. "This is delicious, by the way."

He waits, his eyes level with hers. She's seen this look before and it means, essentially, *Tell me what's on your mind or let's cut the crap and talk about something else.*

"Okay," Tish says, surprising herself by choosing Door No. 1. "Two of my reporters are working on a story that, if it leads where I think it will, could make it harder for the county to approve the new ski area."

"And?"

"And I don't know, a year ago, even a few weeks ago, I would've jumped on it with both feet. But now I'm wussing out. I'm worried it could cost me my business."

"I'm guessing you're not going to tell me what this story's about."

"I can't, Scott. I really do think we're onto something, but I don't like how badly I want us to be onto something. You know? Because if we're wrong, it could really blow up on us."

He cracks an egg for his own omelet and begins stirring it slowly with a fork. "I'm not sure what you want me to say here."

"I need to know how vulnerable I am." She looks up at him. "Do you know, has Bucholtz taken any more steps to call in my loan?"

He's silent a moment, busying himself with his omelet, and Tish recalls his remark about all the rules he's breaking by talking to her about internal bank business. But she doesn't take it back. She needs to know the answer.

"No, he hasn't," he says. "Not that I know of, anyway."

"But he could, right? Pretty much any time?"

"Tish, your line of credit is secured by your ad revenues," he says. "If Bucholtz decides he doesn't like the trendline in your revenues, he can demand repayment of all or part of the loan. Bankers don't like to do that because the end result is usually that the business fails and nobody gets paid, but he can, pretty much anytime, pretty much for any reason."

"I was afraid you were going to say that."

"For what it's worth, I think you should publish your story."

He goes back to his omelet and Tish thinks: *God help me, I think I'm falling in love with this man.* This realization, its undeniable ring of truth, frightens her almost as much as the prospect of Stan Bucholtz shutting down her newspaper.

"I'm just worried he'll put me out of business before I can publish the full story," she says, struggling to return to the business at hand. "Then

I've thrown seventeen people out of work and killed a newspaper I love for nothing."

"Don't worry, I'll give you a heads up if he's about to call in your loan."

"I do worry," she says. "That's pretty much all I do these days."

"Well, I've seen your books and you'd be crazy not to," Scott says. "But what's the point of owning a newspaper if you're not going to publish the news?"

At work that day, Tish sends Gemma up the ski hill with a stopwatch to chart chairlift wait times and chat up servers in the mountain's half-empty restaurants while Tish works the phones tracking down staffers in FrankCo's famously secretive back office. After a few calls, she reaches Lila Parsons, an accountant in the ski company's operations department who used to do the books for Tish at the *Flyer*. It takes some sweet-talking, but off the record Lila confirms what Tish saw with her own eyes on Saturday: Opening weekend crowds are down nearly fifty percent and pre-bookings for Thanksgiving weekend are worse.

That night, Tish takes Gemma with her up onto the roof and together they count twenty lights on Mount Boyd. The next night, they count eighteen and by Tuesday night it's down to just fifteen. Sheldon Dunow and Jimmy Lachlan aren't taking Tish's calls, and no one else at the ski company will discuss security, on or off the record, but Moira is starting to hear sheriff's deputies bitching about losing O.T. as they get pulled off mountain duty. Clearly, Jimmy has lost the argument. FrankCo is bleeding money and it's pulling back on security, hoping Sheldon Dunow is right and the Mother Earth's Avengers have moved on.

The next day, the Wednesday before Thanksgiving, Tish sits down to rough out an editorial using her nightly rooftop security census. It's crude and informal, but she's been watching the mountain every night for a week and the downward trend is clear. By turning a blind eye to the threat posed by the Jack Frost Collective, she writes, FrankCo is not only courting another attack, but also putting the resort's very economic stability at risk.

She's reading over her first draft, the newsroom quiet except for the light tippity-tap of fingers on computer keys, when the phone on Gemma's desk beeps.

"Hey, you've got an admirer," Jen says over the intercom. "He won't give his name, but he says he reads all your stories and wants to give you a big tip on Jack Frost."

"He won't give his name?" Gemma asks.

"Yeah, I'm getting major wackadoodle vibes on this one," Jen says. "The guy sounds like Darth Vader on Quaaludes. You want me to take a message?"

"Nah, I better take it," Gemma says. "Put him through."

"Put Darth on speaker," Moira chimes in. "This one I want to hear."

But Gemma has already picked up. "This is Gemma," she says, then raises a bright, nervous laugh. "Thanks, that's really nice of you to say. I don't think I caught your – "

The uneasy tremor in her voice hushes the room and Tish rises instinctively out of her seat.

"You want me to do *what?*" Gemma asks.

Tish reaches Gemma's desk in three quick strides and hits the speaker button on her phone. Instantly, an artificially deepened voice billows up from the phone: " …. are a peaceful organization. Our dispute isn't with the residents of Franklin or with visitors to the resort. For this reason, we want your newspaper to advise all citizens to avoid flights in or out of Elk County Airport tonight, starting at six p.m."

"What happens if they fly into the airport tonight?" Tish asks.

The line goes silent. Tish could smack herself. She spoke without thinking and now they've lost him, whoever he is. With no other choice, she says, "I'm Tish Threadgill, Gemma's boss at the *Flyer*. What exactly are you going to do at the airport tonight?"

"Put a screwdriver in the gears, of course," replies the low, robotic voice.

"And it will be dangerous to take a flight in or out?"

"Not if your paper gets the word out in time."

"We're a daily newspaper. How are we going to get out the word about an attack tonight?"

"One more thing," the voice says. "The explosive used in the action at the West Fork Power Substation was liberated from the Myrtle Creek Quarry near Roseburg, Oregon. The FBI already knows that, but you can tell them we told you. Goodbye."

"Hold on, wait!" Tish cries. "What are you planning to do at the airport tonight?"

But the line has gone dead. For several seconds, five reporters stare at Gemma's still humming phone. It takes a sixth person, Jen, standing in the open doorway, to break the silence.

"Who *was* that?" she asks.

"I don't know, but I think it's real," Tish says. "That bit about the quarry in Oregon, that sounds right, and it hasn't been reported. Not the name of the quarry."

"Can't we trace the call?" Perry asks.

"Not if he called from a pay phone," Moira says. "By the time the police trace it, he'll be long gone."

The reporters sit with this a moment, that the voice they just heard is a member of the group that's been terrorizing their town for the past two months, and he's warning them to expect more.

"So, what do we do now?" Gemma asks.

"I'll call the FBI," Tish says. "The rest of you, write down everything you saw and heard. Everything, no matter how inconsequential it seems. Drop whatever you were working on. This takes priority."

◆ ◆ ◆

Daniel, the same blandly officious Public Information flack who managed the interview with Art Monkiewicz three weeks ago, meets Tish, Jen, and Gemma at a side entrance to the courthouse before leading them through a maze of corridors to a windowless basement conference room. The room is brightly lit and packed with police, some in uniform, some not, talking into telephones and manning fax machines, but Tish's eye is drawn to Special Agent Monkiewicz, seated at the center of the long conference table flanked by Sheriff Hayes and Cory Carr. She's oddly reassured to see him. The rumor mill had Monkiewicz on a plane for Oregon as soon as FrankCo opened its ski season without a fresh attack, but here he is, tieless, his shirtsleeves rolled to his elbows, ready to get to work.

"Where's the rest of your people?" Hayes snaps.

"We have a newspaper to put out, Sheriff," Tish tells him. "I had everyone write down what they heard. You can interview them later if you want."

"We've just had a credible threat of violence at a public airport," Hayes shoots back. "That goddamn paper of yours can wait."

But Monkiewicz raises a hand to silence him. "She's right, we can talk to the others later," he says. "And we'll need to put a recording device on your office line."

"I very much doubt they're going to call us again," Tish says.

"Probably not, but we need to be ready if they do. In the meantime, why don't you tell us again what the caller said. Everything. Don't leave anything out."

Jen goes first, letting Monkiewicz lead her through a step-by-step reconstruction of her brief conversation with the deep-voiced stranger. The FBI agent is meticulous, having first Jen and then Gemma and Tish repeat every word the caller said, doubling back several times to check if their memories have shifted.

"Ms. Seagraves, why do you think he asked to speak with you?" he asks.

"I have no idea," she says. "He said he liked my stories in the paper."

"But you don't typically cover the Jack Frost stories," he says. "That's more your colleague Moira Mangan's territory, as I recall."

"Gemma's one of our newest reporters," Tish cuts in, "but she regularly breaks stories about the city and the ski company. Obviously, this guy likes what he read."

"I see," Monkiewicz says, making a note on his yellow pad. "About the name he mentioned at the end, Myrtle Creek Quarry – you're sure that's the name he used, Myrtle Creek?"

"That's what I heard," says Gemma.

Monkiewicz's deep-set eyes find Tish and she nods.

"That's the name of the quarry where they stole the explosive they used at the power station, isn't it?" she asks.

Sheriff Hayes clears his throat, but once again Monkiewicz raises a hand to silence him.

"It is, yeah," he says.

"So, are you going to shut down the airport?" Tish asks.

"We'll get to that," he says. "First, though, I'd like to finish my interview, if that's all right with you."

"Sir, I'm asking as a reporter," Tish says. "I need to know what I can put in the paper. Are you or are you not going to shut down the airport?"

"With all due respect, Ms. Threadgill, I'm not sure it's a good idea for you to report any of this just yet," Monkiewicz says.

"I'm afraid that's not your call," Tish says. "I held back that letter, but this time they're threatening to take out the county airport. It'll take two hours to get a special edition onto the streets. Radio and TV can get the word out faster than that. I need to know what we should say."

"You're putting out a special edition?" Carr asks, incredulous.

"I don't know, maybe," Tish says. "We have no idea what any of this means. Are they going to blow the place up? Disable the runways somehow? Whatever it is, people have a right to know and I have an obligation to publish as soon as possible."

"This could all be a hoax," Carr says. "Some guy calls up the local newspaper and says he's going to blow up the airport. How do we know he's actually going to do it?"

"He knew the name of the quarry where they got their explosive, Cory," Tish says. "That hasn't been reported anywhere."

"If you shut down that airport, it'll make the national news again," a voice says from the far end of the room. "That'll cost us half our Christmas business, maybe more."

Tish turns to see Sheldon Dunow at the far end of the conference table, still in a suit and tie, surrounded by papers and Styrofoam coffee cups. When did he get here? she wonders. Did he come in while Monkiewicz was questioning them? Has he been here all along?

"What do you want us to do, leave the airport open and have some lunatic blow up a plane?" Sheriff Hayes says. "What would *that* do to your Christmas business?"

"What I want, Lorne, is for somebody to catch these guys," Dunow says. "We've got nine flights arriving tonight, to say nothing of the private aircraft. That's close to a thousand people sitting in departure lounges in Denver and Chicago watching this play out on TV while you sit here with your thumbs up your asses."

Tish has never seen Sheldon Dunow angry before. Sarcastic, yes. Cutting. Rude. But never actually angry. It's impressive, more a snarl than a shout, all the more frightening because he keeps his voice low and under control.

"Whether we like it or not, Mr. Dunow, this is a credible threat. We can't simply ignore it," Monkiewicz says. "Even if Ms. Threadgill doesn't publish a story, the news is going to get out, and when it does it will cause some panic." He turns to Tish. "So, the answer to your question is yes. We will be closing the airport as of four p.m. There will be no air traffic in or out after that."

"Closing it until when?" Tish asks.

"I don't have an answer for that," he says. "Tonight at least, maybe longer. We'll see."

"All right, then I need to go," she says, standing up. "You're welcome to talk to the rest of my staff and you have my permission to put that recording device on my office telephone, but right now I have a newspaper to get out."

Outside on the streets, tourists are heading back to their hotels, limping by, clutching skis propped on their shoulders. Storm clouds, threatening all day, have cleared, leaving the late afternoon sun to cast the brickwork buildings lining Main Street in a warm golden light. It could be a thousand other winter afternoons in ski country, streetlights glowing, skiers in parkas and watch caps gathered at street corners trading tall tales about that last magical run. Turning onto Mountain Street, Tish wants to shout: *Wake up, people! We're under attack!* But she says nothing and turtles her head down against the cold for the last block to the office.

In the newsroom, Moira has already left for the airport and Chuck is drafting the story about the Jack Frost call while Perry puts together a sidebar laying out the history of the attacks. Tish fills them in on the news from the courthouse, then looks up at the three clocks over the door that give the time in Los Angeles, Franklin, and New York. It's nearly four o'clock local time. She never had any intention of publishing a special edition, which is a practical impossibility anyway. But she's dead serious about getting the story out. No way is she allowing unsuspecting airline passengers to fly into a potential death trap just to protect Sheldon Dunow's bottom line.

Working quickly, she types:

> FLASH – Terror Group Threat Closes Colo. Airport – FLASH
>
> Franklin, Colo., Nov. 19 – Elk County Airport, which services the Franklin ski resort, will close at 4 p.m. today following a "credible threat" of an attack by the Jack Frost Collective, a reputed eco-terror group, according to the FBI.
>
> In light of the threat, the airport will be closed to all air traffic until further notice, said FBI Special Agent Arthur Monkiewicz.
>
> "This is a credible threat," Monkiewicz told the Franklin Flyer in announcing the closure. "We can't simply ignore it."
>
> #### UPDATES TO FOLLOW ####

Tish is tinkering with the lede when she hears Perry say her name.

"You know what's weird?" he's saying. "With the other attacks, you could always point to something from *A Screwdriver in the Gears* that inspired it. You know, like the bombing of the power station or the fire-bombing of Boss Burroughs' house."

"Yeah?" Tish says, distracted. Should she call the Jack Frost Collective a "reputed eco-terror group" or go with the more bland "radical environmental group"? The troglodytes at the AP desk won't like "eco-terror," but she wants this piece to pop and nothing pops like a terrorist attack.

"Well, I've looked, and the Frost gang never hit an airport," he says.

She takes her eyes off the screen, having heard him for the first time. He's right. In the book, the Jack Frost gang torches houses, pours sand into gas tanks, dumps elk's blood on a man's head, and shuts down lumber mills by sticking screwdrivers in engine gears, but they never attack an airport. They never go *near* an airport.

"Wasn't there something about a railway line?" Chuck asks.

"Actually, it's a railroad bridge," Perry says. "Jack and Joey talk about blowing it up, but they never actually do it. Anyway, a railroad bridge isn't an airport."

"Maybe we're overthinking the whole literary reference thing," Chuck says. "They never actually said they were following the book. Maybe it's just something we've put onto it."

"Note it as a question mark in your piece and move on," Tish says. "We'll know soon enough what happens at the airport. For now, we need to focus on reporting what we *do* know, which is that the police have closed it down."

But she turns back to her computer, even more unsettled than before. What if this is a hoax and by rushing to report it she's playing into the activists' hands? All she has to do is wait five minutes and Monkiewicz' statement will be on the wires. Does it matter if Tish Threadgill, editor of the *Franklin Flyer*, breaks the story five minutes ahead of the official FBI announcement?

Hell yes, it matters.

She hits send, shooting her file to the AP aerial on the roof and from there to the regional AP desk in Denver. She forces herself to spend a minute idly checking in with Chuck and Perry about their stories for tomorrow's paper. It is quite possibly the longest sixty seconds of her life, but when she sits back down at Rod's old desk and refreshes her screen, the AP desk has bumped her FLASH notification to the top of the head-line queue.

"Guys, check your AP screens!" she calls to Chuck and Perry.

They do, executing a memorized sequence of keyboard clicks that opens up the AP headline queue on their computer terminals.

"Whoa, that was fast," Perry says. "Who broke this?"

"We did, just now," Tish says. "See the *Flyer* name-drop in the last graf?"

"But it doesn't have the Jack Frost call," Chuck says, scrolling through the story.

"Look at the clock," she says. "It's four o'clock on the Wednesday before Thanksgiving, one of the slowest news days of the year, and environmental activists have just shut down an airport in ski country. Every newsroom in the country is going to jump on this, and we're going to own it. We're going to own it tonight with this story, and tomorrow morning when we break the Jack Frost phone call, we'll own the second-day story, too."

The intercom buzzes on her desk.

"Tish," Jen says. "A news director from WMAQ in Chicago on line one. He says he wants to talk to you about a closure at the airport?"

Tish smiles broadly to her two reporters. "Thanks, Jen," she says. "I'll take it in my office."

For the next two hours Tish takes every call she can, going live to air on local newscasts in Chicago, Denver, San Francisco, and Los Angeles to report, in her calmest, most authoritative tone, that a *Flyer* reporter is on the scene at the airport and that she herself was with the FBI special agent in charge at the moment he decided to close it down. She never mentions the phone call from Jack Frost and she takes care to make Monkiewicz and Sheriff Hayes sound decisive and in control. And she inserts the name of her newspaper into nearly every sentence she utters.

At six o'clock, the time the caller gave for the airport closure, Tish tells Jen to direct all future calls to the FBI, and turns her attention to Moira, who has holed up at a pay phone at the Valley View Shopping Center across the highway from the airfield, calling collect every ten minutes with updates. Already, the airport has been evacuated, and traffic is blocked on Highway 22 for a mile in either direction. A small army of police – FBI, Colorado State Patrol, and sheriff's deputies – are standing around their cars along the security perimeter and dozens more are prowling the airport grounds searching for bombs and other forms of sabotage.

Time ticks by slowly. At first, the reporters race to call any last sources and finish up their stories, but by eight o'clock, their pieces are written and edited, waiting only to be laid into the front page that still lacks the lead story Tish is expecting from Moira.

At eight-thirty, Tish is on the line with Moira when a single-engine Cessna slowly whines up the long valley, flashing a distress signal.

"Guys, hey – pipe down!" Tish shouts. "I think we might have something."

"What is it?" Chuck asks.

"A plane, flying in after curfew," she says. "It won't communicate with the tower."

The newsroom goes quiet, and through the open phone line Tish can hear the crackle of police radios and, maybe, possibly, the distant hum of the descending plane.

"The cops are barricading themselves behind the doors of their cars," Moira says. "They're saying the plane's clearly in distress, but the pilot won't respond to radio. They think he might be carrying a bomb of some kind."

"Mo, you need to protect yourself," Tish shouts. "Get down! Get behind something!"

But there's no answer, just the ambient crackle and hum. Moira, Tish realizes, has left the phone hanging from its cord. Dragging her own long phone cord after her, Tish rushes to the north-facing windows of the newsroom, hoping to see the explosion for herself, but all she can see are the tops of nearby buildings and a dark, moonless sky. A minute passes like this, then another, the newsroom graveyard quiet, all eyes on Tish, watching, waiting.

"Hey!" Moira says, coming back on the line. "False alarm!"

"Talk to me," Tish cries. "What happened out there?"

"Nothing happened," Moira shouts, "The pilot was flying out of Denver when his electronics went kaput. Communications, instruments, everything. He wasn't even flying into Franklin. He just needed to make an emergency landing before he crashed into the Great Divide."

"Wait, what?"

"He's fine, he's fine," Moira shouts. "The runway's lit up like a Christmas tree so he had no problem landing. I don't think he even knew the airport was closed."

"Shit, I thought we had something," Tish says, before she catches herself. "Look, maybe you should come back. I'm not so sure it's safe out there."

"Are you kidding me?" Moira says. "There's no other press this close. You couldn't get me out of here with a crowbar."

But an hour later the airport is still quiet. Perry, the only reporter with family in the state, has already left to drive to Boulder for the holiday, and the *Flyer's* Thanksgiving edition sits camera-ready in the layout room, minus a three-column hole across the top of page one. By eleven, the reporters are at their desks rereading day-old editions of the *Denver Post*, and at midnight Tish orders Moira in from the airport and sends the other reporters home.

"I'll call if anything happens," Tish tells them. "But you need to go home, get some rest. I'm going to need you guys to come in for at least a few hours tomorrow."

"I don't mind staying at least till the press guys come," Gemma says.

"Thanks, Moira and I have it under control," Tish says. "I can give you a ride if you want."

"It's cool, I've got my bike," Gemma says.

"There's ice on the roads," she says. "I can't let you ride through that this late at night."

"I can give you a lift," Chuck offers. "I drove in this morning."

The two of them turn to each other, Gemma surprised, Chuck looking hopeful as a puppy at the pound. Part of Tish hopes she's imagining things because an office romance is the last thing she needs right now. Another part of her, the part that woke up in Scott Sage's bed this morning, hopes Chuck wakes up Thanksgiving morning with something to be thankful for.

"Okay, great," she says. "Get out of here, both of you. I'm serious."

◆ ◆ ◆

Out on the street, Chuck helps Gemma stow her bike in the back of his puke-green 1974 Datsun B210, tying the hatchback lid in place with a bungie cord, and they drive through deserted downtown Franklin in silence, the only sounds the steady *ka-chunk, ka-chunk* of the car's balky transmission. Chuck bought it the summer before he went to college, five and a half years ago, and he knows just enough about engine repair to know there's no plausible explanation for how it can still be on the road. His parents have offered to buy him a new car, have *begged* him to let them buy him a shiny new Camry or Chevy Malibu, but he's perversely proud of his ugly green beater.

"What'd the guy say to you?" he asks, to break the ice. "The Jack Frost guy – before you put the call on speaker, what was he saying?"

"Not much, honestly," she says. "He told me he liked my piece about the security ride-along on Mount Boyd. He said it was excellent journalism."

"It's just so weird, right? That this guy is reading our newspaper. You think he's local?"

"Take a right here," she says, pointing out the turnoff.

They've just crossed the narrow bridge that divides the downtown district from East Franklin, where Rodeo Road begins its winding journey up the side of White Mountain into the town's toniest neighborhood. For a hundred yards, there's nothing, just pine trees and the view out over the slow, black Franklin River. Then the first mansion appears, a futuristic glass-and-stone pile that looks like a mashup of Cinderella's Castle and the Space Station.

"Aren't the cops saying these guys are based out of Oregon someplace?" she says.

"That's what they're saying, yeah."

"You aren't buying it?" she asks.

"What do I know, right? But no. I think they're locals and I think they're fucking with us."

"With this airport thing, you mean?"

"With all of it. It's all one big mind-game. And you know what else? I think it's cool."

Gemma nods, gazing out the car window, and for a moment, he thinks he's gone too far. But he isn't sorry. Chuck knows the Jack Frost gang torched a beloved mountain restaurant, and now they're threatening to blow up a public airport. But he also knows the restaurant was empty when it burned, and when all is said and done, no one's going to get hurt at the airport, either.

"I get that it's wrong, and I can't, like, justify it intellectually," he says. "Whoever did this should spend a long, long time in jail. But I mean, they're right and they're doing something about it. Who does that? Not me, that's for sure."

"So, they're heroes, is that it?"

"No, no, hero's the wrong word. I don't mean it like that."

Gemma still won't look at him. He'd have thought Little Miss Millionaire Vegan, with her hemp-cloth sweaters and animal-free footwear, would be all in for Jack Frost. But right now, he seems to be turning her off.

"This is me," she says. "Next driveway on the right, just past that big cottonwood tree."

Chuck sees no house where she's pointing, only a narrow driveway winding up into a grove of leafless aspen trees. He makes the turn and they start up the hill, the Datsun's under-powered engine struggling on the steep incline until, just as he thinks the car will finally blow a fuse and burst into flames, the driveway curves onto a secluded cul de sac that opens out onto the front yard of a towering fieldstone-and-wood-frame mansion. The house looms over the graveled drive, dark and faintly malevolent. This is a house that requires staff, is Chuck's first thought. His second thought is that he wouldn't be surprised to see a helipad out back.

He pulls to a stop a few feet from the massive oak front door. For a moment neither of them speak and he's left with the sound of the ticking engine and the view out over the lights of the city to the blue-black mountain set against a moonless sky.

"Let me ask you something," she says, leaning over toward him. "If you saw one of these guys and you knew who they were, would you turn them in?"

He fixes her with a gaze, unsure what the right answer is. "You're saying you wouldn't?"

She smiles. "Uh-uh. I asked you first."

"Okay, no," he admits, "I probably wouldn't."

"Me, either," she says.

He has imagined this moment, he has imagined *exactly* this moment, the two of them after a long day, no one expecting them, no one really knowing or caring where they are, alone in his car, fifty feet from her parents' big, empty house – and presumably, Gemma's big, empty bed. She's already leaning over the gear shift, her face just a foot or two from his. All he has to do is close the distance between them and kiss her. But he finds he can't move. The signal leaves his brain, travels down his spine, where – *poof!* – it vanishes, gets diverted into some neural back alley and slams into a brick wall.

"Well, thanks for the ride," she says finally.

"Sure, of course," he says, too brightly. "Any time."

He'd like another shot, one more chance to connect his brain to his limbs, but she's already out the door to retrieve her bicycle from the back of the car. By the time he gets there, she has the bike on the ground and is wheeling it toward the house.

"I could give you a ride in to work tomorrow!" he says.

But this makes so little sense that she just laughs and waves goodbye.

A second later, she has opened the massive oak doorway and rolled her bike inside, leaving him alone on the frozen driveway, warmed only by the flaming pyre of his self-loathing. Upstairs, a curtain moves in a second-floor window. Someone is watching from inside, Chuck is certain, and they're laughing. Gemma is probably laughing with them. What other possible response could there be?

I need to join a monastery, he thinks as he folds himself back into his car. I need to turn my life over to God and minister to the poor and needy. I need to do literally anything but hit on women, whom I will never, ever understand.

Through a slit in the curtains, he watches the pale green Datsun execute a three-point turn and start back down the steep driveway. He'd expected Gemma to come alone, but he had never been worried. If she had invited her friend in, he could have ducked into one of Vicky Seagraves' ballroom-sized walk-in closets until he left. All the same, he's relieved to see Chuck's battered car disappear down the driveway.

He waits for Gemma to peel off her coat and backpack and hang her mountain bike on its hook in the mudroom. Only when she has kicked off her shoes and started into the kitchen does he make his way to the stairs. He can hear her opening the fridge, pouring a glass of guava juice, finding a plate in one of the cabinets. He hangs back until she's engrossed in pouring herself a bowl of the baked veggie chips she likes before he steps through the open doorway.

"Who was that?" he asks.

She whips around, nearly dropping the bag in her hand. "Jesus, Terry," she says. "You scared the hell out of me."

"Sorry, I came up to watch us on the eleven o'clock news," he says. "Is that the guy we leaked the FEC Corp story to?"

"Relax, he's harmless. You saw him. I all but grabbed his crotch and … headlights, deer."

"Have some pity. Maybe he's gay."

"Trust me, he's not gay. He's one of your biggest fans, though. He told me he wouldn't turn you in even if he knew who you were."

"You told him about us?"

She laughs. "No, I didn't tell him about us. He brought it up. He thinks what we're doing is cool, and he's rooting for us to win."

"Well, keep working on him. We need to get that damn story in the paper."

"Seriously, this is what you want to talk about, some stupid piece of land in the middle of nowhere? That's what's top of mind for you at this very moment?"

"You were great, Gemma," he says, relenting. "I mean it. Totally convincing."

She laughs, her slight frame seeming to puff outward at the compliment. "Did you notice how I got her to put it on speaker right away?" she says. "I didn't even have to call her over. She just took the call herself."

He nods, letting her bask in their victory. He has known Gemma Seagraves since she was in kindergarten and he was – whatever age he was when Gemma Seagraves was in kindergarten. He'd trust her with his life, is in fact trusting her with his life, but he does wish her redtailed bitch of a mother had left her with a little more self-confidence.

"I told you we could pull this off," he says. "And I was right. We nailed it. You *nailed* it."

"Tish went live on every newscast from Chicago to L.A.," she says. "And she'll do it all again tomorrow after we run the story about the phone call."

"Yeah, I heard her on the radio. She said they have dozens of cops at the airport. Is that true, you think? Dozens?"

"At least that, yeah, from what Moira was saying," she says. "They'll have to leave some security on the mountain, but you should have a clear field tonight."

He's silent. Gemma knows there will be a separate action tonight, but for security reasons she doesn't know what the action is or who is involved. For security reasons, she doesn't know the identity of any members of the collective, aside from him, and none of them know who she is. It's better this way. They've all taken an oath to accept a long prison sentence before informing on other members of the collective, but he knows just how worthless an oath like that will be for someone staring down ten or twenty years in a federal penitentiary.

"I could come along," she says. "If you need an extra hand."

"You know that's not possible."

"I'm just saying I can do more. Maybe not tonight, but if there's another action, I can be of use. I'd like to do more."

"You're already doing more than enough. You're my eyes and ears at that newspaper."

"I'm your checkbook, Terry."

"No," he says firmly. "You got us all those photos of the ski company's on-mountain security the other night. And you're going to get that FEC Corp story into the paper."

"We would've had it in the paper already, but Tish spiked it. She's done it twice now."

"Right, but you're going to keep at it. You'll figure out who owns that damn property and blast it all over the news. That's why we placed you at that paper."

She nods, brightening again at the compliment. Christ, he thinks. Scratch a wallflower and you'll find a narcissist every time. In truth, Gemma has already caused him to make his single greatest tactical blunder. Troy Martin pushed for leaking the FEC Corp file directly to the local papers. Plain white envelope slipped under the door at night, no names, no fingerprints, no way to trace it. But Gemma dreamed up an elaborate charade so the reporters would think they'd discovered it on their own and found a prep school friend from out of town to put on a wig and cheap prop eyeglasses for the handoff. And to keep Gemma onside, to keep the money flowing, he'd agreed. Six weeks later, the story still hasn't found its way into the paper, and Gemma's school friend, whose name he doesn't even know, could bring down the whole collective if she ever makes the connection.

"It's late," he says. "I better go."

"You want something to eat?" she asks. "I can make you a smoothie, or just like a cup of coffee. You're going to be out there all night."

He smiles. He's about to commit enough Class 1 felonies to get them both put away for decades and she's talking about making him a smoothie.

"You've got a VCR here, right?" he says.

"Don't worry, I'll record every minute. Just local stations or do you want CNN, too?"

He considers this. "Local stations, mostly. They're more likely to stay with the story. But if CNN covers it, I'd love to see that. I want to see all of it."

"You think they'll shut down the mountain?"

"They'll have to, for a while at least. After tonight, they'll have no choice."

"And then what?"

"And then you wait for further orders. Don't do anything until you hear from me."

"Will I hear from you?"

"Eventually, yes," he says. "But don't come looking for me. Don't do anything you wouldn't normally do."

His gear – parka, gloves, a light pack containing wire cutters and incendiary devices – is waiting by the back door. Once he's gathered it all up, he and Gemma walk through the dark yard to a stand of juniper bushes where he has stashed a mountain bike.

"You did good tonight, Gem," he says. "Better than good. That was first-class work."

"Hey, just following the plan, right?" she says.

Standing on her tiptoes, she plants a wet, urgent kiss on his lips. To his surprise, the moment lingers and he feels the press of her small body against his. He slept with Gemma several times during the recruitment phase. It felt weirdly incestuous, like he was sleeping with his sister, but it wasn't unpleasant, exactly. Danger, he knows, is a potent aphrodisiac. But even if he cared to start that up again, which *he doesn't, there's no time. In an hour, he'll be meeting the others south of town where they've stashed the stolen snowmobiles, and an hour after that he'll be at the top of Mount Boyd, waiting for the explosions that will mark the start of the night's action.*

"Go to work tomorrow just like normal," he says, disentangling his body from hers.

"I know," she says. "Don't do anything I wouldn't normally do. I heard you the first time."

"Okay, but the heat's going to be on after tonight. Worse even than after the Highline fire."

"As long as it stops them building in Elkhorn Canyon, it's worth it."

They kiss again, less urgently this time, and he sets off through the aspen trees with the bike. It's a dark, moonless night – a pre-condition for tonight's action – and after only a few yards she disappears behind him. Out of habit, he stops every twenty or thirty yards to check that no one's watching, but no one is. It's past one in the morning and everyone in this part of town went to bed hours ago. When he reaches Rodeo Road, glistening white with frost, he stops to look out across the darkened valley at the FrankCo snowcats grinding their way up and down the lighted ski runs, grooming the freshly made snow. Enjoy it while you can, assholes, he thinks. Then he leans into the pedal and starts coasting down the hill, heading for the base of Mount Boyd.

PART THREE

A Screwdriver in the Gears

"Jack, c'mon, we gotta get moving!" Joey shouted from the idling motorcycle.

Jack stood listening to the roar of machinery overhead. What had gone wrong? Had Joey crossed the wires somehow? Was the fuse defective? In the end, it didn't matter. If he didn't hop on Joey's chopper soon, Sheriff Fontine would arrest them both.

Rummaging in his overalls, his fingers found the flathead screwdriver. Years later, whenever he told this story, Jack would remark on how small the screwdriver was, less than a foot long and three-sixteenths of an inch thick. But it was the perfect tool for his task, and without a second thought, he jammed it between two enormous, clacking gears overhead.

The teeth of the gears met the steel blade of the screwdriver, bending it like a paperclip, but this derailed the gear, which shuddered, then screamed: Skraaaaaak!

"Let's get the hell outta here!" he shouted to Joey.

A Screwdriver in the Gears
Bill Blanning, 1971

Chapter Nine

"Don't look now," Moira hisses, "but I think I just saw Lesley Stahl."

Tish tries to follow Moira's gaze, but all she sees are row after row of TV journalists, mostly white and male and middle-aged, with blow-dried hair and professionally capped teeth, gabbing with friends or shouting into breadbox-sized portable phones.

"Where?"

"Eight o'clock, talking to the fat little producer guy," Moira says. "She was *so* robbed, man. If there was any justice in the world, she'd be in the anchor's chair right now."

"Okay, I've got you beat," Tish says. "Three o'clock. In the cream-colored pantsuit."

"No freaking way – Joan *Didion*?" Moira says, stunned.

"She's probably here for a magazine piece," Tish says. "From what I hear, she used to be tight with Bill Blanning."

"One time in college," Moira says, "I went as Joan Didion for Halloween: cigarette, big sunglasses, a matchbox Corvette around my neck. Nobody got it, of course. Would it be weird if I asked her for an autograph? Because I totally want one."

Tish giggles, enjoying herself. It's so rare to see Moira Mangan fangirling. And she's not the only one. Passing through the lobby of the Hotel Franklin earlier, Tish had spotted her own childhood girl-crush, Barbara Walters, berating a twenty-something assistant producer because her hotel room has a view of the hotel's inner courtyard, not Mount Boyd.

Two weeks after America's most famous non-attack on an airport, the national media has once again descended on Franklin, Colorado, and this time it has brought the A Team. No more Kelly Cherry and little Anderson what's-his-name. Tonight, the Jack Frost Collective will be at the top of the nightly news, third story down from President Clinton and whoever got shot today in Northern Ireland. After drawing the police from Mount Boyd to the county airfield, where for eight long hours nothing happened, the Collectivists struck the ski hill, first detonating a bomb that blew out the pipe supplying water to the snowmaking machines, and then, capitalizing on the chaos that followed, pouring sand into the gas tanks of every snowcat and snowmobile not in active use. In the morning, when the lift operators started Lift #1, they heard a deafening screech of metal as a cable jumped the guidewheels. Someone had placed not a screwdriver, but a specially forged steel ramp between the guidewheels on a tower a thousand feet from the base of the hill, which derailed the cable as soon as the wheels started to turn. Damage to the chairlift was minimal, but FrankCo shut down the mountain to inspect its other lifts and it has remained closed ever since – until today.

At a signal from a black-clad technician at the front of the room, the klieg lights flash on in rapid succession – *boom, boom, boom, boom* – sounding like mortar rounds landing in a distant field, and Patti Murray steps onto the stage in an ill-fitting blazer and skirt, trailed by Rudy Lawton and half a dozen other local businessowners. In the weeks since the Thanksgiving attacks, the Lazy T and Lawton's Drugs have become regular stops for visiting journalists, and Patti's public about face on Elkhorn Canyon landed her a featured spot on *Nightline*. Still, Tish, who has known Patti and Rudy for decades, is disappointed to see the two long-time Elkhorn Canyon foes parade onstage as human props in FrankCo's "Back in Business" press avail. Apparently, two weeks of empty slopes, and even emptier shops and restaurants, were all it took for them to wrap themselves in the comforting arms of the Franklin Skiing Company.

Tish shoots a glance at Jimmy Lachlan, who stands against the far wall, asking with her eyes if this is the big surprise he's been promising all morning. The big Aussie's craggy face remains impassive, but he shakes his head once discreetly, *No*.

Then she sees it. Or rather, she sees *him*. Just behind a beaming Sheldon Dunow, waving to the crowd like a prom king acknowledging his subjects, walks a sad-eyed Russ Canavan, his hands thrust into his pockets to keep them from rubbing together. Tish doesn't give Jimmy the satisfaction, but she knows he's flashing her a small, smug grin.

Tish has known Russ since she moved to town and they even went on one disastrous date back in the eighties, during which he would not shut up about the wonders of deep-tissue massage and warm-oil enemas. His environmental stance, she knows, is completely genuine, but his livelihood is as tourist-dependent as everyone else's in Franklin. No skiers on Mount Boyd, no hundred-dollar massages or daylong wellness retreats, and Russ Canavan is on the first flight back to Fort Lee, New Jersey, trailing hundreds of thousands of dollars in business debts.

"As many of you know," he says when it's his turn at the podium. He stops, adjusts the microphone, and starts over. "As many of you know, my organization, the Mountain Wildlands Coalition, has opposed the development of Elkhorn Canyon for nearly a decade. We still have many questions, but for the past several weeks I, along with other local environmentalists, have been in talks with the Franklin Skiing Company, and they assure us this new expansion is going to be the most environmentally friendly resort in the history of winter sports. So I am here today to announce that the Mountain Wildlands Coalition has voted to endorse the Franklin Skiing Company's plans for expansion in Elkhorn Canyon."

Russ's hands, Tish notices, are not rubbing together. He's beyond that. He looks gutted, like a man who has just emerged from ten hours of police interrogation. As he lists the concessions FrankCo has made – cutting one ski lift from the resort design, eliminating the hotel at the base of the ski hill – Tish's mind travels back to the draft of Chuck and Gemma's FEC Corp story still sitting in a manila folder on her desk. They never found a direct link between the FEC Corp and FrankCo, but unless the owners of FEC Corp really are environmentalists, it doesn't matter. If the ski company buys the FEC Corp property, it could easily accommodate half a dozen luxury hotels, plus restaurants and a decent-sized pedestrian mall.

On the walk back to the *Flyer* office, while Moira burbles on about the cut of Joan Didion's pantsuit, Tish mentally rehashes her conversations with Chuck and Gemma about the FEC Corp piece. Their early take on the story *was* a touch conspiratorial, but that isn't why she spiked it, not really. The first time, she was worried Sheldon Dunow might claw back the advertising lifeline he'd thrown her the day before, and the second time she was afraid Stan Bucholtz would call in the loan on her credit line. In other words, Tish killed the story for the same reason Patti Murray sat down with Ted Koppel and Russ Canavan stood before the cameras and pretended dropping a single ski lift from a two-thousand-acre resort would save one of America's last remaining pristine old-growth alpine forests: She was protecting her livelihood.

"Jen!" she shouts, frustrated. "Why is there a humongous pile of mail on my desk?"

"Because it's been sitting on *my* desk almost a week and you haven't looked at any of it," Jen calls back. "I thought a change of scenery might do it some good."

"Have you at lea – ?"

"I've gone through all of it," Jen says. "There's nothing from Jack Frost. But you need to read your mail."

Chastened, Tish begins sorting her mail while plotting how, and when, she can get the FEC Corp story into the paper. Her window is narrow. For the next couple days, she knows, no one will read anything that isn't about reopened ski runs and returning skiers, but by the weekend the national press will be gone, off to chase the next quirky crisis in flyover country. And for this story she needs the national press. If she's going to blow up her newspaper by breaking a story, she needs all the amplification she can get. So if she's going to run the FEC Corp story, it has to be this week, Thursday or Friday at the latest. Check that. Thursday. It has to run Thursday.

She's halfway through her mail pile, still planning the rollout of the

FEC Corp story, when she comes to a letter on heavy-bond paper from the Colorado Secretary of State:

> Dear Mr. Barlow,
>
> This is to confirm that our office is in receipt of your request for additional documentation from the Colorado Department of Conservation. Pursuant to the Colorado Open Records Act, C.R.S. § 24-72-201-206, you must direct your inquiry to the Colorado Department of Conservation, not to this office.
>
> For your future reference, the address of the Colorado Department of Conservation is ....

Tish reaches for her phone and punches the button that connects her to the newsroom. "Perry?" she asks. "Could you swing by my office for a sec?"

She spends the next minute rifling through the pile for more letters from the Secretary of State. There are two more, all sent the same day, all bearing the same message about the proper office to direct his inquiry.

"You wanted to see me, boss?" Perry says from the doorway.

"What records are you trying to get from the Colorado Department of Conservation?" she says, holding up the stack of letters.

"Why – how come those went to you?" he stammers.

"Because I run a newspaper and I ask my secretary to route all official-looking correspondence through me," Tish says. "You haven't answered my question: What are you requesting from the Department of Conservation ?"

Perry's face drains of color, and for half a second, Tish thinks he might start to cry. "I'm so sorry," he says. "I should've told you, but he said he'd have me fired if I ever told anyone."

"Wait. Who're we talking about here – Rick Sheffield?"

"I'll quit, okay? I'll hand in my resignation today. I'm not hacking it here, anyway."

Rising from her chair, Tish shuts the door with a gentle kick.

"Nobody's asking you to resign," she says. "I just want to know what happened, why you sent in those Open Records requests."

"He told me everything," he says, still fighting back tears. "That night I drove downvalley to see him, he told me the whole story. He found evidence the lynx is still in Elkhorn Canyon, but they deep-sixed his data and wrote the report to say it was only bobcats."

"He told you that?"

Perry nods solemnly. "But you can't use any of it. He made me promise not to tell anyone, not even you. *Especially* not you. If we print it, he'll just say we made it up."

"Okay. But he said it, right?"

"Oh God, I'm not cut out for this," he says. "I'm such a shitty reporter. You see a situation like this and you know exactly what to do. Me – I can't even spell."

"What're you talking about? Perry, you're a great reporter. People talk to you. Even this Sheffield guy talked to you. He wasn't talking to *anyone* and you got him to open up to you."

He brightens a little, testing what she's said against his year at the *Flyer*. It fits because Tish is mostly telling the truth. At heart, Perry Barlow is a big, sweet-tempered child, twenty-five going on twelve. His wife pushes him around, and he can't spell any word longer than five letters, but people sense his vulnerability, his eternal lostness, and want to help him.

"So, we were right all along," Tish says. "The lynx is out there and they're covering it up."

"That's what Rick says, anyway."

"Wow," she says, shaking her head. "You think the world's all screwed up, and then it turns out it's even more screwed up than you thought."

"What're we going to do?" he asks. "About Rick Sheffield, I mean."

"I don't know, I can poke around my sources at Conservation, but I've been doing that for weeks. We'll have to come at it sidewise, I guess."

"Sidewise?"

She laughs. "Right, yeah, that's just what I say when I have no idea what I'm going to do. But look, get these Open Records requests in today. And don't quit on me, okay? You've got the lightest touch with features of anybody I've ever had here. People tell you stuff even when they shouldn't. That's a gift. Don't underestimate it."

As he heads off, wiping his nose on his shirtsleeve like a toddler, Tish flashes again on the FEC Corp story she was just now plotting out how to report. On the surface, the lynx story and the FEC Corp story have no point of connection, except that they both involve Elkhorn Canyon and nobody will talk about them. But maybe that *is* the point of connection. If Tish has learned anything in her years as a reporter it's that human beings are incurable chatterboxes. Usually, half the job is getting them to shut up. But here, in a matter of weeks, two wholly unrelated sets of sources have led her reporters into the same journalistic cone of silence. Coincidence? Possibly. But if it isn't, the FEC Corp story could be the sidewise angle she needs to break open the story of the Canada lynx. Push one, and the other just might pop out.

◆ ◆ ◆

"Does the name FEC Corp mean anything to you?" Tish asks Scott the next morning.

They've been awake since eight when Scott slid a sleep-warmed hand down her bare belly and whispered, *Are you even half as horny as I am?* She was, it turned out, but that's all behind them now, and they're tangled up together in bed drinking their morning coffee.

"No," he says. "Should it?"

"Probably not. I was just wondering if you'd ever come across the name."

"At the bank, you mean?"

The hair on Scott's chest is the dulled silver of steel wool, unlike the hair on his head, which is still, mostly, reddish brown. Tish likes running her hand through it, feeling its tensile strength. It is without a doubt the butchest thing about him.

"I'm just a credit officer," he says. "A *junior* credit officer. There's a lot going on at that bank I don't know about."

"Right, sure. I just figure, if a bank's like any place else in the world, people talk."

He turns to look at her. "No, Tish."

"No, what?"

"No, I'm not going to be a source for you."

She sits up, struggling to look offended. "I'm not asking you to be a source."

"Yes, you are. And it's not going to happen. I don't like Bucholtz any more than you do, but he hired me when I was desperate for a job, and I'm not going to screw him over."

"Okay, you're right. I'm sorry," she says. "It's late. We should be getting ready for work."

"Come on, don't be like that."

"I'm not 'being like that.' I'm stating an observable fact. It's five past nine and certain junior credit officers should be getting dressed for work."

She swings her legs out from the bed and strides naked to the bathroom. Her first three or four steps are quick until she feels his eyes on her backside and slows down a tick, letting him look. In some ways, this is even better than waking up to a horny man. A month into their relationship, Scott still can't stop checking her out. At home, she wraps up in a nightgown or the floor-length kimono, but at Scott's condo she goes everywhere naked, even the living room, with its wide, uncurtained windows. If she flashes the universe a little thirty-seven-year-old boob, so be it. Nothing is going to make her give up feeling desired again.

She showers quickly, brushes and rinses, and returns to the bedroom wearing only a towel wrapped around her hair. By then, Scott is trussed up in a suit and tie, but he still smiles when she enters the room, giving her an appreciative once-over.

"This FEC Corp thing, this is the story you were telling me about, isn't it?" he says. "The story you were afraid to report."

It takes a second, but she remembers their conversation the morning after their first ski date, just before Jack Frost shut down Mount Boyd. She told him she was afraid to publish, and he asked what point there was in owning a newspaper if she wasn't going to publish the news.

"What is it you think they've done?" he asks.

"I don't know, exactly," she admits. "A company by that name bought an old mining claim in Elkhorn Canyon a mile from the base of the new ski hill. They told the family they bought it from that they're environmentalists trying to preserve the land, but they didn't put any easements on it and we can't figure out who owns it."

"And you think Bucholtz is mixed up in it somehow?"

"Scott, look, you were right before," she says. "I can't expect you to risk your job for a story I'm working on."

"Even if there's a file for this company at the bank, I probably wouldn't have access to it."

"So forget it, okay? Go on, it's almost nine-thirty. You're going to be late."

"You better put some clothes on there, lady, or I'm not going anywhere."

She lets out a most un-Tish-like laugh, low and throaty. "Is that a threat or a promise?"

"Both," he says, already loosening his tie.

When Tish makes it in to work, an hour later, she summons Chuck and Gemma to her office.

"What would you say if I told you I wanted to run the FEC Corp story Thursday?" she asks.

"*This* Thursday?" Gemma says.

"We've had this in the can almost a month now," Tish says. "You guys should be able to turn it around in a couple days, right?"

"We've barely looked at it in weeks," Chuck says. "We'll need to go back and double-check everything."

"Take all the time you need," Tish tells them. "If you have to skip some meetings, let me know and I'll have Perry pinch hit for you. Or I can do it. This takes precedence. Oh, and one last thing: Put in a call to Sheldon Dunow and ask if he's aware of this land deal."

"Sheldon Dunow?" Chuck asks. "I thought we were avoiding any suggestion the FrankCo had anything to do with this."

"We are," Tish says. "That's why we're calling him, to give him a chance to deny it."

"But just putting his name in the story will …. " he starts to say before his voice trails off.

"Exactly," Tish says. "Don't call his PR people. Call Dunow directly and print whatever he says, even if it's a flat denial."

"Aye-aye, boss," he says, leaping up from his seat. "He'll be my next call."

A little before three, Tish is having a late lunch and flipping through a copy of *Newsweek* that's been making its way around the office. Franklin made the cover. Or not Franklin, exactly. The story, headlined "The War For Our Forests," focuses on radical environmental activism across the West, but it leads with Jack Frost's non-attack on the Elk County airport and features color photos of the torched Highline Chalet and the disabled Lift #1, with its long line of mangled lift chairs splayed across the snow.

The phone on her desk beeps. "Scott Sage from Franklin Savings," Jen says. "Line one."

Tish sets aside her magazine and nudges the door to her office shut. "Twice in one day wasn't enough?" she purrs into the phone.

"Tish, listen," Scott says, low and insistent, "Bucholtz wants to meet with you tomorrow. He says you might want to bring a lawyer."

"Oh…," she says.

"Tell me, how much cash can you scrape together by tomorrow?"

She pictures Scott at his desk, hunched over his phone like a spy requesting the coordinates of the dead drop. What is she doing to this good, sweet, ordinary guy?

"If I stiffed all my vendors and zeroed out my last mutual funds?" she says. "Twenty-five thousand, maybe thirty."

"That's it – thirty grand?"

"Scott, I'm broke. If I had the money, I'd have paid this off months ago. There's no way you can slow-walk this?"

"I've already made my objections clear," he says. "If I say anything more, he'll let me go a couple weeks early and hand the account off to somebody else."

"Okay, be honest: How much would it take? Realistically. What's Bucholtz's number?"

"I'm not sure he has a number," he says. "If this was just about the money, we would take your thirty thousand and call it a win. But I don't think that's going to work here."

"So, you're saying I'd have to come up with the full $150,000?"

"It's actually closer to one-sixty now. Look, I know you can't get your hands on all of it, but you're going to have to – "

"What if I *could* get my hands on all of it?" she asks. "What if I came up with $160,000 in the next day or two – would this go away?"

"Well, yeah. But if you have $160,000 lying around, you need to tell me where it is."

"I don't have it now. But I might know someone who could give it to me. If I beg."

"That sounds … complicated," Scott says.

"Believe me, it is. It also probably won't work. But I don't really have a choice, do I?"

"Okay, what can I do to help?"

"Right now, nothing," she says. "Or no, I lie. Go back to Bucholtz and tell him I'm freaking out. I cried on the phone, begged you for more time, the whole nine yards. Make it sound like I'm going to walk in there tomorrow and hand over the keys."

"I can do that," he says. "You want to tell me what you're planning?"

"Not especially, no," she says. "I just need you to keep Bucholtz in check, make him think he's winning. Okay?"

They talk a minute more, getting their stories straight, but Tish's mind is already racing, a thousand thoughts competing for her attention. The first to get through after they hang up is the phone call she asked Chuck make to Sheldon Dunow that morning. Dunow hadn't come to the phone, naturally, and a couple hours later a FrankCo PR flack had called back with a carefully phrased denial. This was fine with Tish. What Dunow said on the record about the FEC Corp land deal didn't interest her. She had wanted to see what he would do when he learned the *Flyer* was running a story about it.

And now, maybe, she has her answer: One of her reporters tells Sheldon Dunow they're days away from reporting the existence of a previously unknown parcel of land less than a mile from his company's proposed new ski hill, and five hours later Stan Bucholtz is threatening to call in her loan. So, unless she's wildly misreading the situation, the Dunows know about the FEC Corp property, and would prefer the rest of the world didn't. But that's not even the most interesting part. Tish had thought she might get a call from someone on the FrankCo sales team hinting that they were rethinking their advertising strategy. But no. Dunow had gone straight for Tish's fiscal jugular and tapped Stan Bucholtz to wield the knife. Which means Bucholtz knows about FEC Corp, too, and is working with Dunow to keep it on the down-low. Which means she's sitting on an even bigger story than she thought.

Assuming, that is, she can stay in business long enough to get it into the newspaper.

Tish sits alone in her office, preparing herself for a conversation she's been putting off for five and a half years. Then she reaches for the phone and punches in her father's home number in Connecticut.

◆ ◆ ◆

The last time Tish saw Roland Threadgill, five and a half years ago, he was in Denver for a builder's trade conference and she and Doug had driven down from Franklin to pitch him on investing in the *Flyer*. The *Bulletin* had launched its daily edition six months earlier and Doug planned to ask the old man for a $100,000 loan that would, he believed, allow them to bury Leo Mayer once and for all. First, though, they had to pretend that this was simply a family visit. They ate blood-rare steaks at the Trinity Grille, and watched a Broncos game from corporate box seats high above the fifty-yard line. Then, claiming she needed to get back to Franklin to run the paper, Tish drove home, leaving Doug with their father to make the pitch for the loan.

That night, when Tish arrived at the *Flyer*, there was no message waiting for her from Doug. He didn't call the next day, either, and by the time she reached her father, he was back in Connecticut and couldn't understand what all the fuss was about. He'd offered to loan Doug twice what he'd asked for, her father told Tish, if he and his sister shut down the paper and moved to New Canaan, where he would set them both up in the family business.

For two days, Tish called hotels and police stations and hospitals, hoping someone had seen her brother. On the third day, as she was packing up to drive to Denver to look for him herself, she got a call from the Arapahoe County sheriff's department. A deputy, following up on reports of an unpleasant odor emanating from a motel room on a desolate stretch of I-70 east of the city, had found Doug suspended from a light fixture by his own belt.

"Patricia Threadgill," her father says when he comes to the phone, his cement-mixer growl booming in her ear. "To what do I owe the pleasure?"

"Hi, Dad," she says.

"Dad?" he says, offering up a gruff chuckle. "It's 'Dad' now, is it?"

"Dad, could we maybe not do this?"

"Could we not do what, sweetheart?" he says, all syrupy concern. "You're the one calling me for the first time in five years. So please, enlighten me, what is it that we shouldn't do?"

Tish takes a deep breath, settling herself. Her memories of her father aren't *all* bad, she reminds herself. Even after the divorce, when he mostly pretended Doug and Tish didn't exist, he still sometimes took her for rides through Connecticut farm country on his blue-and-silver Ducati. She can see him even now, crewcut and young in his biker's leathers, his eyes hidden behind mirrored aviator sunglasses, licking an ice cream cone at a farmstand north of Newtown.

"Could we start over?" she says. "I'm sorry I haven't called. When Doug died, it brought up a lot of old stuff, a lot of old feelings. Maybe that's unfair of me, but it's how I felt."

Her father doesn't argue, doesn't accuse or try to justify himself. It's not much, but it's just enough to allow them to fall into a brief, companionable silence.

"What happened with Douglas is a tragedy," he says. "Can we agree on that much?"

"Yes, Dad. That much we can agree on."

"And you think I played some role in that."

"Now wait, I never said that."

"You meant it."

"Well, I guess you're free to draw your own conclusions."

"You told me you never wanted to see me again. You said if I showed up at my own son's funeral, you'd have me thrown out. And then for the next five years you refused to come to the phone or answer any of my letters. Just what conclusion do you expect me to draw from that?"

Tish shuts her eyes, tuning out the ringing phones and chatter on the other side of her office wall. He's right: She'd said all that, and more. She meant it, too. If her father had showed up at Doug's funeral, she'd have thrown him out herself. If she hadn't killed him first.

"He loved you," she says. "He looked up to you. We both did."

"I had no idea he would react the way he did. I thought he was just asking for a loan."

"You made fun of him," she says. "You made fun of both of us."

"I never made fun of anyone," he roars back at her. "You don't know. You weren't there."

"I *was* there," she says. "For a day and a half before I drove back to Franklin, I was there. You said we were like two kids playing store and someday we'd have to grow up and run a real business. You kept counting off all the ways Doug reminded you of Mom. You said it over and over and over, like it was a joke, like it was funny."

The line goes quiet. Her anger is so old, so raw, so ungovernable. Because there were the Ducati weekends, but there was also the Saturday when she saw her father with his two other children in the meat aisle at Gristede's and he walked past Tish and Doug like they were invisible. There was the morning he called Tish to come pick up her mother, who had showed up at his house asking for a hundred dollars to pay an overdue gas bill. Tish found her mother on his porch in a bathrobe and slippers, her once flowing auburn hair pasted to her scalp, her eyes dead in their sockets from the tranquilizers. *I can't have this*, her father had hissed as he handed Tish five twenties plus cab fare home. *You need to take better care of her. I can't have her coming around here looking like this.*

"Why did you call me today, Patricia?" he asks, finally.

"I'm in trouble, Dad," she admits. "That's why. I need your help."

"With the newspaper?"

"Look, I know what you think. And you were right. Okay? Even with all the money in this town, it's hard to make one daily newspaper work, much less two. But I'm here and I'm doing it, and I need $160,000. Now. Today."

"For Christ's sake, Patricia – why? You could do anything. You could *be* anything. Why throw your life away on some crappy little newspaper in East Jesus, Colorado?"

"I'll sign away my inheritance," she says. "If you give me $160,000 now, Mim and Cord can split whatever's left of my share."

"You would do that?" he says, appalled. "Do you have any idea how much money there is?"

"Several million, I'm guessing," she says. "Assuming, that is, I'm still included in the will."

"Of course you're in the will. Jesus, what kind of prick do you think I am? I would never cut a child of mine out of my will."

"Well, all I want is $160,000. Then you can wash your hands of me once and for all."

"Don't talk like that, Patricia," he says. "Nobody wants to wash their hands of you."

Bile rises in her throat, flooding her mouth with the taste of soured milk, as she thinks of the pitch booklet she and Doug wrote for their father five and a half years ago. They'd spent weeks creating charts and graphs and writing bullet-point arguments explaining how they would drive the *Bulletin* into bankruptcy. Doug had spent fifty dollars to have it printed, in color on cardstock paper. Two copies, one for Doug and one for their father. Tish had found them both still in their envelopes on the bedside table of the Motel 6 where Doug had hung himself. The old man hadn't even bothered to take his copy out of the envelope.

"There's only one condition," Tish says. "I need it by tomorrow."

"Tomorrow?"

"Tonight would be better, honestly, but tomorrow will do. After that, it's no good to me."

Chapter Ten

"Chuuuuckles!" Jen warbles over the intercom. "Your mom again. Line two."

Shit, Chuck thinks, a hunk of breakfast bagel turning to sawdust in his mouth. His mother never calls him at work, but there'd been a message slip when he came in saying she'd called at 9:31 a.m., ten minutes before he arrived. And now, half an hour later, she's calling again.

"Could you tell her I'm out?" he says.

"Tish doesn't pay me enough to lie to people's mothers," Jen says. "She's waiting, dude. Line two."

On the other side of the newsroom, Moira is deep into a day-old *New York Times* and Gemma is knocking out a City Hall piece that got lost in the shuffle over the FEC Corp story. Without quite realizing he's doing it, Chuck runs his fingers through his hair, straightening the part, and hits the button for line two.

"Hey, Ma," he says. "This isn't a great time. I'm kind of on deadline."

"Well, hello to you, too, honey," she says. "This won't take long. I'm only calling because when I was reading my *Post-Dispatch* this morning, I came across a very interesting story. Shall I read a little of it to you?"

"You want to read a story to me?"

"Dateline: Franklin, Colo.," she reads, ignoring him. "By Charles Quigley, Jr. and Gemma Seagraves. In this picturesque mountain village rocked by attacks from radical environmentalists, a mysterious organization claiming to be an environmental group has bought a remote parcel of land near a controversial new ski area, but local environmentalists say they've never heard of the group and its purchase contract makes no provisions for preserving the land for conservation."

The lede's been rewritten, and somewhat garbled in the process, but it's their story, all right. In Franklin, the FEC Corp story had hit like a tidal wave, upending the politics of the Elkhorn Canyon ski area proposal and sending the three Denver TV stations into a frenzy of follow-up reporting. But this is different. This is his story, and his byline, in his hometown paper.

"That was in the *Post-Dispatch*?" he asks.

"Page A-12, top of the fold," she says. "I'll clip it out and send it to you."

"You don't have to do that. Just save it and I can see it the next time I'm home."

"No, I'm going to send it to you. Just think how it'll look in your law school application."

Chuck closes his eyes, belatedly realizing where this is headed.

"I'll bet you could make a mosaic of all the versions of this story," she says. "You know, with the mastheads of the newspapers that published it? It'd totally set your application apart."

"A mosaic?"

"Maybe mosaic isn't the word I'm looking for," she says. "More like a file, you know? Something people can flip through, to see how your story went national."

"Ma, look, I'm not going to be making a mosaic or a file or anything else for my law school application."

Across the room, Gemma turns to look at him, her small, red mouth twisted in concern. Even Moira is watching him now over the top of her day-old *Times*, one quizzical eyebrow raised.

"Why are you shouting at me?" his mother asks, hurt.

"Sorry, I didn't realize I was," he says. "It's just, like I said, this isn't a great time. I'm at work and it's crazy busy here."

"Well, you need to start thinking about this. That application's due in February."

"Could we please talk about something else? How are your painting classes? Have you – ?"

But the human freight train Marilyn Quigley just keeps barreling down the track. "Your grandfather spoke to the dean. You sent him that letter explaining why you left."

"No, I didn't," he says. "I never sent the letter. I wrote it, but I never put it in the mail."

"You never sent it?"

"And I'm not going to send it, either," he says, louder now. "I hated law school, Ma. I hated every minute of it, and I wasn't any good at it. That's why I left. I'm doing what I want to do right here, right now, writing stories like the one you saw in the *P-D* this morning."

"Do you have any idea how much newspaper reporters make?" his mother wails.

"A heck of a lot more than a law student who flunks the bar exam," Chuck says. "Bye, Ma. I'm at work now. I've got a Planning & Zoning meeting to go to."

He slams down the phone, feeling a burst of elation. He's free. He's done it, cut the cord, finished the job he started when he walked away from Mizzou Law – and the magic of it is that because he's paying his own bills, there's nothing his mother can do about it.

"That," Moira says, "was a thing of beauty."

When he turns, both Moira and Gemma are at their desks, slow-clapping their approval.

"'Bye, Ma, I'm at work now. I've got a Planning & Zoning meeting to go to,'" Moira says. "Every reporter on earth should have that carved on their tombstone."

She produces a flask from the bottom drawer of her desk and tops up his and Gemma's morning coffee with half shots of whiskey. Word spreads, and before long half the staff is in the newsroom raising toasts to meddling mothers and blowing off law school – everyone, that is, but Tish, who remains holed up in her office, doing what exactly nobody knows. The boss has been squirrelly lately, Chuck has noticed, meeting with her bankers and calling their advertisers to reassure them the *Flyer* is on solid financial footing. Word around the office is that FrankCo slashed its winter ad buy after Chuck and Gemma's story ran, which spooked everyone from the press room guys to the local realtors and hoteliers who advertise in the paper.

When the newsroom party finally breaks up, Chuck remembers that he actually *does* have a Planning & Zoning meeting to attend. He grabs his coat, along with a pen and notepad, but when he stops at the front desk to tell Jen where he'll be for the next two hours, Tish pokes her head out from her office.

"Any chance you can skip P&Z today?" she asks.

Nothing, in fact, would make Chuck happier, but it's an odd request. They need a third-day follow on the FEC Corp story and the county courthouse is the obvious place to go looking for it.

But he shrugs. "It's right before Christmas so it's not like they're going to get a lot done."

"Good," Tish says. "Give me ten minutes and meet me in the third-floor conference room."

"Sure," he says. "Ten minutes, third-floor. What's up?"

Tish radars a look at Jen, who is making a show of being deeply engrossed in the morning mail. "Just meet me upstairs in ten," she says. "And bring Gemma. She should be there for this."

◆ ◆ ◆

The building that houses the *Flyer* is furnished with beige institutional carpeting and water-stained popcorn ceilings. The hallways are scuffed by a thousand bike wheels and running shoe treads, and the bathrooms, one per floor, perennially reek of urine. The building's lone amenity is a glassed-in conference room on the third floor across from a dentist's office and a framing shop. Since dentists and picture framers have little use for conference rooms, it's always empty, and with the Venetian blinds drawn, reliably private.

When Tish arrives, Rick Sheffield is already there, sitting next to Perry at one end of the faux-maple conference table. The field biologist is even smaller than she remembered, slight-built and bearded, with thinning hair and rimless glasses, dressed in a sloppy turtleneck and wide-wale corduroys like the sixties never ended. His face, oatmeal-gray to begin with, blanches white when he sees Chuck and Gemma roll in behind Tish.

"I told you, nobody else," he says, rising from his chair. "Just you and Tish."

"Rick, this is Chuck Quigley and Gemma Seagraves," Perry says. "They wrote the story on the FEC Corp that you called me about. Tish thought they should hear what you have to say."

"I could lose my job," he says. "I'm probably going to lose my job, anyway, but this would be icing on the cake."

"Let me ask you, did anyone see you come up here just now?" Tish asks.

"No, we came up the back stairs," he admits. "Nobody saw us."

"And you can see the blinds are drawn, right?" she says. "Nobody else knows you're here. It's just the four of us and we don't burn our sources, okay? That's a promise."

He looks around, a frightened deer taking a meeting with four hungry wolves. But what choice does he have, really? They've all seen him and Perry has already heard most of his story.

"I don't want my name anywhere near this," he says. "Not even as an anonymous source or whatever. If this helps you track this lady down, great. If not, we never spoke."

"That's fine, Rick," Tish says. "Perry told me you wanted your name kept out of it and we'll respect that. So why don't you tell us a little more about this woman you met. You think she might be Anna Pitlor from the Friends of Elkhorn Canyon?"

She has Chuck's and Gemma's full attention now. The two reporters had been standing in the doorway, looking for an excuse to head back downstairs, but they quickly find seats on either side of Tish and start taking notes.

"She never used the name Anna," Rick tells them. "She said her name was Juliet. I don't remember her saying anything about the Friends of Elkhorn Canyon, either."

"This Juliet, did she give you a last name?" Gemma asks.

"It never got that far," Rick says. "It was just a quick conversation – fifteen, twenty minutes, tops. I'd forgotten all about it, honestly, until I saw your story in the paper."

"Then, can you tell us what she looked like?" Tish asks.

"Thirtyish, maybe?" he says. "Dark brown hair, super athletic. Pretty, too. Not like she could be on the cover of a magazine, but definitely easy on the eyes."

"Anything else – height, weight, build?"

"Medium everything?" He lets out a nervous chuckle. "Sorry, I'm no good at this."

"It's okay," Tish says. "When did you meet her?"

"It would've been sometime in February or March," he says. "I was out in the canyon, finishing up my field work for the lynx study. I'd made camp at this old miner's shack way out in the backcountry, and she just showed up one day. Snowshoed in, which surprised me because that cabin's pretty far up the canyon. No one but hunters ever gets that far, and most of the time not even them. But she said she was snowshoeing through, so I invited her in for a cup of tea. That's when she told me about this piece of land she was scouting out."

"Did she say where it was located?" Tish asks.

"Not that I remember," he says. "I wish to hell I'd asked."

"What about the company that bought it out – could it have been called FEC Corp?"

"Maybe," he says. "I mean, that sounds sort of right, but I wasn't paying that close attention. All I know for sure is she said they bought up an old mining claim in Elkhorn Canyon and now they were offering people shares."

"Shares?" Chuck says.

"That's what she said. Shares."

"Did she offer you any?" Gemma asks.

"No, it wasn't like that," he says. "It was more like she was thinking of buying in. She kept asking, did I think she should buy a share? Like, would that be a smart move?"

"What'd you tell her?" Tish asks.

"I told her I had no idea," he says. "But I do remember saying that if it depended on the ski resort going in, maybe it wasn't so smart. I'd spent a winter out there by then and I was pretty sure the lynx was still resident in the canyon. I never got any direct sightings, none I'm certain of, anyway, but I had scat and fur samples and footprints."

"Wait a minute," Chuck says, looking up from his notepad. "You had evidence the lynx was still in the canyon?"

"Chuck, this part is all embargoed," Tish tells him. "Perry has Open Records requests in to confirm it independently."

Gemma turns on Perry. "You *knew* about this?"

"I told Tish," he stammers. "Rick wouldn't let me use anything he said. He told me he'd deny it if I tried to print it."

"Guys, guys, let's not get sidetracked," Tish says. "We can come back to this, but let's focus on the story in front of us."

"They've deep-sixed all that, anyway," Rick says. "You'll never get your hands on any of it. But I didn't know that then. I had the evidence and I figured once it got out, the state would refuse to sign off on the ski resort."

"And that's what you told her?" Tish says.

"Well, no," he says. "I'm pretty careful about discussing my data before it's published, but I gave her the general gist. And you know what she said? She said, 'What if you're wrong? What if you go back to your data and you realize what you're really looking at is a bobcat?'"

"She wanted you to fake your data," Gemma says.

"No. I mean, we were just sitting outside my little shack drinking tea," he says. "She asked me some more questions about my field work and thanked me. Honestly, I came away thinking I'd saved her a big whack of money. Now, after seeing your story, I'm not so sure."

"And she never offered you any money?" Chuck asks.

"No, no, nothing like that," he says. "We just talked, and then she took off. In retrospect, she did seem awful interested in my lynx study. But a lot of people are. It's interesting stuff."

The reporters take him through the story again, trying to draw out fresh details. Did she say where she lived? The company that bought the mining claim, did she ever say where it was based? Did she mention the names of anyone who worked there? But Rick is getting tired and they learn nothing new. Finally, Perry, who has barely said a word since they sat down, offers to walk Rick back to his car.

"Can I ask you one last question?" Tish says. "Now that you know there's private land near the resort that can be developed, would you consider going on the record about the lynx study?"

Rick looks up at her. "I hear you've been poking around, seeing if anybody else will talk."

"I made a few calls," Tish admits. "Got me nowhere."

"You're not going to get anywhere, either," he says. "Benton and them, they're circling the wagons. If I spoke up now, they'd trash me, say I was disgruntled and crazy and I'm just changing my story because of the controversy."

"What about your notebooks?" Gemma says. "Wouldn't they'd back you up?"

"I don't have any of that stuff anymore, and I don't know where it is," he says.

"What happened to it?" Tish asks.

"I don't know," he says. "You'd have to ask them. But without it, I can tell you there's no case for me to make. Like I told Perry here, a lot of what I found was from bobcats. If you don't have all the evidence – the footprint photos, some of the hair and scat I found – you could argue it's *all* bobcat. Which is exactly what they did."

"But you believe the lynx is up there," Gemma says. "You're sure of that."

"Oh yeah," he says. "I'd stake my reputation on it. I *did* stake my reputation on it, until these bastards hijacked my work."

"What if we find out who's behind the FEC Corp?" Tish asks. "Would that change your mind about going on the record?"

"Look, I'm not going to say no," he says. "But I've got to be honest: As much as I admire what you guys are doing, I could light my whole career on fire here and they'd still get this thing built. And I've got a family to support."

After Rick leaves, plodding down the dingy hall at Perry's side, Tish, Gemma, and Chuck flip through their notes, trying to make sense of what they've heard. Gemma's the first to speak.

"Guys, this is *way* bigger than our original story," she says. "This isn't just some random rich guy cashing in on the new resort. They were selling shares in this thing, and they were using the shares to bribe people."

"Whoa, whoa, slow down," Tish says. "We can't even be sure this is the same piece of land. She never mentioned FEC Corp or the Friends of Elkhorn Canyon."

"He said it *could* be FEC Corp," Gemma says. "He said that sounded right."

"He said he couldn't be sure," Tish reminds her. "This is an anonymous source. If he isn't one-hundred-percent sure, we can't use it."

"It's a property in Elkhorn Canyon that depends on the new ski resort getting approved," Gemma says. "How many of those can there be? And come on, she was trying to get him to take a bribe. That's what all that was about."

"Again, that's supposition," Tish says. "We need facts, Gemma. Hard, reported facts."

"How would it even work – the shares, I mean?" Chuck asks.

"My guess is it's like a limited stock company," Tish says. "Ownership is divided among a limited number of shares, but they're circulated privately, not on any regular stock exchange."

"It's such a perfect way to bribe someone," Gemma says. "You give them a share in land that's worth nothing unless the ski resort is approved – and then it's worth millions."

But Tish is already there, sifting through the implications of what

Rick has told them. And once again the first place her mind goes is Stan Bucholtz. His family goes back three generations in Franklin. His forebears were ranchers, not miners, but he would know about the abandoned mining claims that dot the forests of the Franklin Valley. And he has a subtle mind, devious and perfectly ruthless. If anyone is bribing public officials through shares in a private land company, she thinks, Stan Bucholtz has a hand in it. So does Sheldon Dunow. And Cory Carr.

"We need to get this in the paper, like tomorrow," Gemma says.

"Well, we can't," Tish says. "Not until we have some hard evidence."

"Gem's right, you know they're covering their tracks as we speak," Chuck says. "The longer we wait, the deeper they'll bury them."

Gem. Even with all the other thoughts humming through her brain, Tish notes the contraction of Gemma's name. She'd had the sense that Chuck struck out the night of the airport attack, but maybe not. Maybe he's still up there swinging.

"I'm not arguing with you," she says. "But for now all we have is an anonymous source who says he met a woman who asked him about buying a mining claim. We don't know who she is, we don't know who she works for, we can't even say for sure she was talking about FEC Corp."

Tish grabs her notepad and stands. She's finally out from under her loan from Franklin Savings, but the deep cut in FrankCo ads has the paper in crisis again. She has a long day ahead of her of phone calls to vendors and advertisers looking for an exit ramp. But she feels the tingle in her fingertips she gets when she knows she's going to nail down a major story.

"One way or another, we've got to get this in the paper," she tells the two reporters. "This is priority one. Cover your beats, do your job, but from now on this is the only story that matters."

◆ ◆ ◆

By the time Chuck gets to the courthouse, the Planning & Zoning Commission meeting is half over, and Dana Tieg, still smarting from his big scoop, isn't about to let him copy her notes. After the meeting, Chuck makes the rounds of the courthouse angling for a follow-up to the FEC Corp story, but in the end, he and Gemma have to settle for a rambling piece filled with quotes from locals saying what they think of what the *Flyer* has already reported. This is glorified water-cooler gossip, but it's all they've got for a lead story until a little before five when, with the newsroom jamming against deadline, Chuck gets a call from Troy Martin in the assessor's office.

"You might want to get down here," Troy tells him. "The county commission's official schedule for January just went out."

Chuck laughs. "Let me guess. They're putting off hearings on the resort until the spring."

"Think again, man," Troy says. "The first hearing's set for January 4."

"No way, they're sticking to the original schedule? Even after our FEC Corp piece?"

"I guess they want to jam it through before you guys can dig up any more dirt. The pricks."

When she hears what Chuck has learned, Tish rips up the front page and they're all stuck in the office until midnight reporting on the reignited furor over the Elkhorn Canyon vote.

The next morning Tish joins Scott for a few leisurely runs on Mount Boyd, but by early afternoon she's back in the office with Chuck and Gemma trying to track down the "Juliet" Rick Sheffield met in Elkhorn Canyon and combing through the *Flyer* morgue for suspicious transactions buried in the legal notices.

It's dark by the time she locks up the office and sets off for Scott's condo. It has been snowing on and off all day and there's five inches of fresh powder on the ground. Between the battle over her credit line and the FEC Corp story, Tish has almost forgotten about Christmas, but Franklin hasn't. In a ski town, the weeks before and after Christmas are the highest of high seasons, when, in a good year, every hotel is full, every vacation home is occupied, every restaurant is booked from open to close, and every local is working double shifts to make up for the slack months in spring and fall. This *isn't* a good year. Thanks to Jack Frost, hotel occupancy is down thirty percent, and skier numbers on Mount Boyd are worse. Tonight, though, one week to the day before Christmas, Mountain Avenue is strung from end to end with tinsel and blinking lights and the sidewalks are packed with giddy tourists laden down with shopping bags.

Locals are forever bitching about Christmas Week. Tish herself bitches about it. The long hours. The endless lift lines. The loud Texans everywhere. The impossibility of getting a reservation in a restaurant any time in the last two weeks of December. But the fact is, she thinks as she passes a middle-aged couple in cowboy boots and matching silver chinchilla coats, she lives for this. It's not just that the *Flyer*, even with the loss of the FrankCo ads, is six pages thicker than it will be at any other time of year. It's that Franklin, this sleepy mountain town she's come to call home, is for once alive, vital, pulsing with energy. It's that for two weeks in the dead of winter the world sees the heart-stopping beauty she sees all year.

The next morning, bright and early, she's back in the office with Chuck and Gemma, bashing her head against the brick wall of the FEC Corp ownership structure. All day they work, and all day they get nowhere. Late that evening, with the Monday paper only half-written, Tish springs for takeout from Mountain Hunan: Kung Pao chicken and sweet & sour pork for her, Chuck, and Lydia, and vegan-friendly cashew broccoli with rice for Gemma. They're finishing their meal, splitting a plate of Scott's chocolate-chip cookies, when the phone rings.

"Hey babe, the cookies were a big hit," Tish says, keeping her voice low. "I'm going to be here a little while longer, I'm afraid. I hope you're not too lonely at home all by yourself."

"I'm not lonely," says a familiar robotic voice. "But thank you for asking."

Tish hits the button that puts the call on speaker and snaps her fingers, waving Chuck and Gemma over. "Is this who I think it is?" she asks.

"It is," says the robo-voice. "I'm calling to let you know that I warned the Franklin Skiing Company that it shouldn't run its lifts tomorrow morning."

"Why not?"

"You know why not," the voice says. "We've slipped another screw-driver into the gears."

"On the lifts? Thousands of people ride those things. Somebody could get killed."

"Not if you warn them to stay away."

"You say you've already told FrankCo what you've done?"

"The last time we spoke, I told you we liberated the explosive for the action at the West Fork Power Station from the Myrtle Creek Quarry in Roseburg, Oregon. You reported that the quarry was in Oregon, but not its name or where it's located. That was very thoughtful of you."

"Wait, when you say you're going to – "

But the hum of the disconnected line is already buzzing in her ears.

"That was him, wasn't it?" Lydia asks, poking her head in from layout.

Before Tish can answer, her eyes find the small black tape recorder the FBI installed next to her phone after the attacks the month before. She was supposed to switch it on if she received a suspicious call, but it all happened so quickly and without warning.

"Okay, this changes everything," she says, recovering. "Chuck, I want you to start writing up an account of the phone call. Gemma, start calling around, see if you can get reactions from local pols – Cory Carr, City Council, local skiers, whoever."

"Where are you going?" Chuck asks.

"To call the FBI," she says, heading for her business office.

When Tish reaches the FBI's Jack Frost tipline, the young agent who takes her call patches her through directly to the bureau's local headquarters.

"This is Monkiewicz," comes the voice on the line. "Don't tell me you got a call, too."

"Agent Monkiewicz," she says, surprised. "I didn't realize you were in town."

"I just flew in this morning," he says. "With Christmas coming up, we've been expecting something like this. So, talk to me. Did you get a recording?"

"No, I'm really sorry, it happened so fast. I didn't even think of it until he'd hung up."

"No problem," he says, disappointed. "We have a trap and trace on your phone, so we'll know where the call originated."

"You've got to figure he's calling from a pay phone."

"Right, but at least we'll know which one. And who knows, maybe we'll lift a print off the handset. Now, tell me what he said. Start from the beginning and don't leave anything out."

Tish takes him through her conversation with Jack Frost, line by line. It doesn't take long. She was on the phone with the eco-terrorist less than a minute.

"I'm going to need you to work with us on this one, Ms. Threadgill," Monkiewicz says. "It's imperative that we don't overreact to this latest provocation."

"All due respect, Agent Monkiewicz, we've been over this," she says. "I run a newspaper and my first responsibility is to my readers. These guys are threatening to take out a chairlift. We could be looking at hundreds of people getting injured or killed. I have a duty to report that."

"I understand that. I do." He stops himself, regroups. "Do you mind if I call you Tish?"

"Sure. If I can call you Monk."

"Please do. It's actually the name most people use. So, Tish, the thing you need to understand is that we've had a month to plan for this. The bureau has put some of its top behavioral analysts on this and tonight fits perfectly with what they predicted this organization would do: Call in a threat to a media outlet so we'll shut down the mountain and force the ski company to endure another round of punishing publicity."

"Okay, but this isn't like the airport," she says. "They've already shown they can disable a chairlift. You've seen the pictures of all those lift chairs in the snow."

"They didn't call that action in," Monkiewicz says. "They didn't call in the two earlier bombings, either. The only time these guys called in an attack in advance, it didn't happen."

"So, what, you want me to do nothing?" she asks. "Just sit on the story and hope nobody gets killed on the mountain tomorrow?"

The line goes silent. Clearly, this phone call isn't going how Monkiewicz had planned.

"I have an idea," he says. "Why don't you come in and talk with us in person? I brought one of our behavioral specialists with me. She'll definitely want to talk with you, and I think you'll enjoy talking with her. It'll have to be off the record, but we can do a full debrief on the phone call and you can see a little of what we're seeing."

"No way, you're inviting me, not the other way around," Tish says. "Either we're on the record or I stay here and put out a story on the AP wire about a phone call from an eco-terrorist threatening to take out a chairlift on Mount Boyd."

"Okay, okay," he says, relenting. "I hope you'll see why we need to keep a lid on this, but I don't have a lot of leverage here. We've set up a command center at the ski company office in town. I'll meet you there in ten minutes."

After she hangs up, Tish heads back to the newsroom, where she finds Chuck, alone, typing up the story on the Jack Frost phone call.

"What'd the cops say?" he asks, looking up from his monitor.

"I don't know," she says, a little shell-shocked. "I don't think they believe this is real."

"They don't – Tish, I heard him," Chuck says. "You did, too. That was Jack Frost."

"No, I mean, they don't think the threat is real," she says. "They think Jack Frost is using us to do his work for him."

Chuck blinks several times behind his thick glasses. "Oh, wow. That's just … wow."

"Where's Gemma?" she asks.

Chuck's gaze follows Tish's to Gemma's chair, as if he, too, is surprised to find it empty. "She said she needed to talk with a source," he says.

"They couldn't do it by phone?"

"I guess not. Honestly, I wasn't paying a lot – so, what're you going to do?"

"I don't know," she admits. "He asked me to meet him at the ski company. He's brought some behavioral analyst he wants me to meet."

"What about the Jack Frost story? Lydia's already ripped up the front page."

Tish checks her watch. It's five minutes past eight. The press-room guys won't come for the proof sheets until three a.m. In a pinch, they could come an hour later and still get the first editions on the street by dawn, but that's not a deadline she's particularly keen to push.

"Keep working," she says. "Plan A is we run the Jack Frost call tomorrow. If this behavioral analyst chick changes my mind, I'll let you know."

At eight o'clock on a Sunday night, the lobby of the three-story brick building at the base of the ski hill that serves as FrankCo's local headquarters is empty except for three security guards in sky-blue company fleeces. They aren't local, so far as Tish can tell, and they insist on seeing her driver's license before one of them escorts her up a set of stairs and down a long hallway, where Art Monkiewicz is waiting for her, his deep-set eyes radiating their usual mix of fatigue and beat-cop intensity. He ushers her into a large, brightly lit command center crowded with people, nearly all of them men, some arguing in noisy clusters, others monitoring banks of closed-circuit TV screens. The place writhes with an anxious male energy verging on panic that puts Tish in mind of an anthill under attack from a hungry anteater. But before she can get her bearings, Monkiewicz leads her down a short hallway into a cramped office, where a young woman sits behind a desk making notes on a yellow legal pad.

"You must be Patricia," she says, turning over the notepad. "I'm Ruth Mariucci."

The FBI analyst is about thirty, petite and fine-boned, with a dimpled smile and curly russet hair gathered in a no-nonsense ponytail. One look and Tish knows Ruth Mariucci spends ten minutes in front of the mirror each morning figuring out how she can play down her natural beauty so the men she works with won't spend all day staring. One look back at Monkiewicz and she knows that the men she works with stare at her, anyway.

"Call me Tish," she says. "Monk here does."

Ruth glances over at Monkiewicz, flashing a brief, playful smile. That's all it takes. One flash of the dimple and she might has well have roped him with Wonder Woman's Magic Lasso.

"Please, have a seat," she says, gesturing to an empty chair. "I understand you're the one who took the call to the newspaper office tonight."

"That was me," Tish says. "I'm sorry I didn't record it."

Ruth waves this off. "That's okay. Just tell me what he said."

Ruth Mariucci, Tish quickly realizes, would make a first-rate newspaper reporter. She looks her directly in the eye and asks soft, insistent questions. More importantly, she actually listens to Tish's answers. For months now, with Sheriff Hayes, with Monkiewicz, even with Jimmy Lachlan, Tish has had the sense they were filtering what she said through their own view of the case. Here, for the first time, she's talking to a cop who hasn't already made up her mind.

"This is the second call they've made to your newspaper, am I right?" she says when Tish finishes her story.

"That's right," Tish says. "The first note after the Highline Chalet fire went to both papers, but since then they've called us twice."

"Any idea why they would single you out?"

"I don't know. I mean, our paper's been pretty squarely anti-Elkhorn Canyon. Maybe they feel we're more politically simpatico."

Ruth makes a note on her pad. "I find it interesting that the caller joked with you about being lonely," she says. "And on the earlier call, he complimented one of your reporter's work. There's a strange kind of chumminess to it, like he's trying to build a rapport."

"You think he could be someone we know, someone from around here?"

"I suppose that's possible," Ruth says. "Although it's unlikely that you actually know him. Even with the voice masking, if you had a previous relationship, he wouldn't want to risk you identifying him. But it does suggest he sees himself as your social equal, someone who *could* be your friend, if the circumstances were different."

Tish hasn't thought of it this way, but it strikes her as exactly right. Jack Frost was calling in a death threat, but his tone was cheerful and friendly, like he was inviting her over for a beer.

"We believe we're dealing with a group of white, highly educated people, most likely in their twenties or early thirties," Ruth says. "There's some uncertainty in the data over their base of operations, but what is clear is that, as a group, they could be from here. Whoever these people are, they share the prevailing ethos of this town – its politics, its concerns about the environment, its anti-establishment views."

"Which is why you don't think he's going to take out a chairlift tonight?" Tish asks.

"These are folks who have read deeply in the literature of environmental activism and nonviolent protest," Ruth says. "They are explicitly modeling themselves on Jack Frost, the hero of Bill Blanning's novel. No one gets hurt in that book, ever. Jack Frost wins his battles by making fools of his enemies. By tricking them into defeating themselves."

"Okay, but what if they're getting tired of playing by their own rules?" Tish asks. "Or if one of their members decides to go rogue?"

"If they wanted to take out one of those lifts, they'd just do it," Monkiewicz cuts in. "But then they'd actually have to do it – and you saw that room back there. As I say, we've been gaming this out for weeks. There's surveillance all over that mountain and the ski company's got people checking and re-checking every piece of equipment. Even if the activists were able to sabotage a chairlift, security would pick it up long before the mountain opens."

"This way they achieve the same end, just with a phone call," Ruth says. "You put out the word to the AP and it makes the eleven o'clock news in every city west of the Mississippi."

Tish eyes the two FBI agents, the dumpy ex-DC beat cop and the soft-spoken, be-dimpled criminal profiler. "I'm guessing the ski company is pushing very, very hard to avoid another shutdown," she says.

"Mr. Dunow has made his views known," Monkiewicz admits. "But that's not why we're making this call. This is coming from Quantico, from the work they're doing there."

"Can I ask?" Tish says, turning back to Ruth. "You said there's some dispute in the data about where they're from. Are you saying the activists might not be from Oregon, after all?"

Ruth's eyes find Monkiewicz's. Whatever her question is, his unsmiling expression says, the answer is no.

"As I'm sure you know, our work here is extremely delicate," she says. "Agent Monkiewicz and I have tried to be as candid with you as we can, because, to be frank, we need you on our side tonight. But the more of what we say that shows up in print, the harder it's going to be for us to catch these guys."

"On background, then," Tish says. "Are you looking at this now as a locally run operation?"

"I think I've already said enough," Ruth says. "But you're an intelligent person, Tish. Ask yourself: Why now? Why tonight? Yes, it's Christmas Week. Yes, the mountain's crowded. But what else is going on right now? What else might have set these folks off?"

"You think they're reacting to the county's decision to go ahead with the Elkhorn Canyon vote," Tish says. "That hasn't hit the wires yet, so you think they're here in town, responding to local events."

"Ruth's right, we've said enough already," Monkiewicz says. "You're here tonight because we didn't want to see your newspaper turned into a weapon in these guys' arsenal. But you have to understand: They're reading everything you write. If you report what you've seen and heard here, that helps them. It helps them a great deal."

Tish holds out a little longer, but in the end she agrees to keep the Jack Frost phone call out of Monday's paper in exchange for an exclusive story on the investigation after the Jack Frost gang is arrested. But on the walk back to the *Flyer* office, all she can think about is what Ruth said about why Jack Frost chose tonight to call. The FBI profilers must have heard that the county was proceeding with the Elkhorn Canyon vote, and put her and Monkiewicz on the first plane to Colorado. And then just as they'd predicted, Jack Frost called in a threat.

They're reading everything you write, Monkiewicz had told her. Which means, wherever the Jack Frost gang originally came from, wherever they might have bought or stole the components for their bombs, some of them are in Franklin following the news in the local papers. And not just any local paper, but the *Flyer* in particular. Twice now, Jack Frost has called the *Flyer*, and as far as Tish knows *only* the *Flyer*, speaking to Gemma the first time and the second time to her. When she gets back she needs to talk with Gemma again about what the caller said to her – except, she recalls, Gemma is out tracking down a source. The thought pulls Tish up short half a block from the *Flyer* building. What source could be so important that a reporter would leave the newsroom just as a major news story is breaking? Why didn't she tell anyone where she was going? And where the hell is she now?

At that very moment, Gemma is tramping through foot-deep snow-drifts in a vacant campground south of town known as The Tipis. She had ridden her mountain bike to the point where the county snowplows turned around, about a mile from the city line, then ditched the bike in some bushes and walked the last quarter mile past a pair of snow-covered horse barns and a ramshackle trailer court, home to several dozen Mexican families who work off the books in Franklin's restaurants and hotels.

She's not supposed to know Terry camps out here, but she followed him home one morning after he'd spent the night at her mother's not long before the airport action. As soon as she saw where he was heading, she realized how perfect it was. In Franklin's earliest days, Ute Indians erected their tipis on the land in the summer months while they hunted and fished in the creeks that ribbon the narrow valley south of town. A century later, the site of their ancient village has become an unlicensed campground popular with locals willing to spend the summer in a tent to avoid paying rent in town. The family that owns the property has tried for years to build tourist cabins there, and for years the county has denied them permits to construct anything more permanent than a fire ring. So every fall, when the weather turns, the campground empties out and the remote, wooded meadow reverts to snowbound wilderness.

Now, on a Sunday night deep in December, the campground is desolate and still, the only sound the muffled gurgling of the Franklin River at the far end of the meadow. Surveying the snow-blanketed meadow by the weak light of her bike lamp, Gemma worries, not for the first time, that Terry isn't here. Once, when he was living with her that summer, he'd pointed out a graceless Swiss-chalet-style mansion eight driveways down from her mother's house and told her he'd crashed there for two weeks in April, bedding down in the basement and eating through the canned goods in the pantry. But it's Christmas Week now, so empty homes are going to be hard to find, even on Rodeo Road. Sure enough, halfway into the clearing, Gemma spots snowshoe tracks leading toward the river, where a silver-and-white tent hides behind a grove of blue spruce trees a few yards from the river's edge. The tent is dark, with snow piled in drifts around the sides, except at the front where boot prints have cleared a narrow path to the tent's entrance.

"Terry?" she calls. "Terry, you in there?"

Nothing, just the gurgling water and a faint echo of her own words through the trees. She's covered in snow, her feet are freezing in her faux-leather boots, and every atom in her body screams to head back to the warmth and safety of the *Flyer* newsroom, where she knows Chuck and Tish must be wondering where she is. But she forces herself to kneel down and unzip the outer rainfly.

In one corner of the cramped two-man tent, she sees Terry's backpack set atop his winter sleeping bag. In another corner sits his "kitchen": a single-burner propane stove, saucepan, plate, cup, and spork, along with a stack of military-style MREs. Terry never talks about his military service, but she knows he fought in Desert Storm. Before that, she gathers he was Special Forces, posted somewhere remote and cold – Scandinavia, maybe, or northern Asia. During the weeks he lived at her mother's house, when he wasn't sharing Gemma's bed, he slept in the maid's room, his belongings laid out neatly on the floor, almost exactly as they are here. If a wolf could shop at a Army-Navy Surplus store, Gemma thinks, this is what his den would look like.

But as she angles her bike lamp around the tent's interior, she spots what she missed at first glance: a sky-blue parka and black snowpants wrapped in plastic atop the sleeping bag. Bending down for a closer look, she sees a FrankCo I.D. badge bearing the name Richard Cutler below a blurry photo of Terry on a lanyard around the neck of the parka. On the floor of the tent beside the snowsuit sits a red-and-black Sawzall electric saw.

She hears boot stamps in the snow behind her. Scrambling out from the tent, she searches the dark woods for someplace to hide, but it's too late. Her own boot tracks lead straight here. She's zipping the tent closed when the boot stamps stop and a flashlight beam finds her.

"Terry, it's okay," she says. "It's just me."

"Gemma?" he says, stunned.

He's standing at the edge of the clearing in his broad snowshoes, a flashlight in one hand, an unsheathed hunting knife in the other. She can't see his face, but she doesn't need night-vision goggles to know he's not smiling.

"How did you find – ?" He stops himself. "Fuck it. Who cares how you found me. Gemma, this is crazy. This is the kind of thing that gets people caught."

"What *I'm* doing is crazy?" she fires back. "How about showing up at a heavily guarded ski resort with a Sawzall in your pack?"

"Hey, it's not as crazy as you think," he says. "I've been up on the mountain the last three nights – just walked out of the woods onto a ski run. There's so many people working up there they have no idea who's who."

This silences her. Terry's audacity frightens her, but, deep down, it thrills her, too. Which frightens her even more. She believes in the cause, she wants to see FrankCo stopped and the lynx saved, but she also knows she will follow this man essentially anywhere.

"This isn't part of the plan, Terry," she says.

"You don't know the plan," he says. "You never did. That wasn't your role."

"Whatever it is, I know it doesn't involve hurting anyone. You must have told me that a thousand times, that nobody would get hurt."

"Nobody's going to get hurt. I called the company and your boss at the newspaper. They'll shut down the mountain. It'll cost the Dunows millions, but nobody's getting hurt."

"What if they don't shut it down?" Gemma asks. "You burned them with that airport thing. They might decide you're bluffing this time."

"Oh, they'll find it in the morning before the mountain opens," he says. "This won't be like the last time. That Sawzall makes a huge gash in the metal. It'll be pretty hard to miss."

"What if they don't see it?" she says. "What if they miss it and somebody gets hurt? What if somebody gets killed?"

"Well then," he says, "I guess some things are out of our control."

All that spring and summer, while they were sharing her bed and he was unfurling his plans, Terry had read her his favorite passages from *A Screwdriver in the Gears*. How the Jack Frost gang had removed all the furniture from Boss Burroughs' house before they torched it. How they'd decided against blowing a railroad bridge because someone might try to cross it after it fell. How, over and over, they disabled vehicles and forest-killing machinery without ever putting a single living thing in danger.

"Please don't do this," she says. "We're winning. We're so close now."

"Bullshit," he says. "The county's holding its hearings right on schedule. Nothing's changed. They're just going to bull right through."

"You don't know," she says. "You don't know what we've been working on. We found a source who told us about the owners of that piece of land in Elkhorn Canyon. They split it up into shares and used the shares to bribe people."

He stares at her in the dark. "They used it for bribes?"

"That's what we think. We've got – "

"That's what you *think*?"

"Terry, listen, we talked to a source," she says. "I was there, I heard him, but he's not ready to go on the record. We'll get there, though. It might take a couple weeks, but we'll get the story. But if you do this tonight, none of it will matter."

Gemma has no idea if this is true. She has no idea what would or would not happen if Terry Albrecht hurts or kills someone on Mount Boyd. All that matters is that he's listening to her.

"You think you can get this story?" he says.

"I know we can get it."

"When?"

"I don't know exactly, but it won't be long. We're really close."

"The first hearing is January 4, Gemma. That's two weeks away."

"We'll get it before then, I promise," she says. "But you have to stand down. You have to stay home tonight, or we'll lose everything we've worked for."

Terry trains the flashlight on her, searching for signs of deception. At last he lets it fall to his side. "All right," he says. "But I'm not waiting forever. You don't know the whole story, Gemma. You think you do, but you don't."

"What're you talking about?" she asks. "What story?"

"The Jack Frost story," he says. "There's more to it that nobody knows. Blanning pussied out and burned the whole thing before anyone could read it, but he told me the story. It doesn't end the way everybody thinks."

The ride back is treacherously slow on the iced-over roads south of town. Outside Lawton's Drugs, Gemma locks her bike to a *Daily Flyer* news box and ducks inside to warm up and plot her next move. In the rear of the store, at the end of the toothpaste aisle, she checks herself out in an anti-shoplifting mirror. Her boots and gloves, made from recycled waste products, are more or less waterproof, but her jeans are soaked through and her face and hands are burned red from the cold. There's no way she can go back to the office, not looking like this.

There's a pay phone in the back next to the public bathrooms. She buys a pack of Juicy Fruit gum to break a dollar bill and dials the number for the *Flyer's* office line.

"Newsroom," Tish says, picking up on the third ring.

"Tish, hey – it's me, Gemma."

"Hey, where are you?" Tish asks. "Chuck said you went to find a source."

"Yeah, I struck out," she says. "I've been looking everywhere. I couldn't find him."

When Tish doesn't answer right away, panic prickles up Gemma's spine: Her story makes no sense. Nothing she's doing makes any sense. She's been lying for months, lying to everyone about everything, and now when it matters most, she's losing her gift for it.

"This source," Tish says, "you want to tell me who it is?"

"I'd like to, but it's … it's kind of delicate."

"Delicate, how?"

"He's a local guy and he's worried about having the cops crawling all over him. I promised I wouldn't give out his name."

"Okay, you know what?" Tish says. "I've got a million balls in the air right now, and so do you. We can talk about this later."

Relief washes over Gemma, warm as bathwater. "Okay, cool," she says before Tish can take it back. "So, where are we with the Jack Frost call?"

"I spiked the story. We're going with the front page we had before the call came in."

"We're not running anything at all?"

"Not tonight. I got Monkiewicz to agree to give us the exclusive once Jack Frost is caught. But for now, he persuaded me the activists are using us to get at FrankCo."

Gemma thinks of Terry in his lonely tent in The Tipis with his Sawzall and his rage at the Dunows. It's just as she'd feared. If she hadn't gotten to him tonight, he might have disabled a chairlift. He might have killed somebody.

"That's probably the right call," she says. "So, what do you need from me?"

"Your pieces are done, right?" Tish asks. "The City Hall piece and the Elkhorn Canyon vote roundup you did with Chuck?"

"They're both in," Gemma says. "But I can come in to help write headlines if you want."

"Nah, why don't you call it a night?" Tish says. "It's going to be a long week. You should get some rest."

Gemma signs off, too relieved at not having to face Tish to consider why Tish might not have wanted to face her. Instead, as she unlocks her bike and points it in the direction of Rodeo Road, she thinks again of Terry and his parting words about Jack Frost. Like everyone else, Gemma knows the legend of Bill Blanning's unwritten sequel to *A Screwdriver in the Gears*. The story Blanning has told in a hundred magazine profiles is that he kept starting the second Jack Frost book but "never could get the characters to talk to each other."

But that's not the story Terry's telling now. And one thing Gemma knows for sure about Terry Albrecht is that he once knew Bill Blanning. It's been a decade at least since they last spoke, but Terry knew him, and knew him well. Maybe he knows something about the famous unwritten sequel that no one else knows.

Chapter Eleven

Tish can't sleep that night, waking again and again out of the same dream in which a small boy falls screaming to his death from a derailed chairlift. But the police scanner on her bedside table stays quiet all night, and when she calls Jimmy Lachlan the next day, he tells her the only incidents on the mountain are a snowboarder who slammed into a tree and a 68-year-old retired schoolteacher rescued outside Herbie's Hideaway after fainting from altitude sickness.

Tish is back to sleeping in her own bed for now because Scott has his daughter Melanie for the holidays. He'd wanted to introduce them, maybe even have Tish over for dinner one night, but Tish nixed the idea. Too soon, she told him. What she didn't say, what she didn't know *how* to say, is that the prospect of meeting Melanie fills her with panic. This isn't like meeting a guy's parents, which she's done a million times. This is his daughter, who could hate her. She could decide Tish isn't nice enough or pretty enough or too mean or too bossy or simply hate her for no reason at all, and that would be that. Given a choice between Melanie and Tish, Scott would pick his daughter a hundred and ten times out of a hundred. And Tish could lose the first man she's let herself care about since Doug died.

To distract herself, she focuses on filling the pages of the *Flyer* with copy and helping track down the woman Rick Sheffield met in Elkhorn Canyon last winter. The whole staff is working the story now, Moira asking sheriff's deputies if they've run across a pretty, brown-haired woman named Juliet, Perry making the rounds of outdoor outfitters to see if anyone recalls renting her snowshoeing equipment. Chuck and Gemma blow the better part of two mornings reading guest registries for the months of February and March at a dozen local hotels. But it's a needle in a haystack, and what little they have to go on – thirtyish, brown hair, athletic build, pretty, likes snowshoeing – describes half the female population of Franklin.

Tuesday morning, before everyone heads out on assignment, Tish calls Gemma into her office. The girl is looking tired, Tish thinks. Or maybe *tired* isn't the right word. Stressed. Overworked. Her mousy blonde hair is tied off in a messy ponytail and her skin is breaking out, her chin and forehead dotted with angry pimples. Tish tries to remember the last time her own face broke out, and the answer comes to her with the force of a slap: It was the week her brother died.

"I know you've got a lot going on," she says after Gemma takes a seat, "so I won't take up too much of your time."

"But you'd kind of like to know where I disappeared to Sunday night," Gemma says.

"We could start there," Tish says.

"I'd rather not use names if that's okay with you."

"Okay. I can live with that."

Already, though, Gemma is worrying a fresh pimple on her chin. She seems unaware she's doing it, as if her hand and face belong to another person, but it's mesmerizing to watch, her thumb and long forefinger pinching and rubbing the skin raw.

"So, a couple weeks ago," she says, rubbing away, "I got a call from a guy – let's just say he's someone I know from growing up here. Anyway, he told me he might have some info about Jack Frost."

"What kind of information?"

"That's the thing," she says. "He was super-vague and so many people around here say they've seen Jack Frost. He's like the Bigfoot of environmental extremists."

"But then, when the call came in the other night, you tried to contact him."

"I figured it was worth a shot, right? But when I went where he told me to go, he wasn't there. I waited almost an hour, but he never showed."

By now Gemma has popped the pimple on her chin and it's bleeding. Not much, just a trickle, but Tish reaches for a Kleenex and holds it out to Gemma.

"You're bleeding," she says, touching her own chin to show where.

"What?" Mortified, Gemma grabs the tissue and dabs it at her face. "Ew, gross."

"So, um," Tish says, trying not to stare, "have you told anyone at the FBI?"

Gemma looks up from the bloody tissue, lost. "The FBI?"

"This source of yours, have you said anything about him to the police? They might be able to use his info."

"Oh right," Gemma says. "No, I haven't. I'm not going to, either."

"Because he's a source?"

"Right. But he's more than that, really. I've known him for a long time, and he came to me because he knew I wouldn't sic the cops on him."

Tish nods. If she's telling the truth, Gemma's clearly in the right here. So far as she knows, her source has committed no crimes, and alerting the FBI would trigger weeks of surveillance and harassment. But Gemma doesn't look to Tish like someone who's telling the truth. She looks like a scared twenty-two-year-old badly out of her depth.

"These guys have done some pretty reckless things," she says. "If you have any information that could save lives, you're going to have to weigh where your responsibilities lie."

"Of course," Gemma says. "I'm not going to let these guys get away with hurting anyone."

"And look, you can't just take off like that without saying where you're going," Tish says. "You're my employee. What you do on your own time is your business, but when you're working on a story for this paper, I need to know where you are at all times. Are we clear?"

"Loud and clear. It won't happen again, I promise."

"All right then," Tish says, standing. "Let's go find this Juliet chick."

◆ ◆ ◆

But they don't. They don't find anything, and the days leading up to Christmas devolve into a frantic scramble to fill hundreds of inches of empty news columns in a city where nearly all public offices – county, city, state, federal – are closed for the holiday week. The town's awash in rumors, inaccurate in nearly every particular, of the phoned-in threat to the ski company Sunday night. Normally, Tish would throw every reporter she has at a rumor like this, but she's still bound by her agreement with Monkiewicz, and in any case she isn't eager poke the bear, for fear that news of Jack Frost's *other* call, to her newsroom, will leak out. All of which leaves her with nothing but page after page of snow reports and feel-good features about plucky locals making the most of this year's bummer of a ski season.

Christmas falls on a Saturday this year, which means that, for once, her staff doesn't have to draw straws for who will work on the holiday. Scott still has Melanie, so Tish hosts a potluck "Orphan Christmas" at her apartment for Chuck, Gemma, and Jen. Moira comes, too, bringing along a sheriff's deputy, Derek Hines, she's been dating on the down-low for the past two months, and for a few hours the six orphans drink spiked egg nog and watch *It's a Wonderful Life* and forget all about Jack Frost and the FEC Corp.

Once or twice, though, late in the evening, Tish takes her eyes off the screen and watches Gemma at the end of the too-small couch sitting between Moira's hunky cop and Chuck. She's been keeping tabs on Gemma all week, cocking an ear when she takes a phone call in the newsroom, discreetly checking Jen's log sheets of Gemma's comings and goings. She hasn't learned much. Yes, Gemma left the newsroom in the middle of a breaking story, and, yes, she's been looking a little rough around the edges since, but then she hasn't had a real day off in weeks. No wonder she's tired. In three months, this hair-chewing rich kid has gone from a grass-green intern to helping to break an enterprise story most reporters wait a lifetime to get.

Maybe, Tish thinks, watching Gemma cheer for Jimmy Stewart to win back Donna Reed, *I need to back off and trust her. Maybe I need to just let her do her job.*

So she does. Not completely, but she quits peeking at Jen's log sheets and pricking up her ears every time Gemma takes a call in the newsroom. Which is why, on Wednesday afternoon, just as she's about to crack her daily cup of blueberry Yoplait, when she overhears Gemma tell Jen she's heading out for a City Council meeting, Tish's first impulse is to let it go. After all, the Franklin City Council does hold working sessions most Wednesdays, and sometimes they go all afternoon. But that morning's paper is right there on her desk, and it only takes a second to flip to the back page where the agendas for local government meetings appear in seven-point agate.

The Franklin City Council, Tish is relieved to learn, is in fact scheduled to meet from one to five that afternoon. But then her eyes drift down few lines to the agenda items:

1-3 p.m.: Executive session – public not invited

"Well, fuck a duck," Tish says aloud, startling herself. But she's out of her chair and heading for the door before she has time to wonder where that one came from.

"I'm going to go grab some lunch," she tells Jen.

Her receptionist looks up at her, eyes wide. "You're going *out* for lunch?"

"A person can only eat so much blueberry yogurt," she says. "You want anything?"

"Thanks, I'm good," Jen says. "Don't forget, you've got Rudy Lawton at one-thirty."

"Yeah, I know," Tish says, halfway out the door.

But as soon as she's out of Jen's sight, she stops to check her watch. It's twelve-forty-five. She'd completely spaced the meeting with Rudy, which is a problem because she can't afford to blow him off. Two days ago, the pharmacist told Kendra Graves, Tish's ad manager, that he was considering taking his business across the street to the *Bully*. Which Tish knows he would never do. But what if he did? Losing the half-page Lawton's Drugs ad would be bad enough, but coming so soon after FrankCo pulled its ads, another high-profile defection might look like the start of a stampede.

Five minutes, she tells herself. *I'll see where Gemma is going, grab a bagel, and be back in time to prep for the meeting with Rudy.*

Cutting down the slush-strewn alley that runs alongside the *Flyer's* building, Tish emerges onto Union Street just in time to see Gemma cross Mountain Street, heading north. This time she says it in her head: *Well, fuck a duck.* If Gemma was really heading to City Hall, she would've turned right on Mountain toward Main. So now Tish has a choice to make. She can follow Gemma on foot or run back to get her car. Or she can forget all this "Spy vs. Spy" crap, buy her bagel, and head back to the office.

She goes for her car. It's parked behind the building in one of two spaces reserved for *Flyer* staffers and she's out onto the street in under a minute. There's only one way in or out of town, and if Gemma is driving, not walking or taking her bike, she can only be in one place: on Main Street, heading north toward Highway 22. Sure enough, pulling onto Main, Tish spots a sleek black BMW 325i two blocks ahead of her. The car belongs to Gemma's mother and the few times Gemma has driven it to work, she's had to endure endless ragging from the rest of the staff, who, like Tish, all drive second-hand beaters one blown gasket from the scrapyard. Right now, though, all that matters to Tish is that the car is black and shiny and just clean enough to stand out from the mud-splattered Jeep Wranglers and Ford F-150s on the road out of town.

She hangs back, maintaining the two-block distance, silently willing Gemma to peel off at the Valley View Shopping Center. But she doesn't. She passes the mini-mall and then the airport itself, and opens up the

Beamer's finely tuned German engine for the long straightaway. Tish considers peeling off herself. It's nearly one now, and if she's going to make it back in time to meet with Rudy Lawton, she only has a few minutes before she needs to turn around. But she keeps driving, maintaining a safe two hundred yards between herself and the black Beamer, as the minutes tick past.

Fifteen agonizing miles later, Tish is looking for a spot to turn around, racking her brain for good reasons why she might have been held up on her bagel run, when she sees the BMW slow down and ease into the exit lane for County Road 4 into Gilburne Canyon.

Tish slows, too, pulling into the parking lot for the Gilburne Saloon as the BMW disappears over a slight rise into the canyon. At last she understands where Gemma is going. Gilburne Canyon is true cattle country. Aside from a sprinkling of B-list actors and rock musicians, the only people living on County Road 4 are ranchers who want nothing to do with the resort and its intrigues. Gemma isn't going to meet any of them. She's going to see Bill Blanning, the creator of Jack Frost.

Half a mile past the Gilburne Saloon, Gemma flashes on a memory of driving this same road with her beloved Irish nanny, Dierdre, on the way to horseback-riding lessons at a dude ranch at the far eastern end of the canyon. She was just seven or eight, and she can't say for sure if she's been back since. Gemma's parents divorced when she was three and she and her mother bounced between Chicago, Santa Barbara, and Curaçao before settling in Franklin when Gemma started first grade. For eight years, until she went East for prep school, Franklin was ski lessons in winter and dirt bike races on Rodeo Road in summer. Not Gilburne Canyon. Not cattle barns and branding sheds. She's twenty minutes from her childhood home, but for all she knows about the place, she could be driving through Outer Mongolia.

But even she knows how to find Bill Blanning's driveway, with its famous warning signs and its even more famously unlocked front gate.

When she called the night before, she'd introduced herself not as a reporter for the *Daily Flyer*, but as Victoria Seagraves' daughter. As far back as she can remember, whenever Bill Blanning's name came up, and sometimes when it didn't, Gemma's mother has gleefully recounted the torrid fling she had with the author in the 1970s. Her mother tells a lot of stories, not all of them true, but this one Gemma believes. Her mother has always been a relentless starfucker, and from what Gemma has heard of Blanning, Vicky Seagraves circa 1975 sounds like she was just his type: beautiful, wild, and forever flying on one illicit substance or another.

Gemma scans the bleak snowfields on either side of Blanning's driveway for the Rottweilers she's heard so much about, but nothing stirs until she's parked next to his battered blue Ford pickup, and even then it's just Blanning, in faded jeans and a red-checked lumberman's jacket. The dogs, she sees, are lined up in the window, their wet noses pressed to the glass, watching.

"I was expecting someone, you know, a bit younger," he says when he shakes her hand.

"Younger – why?" she says.

"Well, your mom and me – if she's the one I'm thinking of – that wasn't until '75 or '76."

Gemma had dropped her mother's name to disarm him, to signal that she comes in peace, but now, too late, she realizes how it must have sounded to Blanning.

"Oh God, I'm sorry," she says. "Is that why you think I'm here?"

"It's not?"

"No, my dad's in Chicago," she says. "I don't see much of him, but he's definitely my dad. I have his blonde hair and green eyes. That's not why I'm here."

"Why are you here, then?"

"I want to talk with you about Terry Albrecht."

For the briefest moment, the cocksure grin dies on Blanning's lips. Then, just as quickly, his hooded eyes narrow. "What is this? Are you some kind of cop?"

"No, I'm a reporter with the *Flyer*," she says. "But I have no intention of writing about this. I'm a friend of Terry's, and I'm trying to stop him from doing something stupid. And I think you know what I'm talking about."

He stares her down, his thoughts almost audibly whirring and clicking. He *does* know what she's talking about, that much is clear. The question is what he's going to do about it. She has all but outed herself as a member of the activist cell terrorizing the Franklin Valley, and one word from him and the police could put her and Terry, and possibly three or four others, behind bars. But she can see he's curious. It's there in his narrow, sun-battered face. In three long months, no one else has said the name Terry Albrecht.

"Five minutes," he says, jerking his thumb in the direction of the door.

The four dogs pile into the doorway, whining and mewling, but Blanning scatters them with a brisk wave of his hand. This is Gemma's first time in Blanning's home, and like Moira before her, she's struck by how civilized it looks. A bottle of Wild Turkey and some unwashed water glasses sit on a side table and a stack of papers have been tossed across the floor, but otherwise the place is spotless, every corner swept, every book in its place on the shelves. The front room has a staged quality, as if she's stumbled into a museum dedicated to a long-dead writer and any minute now a matronly docent will appear to tell her where the great man wrote his books.

"Want something to drink?" he says.

This isn't a question and he doesn't wait for an answer, just heads for the side table, the dogs trailing after him like four worried ducklings, and pours out a generous shot of Wild Turkey.

"You knew about Terry from the start, didn't you?" Gemma says.

He downs the whiskey in a single gulp like medicine and refills the glass, eyeing her.

"Look, nobody knows I'm here," she says. "Trust me, the last thing I want to do is put any of this in the newspaper. I'm deeper into this than you'll ever be."

"No, I didn't know, not at first," Blanning says at last. "I hadn't seen him since he was a kid. Last I heard he was in the Army, killing A-rabs. So I figured it was what the cops said, this outfit out of Oregon, the Mother's Little Helpers or whatever they call themselves."

"But then?"

"Then he burnt up that restaurant and set all the furniture out on the lawn."

"And he got that story from you?"

"I told it to him right on that sofa there," he says. "I read it to him – like a bedtime story, you know? Terry loved all my Jack Frost stories, but that one, he couldn't get enough of it. So when I heard about that restaurant going up, I knew. It was like he was talking to me, telling me a joke."

"I'm guessing the cops have been by here dozens of times since then."

"Yeah, I keep waiting for those bozos to put two and two together," he says. "I mean, everything that kid knows about Elkhorn Canyon, I taught it to him. And it's not like I'm the only one who knows he was coming around here. But so far nobody's breathed a word. You know why? People out here want Terry to win. They're like me, too lazy and broke-dick to do it themselves, but they're glad somebody's doing it."

"I want to help Terry, too," Gemma says. "I'm worried about him. The last time I saw him, he told me about another Jack Frost story, one nobody knows about."

"I see," he says, setting down his glass.

"You know what I'm talking about, don't you?"

"What'd he tell you about this story nobody else knows about?"

"Not much," she says. "Just that you burnt it before anyone could read it and it doesn't end the way everybody thinks."

"You know what?" he says. "It's been swell visiting with you, Ms. Daughter-of-Vicky-Seagraves, but I think your five minutes are up."

"Mr. Blanning, please, I need your help," she says. "When I saw him, Terry was talking about taking down a chairlift and it didn't sound like he cared if anyone got hurt."

"So, you can use a fucking telephone. Call the cops, turn him in."

"You know I can't do that. I'd spend the next ten years in prison, and so would a lot of other good people."

"What makes you so sure *I* won't drop a dime on you?"

"If you were going to call the FBI, you'd have done it months ago. Tell me about this other story. Is this the second book? Is that what he's talking about?"

"He was just a little kid," Blanning says. "Nine, ten years old. How was I supposed to know he'd commit the thing to memory? It was a story – just a stupid story. I had the good sense to burn it in the sink before anyone could publish it."

"Okay, but why? Why'd you have to throw it out?"

"Aw, hell. You're too young to understand."

"Try me."

He picks up the shotglass, and sets it back down again. "There was this moment," he says, "this one, brief moment, before Watergate, before the oil embargo, when it felt like we were winning. We got the EPA. We got the Clean Air Act and the Clean Water Act. They were opening up wilderness areas right and left. There was just this momentum, and it felt like maybe America was finally coming to its senses. That's why I wrote *Screwdriver* in the first place, to keep the ball rolling."

Gemma is quiet now, letting him talk.

"And I don't know, it's hard to explain," he says, "but some part of me always thought if you stopped Boss Burroughs, if you showed the world what a shitheel he was, you could save the forests, you could save pristine valleys like this one. But I was wrong. Boss Burroughs isn't the problem. The problem's everybody else. The problem is *us*. So one day I wrote a scene where Jack Frost sets off a bomb under a Jeep and it blows a guy's leg off."

She closes her eyes, seeing it all now. This is the story Terry is carrying with him, the one no one else knows about: Violence makes sense. Violence works.

"I was just so damn angry," Blanning says. "We'd done everything right. Marched in the streets, signed petitions, gotten laws passed. We played by the rules, and it didn't change a damn thing. So a few pages later, I had Jack set off another bomb under a guard shack at the lumber camp, and this time it kills six people."

"Six people?" Gemma says.

"I know, I know," he says. "It stopped the book in its tracks. I mean, it wasn't only that. There were other things. But I didn't know where to go next. I still don't."

"But you told Terry that story," she says.

"Sure, I told him," he says. "I told him all my stories. I loved that kid."

"Well, he never forgot it," she says. "The last time I saw him, he had a FrankCo uniform and a Sawzall. I didn't see any explosives, but that doesn't mean he doesn't have any."

"So, what do want me to do about it?"

"I want you to go see him," she says. "He's staying at The Tipis, south of town. He camps out there, along the river."

"The Tipis, huh?" Blanning says with a chuckle. "That takes some balls this time of year."

"At the paper, we're working on a story that could blow the plans for the new resort out of the water, but it's going to take some time," she says. "That's why I'm here. I need you to talk to him, tell him to hold off until we can get that story into the paper."

"What makes you think he's going to listen to me?"

"He looks up to you, you know that. This whole campaign, it's halfway to show off for you."

He picks up his glass again, studying it. There isn't enough whiskey in fifty glasses, Gemma senses, to drown his desire for all of this to go away.

"All right, I'll go see him," he says, relenting. "I'm not saying it'll do any good, but I'll do it. He needs to knock this shit off before somebody gets hurt."

Gemma thanks him, and tells him again where to find Terry, but she isn't sure she believes he'll go. Once upon a time, Bill Blanning was a high-country Thoreau, surviving two winters in the raw woods with nothing but a rifle and a few traps, but that was forty years ago. Now, he's a sad old drunk who would starve to death in a week if it weren't for the young women who cook and clean for him and buy all his food.

That night, after she hands the paper off to Lydia, Tish pulls her Toyota onto Main Street and drives the fifteen miles to Gilburne Canyon. Blanning's Rottweilers find her three-quarters of the way down the driveway to his ranch house, snapping and snarling and flinging their huge paws at the windows of her car. It's loud and it's terrifying, but Tish has visited Bill Blanning often enough to know this is just how his dogs get their exercise. All the same, she keeps the doors locked and windows rolled up until the door swings open and a young woman stomps out onto the porch, aiming a twelve-gauge shotgun at Tish's windshield. She's young, in her early twenties, her long legs bare under her terry-cloth bathrobe, her dirty blonde hair billowing out from under a navy watchcap. Still, Tish thinks as she rolls the passenger-side window down a few careful inches, she looks like she knows her way around a twelve-gauge shotgun.

"Hi there," she shouts over the snarling Rottweilers. "My name is Tish Threadgill, and I'm with the *Franklin Flyer*. Could you call off Bill's dogs, please?"

"A reporter?" the girl shouts back. "What the hell're you doing out here? This is private property, lady."

"I'm aware of that," Tish says. "Could you please call off the dogs? It's hard to talk with them snapping and growling like that."

The girl is still a moment, then brings two fingers to her lips for an ear-splitting whistle. The dogs respond instantly, falling back from the car and retreating to the porch, whimpering.

"All right, I called them off," she says. "Now, what's this all about?"

As she cautiously extricates herself from the car, Tish sees – or rather, tries very hard *not* to see – that the young woman's bathrobe has fallen open at the waist, revealing a strip of pale flesh and a pair of men's boxer shorts.

"I want to have a word with Bill," Tish tells her. "One of my reporters drove out here to see him today. I want to ask him why."

"Wait – *who* came out here?"

"Her name's Gemma Seagraves. She works for me. I'd just like – "

There's a shout from inside and Bill Blanning comes clattering onto the porch, fully dressed in jeans and a red-checked coat. "All right, all right," he says. "I'll handle this, Elsa."

"The hell you will," Elsa says. "Who *is* this lady? And who the fuck is Gemma Seagraves?"

"How about you go inside and feed the dogs?" Blanning says. "They worked up a pretty good appetite just now."

"Is this why you didn't want me around today?" Elsa shoots back. "So you could shack up with this Gemma chick?"

"I said, go inside and feed the dogs," he tells her, taking the gun from her hand. "And while you're at it, you might want to put on some clothes."

Elsa hitches her robe, her expression fixed at some midpoint between irate and humiliated. Tish has heard the stories about Bill Blanning and his ranch girls and has even seen a few draped over him in back booths at the Gilburne Saloon, but this one is young enough to be his granddaughter. She's pretty, too, long and lanky, with milk-white skin and big blue doll's eyes. Fame is weird, Tish thinks. *People* are weird.

"When she's gone, you and me are gonna talk," Elsa says, struggling to recover her dignity.

"Fine, we'll talk," Blanning says. "Now, get the dogs inside and make yourself decent."

It takes her a moment, her eyes boring livid holes into Blanning's forehead, but finally Elsa whistles for the dogs, who waste no time racing inside ahead of her, their fat tails wagging as if they'd heard what Blanning said about being fed.

"I sent her inside," he says, coming down from the porch. "Now, you need to go on home."

"I followed Gemma here today," Tish says.

"You did what?"

"You heard me," Tish says. "I want to know what you two talked about."

Blanning chuckles, shaking his head. "I should've known that girl'd bring trouble."

"Yes, you should have," she says. "Now, either you tell me what you two talked about or my next call will be to Art Monkiewicz so he can come out here and ask you himself."

"And tell him what? That one of your reporters came out and asked me some questions?"

"She sneaked out here to see you, Bill," she says. "She told my secretary that she was going to a City Council meeting and drove out here instead."

"You know, I've never been a newspaper editor, but I think that's what I'd want my reporters to do, go out and find stories."

"What story was she trying to get?"

He looks out at the dark field as if he's hoping a fleet of alien spacecraft will swoop in and save him from having to answer the question. But there's nothing out there but cattle and snow.

"She had a theory that these eco-terror folks might have been motivated by something else I wrote, something that never got published," he says.

"Your second Jack Frost book? I thought you burnt that up."

"That's what I told her. I tossed that thing into the fire twenty years ago. Nobody but me has ever laid eyes on it, and I only did long enough to realize it was the dumbest thing I ever wrote."

"Where did she get the idea that Jack Frost had seen your other book?"

"She's your reporter. Ask her."

"I will," Tish says.

"Of course then you'll have to tell her you followed her out here. I don't imagine she'll take that very well."

"What was in this book you abandoned?" Tish asks. "Why'd you throw it out?"

"I told you, ask your reporter," he says. "I'm done talking to you. If you're not back in that car of yours in one minute, I'm going to call those dogs back out and *make* you go."

"Bill, I need to – "

He puckers his lips into a whistle, and there's a thunderous crash from inside as the four dogs bound out from the kitchen in the direction of the front door.

"Okay, okay," Tish says, holding up her hands. "You've made your point."

"Wise girl," he says. "If I see you out here again, I'm not calling them off. Understand? That goes for the rest of your staff, too. I'm done talking to you people."

On the drive back to Franklin, Tish tries to make sense of what Bill Blanning told her. Tales of a second, unpublished Jack Frost book are almost as old as his first Jack Frost book, but Tish can't recall anyone saying what the second book was about. If she'd ever given it any thought, which she hasn't, she would have said Blanning took the publisher's money and never wrote a word. That Bill Blanning actually wrote a sequel to his most famous book and that members of the Jack Frost Collective might have read it and been influenced by it – this thought never has crossed her mind, and she can't begin to imagine why it would occur to Gemma Seagraves.

But Blanning's right that she isn't looking forward to asking Gemma about it. It's not just that it would mean admitting to Gemma that she followed her to Gilburne Canyon. It's that doing so will tip Gemma off about her suspicions. If Tish is right, and Gemma is up to something, tipping her off would put an end to any chance of figuring out what it is. And if she's wrong, if Bill Blanning is telling the truth and Gemma is guilty of nothing more than running out a particularly unlikely journalistic ground ball, Tish risks losing one of the most naturally gifted reporters she's ever had.

◆ ◆ ◆

Before work the next morning Gemma rides her mountain bike out past the horse barns and the dilapidated trailer court south of town, tramping the last quarter mile through knee-high snowbanks to The Tipis. But when she gets there, Terry's campsite is empty. She can make out his snowshoe tracks crisscrossing the open meadow, and the small rectangle of bare ground near the riverbank where he'd made camp, but his tent, his pack, his bike – all of it's gone.

For the first time, Gemma thinks about running. She has known from the start that getting caught could mean years in prison, but until now she has never seriously considered that they might get caught. Terry is too smart for that, his actions too well planned out. Now, she realizes she doesn't know what Terry's real plans are, and she's beginning to suspect he doesn't, either. If, God forbid, Terry ends up hurting someone, she could spend decades in prison. If he kills someone, she could spend the rest of her life there.

Gemma hasn't spoken with her mother in months, and their relation-ship, never cuddly, has recently veered toward the non-existent, but if she were ever truly in trouble, she knows her mother would take her in. It doesn't hurt that her mother's last known address was in Curaçao, a Caribbean island nation with no extradition treaty with the United States. But does she really want to live a life on the run – with her mother, of all people? And what about Terry? She has never kidded herself that Terry cares about her the way she does for him. For Terry, Gemma knows, she's a bank account, a walking credit card he can tap whenever he needs to establish a false identity or bankroll a road trip to Oregon. But he listened to her when she begged him not to carry out the attack before Christmas, and he knows she's working on a story that could put a stop to devel-opment of Elkhorn Canyon once and for all. If she runs now, that story might never make it into the paper. And then who is going to stop Terry?

Two hours later, she's at her desk in the newsroom when her phone beeps.

"Hey, Gem," Jen says over the intercom. "Terry from Gilburne, line two."

Gemma stares in disbelief at the blinking red light on her phone. "Who?"

"Terry from Gilburne," Jen says. "You holding out on us there, Seagraves? Rolling in the hay with some cute ranch boy down there?"

Gemma allows herself a quick room-check. The newsroom is blessedly empty, all the reporters on assignment except Perry, who is at his desk banging out a feature story, worrying over his spelling dictionary.

"Umm ... Perry?" she says.

He looks up from his dictionary, his long eyelashes batting slowly, until, as if catching up on some internal tape delay, he hears what Jen said.

"Oh, right, sorry," he says, hopping up out of his seat. "I'll ... uhh ... go see how Lydia's doing in paste-up."

Gemma thanks him and waits for him to disappear through the newsroom doorway. When she's sure he's gone, she takes a deep breath, settling herself, and reaches for the phone.

"Hello, this is Gemma."

"She off the line?" a husky male voice asks.

"Who?" Gemma asks. "Oh, right. Yes, it's just you and me. Who is this?"

"You know who this is," the man says, and she recognizes the whiskey-roughened voice of Bill Blanning. "I'm giving you a head's up. Your boss followed you out here yesterday."

"She – what?"

He ignores this. "I told her you asked me about the other Jack Frost book, and I said nobody but me has ever seen it," he says. "If I had to lay odds, I'd say she bought it, but if I were you I think I'd find your friend pretty quick."

For a moment, Gemma is unable to speak. She's back at Terry's deserted campsite hearing the gurgling stream, thinking about running. Where would she go? How would she do it? If she did, could she ever come back?

"I just got back from trying to find him," she says, lowering her voice to a whisper. "He's gone. The campsite's empty."

The line goes ominously silent.

"There's a few other places I can check," she lies. "And I'm really close on that news story, the one I told you about. If I can get that into the paper, he'll stand down, I know he will."

"Then I suggest you get on that," he says. "Because I'm not getting dragged into this. I don't mind playing dumb for a little while, but if this starts getting hot and heavy, I won't think twice about giving you two up."

"Don't do that, please," she begs. "Not yet."

"I love that kid," Blanning says. "And I respect the hell out of what he's doing. What *you're* doing. But I'm too damn old to go to prison."

Before Gemma can answer, the line clicks dead.

Chapter Twelve

On Friday morning, Tish drags herself out of bed at seven to brown chicken thighs and fry lardons of bacon for coq au vin while Charles Gibson and Joan Lunden ring out 1993 on *Good Morning America*. Melanie has been home in Fort Collins since the Monday after Christmas so this isn't Tish's first night back with Scott, but it will be their first New Year's Eve as a couple and she wants to cook dinner for him for once, if it kills her.

Which it very nearly does. Tish owns exactly one cookbook, a sauce-spattered copy of Julia Child's *Mastering the Art of French Cooking* that her mother, during her manic phases, had used to fill their refrigerator with boeuf bourguignon, vichyssoise, and cassoulet. These dishes, fatally undercooked or missing a crucial ingredient, sat uneaten in the fridge until Doug or Tish quietly tossed them out. Twenty-five years later, Tish can see why her mother never could make the recipes work. For the coq au vin, Tish first has to cut up a roasting chicken and marinate it in wine and stock. Next, she has to fry the lardons. Then the chicken. Then, incredibly, she has to pour a shot of cognac over it *and light it on fire*. And that's before she gets to the beurre manié, whatever that is.

It's exhausting, and she has a newspaper to run. At nine, she shoves the half-finished stew in the fridge, grabs a shower, and heads in to work, where two baby-faced FBI agents, conspicuous in their navy blue suits, sit on either side of Jen at the reception desk. This is Monkiewicz's doing. He's been fighting to put agents in the *Flyer*'s office all week, and now on New Year's Eve, Tish has finally given in. All day, the agents prowl the office scanning the incoming mail and monitoring Jen's calls in case Jack Frost phones in a new threat.

They're still there at eight that night when Tish sends Lydia home, shooing her and the two supremely bored FBI agents out the door, with directions for them to hit the Summit Tavern for the start of the annual New Year's Pub Crawl. After they leave, she spends an hour in her office catching up on paperwork. Scott is due to come by for a late dinner at ten and he's made her promise she won't so much as mention the newspaper until Sunday morning. It's a promise she intends to keep. She has bought not one, but two bottles of Veuve Cliquot, the pricey French Champagne Scott has turned her onto, and she plans to get expensively trashed and sleep in till noon.

A little after nine, she puts away her spreadsheets and makes a final pass through the office, dousing lights and turning off machines. She's in layout checking the proof sheets for Saturday's paper when she hears the faint tapping of computer keys coming from the newsroom.

"Hello?" she calls out.

The typing abruptly stops, leaving only the hum of the building's ancient heating system.

"Hello?" she says again, heading for the newsroom. "Is somebody here?"

More silence, then: "It's me. Gemma."

When Tish reaches the newsroom, Gemma is standing a few feet from her desk, hands behind her back, as if to demonstrate that they're not doing anything. She looks awful, her eyes glazed with exhaustion, the acne that a few days ago dotted her chin and lower cheeks now colonizing the rest of her face, turning it a high, mottled pink. Even her smile looks tired. And guilty.

"Sorry," she says. "I thought you'd gone home."

"I thought *you'd* gone home," Tish says.

"I did, but then I came back. I needed to catch up on some City Council stuff."

"Gemma, it's New Year's Eve."

"I know, I know. I'll go out later. I just figured it'd be quiet here and I could get some work done, you know?"

Gemma's desk is piled high with old newspapers and open file folders, but at the top, nearest the computer keyboard, Tish spots a folder marked in large red letters: "FEC Corp misc." Taking a step closer, she scans the story on Gemma's monitor, picking out the words "Elkhorn Canyon property" and "apparent bribes" and "the *Flyer* has learned."

"What the hell?" she asks. "You're writing up the FEC bribery story?"

"I was just roughing it out," Gemma says. "I wanted to see what we have so I could talk to you about it."

In her mind's eye, Tish sees Gemma's black BMW slowing down for the turn into Gilburne Canyon. The question is right there, waiting to be asked, demanding to be asked.

"I saw you," she says. "The other day, I followed you when you went to see Bill Blanning."

She wills Gemma to look confused or insulted, but she just opens her mouth and closes it again wordlessly, caught.

"You promised me," Tish says, angry now. "You told me to my face you wouldn't go off on your own without letting me know and then you went and did it."

"I'm so sorry," Gemma says. "I got another tip from my source. I should've told you. I don't know why I didn't."

"What's his name?" Tish asks. "Your source – I want to know his name."

"It's Richard," Gemma says. "Richard Cutler. I finally tracked him down a couple days ago, and he told me he'd heard Jack Frost knew about another book Blanning had written, one that turned violent in the end. I should have known he was full of it. But I wanted it to be true. I wanted to be the first one to get it in the newspaper."

The girl is crying now, Tish realizes, quiet, wrenching little chest-chokes.

"What happened?" she asks, softer now.

"Oh God, it was so ridiculous," Gemma says. "I drove all the way down there and got past those horrible dogs, and Blanning – he just laughed at me."

"He laughed at you?"

"He said he'd thrown that book in the fire twenty years ago so there was no way these guys could've ever seen it." She looks up at Tish, tears streaming down her cheeks. "I screwed up. I know I screwed up, and I don't even know why. I just wanted to bring in a big story."

Tish fights to hold onto her skepticism, her nagging sense that this is all an elaborate performance, but she's overcome by the sheer *thereness* of the young woman in front of her, red-faced and snot-smeared, dissolving into tears. Whatever else is going on, this is a girl in crisis. So, she does the only thing she can think to do, which is to lay a hand on Gemma's shoulder and mouth soothing platitudes until Gemma finally, mercifully, breaks it off to reach for a box of tissues.

"Gemma, I have to ask," Tish says. "What's really going on here?"

She looks up from her tissue, on alert again. "What do you mean?"

"I don't know," Tish says. "For a couple weeks now, you've seemed on edge. Really manic and fragile. And now this. I have to be able to trust the people who work for me."

"You *can* trust me," Gemma says. "I know I've let you down, but you have to believe me, it's only because I'm trying to get all these stories into the paper. The county's holding its first hearing on Elkhorn Canyon on Tuesday."

"And I told you, we're going to run the FEC bribery piece."

"By next Tuesday?" Gemma asks. "Tish, we *know* they're corrupt. We know they made payoffs. That woman Sheffield met, she was trying to bribe him – we know that."

Tish thinks, suddenly, of the blue-gridded proof sheets of the Saturday paper in the layout room. She's being paranoid, she knows that. Even Gemma, strange as she's been acting, would never try to sneak a story into the paper while Tish was asleep. But the fact is, the press guys won't be here till three, and between then and now anyone could rip up the front page and paste in a new one. All it would take is some heated wax and an X-Acto knife.

"We have more time than you think," she says. "It'll take two or three hearings before they can vote on Elkhorn Canyon. That gives us a month, maybe more."

"But, Tish – "

"No more buts," Tish says, shutting her down. "It's New Year's Eve. You need to get out of here. Go hit the pub crawl, go home and watch the ball drop on TV, I don't care. You've been working way too hard. Now, give me your keys."

"My keys?"

"I don't want you coming in to work tomorrow," Tish says. "You don't set foot in this office again until I get in on Sunday morning. Got it?"

She stays at Gemma's side until they've switched off the last of the lights and walked out into the corridor, Tish turning the key in the main lock and the deadbolt. Doug had the second lock installed years ago following a rash of break-ins, and only three people have keys: Lydia, the chief pressman, and Tish herself. No one's getting at the proof sheets for Saturday's paper.

When she gets home fifteen minutes later, the front door to Tish's apartment is ajar and Scott is standing at her kitchen counter snapping the ends off green beans as the coq au vin bubbles behind him on the stove.

"Perfect timing!" he calls to her. "The chicken's almost ready. I hope you don't mind, but I added some herbs and a little extra cognac."

She tells him it's fine. And it *is* fine, even the fact that Scott let himself in with the key she keeps under the mat, which he's never done before. She isn't prepared to decide what she thinks about that yet, not after the day she's had, so she just kisses him hello and busies herself setting the table and popping the first of the two bottles of Veuve Cliquot.

It's New Year's Eve, she tells herself. Gemma can wait. For now, her only job is to eat a big meal and drink herself into oblivion on overpriced Champagne. But all Scott has to do is look up from his green beans and say, "Long day?" and it all comes tumbling out, starting with finding Gemma in the newsroom writing up the FEC Corp bribery story. To make that make sense Tish has to work back to explain what Rick Sheffield told them after they published the *first* FEC Corp story, then how Gemma disappeared the night Jack Frost called, and how she'd disappeared again two days ago to go talk to Bill Blanning.

"So, in other words, just another boring day at the office," Scott says.

Tish laughs, but it has a strangled quality. She's in trouble, she realizes. Deep, deep trouble.

"You think she's involved somehow?" Scott asks.

This, of course, is precisely what Tish has been thinking, that Gemma is somehow mixed up in the attacks on the ski company. But how? And *when*? Last she checked, Gemma was putting in sixty hours a week at the *Flyer*.

"She's just a kid," she says. "This poor little rich girl from Rodeo Road. I can't see her torching restaurants and blowing up power stations."

"So, maybe she's their moneybags," he says.

"Like, she's raiding Daddy's bank account to finance the attacks?"

"They're getting their cash somewhere, right?" he says. "It's expensive, running a campaign like this. Have you talked to the cops about any of this?"

"Your water's boiling," Tish says, nodding to the stove.

It's true: The saucepan at the rear of the stove is billowing steam. With a shrug, Scott scoops his pile of green beans into a stainless-steel steamer tray and drops it in.

"You think I should, don't you?" she says. "Call the cops."

"You know what I really think?" he says. "I think you're probably right that girl's guilty of nothing more than wanting to be a star reporter. But I also think it doesn't matter. You aren't going to turn her in. You'd never turn one of your own people in to the cops – not unless they shot somebody on the courthouse steps." He reaches for a pair of tongs. "White meat or dark?"

"Dark," she says. "Let me have that thigh there. Maybe that drumstick, too."

He serves the chicken, a thigh and drumstick for her and a breast for himself, before ladling wine-dark sauce onto the scoops of mashed potatoes that were supposed to be his only contribution to the meal. Tish is surprised how good it smells, tart and savory, with a tang of fermented fruit, and she realizes she hasn't eaten since her lunchtime Yoplait, ten hours ago.

"Look, I'm on your side," Scott says, handing her a plate. "If even half of what you're saying about this bribery thing is true, that's a hundred times worse than some kids blowing up a power station out in the woods. You know that. I know that. Now, it's New Year's Eve, and I'd like to eat this delicious meal you've prepared for us."

But the meal is a slog. The chicken is fine, a little soggy, perhaps, from sitting all day in the fridge, but edible. Good, even. But after her first few famished bites, Tish tastes nothing, her mind replaying her conversation with Gemma in the *Flyer* newsroom. There's no way mousy Gemma, with her recycled-waste boots and pimply chin, is a terrorist, but what about this Richard Cutler character she's been talking to? The name rings no bells for Tish, which is strange if, as Gemma claims, he's a local. Maybe, she thinks, Cutler's the one she should be keeping an eye on, not Gemma.

"Dessert?" Scott asks.

Tish looks up from her plate, blinking, lost. "What?"

"Dessert," he says. "The dish, often sweetened, commonly served after the main meal?"

"Right, sorry, of course," she says. "Let's have dessert. What're we having?"

Wrong question. They're having crème brulée, which she should know because Scott has been talking about it more or less nonstop since she surprised him with a baker's torch and half a dozen butane cartridges for Christmas. She clears their plates, knuckling back thoughts of how she can track down Richard Cutler, as Scott unpacks the small silver torch from its leatherette kit bag, gleeful as a nine-year-old with a new model train. He sprinkles half a tablespoon of vanilla sugar onto the pre-made custard in each ramekin, and then, narrating his actions step by step, he fires up the handheld torch and chars the vanilla sugar a dark, even brown.

"Ta-da!" he says, clicking off the blue flame.

Tish suppresses a laugh, wondering how she, of all people, ended up with a man who takes his food nerdery so seriously. But she dutifully cracks the shell of caramelized sugar with her spoon and brings a quivering dollop of custard to her mouth.

"Oh, wow," she says.

"Good?" he asks.

"This is amazing," she says, spooning in another creamy mouthful shot through with crackly bits of caramelized sugar. "Scott, you need to open a restaurant. I'm serious."

That's when she feels it: an unexpected hardness, a rigidity where there should be give. Digging the spoon deeper, she strikes it again, and this time her eyes catch a brief metallic flicker.

"Oh God, oh no," she says, digging through the custard. "Scott, tell me this isn't…."

But she can see it plainly now in the flat of her spoon: a thin gold band swimming in vanilla custard, topped by a small white diamond.

"You don't have to say anything right now," he says. "I just want you to think about it. I want you to think about what a life with me would be like."

"Now?" she shrieks. "You're springing this on me *now*?"

She's shocked by the violence in her own voice. It shocks Scott, too, and his face, smiling seconds ago, collapses in on itself.

"Oh God, I'm sorry," she says. "I love you, Scott. I don't say it enough, but I do. I love you, but I don't know, I don't think I can deal with this right now."

"Can't deal with it because you don't want it?" he asks. "Or can't deal with it because you have too much going on to think about it right now?"

She starts to tell him it's Door No. 2, definitely, but the words catch in her throat. The weight of the last year, the weight of the five and a half years since Doug died, hits her all at once, like a building falling on her. For five and a half years, she's worked seven days a week without taking a vacation. For five and a half years, she's eaten the same lunch every day and stayed at the office until midnight every night. For five and a half years, she's pushed away every man who tried to get close. And it all seemed totally normal, like this was how her life was meant to be.

"I know we've only been seeing each other a few months," he says, "but I've been thinking about this ever since Melanie left. I'm almost forty here, Tish. I don't want to wait. I'm sick of waiting. I've wanted this since the first time I met you."

"Scott, it's okay," she says. "I don't want to wait, either. The answer's yes."

His eyes flash up at her. "What?"

"The ring, the custard, the whole deal: The answer is yes," she says. "I mean, I think you're out of your mind to want to marry me, but if you'll have me, yes, I'm yours."

They kiss, both of them laughing now, and then Scott insists on washing the ring off in the sink so he can get down on one knee to formally pop the question. She tells him yes, again, and they crack the second bottle of Veuve Cliquot to toast the occasion. After that they're up for hours, talking and planning. The wedding, they decide, will be that summer, but they'll keep separate apartments until next fall. On this point Tish is adamant. Melanie spends her summers with her dad and Tish wants to give her as long as possible to get used to the new woman in Scott's life. Then there's the honeymoon. This is Scott's non-negotiable. Tish hasn't had a real vacation since her brother died, and in the five years since his divorce, Scott has spent all his vacation time caring for his daughter. They need to get away, just the two of them – no newspaper, no Melanie. A beach vacation in Bali. Rock climbing in Mexico. Two weeks cycling through Provence.

"I'd love to cycle through France with you," Tish says. "But if you talk with my banker, I think you'll find I'm flat broke."

"I've got my year-end bonus coming," Scott says. "That plus my savings would pretty much cover the whole trip."

"Scott, Stan Bucholtz isn't going to give you a bonus," Tish says. "Why would he? You're out of there at the end of the week."

"He has to give me something," Scott says. "I originated $8 million in loans last year. And now that you've paid down your credit line, my delinquency rate is pretty near zero."

"I'm not so sure Bucholtz is counting that one as a win," Tish says.

Scott is quiet. Two weeks ago, when Tish showed up with her check for $160,000, Bucholtz had shaken hands all round and walked out. They were meeting in Bucholtz's own office, but he left Tish alone with Scott and the bank's lawyers and wouldn't come back until she left.

"He has to give me something," Scott says again. "Bucholtz's greedy, but he's not stupid. He can't afford to have me leave pissed off. I know too much about how he operates."

Now it's Tish's turn to go silent. He knows now about the shares in the FEC Corp, and he knows that she suspects Bucholtz is at the center of it all. If Scott was willing to be a source on that story, she'd gladly trade two weeks in the Pyrenees for whatever he could find in Bucholtz' files. But she decides, for now, not to go there.

"If your ransom money gets us to France this summer," she says, "sign me up."

Over the long weekend, while Tish is putting out the Monday and Tuesday papers, Scott stays home writing up the annual report Bucholtz will use to set his year-end bonus. In theory, these bonuses, which range from token payments of a few hundred bucks to the junior tellers and secretaries to thousands of dollars for the bank's senior officers, reflect each employee's contribution to the bank's profit that year. In fact, as everyone knows, you get whatever Stan Bucholtz feels like giving you, not a penny more or less. But Scott labors over his report all through the holiday weekend, totting up his successes and shamelessly heaping praise on Bucholtz for his bold vision for the bank.

"I think I'm going to get four grand," he tells Tish when she drops him off at work Tuesday.

"In your report, you ask for eight," Tish says.

"That's what I *should* get. Bucholtz'll give me half that. It's the least he can get away with."

Tish doubts that he'll get even that, but she plants a wifely kiss on his cheek and sends him on his way. It's a big day for her, too. That night, the Elk County Commission is holding its first public hearing on the Elkhorn Canyon ski resort, which means she and Chuck will be up half the night writing stories for the Denver papers, and if they're lucky, for *USA Today* and its national chain of satellite papers.

At Franklin Savings, Scott spends most of the day training his replacement, a long-serving teller named Steve Rodriguez, while Bucholtz holes up in his office with the compensation committee. When the clock hits five, Dave Felton, the bank's head of security, escorts the last customer to the front door, and the tellers start counting out their drawers. Usually, this is a rushed process, the speedier tellers helping the laggards so they can all go home, but today no one's leaving until everyone gets their bonus envelope, so they take their time, counting and recounting the stacks of cash, gossiping in nervous whispers about what they're going to do with their bonuses until five-thirty when Bucholtz cracks the door to his office and the building goes silent.

As Bucholtz makes his way down the row of teller's windows, glad-handing and back-slapping, Scott empties out his desk, packing up his photos and pens and making sure his files are ready for the handover at the end of the week. Janny Lewis, a member of the compensation committee and one of Scott's oldest friends at the bank, stops by his desk to coo over his photos and give him a hug. "If it was up to me," she whispers in his ear, "you'd get *twenty* thousand."

"Mr. Sage," Bucholtz says, extending a veiny, mitt-like hand for Scott to shake.

Bucholtz is a short, blunt-built man in his middle fifties, with a pendulous gut and the forlorn, bottom-heavy face of a British bulldog. He's a wealthy man now, but he was raised on a failing cow-calf operation just north of the city limits, which his father, a legendary drunk, lost in foreclosure, with half the land going to the county for a new airfield and the other half to the developer who built the Valley View mall. Bucholtz makes a point of telling this story to every new hire, along with the kicker that, years later, when the developer himself went bankrupt, Franklin Savings ended up holding the note for the land.

"I want to thank you for everything you've done for me, Mr. Bucholtz," Scott says, standing up to shake the older man's hand. "I'll always value my time here at Franklin Savings."

"I'm sure you will," Bucholtz says. He laughs abruptly, exposing a row of cigarette-stained teeth. "You're not going to start poaching any of my clients now, are you?"

"No, sir," Scott says. "I would never do that."

In fact, half a dozen of Scott's best clients have already committed to following him to Mountain Equity. This fact, known to both of them, fills the growing silence broken only by the nervous jingling of change in Bucholtz's left trouser pocket.

"Well, son, I'm sorry to see you go," he says, handing him a plain white envelope. "Please take this as a token of my esteem and affection."

This, in Scott's experience, is always the awkward part. Do you rip open the envelope right there at your desk? Do you stuff it in a coat pocket and open it in the privacy of your car? In the past, Scott always waited, but this year he'd like to know how pissed off Stan Bucholtz is at him, and in turn, how pissed off he should be at Stan Bucholtz. So, taking a letter opener from his packing boxes, he slits open the envelope and pulls out the check, which reads:

ONE DOLLAR and no/100 cents

Scott looks up to see Bucholtz watching him from the doorway of the next cubicle. Their eyes meet, just for an instant, before Bucholtz tips an invisible cap and disappears behind the frosted glass partition.

◆ ◆ ◆

Halfway across town, Terry Albrecht leans against a TV news truck a block from the Elk County Courthouse watching the crowds of locals stream up the granite courthouse steps. In the past week, he's dyed his close-cropped red hair a dark chestnut brown and grown a mustache, also dyed. Tonight, he's added a pair of horned rim glasses, a cheap puffy jacket, jeans, and Carhartt work boots, all chosen for maximum invisibility. The police, he knows, will be staking out the meeting, scanning the crowd for familiar faces and making note of unfamiliar ones. But Terry isn't worried about being recognized. At six-two, with the tapered frame and cut muscles of an ex-Marine who trains daily in full pack and boots, he looks nothing like the pale, doughy boy whose crippling stutter kept him forever on the sidelines at Franklin Elementary.

Still, in terms of operational security, this is madness. For most of the past year, he's operated at the margins of his hometown, moving at night whenever possible and camping out in the woods or in the maid's room of Gemma Seagraves' Rodeo Road mansion. If he crosses the street and climbs the courthouse stairs, he'll be stepping out of the shadows directly onto the field of battle. And for what? Any information he could possibly glean from this hearing will be splashed across the front pages of the two local papers tomorrow morning. And if he wants to watch the hearing for himself, he can tune in to the eleven o'clock news on any of the three Denver TV stations, whose live trucks line Main Street for a block on either side of the courthouse. This, he knows, is precisely the lapse in judgment his pursuers have been hoping for, and yet, just as the hearing is about to start, he crosses the street and joins the stragglers scurrying up the courthouse steps.

Inside, the high-cielinged courtroom is laid out like a church, its twenty rows of spectator benches set off from the lawyer's tables and jury box by a low wooden partition. Tonight, the jury box has been set aside for the TV cameras trained on the front of the room, where the desks usually reserved for the bailiff and court stenographer now seat four of the five county commissioners, with the fifth, commission president Cory Carr, seated high atop the judge's bench, banging a mallet-like gavel to bring the meeting to order.

"Quiet, please!" he is shouting. "Folks, in the interests of getting you home at a reasonable hour, I'd like to bring this hearing to order."

Terry finds a spot along the rear wall, half obscured by a faux-marble pillar, where he can be sure he won't be caught on camera, and surveys the room for police. He sees Sheriff Hayes in his tall white Stetson, along with half a dozen uniformed deputies and a similar number of clean-cut young men in navy blue suits that might as well be uniforms. The FBI agents are stationed along the walls, their eyes roaming the room the way his are. In the front row, in full makeup like a movie star, sits Kelly Cherry, the dim bulb correspondent for Channel 4 in Denver, and beside her, the less blonde, more competent Tish Threadgill, whose newspaper has been so useful to his campaign. Between Threadgill and the gangly, Frankenstein-browed kid who took so long to report on the parcel of land in Elkhorn Canyon, he spots Gemma Seagraves. Terry is surprised, but only slightly. County politics isn't her beat, he knows, but if he was her, he'd do whatever he could to be here, too. Still, he burrows himself in a little deeper behind his faux-marble pillar. The last thing he needs now is for Gemma to see him.

"Thank you," Carr says when the chatter and cross-talk finally dies out. "I want to welcome you to the first public hearing on a proposal to build a new skiing area in Elkhorn Canyon."

His last words are drowned out by angry shouts, which Carr beats back with a renewed round of gavel pounding.

"You will all have your chance to be heard on this issue," he says. "If not tonight, then at the hearings that will follow this one. But first, tonight, we need to hear from the proponents of the new resort" – more catcalls, more gavel-pounding – "I am going to have to ask all of you to settle down and listen to the plan Mr. Dunow and the Franklin Skiing Company are proposing."

He says more, but Terry hears none of it because, following Carr's gaze, he sees the shaved-bald head of the youngest Dunow brother at one end of the plaintiff's table. Dunow is seated in three-quarters profile so Terry can make out only his rounded cheek and a single impish blue eye, but it's unmistakably him. And at last Terry understands why he decided to come.

◆ ◆ ◆

For the past hour, Scott has been stuck in his glass-walled cubicle explaining his personal filing system to Steve Rodriguez, who stayed behind while the rest of the office hit the Franklin Hotel bar to blow their bonus bucks on watery martinis and Long Island iced teas. Finally, though, Rodriguez excuses himself to catch the last round at the Franklin, leaving Scott alone in the shuttered bank building.

Company policy requires at least one security guard to remain on duty until the last employee goes home, but Bucholtz hates paying the O.T. and the bank's senior staffers routinely send the guards home when they work late, knowing Bucholtz won't complain so long as they lock themselves in and call the head of security when they leave. So for now Scott has the building to himself – just him and the security cameras. There are three: one trained on the front door, one on the teller windows, and a fourth on the entrance to the bank vault. There are actually two more Scott isn't supposed to know about inside the vault, but since he has no intention of entering the vault, these don't concern him. He knows only that that he has to steer clear of the teller cameras, which requires him to skirt past the glass-walled cubicles belonging to Janny Lewis and the other senior officers on his way to his ultimate destination, which is Stan Bucholtz's office.

The bank president's office is secured with a programmable combination lock, which would stop Scott cold if Bucholtz had ever bothered reset the combination or used an entry code more complicated than the four letters of his first name: 7(S)-8(T)-2(A)-6(N). So, the door's no problem. The problem is that Scott doesn't know precisely what he's looking for or where to find it. And his time isn't unlimited. On nights when an employee is working late, Dave Felton usually swings by around eight to make sure everything's locked down for the night, but he's been known to show up as much as half an hour earlier, which gives Scott forty minutes to find whatever it is he's looking for and get out.

There are two filing cabinets behind Bucholtz's desk, one unlocked and one secured with a standard key lock. Scott spends five anxious minutes searching Bucholtz's desk and the desk of his secretary for an extra set of keys before resigning himself to the unlocked cabinet. But, as he feared, he finds nothing of interest in the files, just reams of routine correspondence and inter-office memos.

This leaves the safe. It's built into the wall and fairly compact, two feet wide and a foot or so in height. Scott has only seen it open once, two or three years ago, and he's never been in the room when Bucholtz was opening or closing it, which doesn't give him much to work with. He knows only that it's a combination lock whose numbers run from 0 to 99. He's attended enough celebrations in the break room with sheet cake and unspiked punch to know that Bucholtz's birthday is May 16, 1938, and he tries variations on those numbers: 05-16-19-38. When that gets him nowhere, he tries variations on Bucholtz's first and last name. But it's fruitless. He doesn't know how many turns are required to open the lock, or even whether the correct solution starts with a left or a right turn.

He checks his watch. Twelve minutes after seven. The earliest Dave Felton would come is seven-thirty, so, in theory, Scott has eighteen minutes to properly trash his boss's office, smash the rows of eight-by-ten glossies on his brag wall – Bucholtz with Chrissie Evert, Bucholtz with Senator Hank Brown, Bucholtz with Ronald Reagan – and toss every sheet of paper in the unlocked filing cabinet onto the floor. But quite apart from the grievous damage this would do to Scott's career, a trashed office is kid's stuff. If Tish is right that Bucholtz and his cronies bought an old mining claim a mile from a proposed ski resort and then sold off pieces of the property as bribes to ensure the resort would get approved, the proof is probably sitting in Bucholtz's wall safe. Getting it into Tish's hands, and onto the front page of her newspaper, would pay Bucholtz back not just for the puny bonus check and the way he's treated Tish, but for the way he and the other men in his circle behave as if Franklin is their own personal fiefdom, to do with as they please.

Scott is taking one last shot at the combination, trying first Bucholtz's wife's name and then the names of his children, when he turns back to look at the top left-hand drawer of Bucholtz's desk, which hangs partway open. He must have left it like that when was searching for the keys to the filing cabinet, and now, on a hunch, he opens it all the way and runs his hands along the sides and top. Sure enough, at the top of the drawer, hugging the underside of the desk, his fingers find a thin metal retractable shelf, onto which is taped a single sheet of paper full of neatly typed names and telephone numbers. At the bottom of the sheet, he spots a row of letters and numbers: R37-L55-R67-L86-R47. Scott studies these a moment, then barks out a laugh. On a telephone touchpad, the numbers spell out F-R-K-L-N-S-V-N-G-S.

Inside the safe, he finds eight stacks of fifty- and hundred-dollar bills, still in their original bands, about fifty thousand dollars by his eyeballed estimate. He also finds a gold watch, a diamond-studded tie clip, and a slightly scuffed baseball with the words "2,500th hit" scrawled on the side over Pete Rose's signature. After carefully noting the location of each item, he pulls them out to get to a pile of file folders on the bottom of the safe. It's seven-twenty now so he moves quickly, flipping through the folders until he comes upon one near the bottom marked "FEC". The folder contains an Elk County property deed, along with a lengthy legal brief detailing the parcel's ownership history dating back to October 12, 1886, the day Byram Milton patented a mining claim to ten acres of federal land in Elkhorn Canyon. Below this, sits another stack of legal documents pertaining to the incorporation of FEC Corp in the Cayman Islands. And then, at the very bottom of the file, he finds a single sheet of Franklin Savings letterhead, on which Bucholtz has scrawled the word "Ownership" and listed eight names:

S. Bucholtz – 25%

Sheldon Dunow – 15%

Harley Dunow – 15%

Foster Dunow – 15%

Cory Carr – 10%

Deborah Benton – 10%

Leonard Mayer – 5%

Kenneth Carlisle – 5%

Fifteen minutes later, when Dave Felton unlocks the front door, Scott is powering down the copy machine after running off a copy of the complete file, which is now stowed in the bottom of his briefcase.

"Hey there, Mr. Sage," he says. "You're working late."

"Yeah, cleaning out my desk," Scott answers. "I had no idea I'd collected so much crap."

On the street, he half-expects an alarm to sound and a fleet of police cruisers to come flying around the corner, sirens blaring, but it's just another quiet, moonlit Tuesday night in Franklin, Colorado. In in the morning, he'll personally walk the FEC Corp file over to the *Flyer's* offices. He'll ask Tish to hold off publication for a week, to let him get started in his new job at Mountain Equity. Not that it will make much difference. It won't take Bucholtz long to figure out the source of the leak. But by then, with any luck, he'll be too busy defending himself from bribery charges to go after Scott.

For two hours Terry has willed Sheldon Dunow to speak, and for two hours the bald, paunchy FrankCo executive has sat at the plaintiff's table, nodding sagely as his lawyer, Kenny Carlisle, drones on about the proposed new ski area. Every few minutes, Carlisle's monologue is interrupted by angry shouts and catcalls, which Cory Carr silences with his gavel and threats of removal. But Terry long ago stopped listening to what the lawyer has to say. It's as if he's standing under ten feet of water, the raucous proceedings a distant murmur, as he recalls the day twenty years ago that he first met Sheldon Dunow. His mother had pointed him out on Mount Boyd. "That's little Sheldon," she said. "And over there, those are his brothers, Foster and Hal."

"Little Sheldon," she'd called him. It made sense. The two older boys were tall and athletic, clearly at home on the slopes, but Sheldon was short and fat, like Terry himself. Except that, unlike Terry, he wore designer gear and owned Rossignol Stratos, that year's "it" racing ski. The Rossis were half a foot too long for him, and twice, from the chairlift, Terry watched him cross up his skis and tumble twenty yards downhill, landing in a heap of ski poles and twisted limbs.

After the second wipeout, Terry followed Sheldon down Gravy Train, and when he saw the boy alone in the line for Lift #1, he fell in behind him.

"I know who you are," he said.

Sheldon turned around slowly, looking him up and down. "Good for you," he said. "You want an autograph or something?"

"You're my brother," Terry said.

The other boy's pudgy face pinched into a sneer. "What are you even talking about?"

"You're my brother," Terry said again. "My dad is your dad."

"Is there a problem here?"

Terry looked up to see a grown man, tanned and bearded, wearing mirrored shades and the distinctive red-and-black parka of the Mount Boyd Ski Patrol. He had skied over from the base of the lift and now stood between them.

"No, no problem," Sheldon said. "This guy's just a total freak."

"Look, I don't know who you are," the bearded ski patroller said to Terry, "but if you don't want to get your pass pulled, you need to find somebody else to bother, okay?"

"Oh, fuck you," Terry shouts. He looks around the crowded courtroom, startled. Had he said that out loud? Luckily, the hearing is in the midst of one of its periodic outbursts, a group of grunge-outfitted activists shouting down Kenny Carlisle while Cory Carr bangs his gavel to silence them, and the heads that had turned in Terry's direction quickly look away again, caught up in the drama at the front of the room. All except one, in the front row, a sallow, acne-pitted face framed by an unruly mop of limp blonde hair.

◆ ◆ ◆

"What is it?" Tish whispers.

Gemma ignores her, twisted around in her seat, her eyes fixed on the courtroom's rear wall.

"What's wrong?" Tish asks again, louder.

She follows Gemma's gaze to a tall, broad-shouldered man in jeans and a puffy jacket pushing through the crowd toward the exit.

Thwack!

"That is enough!" Sheriff Hayes thunders. He's standing beside Cory Carr on the judge's bench, holding a polished wood truncheon over his head, ready to bring it down again. "The next person who interrupts a witness or speaks out of turn will be forcibly removed and arrested. Do I make myself clear?"

As he's speaking, sheriff's deputies deploy to the front of each aisle, armed with night sticks of their own. In the silence, Tish reaches for Gemma's pad and writes: "Who?" Gemma stares at the word as if it were written in hieroglyphics, but she finally takes the pad back and writes: "Cutler." It takes Tish a moment, but then it comes to her: *Richard* Cutler. Gemma's source, the one who claimed to have an inside track on Jack Frost.

By then, Gemma has pulled herself up from her seat and started edging through the crowd. Following her, Tish has to fight her way to the door, and only once she reaches the landing and starts down the stairs can she move at full speed. Outside, the January night is bitter cold and she's left her coat upstairs. She's coming down the courthouse steps, wishing she'd thought to bring gloves, when she sees Gemma on the sidewalk looking both ways along Main Street.

"You lost him?" Tish asks.

Gemma wheels around, her eyes wild in the reflected light of the courthouse windows. She isn't crying, not yet, but she isn't far from it, either.

"It's all right," Tish says. "You can call him in the morning."

"No, I can't," Gemma says. "He doesn't have a phone."

The girl turns back to look out at the darkened street, leaving Tish to contemplate this latest nugget of information. Earlier that week, she had searched for Cutler in the Franklin phone book and come up empty. Does this mean he's homeless? Living in a remote shack somewhere? She wants to ask – she knows she has the right to ask – but not here, not now.

"Come on, it's cold," she says. "Let's go back upstairs, finish covering this hearing."

"What's the point?" Gemma asks. "You saw Carr, the way he's lapping up whatever that lawyer's dishing out. It'll take a few more weeks, but this is a done deal."

Tish wants to argue, but she's seen Carr's body language, too. He would never admit it, on or off the record, but he already has the votes he needs.

"We'll stop them," she says. "We'll get that bribery piece into the paper."

Gemma doesn't respond, and Tish feels frustration radiating off her, hot as a sunlamp. They've had the bribery story for three weeks now. Juliet, the woman Sheffield met in Elkhorn Canyon, is a ghost, and without a corroborating source, without a smoking gun of some kind, they'll never find enough to publish.

"Let me get my coat and I'll help you find him," she says. "He can't have gone far."

"You know what? Forget it," Gemma says. "You stay here with Chuck. I'm going home."

"You sure? If we split up, I'm sure we can find him. Why'd he come here tonight, anyway?"

"I have no idea," Gemma says. "Look, it's not worth it. He's gone. I'll come up and give you my notes, but then I'm out of here."

But she doesn't move, not right away. She just stands there, impervious to the cold, searching the empty street as if she expects the tall man in the puffy jacket to step out into view under the halogen lights.

Chapter Thirteen

"Ohhh, Gemma-bear," Jen coos over the intercom the next morning. "It's him again."

"Who?" Gemma asks.

"Terry Albrecht," Jen says. "Your ranch-boy dreamboat from Gilburne Canyon."

This time when Gemma looks over her shoulder the newsroom isn't nearly so empty. Chuck's still sleeping off his long night at the courthouse, but Moira and Perry are pounding out copy and Tish is on the phone at Rod's old desk, talking with a source.

"Does he wear his hat and spurs to bed?" Jen asks. "You can tell us. We won't judge."

"I'll take it," Gemma says, to shut her up.

"Line one," Jen says, and before Gemma can stop her, she's singing, "Happy traaails to … "

"Hello, this is Gemma," she says, hitting the button for line one.

"Sorry about the name. I wanted to make sure you took the call."

It's a man's voice, reedy and young. Definitely not Bill Blanning, but not Terry, either. It's no one she knows, a fact that sends a fresh shudder down her spine because, whoever it is, he knows about Terry.

"I saw you with Terry once," he says. "It was just the two of you riding bikes down along the river, maybe three or four months after he got here. Then that day when you came into the assessor's office with Chuck Quigley, I put two and two together."

Gemma rummages around in her brain for the name: Troy something. Troy Martin. And then it all makes sense. Troy Martin must have tipped Terry off about the FEC Corp property, then stood by, the ever-helpful civil servant, while she and Chuck tried to figure out what it meant. But why is he calling now?

"Well, I'm very sorry, Mr. Albrecht," she says, keeping it light. "I'd love to hear more, but I have a meeting in a few minutes."

"He's taken some explosive," Troy says. "I don't know what he's going to do with it."

Gemma cuts another glance over her shoulder. Moira and Perry are still working away, oblivious, but Tish is off the phone now, flipping through the Franklin phone book.

"There were two kilos left over after – well, you know," Troy says. "It's been sitting in a shed in my back yard. Terry came over last night, talking all this crazy shit about the Dunows. He was freaking me out, so I told him I'd dumped the explosive. But when I checked this morning, it was gone. I had some blasting caps out there, and they're gone, too."

"You're sure?"

"Yeah, I'm sure," he says. "I didn't know who else to call. Last night, he kept talking about how time was running out and the game has changed. He must've said it a hundred times."

"What did he say, exactly?"

"Just that," Troy says. "He kept going on and on about Sheldon Dunow and how time was running out. I asked him what that meant, and he just said, 'Time's up, buddy. The game has changed.'"

"I think I might have an idea where's going," she says. "Can you meet me at the gondola?"

"The gondola?" he says. "You think he's heading for the mountain?"

"I don't know, it's just a guess," she says. "Wherever he's heading, we have to stop him."

Troy starts to answer, but Gemma hangs up on him and closes out the file she was working on. She's pulling on her coat and gloves when she senses Tish's eyes on her across the room. When she turns, Tish is still sitting at Rod's old desk, the tiny local phone book on her lap.

"Everything okay?" she asks.

"Yeah, yeah, all good," Gemma says. "I have to run out for a sec. I'll be right back."

Her boss tilts her head, raising an eyebrow in question.

"Oh no, not that," Gemma says. "*Totally* not that. This is a guy. A boy. We're ... he's ... he has something he wants to give me."

She smiles, awkwardly. Tish, she realizes, must have heard Jen say Terry's name over the intercom, but the name can't mean anything to her. Can it? She doesn't have time to worry about that. She has to go, now.

"Sorry," she says, heading for the door. "I gotta fly."

◆ ◆ ◆

As soon as she's gone, Tish tosses aside the Franklin phone book, which, as she'd expected, contains no listings for Terry Albrecht in Gilburne Canyon or anywhere else, and heads for her business office, blowing past Perry Barlow and his infernal spelling dictionary.

Terry Albrecht. From the moment she heard the name over the intercom it has tugged at her, tickling an ancient, half-buried memory. Now, in her office, she pulls the framed copy of the first edition of the *Franklin Daily Flyer* from the wall, and sure enough, there it is in the cutline to the muddy Polaroid she and Doug had pasted in at the top of the page:

Tanya Albrecht, 35, and her son, Terence, age 14

◆ ◆ ◆

Gemma has been waiting on the pedestrian mall that surrounds the Motherlode gondola less than a minute when she sees Troy Martin jogging up Mountain Avenue, waving to her. When Chuck introduced them at the assessor's office, she had only pretended to remember Troy from

Franklin Elementary, but now, seeing him weaving through the crowds of tourists, she flashes on a memory of a scrawny, towheaded fourth-grader out behind the portable classrooms smacking a tether ball around and around on its steel pole, a portrait of loneliness at age nine. She doesn't remember seeing him with Terry, but it makes sense, two outcasts finding each other on the playground while their classmates played freeze tag and kickball.

"Oh man, am I glad to see you," Troy says, out of breath. "I didn't know who else to call. The other guys wouldn't pick up."

The other guys. Gemma has known all along that there were others, and she assumed from the scope of the actions and from the extent of the out-of-town travel she had financed that there were at least three or four. She's dying to ask their names, but that will have to wait. First, they need to find Terry.

"I think he's going to take out the new ski patrol hut," she tells him.

"The new ... Jesus, why?"

"They just finished building it, and I took a million pictures for the paper," she says. "Terry has a copy of the contact sheet."

"Okay, but why there?"

"Blanning wrote another book," Gemma says. "Nobody's ever read it, but he told the story to Terry before he burned it. And in one of the scenes, Jack Frost blows up – " She stops, her eyes trained on Mountain Avenue. "Uh-oh."

"Uh-oh, what? What does Jack Frost blow up?"

"No, not that. It's my boss, she's coming this way. We have to go."

"What're you talking about? Why is your – "

"She hasn't seen us," she says, pushing him. "Move. Let's get on that gondola."

But she's wrong. Tish has spotted them. She throws a hand in the air, shouting Gemma's name, but she's more than a block away and the street is packed with skiers on their way to the gondola for their first trip up the mountain. None of what Tish is seeing is making any sense. In his childhood photo, Terry Albrecht was a redhead, but the man Gemma is with has dark brown hair, closer in shade to the man in the puffy jacket she saw leaving the hearing the night before. Even if he's dyed his hair, why would he meet Gemma in quite possibly the most public place in town, and why, after all his voice-masked calls, would he use his real name?

By the time she climbs the brickwork stairs and crosses the crowded mall, Gemma and her companion have already boarded a gondola car heading up the mountain.

"Stop the gondola," Tish shouts, grabbing the first FrankCo security guard she can find. "I think that's Jack Frost! He's heading up the mountain."

"You think it's *who*?" the security guard asks.

"Jack Frost!" she shouts. "The guy that burned down the Highline Chalet – I think he's on that gondola. You have to stop him."

"Whoa, whoa, slow down," he says, hustling Tish away from the other skiers. "Now, tell me again what you think you saw."

"I think I saw Jack Frost," she says. "I know who he is now. His name is Terry Albrecht and he's Hank Dunow's illegitimate son. He's doing this to get back at his family, who cut him out of his inheritance."

The security guard towers over her, his ink-black unibrow knitted in confusion. To this man, Tish realizes, she sounds completely insane.

"Look, I'm not just some nut," she says. "My name is Tish Threadgill, and I'm the editor of the *Franklin Flyer*. You know the *Flyer*, right? We're one of the local papers here."

"Ma'am, we take all potential security threats seriously," he says, with patronizing slowness. "Why don't you tell me what you think is going to happen today?"

She opens her mouth, but nothing comes out. What *does* she think is going to happen? An attack? Not likely, given that Albrecht identified himself by name when he called. So, what then? She heard Gemma take a call from someone named Terry Albrecht and she pieced together Jack

Frost's identity, but she was only able to pick up parts of Gemma's side of the phone call. All she knows for sure is that, whatever Gemma heard, it frightened her enough to run out here to meet this man at the base of Mount Boyd.

"Listen, I want you to call Jimmy Lachlan," she says. "You know who he is, right? Director of mountain security?"

Officer Unibrow offers up a bland smile. "I know who Mr. Lachlan is, yes."

"Okay, great," she says. "I want you to call him and tell him Tish Threadgill has identified a man she believes is involved in the attacks on the ski company."

"Ma'am, can I ask, what makes you – ?"

"I could, but it's a really, really long story," she says. "Just tell Jimmy this man's on the gondola and he needs to detain him and question him. Okay? He has dark brown hair and he's wearing a light-colored parka, maybe blue or gray. And he's with a woman named Gemma Seagraves. She has short blonde hair and she's wearing a dark brown coat and gloves."

"I'll put in the call to Mr. Lachlan right now," Unibrow says. "And, look, we can stop the gondola. If you think our guests are truly in danger."

"No, don't do that," Tish says, edging toward the terminal building. "There's other people in there with them. Just tell Jimmy to stop them at the top of the mountain. He's met Gemma before. He'll know what she looks like."

"Where are *you* going?" Officer Unibrow asks.

But Tish is already gone, making a dash for the last open gondola car.

"Hey, what do you think you're doing!" he shouts, chasing after her. "Stop right there!"

By the time he reaches the boarding area, Tish has flashed her season pass to the young liftie and hopped into a gondola car just before the doors closed. Seconds later, the car shoots out of the terminal building and they're aloft over the lower slopes of Mount Boyd.

Tish turns to her fellow passengers, a family of four, Mom and Dad and two pre-teen girls who, it occurs to Tish, should be in school right now. All four stand angled away from her, eyes bright with panic, as if Tish herself might explode.

"Hey, folks," she says brightly. "Is this your first time skiing Mount Boyd?"

♦ ♦ ♦

The thirteen-minute gondola ride up the eastern face of Mount Boyd is both uneventful and harrowing – uneventful because it's another perfect bluebird day, windless and cold, not a cloud in the sky; and harrowing because Tish has only just finished learning the names of her rattled fellow passengers when it occurs to her that Gemma and Terry Albrecht could panic and set off a bomb that brings the whole long string of gondola cars plummeting to Earth. Not that this is very likely. Taking down the gondola would be an act of suicide, and nothing Jack Frost has done so far suggests they intend to kill others, much less themselves. Then there's the fact that she isn't even sure the man with Gemma *is* Jack Frost. He could be Richard Cutler. Or he could be Terry Albrecht, but not involved in the attacks on the ski company. Whoever he is, he must have seen Tish try to stop the gondola, and he has to know security will be looking for him when they reach the top. If that is Terry Albrecht with Gemma, and if Terry Albrecht is Jack Frost, he has to be feeling cornered, which makes him dangerous.

But the gondola just soars quietly over Mount Boyd's ridges and false peaks as Tish chats up her fellow passengers, who flew in that weekend from Lubbock, Texas, and who, she's mildly shocked to learn, have told their children's teachers they're in Dallas at a funeral. As they near the Highline terminal, she spots eight or nine FrankCo security guards and ski patrollers clustered around two smaller figures, who, upon closer inspection, turn out to be Gemma and the man she met at the base of the mountain.

Tish waves a hasty goodbye to the truant Texans and runs out onto the slushy snow.

"What the hell, Tish?" Jimmy shouts as soon as she's in earshot.

He's standing between a pair of FrankCo security guards, his hand on the arm of Gemma's brown-haired friend. Gemma's there, too, further back in the pack, arguing with one of the ski patrollers.

"I think that's Terry Albrecht," she says. "Or his name might be Richard Cutler. Either way, he's mixed up in the Jack Frost thing."

"Tish, I know this guy," Jimmy says. "His name is Troy Martin. I've seen him around the courthouse. He works for his mom in the assessor's office."

Tish is close enough now to see that this might actually be true. It's been years since she's worked regularly in the courthouse, but in the man's slate-gray eyes and the defiant set of his jaw, she sees the familial outlines of the county's longtime assessor, Clarice Martin.

"I told you Troy wanted to see me," Gemma calls from the back of the crowd. "He had something he wanted to show me."

"Then why'd he give his name as Terry Albrecht?" Tish asks.

"It was a *joke*," Gemma says. "I told him about that story you and Doug wrote, and it was like an inside joke for us. So I'd know who was calling without him giving his name to Jen."

"All right, look – " Jimmy starts to say.

"No, you look, Jimmy," Tish says. "Gemma's my employee and she's been acting very strangely lately. And this guy called our office using the name Terry Albrecht. Doug and I wrote a story about him years ago. His father was Hank Dunow. He and his mother were cut out of the inheritance and now I think there's a chance he's back getting his revenge."

"Okay, but this guy *isn't* Terry Albrecht," Jimmy says.

"Right," she admits.

"He isn't Richard Cutler or whatever, either," Jimmy says. "I know him. His name is Troy Martin, and he brought a friend up here to look at the view. That's hardly a crime."

Tish feels a tickle of panic along the back of her neck. Has she lost her mind? Has she just chased one of her own reporters all the way up Mount Boyd, and sicced FrankCo security on her, because she wanted to meet a new boyfriend on the sly?

"Say, what's all the hubbub?"

Tish turns to see a short, round, hairless man in a sky-blue parka and black powder pants pushing toward them through the snow.

"Mr. Dunow, good to see you, sir," Jimmy says, unable to hide his surprise.

"Awful lot of security all in one place," Dunow says. "Might look a tad menacing if you're just coming off the gondola to ski."

"We were just about to break it up, sir," Jimmy tells him.

"What seems to be the problem?" Dunow asks.

"Nothing, sir," Jimmy says. "Just a little mix-up. Tish here was concerned – "

"Sheldon, what're you doing on the mountain today?" Tish asks.

"Me?" He chuckles. "I'm meeting and greeting our many fine visitors. It's a new policy. No more hiding out from mean old Jack Frost. I'm out here pretty much every morning now."

"Where?" Gemma asks.

"No – *don't*," Troy hisses.

Gemma ignores him. "Mr. Dunow, where do you set up every morning?"

"Just over there," Dunow says, pointing across the Highline Bench. "We've set up a little hot-cocoa stand in front of the new patrol hut. Dad used to do the same thing, mingling with his customers. They loved it."

By now Gemma and Troy have locked eyes, his jaw set, his head shaking furiously.

"Gemma, what the hell's going on?" Tish shouts.

"*No*," Troy hisses.

But Gemma shakes him off, and Tish sees all over again how young she is – a child, really, and in way, way over her head.

"Clear the area around the ski patrol hut," Gemma says. "There could be a bomb there."

Troy Martin chooses this moment to break free and take off for the gondola terminal. The three ski patrollers who give chase are on skis and

266

Troy's in low-cut boots so he barely makes it twenty yards before they tackle him to the snow.

"What kind of bomb?" Jimmy asks Gemma.

"I have no idea," she says. "All I know is Terry got his hands on some explosive last night and he hates the Dunows. If he's here today, I'd be willing to bet he'd target Mr. Dunow."

A pair of ski patrollers set off across the Highline Bench, shouting for people to clear the area, and in seconds the Highline is in chaos, skiers running from the white-painted patrol hut, screaming and carrying small children. Most are on skis and can glide easily down Gravy Train or the Highline Highway, but others stay behind, struggling to step into their skis or running in panicked circles, collecting up children and shouting the names of their wives and boyfriends.

"That's him!" Gemma shouts, pointing across the snow. "That's Terry!"

Tish sees him instantly, the same tall, broad-shouldered man she'd spotted leaving the public hearing the night before, except now he's wearing the sky-blue parka and black powder pants of a FrankCo security guard. He looks up when Gemma calls out his name, but there's no panic in his movements. He calmly steps into a pair of skis, sets his poles in the snow, and glides off in the direction of Gravy Train.

"Stop him! Stop him!" Jimmy yells. "Stop that man!"

The ski patrollers who had been clearing people from the patrol hut turn their skis downhill and race after him, with several more close behind. The area around the patrol hut is still in pandemonium, but Tish sees Jimmy rushing from ski rack to ski rack, tossing skis and poles out of his way as he goes.

"What're you doing?" she shouts.

"What do you think I'm doing?" he says. "I'm going after him."

"*How?*"

"You can snowboard, can't you?"

He holds up two snowboards left behind by someone taking a cocoa break, one a pink-and-blue Burton Air, the other a black Sims. He tosses the Burton Air her way and starts strapping his Sorel boots into the Sims.

Behind them, the patrol hut is mostly clear now, only two or three patrollers standing at a safe distance barking orders into walkie-talkies. Twenty yards away, Gemma stands alone, staring up at the white structure, tears streaming down her face. With one step, and then another, she begins backing away toward the gondola.

"See you down there!" Jimmy calls to Tish and shoves off down the mountain.

Tish looks at the Burton board at her feet. She can't even remember the last time she rode a snowboard. Her brother Doug, ever the rebel, had been an early adopter, and he'd talked Tish into buying a board, but after he died Tish had quietly gone back to her skis. That was years ago, but she hasn't forgotten how to strap herself in. She tightens her Sorels, hoists herself up, but she has barely even started down the hill before she catches an edge and pitches forward, driving her bare hands into the snow.

Two seconds later she's up again, leaning on her front foot with more confidence and picking up momentum. She scrubs speed on both heels, a little awkwardly, but before long, muscle memory takes over and she's moving faster, chopping her way down the hill, zigzagging toward Gravy Train, where she can see Jimmy Lachlan expertly bombing around the first dogleg turn. She takes another digger just before the turn and skids twenty freezing yards, grasping at the hill above her, the snow piling up in her pants. But – hands, knees, hop – and she's back on her feet, fanning out the snow chunks and starting off. Soon she's careening around the dogleg, clenching her frozen hands into fists.

A hundred yards downhill, she sees Jimmy and half a dozen patrollers spread out along the yellow-painted wooden barrier that marks the closed entrance to the South Peak bowls. Tish makes one last turn and slides over to them.

"Where is he?" she shouts.

Jimmy doesn't answer, just points at a tiny, blue-jacketed figure cruising down the center of the deep, snow-covered bowl. Albrecht's clearly an expert skier, cutting smooth, fast turns through the powder, catching microseconds of air whenever he hits a mogul underneath. If Tish didn't know better, she'd say he was having the time of his life.

"You're just going to stand there and watch him go?"

"He's not going anywhere," Jimmy tells her. "We've called the sheriff and the FBI. They'll be waiting for him when he gets to the bottom."

"This is a huge valley," she says. "Somebody needs to follow him, see where he ends up."

"No way, check out that canyon rim," one of the ski patrollers says, pointing to it. "That's six weeks of snowpack right there hovering on top of ball bearings."

But Tish is having none of it. "You of all people, Jimmy Lachlan," she says. "You're the one who used to take me down into that bowl."

"Almost put myself in a wheelchair doing it, too," he says.

Tish looks again over the barrier. The blue-jacketed figure is halfway down the long slope, four or five hundred yards from the dense forest that carpets the bottom half of Mount Boyd's southern flank. Once he's in there, he'll have fifty square miles of rugged alpine forest to hide in. If he's strong enough, and if he has the right gear in his pack, he could hike over Milton Pass and lose himself in the trackless wilderness of the Continental Divide.

"Oh, for God's sake," she says. "Do I have to go after him myself?"

But her words are drowned out by a tremendous, air-eating boom. The sound rolls down the sides of the mountain, shaking the earth under their feet and sending powder showering down from the branches of the trees. *It's the bomb*, Tish thinks, but she barely has time to complete that thought before she hears a second, louder explosion, a slashing, rivening sound, like someone has taken hold of the very fabric of the world and ripped it in two.

"Avalanche!" Jimmy shouts, pointing to the western rim of the canyon, where great gouts of snow have begun calving off from the ledge and pouring into the bowl. Each new crack in the wall of snow pulls more down with it, like a long white sheet tumbling from a clothesline. Tish looks again at the small blue figure at the bottom of the chute. He's skiing faster now, his turns tighter and more reckless. If he can reach the tree line before the avalanche, the forest might slow the advancing snow enough for him to escape.

But it's gaining on him, a raging tide of snow cascading down the steep cliffs of the canyon, shaking the ground, blotting out all other sound. It occurs to her that it has enough force to bury him, or bring the trees with it. She watches Albrecht veer east, trying to ski away from the falling snow, but the canyon's neck is too narrow and its sides too steep. For one heart-stopping second, he skis through the torrent of snow like a surfer riding a crashing wave before at last he pitches forward, and Tish watches the tiny blue figure tumble over and over until he vanishes under the rolling carpet of white.

Franklin Daily Flyer

August 4, 1994

GUILTY AS CHARGED!

Former Elk County Official Admits Role in Bribery Plot

By Patricia Threadgill

Daily Flyer Editor

Disgraced Elk County Commission President Cory M. Carr pleaded guilty Tuesday to charges that he accepted bribes as part of an elaborate scheme to rig the vote in favor of a massive expansion to the Mount Boyd ski area and profit from a secret development deal associated with the new resort.

As part of his plea deal, Carr will testify against his fellow defendants in the Friends of Elkhorn Canyon bribery scheme, including Deborah Benton, a former district chief with the Colorado Department of Conservation; Stanley Bucholtz, former president of Franklin Savings & Loan; and Harley, Foster, and Sheldon Dunow, the three brothers who until recently controlled the Franklin Skiing Company.

"Your honor, I am acutely aware of the damage my actions have caused to my community and to the public's trust in elected officials," Carr said during a court appearance Tuesday. "Dr. King once said that the arc of the moral universe is long, but it bends toward justice. For too long I behaved as if this maxim did not apply to me. Clearly, this case shows that it does."

The bombshell bribery case, brought to light last winter by exclusive reporting in the *Franklin Daily Flyer*, effectively killed the ski company's proposed Elkhorn Canyon expansion, which, in turn, caused the Dunow brothers to lose control of the company they inherited from their father, Franklin Skiing Company founder Henry R. Dunow. The company is currently up for sale, with rumors of interest from a consortium of New York-based investment firms and a Japanese soft drink manufacturer.

In the minds of many Franklin residents, the Friends of Elkhorn Canyon case is inextricably linked to the Jack Frost Collective and its violent campaign of bombings and sabotage aimed at blocking the proposed Elkhorn Canyon expansion. The outlaw collective's leader, Terence Albrecht, died in January in an avalanche triggered by the explosive impact of one of his own bombs.

Albrecht's terror campaign is believed to have been principally financed by former *Daily Flyer* staff writer Gemma Seagraves, who disappeared under suspicious circumstances the day Albrecht died. Seagraves' present whereabouts are unknown, but FBI investigators have confirmed they are following up on reports that she may have stayed for a time with her mother, Victoria Seagraves, on the remote Caribbean island of Bonaire, near Curaçao.

Under the plea deal, Carr agreed to name

story continued pg. 10

Franklin Daily Flyer

March 16, 1995

A Note to Our Readers

On Friday, Franklin's two newspapers, the *Daily Flyer* and the *Daily Bulletin*, will merge into a single company and the *Bulletin* will cease publication.

The newly constituted *Daily Flyer* will move into the *Bulletin's* former offices at 135 Main Street and *Flyer* editor-in-chief Patricia Threadgill has pledged to retain as many *Bulletin* staffers as possible in the new entity. Longtime *Bulletin* editor Leonard R. Mayer, now serving a six-year sentence at the Colorado Territorial Correctional Facility in Cañon City for his role in the 1993 Elkhorn Canyon bribery scheme, has relinquished his remaining shares in the *Bulletin* and will play no role in the new company.

With the merger complete, Threadgill plans to take an extended maternity leave to care for her newborn son, Douglas. In her absence, questions on business matters should be directed to advertising manager Kendra Graves and editorial questions should be directed to *Flyer* interim editor Moira Hines.

Acknowledgements

A lifetime ago, I worked as a reporter at the *Aspen Daily News*. The *Franklin Flyer* of this novel is not the *Daily News* any more than Aspen, Colorado is Franklin, but I loved that job and I've drawn on what I learned in my two and a half years there for this book. Indulge me in a shout-out to the people I worked with at the *Daily News*, from the O.G. staff of Hal Clifford, Greg DiTrinco, Eve Byron, and Mindy Landis, to reporters and editors who came later, including Scott Broom, Jeanne McGovern, and Brent Gardner-Smith.

What a gas it was to work at that crazy little newspaper.

As I was writing, I drew on several books about environmental activism and the Colorado mountains, including Daniel Glick's *Powder Burn*, Hal Clifford's *Downhill Slide*, Susan Zakin's *Coyotes and Town Dogs*, Ted Conover's *Whiteout*, and Michael Childers' *Fire on the Mountain*. Childers, an associate professor of history at Colorado State, also took time to talk with me about ski resorts and environmental politics. I would also like to thank Brent Gardner-Smith, my old *Daily News* colleague, for talking with me about ski towns and environmental activism, and Erin Prime Lamson for talking with me about bank security systems. All errors are, of course, mine.

Carrie Paterson, Catherine Baab-Muguira, Lauren Nossett, and Kirsten Lunstrum read early versions of *We Bring You an Hour of Darkness*, and Carrie liked it so much she took it on for her publishing house, DoppelHouse Press. I cannot thank Carrie enough for her hard work in producing and distributing the book you now hold in your hands.

It's a cliché for a writer to say his book wouldn't exist without his wife's support, but here the cliché is true: This book would not exist were it not for Eva Busza. She was the one who said my tall tales of working as a reporter in Colorado would make for a good book, and she was also the one who insisted that the protagonist of my next novel had to be a woman. What she doesn't know, what she won't know until she reads this page, is that the heroine of this novel is based, just a little, on her.

Michael Bourne has been a contributor to the *New York Times*, *The Economist*, *Tin House*, and *Literary Hub*, among other publications, and has had his stories published widely in literary magazines. His debut novel *Blithedale Canyon* received rave reviews in *Publishers Weekly*, *Zyzzyva*, and *Rain Taxi*, which called it, "A clever blend of literary fiction with elements of crime and noir … [whose] cinematic quality comes from characters that demand a performance." He lives in Vancouver, Canada, with his wife and son. *We Bring You an Hour of Darkness* is his second novel.